Brown, Stick Around

Thérèse St. Clare

Cover Photograph by Britt Smith Photography

Library of Congress Registration Number: TXu 1-903-274

ISBN-13: 978-0692263150 (Amazon.com)

ISBN-10: 0692263152

This book is dedicated to my parents who fueled my imagination.

Chapter One

"See, Blanche, you're brown… so you can stick around."

As her mother's words echoed in her mind, the memory seemed so vivid. She was four years old at the time and sitting on the corner of the mattress at the foot of the bed in her parents' bedroom. She flinched as her mother roughly brushed her hair to remove all the tangles before pulling the strands tightly against her scalp into two French braids, one on each side of her head.

Each time Blanche had recalled that memory through the years, she had always focused on comparing her own complexion to that of her mother's fair skin. Studying their images in the dresser mirror this time, Blanche focused on her mother's face instead as her mother repeated the prejudicial poem to her.

> "If you're white, you're right.
> If you're black, go back.
> If you're brown, stick around!"

Though there was a lilt in her mother's voice, Blanche could only describe the facial expression she remembered as a sneer. Recalling that moment in her life and the feelings of self-loathing it had planted, Blanche realized why her own self-image was so negative.

Raised in an area where the young children of African-American descent were typically blond, light-eyed, and sport straight or wavy hair, Blanche's café au lait complexion and tightly curled, mahogany mane branded her an oddity. To be accepted in Creole circles, one has to have the right skin tone or the right hair, preferably both. Poor Blanche was born with neither. Her own mother had labeled her as one who was allowed to just stick around.

With memories like these as well as others clouding her mind, Blanche struggled to clear her head and focus. How would she ever manage to impart positive self-images to her students if she couldn't muster a single one of herself?

This was the first day of the summer session and Blanche felt she had already failed the one course she had elected. When the professor asked each student to recall the earliest memory that triggered the development of their current self-image, the rhyme her mother recited plagued her mind. Blanche couldn't recall any positive images she had held of herself as a child. Going through puberty had been dreadful for her. She had felt so ugly, so awkward, so ashamed... Remembering those days, Blanche knew from her own experience how important self-esteem was as a teenager developed a unique personality and transitioned into adulthood. It was part of the formula that fed future success or failure.

"Keep thinking, Blanche," she scolded herself. "There must be some childhood memory related to your self-image that is good."

All of the other students had jotted down their notes and laid their pens on the desk signaling the assignment was complete. Blanche nervously bit at the cap of her own pen. Was she the only one still struggling to think of a story to share with her classmates? When she glanced up at the professor, she could tell he was growing impatient.

"Ms. Aubert, this isn't a contest. You don't have to decide which memory is the best or which is your favorite. I'm asking you to share one of your earliest experiences. Just pick one."

"Pick one?" Blanche thought, "How could she confess, in front of all these strangers, her problem was she didn't have even one?" Well, she didn't have one that was positive. The instructor hadn't specified that it had to be but she would have been too embarrassed to share the thoughts that were going through her head. Maybe this class wasn't the best choice for her after all. Blanche was certain the professor was not able to fathom that people who needed help themselves could actually be among the students present today. Maybe the class was best suited only for those that already possessed positive self-images. After all, the goal was to enhance the skill sets of people who worked with adolescents, not to serve as a group therapy session for adults.

Thankfully, a tone came across the intercom system signaling the end of that class period. The professor was visibly upset they hadn't made more progress that first day and Blanche was confident, per the look he cast her way, that he felt it was her fault. He quickly announced a reading assignment and a self-assessment profile that needed to be completed. Blanche gathered her things and stuffed them into her briefcase. As she walked out the room among her peers, she listened to their conversations.

Based on introductions and what she was now overhearing, the majority of the class was white, obviously middle to upper class, and married. To her, this was a group that typically possessed very positive self-images. Most were teachers who worked in inner city schools and truly desired to give back to their community by helping underprivileged children. Several were tall, thin, well-groomed, blond and blue-eyed. From Blanche's perspective, they epitomized the long revered image of beauty in America. In contrast, the image of a brown-skinned, nappy haired four years old looking in the dresser mirror and hearing her mother's voice echo, "You can stick around," flooded her thoughts again as she glanced at some of her classmates opening the doors of their luxury sedans and SUVs. The feeling of self-loathing began to rise as tears threatened to fill her eyes.

"Come on, Blanche! Pull yourself together!" She scolded herself again, "You're just as competent, and you can do this. You HAVE to do this for the children's sake." Taking several deep breaths, she put her shoulders back and tried to walk with more confidence towards her six-year-old Malibu.

Chapter Two

Pulling under the carport of her childhood home, Blanche sat listening to her favorite song on the radio. She wanted to delay going into the house as long as possible. She was feeling depressed over her inability to complete such a simple classroom assignment. She had been excited when the principal came to her at the end of the school year and informed her of his decision to add another member to their staff, a counselor for the sixth through eighth grade students. In addition, the person would be responsible for guiding the eighth graders and their parents through the completion of their high school entrance qualifications packages and scholarship applications. Writing recommendation letters on their behalf would be essential to some of the students gaining admission to the high school of their dreams making it important to have someone in the position who knew the students well. He envisioned this faculty member could also serve as a resource to the other teachers.

Blanche thought it was a great idea. Immediately she began blurting out her thoughts regarding some of the responsibilities she felt the counselor should have.

"Could they conduct activities during the monthly student assemblies that would help create positive peer pressure? Could they bring in speakers for the parent-teacher conferences to share information with the parents?"

Realizing she was speaking nonstop on the proposal, she looked apologetically at the principal and fell silent.

"Blanche, you seem so passionate about this."

"I am. Parents need to understand how just one word can hurt a child forever. They need to know how to be helpful and supportive, especially during these formative years. I don't think any parent was ever given a manual when their first born was placed in their arms. We can close that gap."

"I've also noticed that the older kids seem to flock to you. They're at ease with you."

Blanche put her head down. She didn't want the principal to feel she had been interfering with another teacher's students.

"Sometimes they're just looking for someone to listen to them…. They just need to be heard."

"That's why I want you to take the job, Blanche. You seem to be in tune with these kids. You grew up in this parish. You know the changes that have happened here. I feel you're the best person for the position. You understand what we are about and what these kids and their parents need."

Blanche looked up shocked that he had offered her the opportunity.

"But my degree is in early childhood education, not counseling."

"With your passion, I don't doubt you will find a way to close any gaps in skill sets that you need. I want you to take the job." He looked into Blanche's eyes and stated sincerely, "We need you to take this job."

In her excitement, she accepted the assignment without a second thought. Now she was concerned she would disappoint the principal and fail the students.

The banging on the kitchen window pane startled Blanche.

"What's wrong with you? Why are you just sitting in the car like that? Why aren't you coming inside?"

Blanche's mother Sherrie was screaming at her and motioning to her angrily with her hand to come into the house. Reluctantly, Blanche gathered her things and headed to the side door. Before she managed to slip the key into the deadbolt, her mother flung the door open eyeing her with a frown and assessing her from head to toe.

"Where have you been?" she scowled at Blanche.

Walking past her through the tiny kitchen and into the living room, Blanche placed her briefcase on the side of the coat rack and tried to answer her mother calmly.

"Mother, this was the first day of the class I signed up for at the community college. Remember? Since I'm going to be a counselor next year, I'm taking the psychology course that is supposed to help guide teachers, counselors, or anyone who deals with adolescents on how to help them sustain a positive self-image as they struggle through puberty."

"That's a waste of time. All those children need is a good beating on their behind with a belt instead of all that psychological mumbo jumbo. It's stupid of you to waste good money on that foolishness. I don't understand why you accepted that job. You should have stayed teaching the fourth grade class. When the principal realizes a counselor is a wasted salary and just takes a ruler to those children and makes them behave, you'll be out of a job. Then, what are you going to do? Sit around the house growing fat and lazy. That lil' money your father left you won't last forever."

"Mother, most schools have counselors now. We just couldn't afford to staff the position until this year. It's not just about dealing with the children who misbehave. Let me explain...."

Sherrie cut her off, "I don't have time to listen to that nonsense.... Anyway, Colin called. He and Maria have to go to Texas for at least eight weeks. There have been several burglaries in the neighborhood of the house they have in New Orleans so they're concerned about Autumn staying home alone. They were wondering if you were free for the summer and wouldn't mind spending it in New Orleans. I told them you didn't have anything to do and would be happy to help them out. They're coming to pick you up Saturday morning because they fly to Texas on Sunday.... Colin wanted to pay you for coming. I told him forget about paying you anything. That's what family is for, to help out when we are needed. No way can they leave that precious baby all by herself."

Blanche's mouth dropped open, her eyes grew wide, and her chest muscles began tightening. She wanted to scream a response but held it in knowing she couldn't disrespect her mother. She had started learning that lesson at an early age. As far back as Blanche could remember, her mother had taught her that back talk would not be tolerated. She didn't spare taking a belt to Blanche's backside to ensure her expectations were understood. Sherrie had used harsh discipline so often that her daughter learned the lessons well. Blanche fought to retain control of her emotions. Responding slowly so her voice remained calm and didn't come across as backtalk, Blanche chose her words cautiously.

"Mother, Autumn would not like being called a baby…. She is a college student…. And, I'm not free for the summer. I'd love to help Colin and Maria out, but I don't think they would expect me to change my plans. Did you tell Colin I have a new job? Did you tell him I'm taking this class?"

Sherrie cut her off again and snarled in response to Blanche's logic, "What you're taking is a waste of time. Drop out that nonsense and start packing. Colin is too good to us for you to not help him out in his time of need. Ever since your father died, he's always been there when we needed anything… Doesn't family mean anything to you anymore or just those tee-negs?"

Sherrie emphasized the last words, her voice deepening to a throttle.

Blanche cringed at the derogatory reference. Creole wasn't a written language so she wasn't sure how the words should be spelled but Blanche knew all too well that tee-neg was Creole for little nigger.

Recalling how she had felt as a young child when called a tee-neg, Blanche wanted to defend her students. She wanted to yell at her mother that these children were not tee-negs. In her mother's eyes, the church parish where Blanche and Colin had attended grammar school had "changed its complexion." That phrase meant the lighter skinned children were now attending what had been traditionally all-white schools or had moved to the suburbs. Left in the inner city and attending the school where Blanche worked were those who were poorer and most often darker skinned.

Blanche loved each of her students as her own. The children were well behaved and had loving parents who were truly interested in assisting any way they could so their children would be prepared to succeed in life. Parent-teacher meetings were always well attended and usually both parents came. How could her mother make such judgments based solely on skin tone? These weren't bad kids. They were only poor so lacked alternatives.

"Well?"

Blanche stopped reminiscing at the sound of the harshness in her mother's voice. Glancing towards her, Sherrie was standing in a demanding manner. Her back was stiff, her arms were crossed, and her facial expression was unyielding.

"What time is Colin coming?" Blanche choked up as she struggled to get the words out.

"They should arrive about noon. I'm cooking him some smothered okra, his favorite dish, so they can eat lunch before you all drive back to New Orleans. They're just picking you up. I told him you could catch the bus but he insisted on coming for you anyway," she muttered disgustedly.

"I'll be ready…" Blanche responded in a whisper fighting to hold back her tears. She did love her students, but the class was definitely not getting off to the best start. Also, she didn't want to disappoint Colin. She would call the registrar's office in the morning and cancel. Since she had only attended the one class, she would be able to apply for a full refund. As she went to her room to pack, the look of triumph on her mother's face caused her to feel even more depressed.

Sitting in her bedroom did nothing to raise Blanche's spirits. The room was painted a pale grey. Her mother always said they needed to pick practical colors that would last and not show dirt. Her bedroom set had been her grandmother's. Blanche felt she should be proud to have something that many would consider an heirloom but sturdy was the only adjective Blanche could think of to describe the bed. Often, she would sit and just gaze in the Sunday paper longing to have something different, something modern, something hers. One day when she was shopping with her mother at a local variety store, she showed her pictures she wanted to purchase and hang on the walls.

"We don't need any dust catchers in the house. I work hard enough as it is keeping that house clean."

Her mother had responded in a way that Blanche knew not to counter with the fact she was responsible for the cleanliness of her room so this was no added work for her mother. Knowing better than to back talk, Blanche's walls only showcased her favorite picture of her father and her high school and college diplomas. She missed her Dad so much. She had so many fond memories of him.

As tears began flooding down her cheeks, she fought to push the memories to the back of her mind. The one that stood out the most happened when she was thirteen years old. It was the last time her mother had whipped her with the belt.

That incident marked the beginning of a period that was too painful for Blanche. She didn't want to recall anything more. If she did, she knew she would not make any progress packing. She had to stop dwelling on that part of her past.

Chapter Three

When Colin, Maria, and Autumn arrived Saturday morning, Sherrie acted as if she was entertaining royalty. Autumn's auburn hair and fair skin was all that was needed to make her precious in Sherrie's eyes. Having met her for the first time at Colin's wedding, Blanche knew she was indeed a beautiful young lady but wondered if her mother would ever see beyond the skin tone and hair color to the true inner beauty the girl possessed. After the tragedy Colin experienced which ended his first marriage in divorce, Blanche was ecstatic when he met and married Maria. Maria's twin daughters Autumn and Aubrey had filled the void in his life. She wondered if her mother would have been so quick to volunteer Blanche's services if Autumn had been Blanche's skin tone, a tee-neg allowed to only stick around.

When Maria approached planting a kiss on her cheek and hugging her tightly, Blanche tried not to think of her own childhood.

"Blanche, thank you so much for being willing to do this for us. We both have to go on this assignment and we were so worried about leaving Autumn alone at night. I know they still haven't caught the people responsible for burglarizing the houses in our area because, every week, we see another incident in the section of the newspaper where they list the police reports. Colin thinks, based on what he's read in the newspaper, it's just teenagers bored for the summer and spending their days breaking into other people's homes to amuse themselves. I can't fathom they would be doing such things just for entertainment. They would be risking getting a police record. Regardless of who the culprits are, it's still a scary feeling.... I don't think I would be able to focus on my job responsibilities worrying if some gang was breaking in while Autumn was home alone.... Colin could tell my nerves were on edge and suggested we call and see if you were free and if your mother felt she could bear being without you for so long."

Maria glanced over to where Sherrie was doting over Autumn.

"I was so relieved when Colin told me your mother said you didn't have anything to do this summer. Autumn is taking two classes to get ahead on her college credits. If she wasn't already enrolled in the summer session, we would have just brought her with us."

Blanche opened her mouth to state she was also in a summer session but seeing the fear turn to relief in Maria's eyes, Blanche's heart went out to her, and she wasn't sorry she had dropped out.

"It was no problem, Maria. I'm happy to help you and Cole out." Blanche used the truncated nickname they had given Colin when he was a child.

Overhearing Maria's words, Sherrie stopped the barrage of Creole she was speaking to Colin and focused on Autumn again.

"What are you taking, cher?" Sherrie questioned.

Smiling, Autumn replied, "I'm majoring in psychology so one of my classes is focusing on adolescent psychology. The other is a class on novels set in New Orleans which will complete my English requirement."

"Oh, my God... Why did the child have to say she's in psychology?" Blanche thought. She hung her head embarrassed for her. She just knew a lecture from her mother was about to follow.

"That's beautiful. You have a smart, young lady here, Maria."

Anger rose in Blanche's chest. She started to comment using as sarcastic a tone as she could, "How in the blanking world was it so beautiful for Autumn to actually major in the subject and a complete waste of time for Blanche to take one lousy class on the topic?" Blanche swallowed the words she wanted so desperately to utter. Fighting to control her anger, she took so many deep breaths that she became heady. Maybe her mother was just being polite for Maria's sake, but deep down, Blanche knew differently. There always seemed to be a different standard when it came to her, her own daughter.

Colin still knew her too well. He sensed something was wrong so walked over immediately. He put his arm around her shoulder, pulled her close to him, and kissed her on the forehead. She began feeling better, and his arms were comforting. Whenever Colin was around, she felt truly loved.

"Is everything alright, cous?"

Blanche liked when he used a shortened version of the word cousin to address her.

"Sure," was all she could manage to respond to keep from bursting into tears. Hugging Colin back, she thought that maybe this would work out alright after all. Maybe she needed time away from her mother. Getting out of such a negative environment for the summer may be all the therapy and support required for her to start her new job with a positive attitude instead of feeling doomed to failure. Maybe she would learn even more than the community college course would have covered if she could borrow Autumn's textbooks. On days Autumn didn't need the book for class, Blanche could read the information and make notes. Being her major, Autumn probably still had the old text books from other psychology courses and Blanche could study those as well. Her spirits lifted at the thought.

"Ready to go?" Colin looked into her eyes still sensing all was not well.

"Yes, I'm all packed. I'll show you what I'm taking."

Colin followed Blanche to her bedroom where she pointed to her large items. He grabbed her biggest suitcase and overnight case before going outside to pack them in the trunk of his car. Meanwhile, Sherrie was loading Maria and Autumn's arms with plastic bins she had filled with smothered okra, rice, and slices of homemade sour cream pound cake. They finally managed to get everything and everyone settled in the car.

As Colin backed the car out of their driveway and Blanche waved good-bye to her mother, she began to feel she was embarking on a new adventure. She and her mother had never been separated for more than a couple of days. At first, she felt anxious, but the anxiety changed to a feeling of excitement. She was light hearted as if a weight had suddenly been lifted from her shoulders. But, most of all, as she took in a deep breath and exhaled it slowly, she suddenly felt free.

Turning to hold conversation with Autumn and to begin formulating their plans for the summer together, she was surprised to see that Autumn had already curled up against the door on her side of the car and was fast asleep. That didn't matter. After all, they would have at least eight glorious weeks together.

Chapter Four

Blanche's excitement grew as each mile passed distancing her further and further away from her mother and her hometown of Lafayette. She watched the road signs which indicated the miles to New Orleans were getting shorter and shorter. The only time she had previously visited the city was for Colin's wedding to Maria. Maybe, this time, she might even be able to play tourist; she could visit museums, eat beignets, and ride a streetcar. Blanche was beginning to feel happy...

When Colin began to drive across the spillway, the waterway that was the final approach on Interstate-10 East into the New Orleans metropolitan area, he glanced at Blanche in the rear view mirror.

"Cous, what's your favorite entree?"

Blanche had to think about it for a while. She wasn't accustomed to being asked what she wanted. Her mother made the grocery list and planned all their meals. When she was little, it was eat what she fixed or you didn't eat at all. She may have also suffered the harsh consequences of having wasted good food if she didn't eat what her mother put before her. Blanche looked up and caught Colin eyeing her in the mirror.

"I like crab," she responded hesitantly.

"Great! There's a seafood restaurant built on stilts at the edge of Lake Pontchartrain. They have the best crabmeat au gratin dish in the city. We'll go there for dinner."

"I never had an 'au gratin' before. Mother just fixes stuffed crabs sometimes. How is it prepared?"

Maria turned as much as she could under the restrictions from the seat belt to face Blanche as she spoke.

"Oh, Blanche, you're going to think you died and went to heaven. It's an oval casserole dish filled with lumps of crabmeat in this buttery, creamy, cheesy sauce with a slight hint of white wine. It's my favorite way to have crab."

"Wine?" Blanche hesitated before continuing, "My mother doesn't allow me to drink except for the holidays. I can have a little wine sometimes with Thanksgiving dinner and a cup of spiked egg nog for Christmas Eve."

Colin glanced at her once again in the rear view mirror but this time his face was stern.

"Cous, you're almost thirty. There is nothing wrong with drinking in moderation."

Blanche thought to herself, "But, what if my mother finds out?"

As they pulled into the restaurant's parking lot, Blanche shook Autumn's arm gently, and she stirred. Seeing where they were, Autumn stretched and perked up quickly.

The parking lot had oak trees shading the area that had to be at least a hundred years old. A small park was opposite the lot with picnic tables set up. You could sit in the cool of the trees and enjoy the beauty of Lake Pontchartrain. Several play sets were clustered together at one corner of the park. A volleyball net was hung on the opposite corner. It was a lovely site for a family outing.

"This way," Colin called to Blanche as he took Maria's hand in his and led the way to the restaurant with the longest boardwalk.

Entering the front door, they were greeted by the hostess, and Colin requested window seating. They had arrived at sunset, and Blanche told them she had never seen anything so breathtaking. The sun appeared to be sitting on the edge of the lake. The sky was streaked with shades of oranges, yellows, and reds. It was so peaceful watching the sun slowly dip below the skyline while the sea gulls dove into the water searching for food.

Colin placed the orders for all of them and requested a bottle of wine. When the waiter brought the wine, Colin performed the usual ritual of swirling a sample to test the bouquet before taking a sip and nodding to the waiter that he was accepting the bottle. Blanche began to panic when the waiter set a wineglass in front of her place setting as well. Not knowing what to do or say, she just sat stoically. Though Blanche knew Autumn was under the legal drinking age by state law, she appeared totally nonchalant when he set a wineglass in front of her and filled it to the halfway mark. As conversation began and the trio sipped their wine, Blanche followed suit not wanting to be wasteful. She reached for her glass carefully holding it by the stem as Autumn did. She had heard one of the teachers at school commenting you had to hold the glass by the stem so the warmth from your hand didn't alter the flavor of the wine. She took her first sip, then another.

"This tastes good," burst from her lips before she realized she had uttered the words. If she had a fair complexion like Autumn's, she knew her cheeks would be turning the brightest red right then.

"I'm glad you approve of the selection, cous."

"I think a Gewürztraminer compliments crab so well," Maria was saying as the waiter approached with their order.

The first bite of Blanche's dish was heavenly just as Maria described. On the drive from Lafayette, Colin and Maria had told Blanche all about their careers and the special job assignments each had. Over dinner, the conversation focused more on the personal aspects of their lives.

Colin and Maria owned two houses. Colin had a larger home on the northern shore of Lake Pontchartrain in Lacombe, Louisiana. This was where they stayed the majority of their time and on weekends. Pointing to an imaginary spot across the lake, Colin told Blanche roughly the area where their main house was situated. He promised they would spend a weekend there when he and Maria completed their assignment and before Blanche returned to Lafayette. The house where Blanche would be staying was the home Maria owned before she and Colin got married. This was where Maria had raised the twins Autumn and Aubrey, as a divorced mother before she met Colin. Aubrey had applied and been accepted for an internship in New York City so was not home for the summer. Though Autumn typically stayed on campus as a convenience, her dorm was being renovated, forcing her to move out and spend the summer at home. Blanche's days would basically be spent however she wanted them to be. Colin and Maria just felt more at ease having someone else present.

As they talked, Autumn mainly smiled politely, occasionally making a comment.

"She's so sweet, so innocent," Blanche thought, "... a child that always tries to please her parents. No wonder they were so proud and worried about leaving their little angel all alone."

Blanche wasn't that much older than Autumn, but since she had finished college and was in the work force, she felt she would be able to guide her young protégée. She could even practice her counseling skills if Autumn needed to talk. They could have intellectual discussions based on her adolescent psychology class. Maybe Blanche could even attend a class as a guest since it was too late for her to sign up herself. She was getting more and more excited about the possibilities the summer held.

The waiter came and refilled their glasses. A second waiter accompanied him holding a tray displaying the desserts they were offering for the evening. As each dessert was described, Blanche began to think she would not be able to decide because they all sounded so delicious. Maria was trying to pick between the Tiramisu and the white chocolate iced, raspberry filled layer cake. Autumn loved the raspberry meringue lemon pie tart but was also tempted by the vanilla ice cream topped chocolate, walnut brownie. Since the poor waiter's arms were about to give out holding the heavy tray, Colin, as usual, took control.

"Bring one of each with plenty of saucers and spoons so they can split the desserts. Ladies, just have some of it all."

All three laughed knowing that was the perfect solution.

Blanche discreetly watched the way Colin and Maria interacted. She was impressed the most by the little things she picked up on between them: the way he took her hand in the parking lot as they walked side by side, the way their eyes seemed to lock on each other, a smile following a whisper in the ear, the occasional gentle pat on the back of a hand, leaning towards her with his arm around the top of her chair. She remembered her father trying similar little gestures with her mother but her mother always seemed to shrug him off. Blanche wondered if anyone could ever feel that way about her. How nice it must be when the feelings are mutual, she thought.

While the ladies busied themselves dividing and consuming the desserts, Colin paid the bill and sipped a cup of café au lait. By the time they were leaving the restaurant, Blanche had never felt so full and so mellow.

"Cole, thank you for a lovely dinner…"

"Cous, I'm glad you enjoyed it. If you enjoy this visit, you are welcome to come anytime."

When Maria promptly added, "Our door is always open. We'd love to have you, Blanche," Blanche knew her words were sincere.

As they exited the restaurant, the waiter met them at the door and was overly enthusiastic when expressing his thanks for them dining that afternoon and wishing they would return soon. Colin had worked as a waiter while in college to help cover his living expenses so Blanche knew he was generous, especially if the waiter or waitress expressed they were in school. This waiter's exuberance made Blanche curious about the size of the tip Colin must have left.

Chapter Five

When Colin took the exit off the interstate that would lead to Maria's house, Blanche noticed the East New Orleans regional library was within easy walking distance. When Blanche commented on the fact and expressed she would love to see what resources might be available on counseling adolescents, Maria promptly dug into her purse, pulled out her library card, and passed it over the seat to Blanche.

They also passed a large municipal park. Thought it was dark, high mast lighting flooded the tennis courts, and people were still playing. Autumn mentioned the park had an indoor swimming pool and a hiking path if Blanche was interested.

When they arrived at the house, Colin retrieved Blanche's suitcases and brought them into Aubrey's room, the bedroom Blanche would be using during her stay. Maria asked Autumn to show Blanche around the house since she and Colin needed to retire to their bedroom to finish packing their suitcases for the trip to Texas the next day.

Blanche glanced around the room they first entered and thought it was as beautiful as any she had seen in magazines. The sofa and love seat were upholstered in pale blue leather. The room was painted a light tan, and jade green antique satin drapes covered the window and the French doors leading to the sun room. An Aubusson rug over the oak block flooring was the center of attraction and served to unitize the color scheme in the room. The rug was pale cream with a border and center woven with shades of blues, tans, greens, and deep peach. Large overstuffed pillows of the same shades were strategically placed on the sofa and love seat. Afghans draped across the back of the sofa sported the room's color scheme and gave a warm, homely feel. A double tier Italian steel, brass, and glass table added a touch of elegance without taking away from the room's size. Maria had placed a small wrought iron side table in the space leading to the French doors separating the love seat and sofa. A crystal lamp softly lit the room. Oil paintings of floral centerpieces decorated the walls, the flowers reflecting the same colors of the rug. A television was opposite the sofa flanked by a pair of bookcases. Silk ivy plants were atop each bookcase, and a couple of larger silk plants were positioned strategically around the room. A picture of the twins was hung above a piano on the right as you entered against the wall by the door leading to the kitchen. A small curio cabinet housed the treasures Maria had collected over the years, one of which was a crystal frame displaying the girls' baby pictures. An antique sewing machine was in the foyer. Autumn said it had been her great-grandmother's. An old-fashioned laced doily covered the top, and pictures of the twins at different ages were on display.

Autumn led Blanche through the main room into the kitchen showing her what was available in the pantry and the refrigerator as well as where the glasses, plates, pots, and utensils were stored. Beyond the kitchen was an indoor laundry room. Off of the main room was the sun porch sporting two skylights. Blanche imagined how lovely it would be at night to relax in the lounge chair and just watch the moon and stars. Returning to the main room, Autumn pulled the remote controls and stepped Blanche through the process of accessing the various cable channels, including using the receiver and selecting pay per view options. She gave her a copy of the latest cable guide so Blanche could see what movies would be playing while she visited. Taking the guide from Autumn, the cover story was a movie Blanche had wanted to see but was never able to since her mother hated suspense films.

"I wanted to see this movie so bad. It looked great based on the ads on television."

"I saw it, and it was good. It kept me on the edge of my seat." Checking the listings, Autumn continued, "It's coming on in about thirty minutes. Why don't you nuke some popcorn and watch it? The house is at your disposal. Enjoy yourself. Most of this stuff rarely gets used."

"Thank you, Autumn. I'll hurry and unpack so I can be back in time."

"I'm going in my room. Just knock if you need anything."

It wasn't long before Blanche could hear a stereo booming behind Autumn's closed door and the chatter of a phone conversation when there were breaks in the music.

Aubrey's room was everything Blanche's room back home wasn't. The walls were painted a cheery cotton-candy pink that contrasted with the white window casing and doorframes. The room was furnished with gold accented, white French provincial furniture. Blanche learned later the furniture had been Maria's when she was a child. The white draperies that hung on the window had a pattern of grey ribbons and pink roses. The window bench seemed the perfect spot to curl up with a book. A desk in one corner of the room had an assortment of novels, reference books, and personal treasures her mother would call dust catchers. The room also had a television and stereo. Blanche felt she could spend the entire summer in this one room and be content.

While Blanche was unpacking, Maria knocked softly on the door.

"Please come in," Blanche called.

Maria opened the door just enough to pop her head into the doorway.

"I was just checking on you. Do you feel comfortable where everything is? Is there anything you need?"

"No, everything is wonderful, Maria. Thank you. I'm just unpacking and then I was going to catch a movie."

"Then I'll leave you alone to settle in. Colin and I are just about finished our packing. The round trip today has us worn out so we're calling it a night…. Our plan for tomorrow is to attend the ten o'clock Mass so you need to be ready to leave about 9:45; then Colin would like to take you to this pancake house which is a traditional breakfast spot here in New Orleans. After breakfast, we need you and Autumn to drop us off at the airport. Is that ok with you?"

Colin walked up behind Maria.

"Are you settling in, cous? If you forgot anything and we don't have it here, that pharmacy we passed right off the exit is opened twenty-four hours."

"No, everything is great. Thank you, again," was all Blanche could think to say.

"Then we're hitting the sack. See ya' in the morning," Colin responded before entering the room and giving her a quick hug.

After unpacking, Blanche went to the kitchen and selected a bag of extreme butter and a bag of cheddar cheese popcorn from the variety in the fully stocked pantry. In one of the kitchen cabinets was a large, white ceramic bowl with popcorn glazed on the surface in black letters. Popped kernels scattered around the lettering completed the decoration. She popped each bag and emptied the hot, buttery, crisp morsels into the bowl. Grabbing a can of root beer from the refrigerator and a handful of napkins out the holder on the kitchen table, Blanche retired to the family room and cut on the television using the remote. The movie was about to start.

She never thought of how simple a pleasure it was to watch a program uninterrupted. At home, her mother chattered constantly during television programs or was always demanding something. Usually, she needed Blanche's help right at the time it was critical not to miss the next scene of her favorite television series.

"Fix me a cup of tea, Blanche," Sherrie would scream from her bedroom.

"In just a minute, Mother…"

"I need it now. You know I have to take my medicine on time."

Why five minutes made the entire world come to an end, Blanche would never know. She had finally given up on hopes of watching her favorite series and would just read at night. Like that, it didn't matter how many times her mother interrupted.

Colin and Maria's home felt like she had escaped to a real movie theater. The pantry housed every version of microwave popcorn from natural to caramel to extreme butter. The big screen television had stereo surround sound. Colin and Maria seemed to have subscribed to every movie channel that was offered, so all the recent box office hits were just a click away using the remote from her comfortable position on the overstuffed sofa. At home, the only times she got to see movies were when one captured her mother's interest, and they would go to the theater together. Sherrie usually picked a musical at the neighborhood cinema that only played the old classics and then would talk through the entire film.

As the murder mystery began to unfold, Blanche felt like she was having her first real vacation. Leaning back against the fluffy pillows wrapped in an afghan with a huge bowl of extra butter and cheesy popcorn mixed together propped on her lap, she thought, "This is going to be the easiest, most stress free, enjoyable, and relaxing summer of my life."

Chapter Six

Sunday morning, Blanche got up early so she would be ready by eight o'clock. She sat on the window bench reading a novel she had selected from Aubrey's bookcase. She had purposely left the door to Aubrey's bedroom open so everyone could see she was ready whenever it was time to leave. About eight thirty, Colin walked past.

"Good morning, cous. Did you sleep well?"

"Yes, I slept fine. This mattress is so comfortable. It's like sleeping in a cloud."

"It's what they call a pillow top. The first time I slept on one of those, we went out the very next weekend and bought new mattresses for all the beds. They are great."

Stepping back out the room, Colin walked a few steps and Blanche heard him pound on the door of Autumn's room and speak in a no nonsense tone of voice.

"Autumn, it's time to get up! And I mean now."

An automatic percolator had been set to brew. Based on the sounds she heard, Blanche knew Colin had continued on to pick up the Sunday morning paper outside the front door and to enjoy a cup of his favorite coffee blend before they were off to church.

About twenty minutes later, Maria walked past, poked her head in the door and wished Blanche a good morning before stepping down the hall to Autumn's room. She entered without knocking. Blanche stepped to the door and eavesdropped. Blanche heard Maria kiss Autumn and start whispering, "What time did you go to bed? You knew you had to get up early. We can't miss Mass. You need to get ready." Autumn moaned some reply. Blanche scurried back to her seat on the window bench and was situated reading her book again right before Maria walked back to her own room hooking an earring to her ear as she passed the bedroom where Blanche sat.

About 9:15, Blanche heard Autumn finally stomping from her bedroom, entering the bathroom, and slamming the door. Blanche couldn't believe it when she heard the shower turn on. By then it was nearly nine thirty. Did she have time to take a shower? Were they going to be late for Mass? She sat nervously on the bed unable to focus on her novel. A few minutes later, Colin pounded on the bathroom door, and his voice was louder and sterner.

"Autumn, it's 9:30. Let's move it!"

Then he peeked in on Blanche and spoke softly and lovingly, "Care for a cup of coffee, cous?"

"No, I'm fine." Blanche replied nervously. She grabbed her purse and went to sit in the family room indicating she was ready. About nine forty, Cole packed the suitcases in the back of Autumn's car while Maria joined Blanche on the sofa. Five minutes later, Autumn finally emerged. She had donned a skirt and summer sweater but was still wearing bedroom slippers and carrying an assortment of items in her arms.

Colin looked at her shaking his head and stated that he would drive. Maria sat next to Colin on the front seat. When she got in the back seat of Autumn's car, Blanche wondered how often she finished dressing in her car. Several pairs of shoes were on the floor. Autumn dug through the stack and retrieved a pair of high-heeled white open toed slip on sandals and changed from her bedroom slippers. On the back dash was a make-up mirror. Autumn dropped the assortment of make-up and hair items from her arms onto the seat between them. Balancing the mirror between her thighs, she managed to put her make-up on perfectly in the moving vehicle selecting from eyebrow pencils, eye shadow, lipsticks, and rouge. Tugging a comb through her thick, wavy locks, she pulled her hair up into a bun and used what looked like a chopstick to hold it secure. The church was only five minutes away. By the time they pulled into the parking lot, she was presentable. Blanche had sat silently amazed as she watched her.

After Mass, Colin introduced Blanche to the pastor and several people he and Maria knew in the parish. Everyone gave her such a warm welcome, Blanche felt as comfortable as she did in her home church parish in Lafayette.

The pancake house where they ate had been in business for over seventy-five years. Though it was now approaching the lunch hour, it was still packed and serving breakfast, which was available twenty-four hours a day. They had to wait over fifteen minutes before they could get a table for four. When they were finally seated and the waitress tossed menus into their hands, Blanche had never seen so many choices. Besides plain pancakes, there were over ten toppings available. All of her favorite things to eat were among those listed – fresh strawberries, blueberries, praline pecans, and sliced bananas. As a waitress passed with a plate piled high with French toast, Blanche saw the servings were very generous, and everything seemed to be topped with whipped cream.

"If we keep eating like this, I'm going to have to walk down to the park we passed and get in some exercise."

"Blanche, I wasn't thinking." Colin pulled out his wallet and fingered through several cards. "I do have a membership in one of the local health clubs. Here... It does include spa services if you ever want a facial, manicure, pedicure, or a massage. You just have to call the member services number and make an appointment."

"Massage?" Blanche repeated the word timidly.

Autumn glanced at her, "If you're ever stressed, you have to go. During finals last semester, I was so tense. I made an appointment, and when I got up, my body felt limp. I was so relaxed I could barely walk."

"Cole and Maria, I don't know what to say. I feel like I died and went to heaven."

Maria patted the back of Blanche's hand, "Just keep our Autumn safe until we return."

Autumn returned the most pleasant smile when Blanche glanced her way.

Blanche thought, "That won't be hard at all. She is such a sweet little angel."

Colin pulled an envelope out of his inside sport coat pocket. "I meant to give you this at home and forgot. Here's a little spending money for groceries and anything the two of you need. If you run low, Autumn has access to an account."

Blanche slipped the envelope into her purse as the waitress approached to take their order. She settled on the buckwheat pancakes with fresh bananas, chopped toasted pecans, praline sauce, and whipped cream. Autumn ordered the pigs in a blanket. Maria tried the orange crepes, and Colin selected a three-cheese omelette with hash browns and bacon. All the plates were passed around so everyone could take a sample of the various dishes. Blanche couldn't believe how quickly she had become a part of Colin's family. This summer with Autumn would be like having the little sister she always wanted. When they walked out the restaurant, they swapped seats. Autumn was in the driver seat with Blanche in the front passenger position. Maria and Colin sat in the rear seat so they could just be dropped off at the check-in point.

On the way to the airport, Maria pointed out several places of interest to Blanche so she could begin planning how she would spend her time in New Orleans. Autumn was an excellent driver. She maintained a proper distance based on the "four second rule," used her signals, and stayed five miles below the speed limit. The radio was so low Blanche couldn't even hear it if they held conversation. Pulling up the ramp, Autumn safely maneuvered the car into one of the few empty spaces. A skycap immediately rolled a luggage carrier over and began loading their suitcases as soon as Autumn popped the trunk open. Colin allowed him to stack the pieces while hugs and kisses were exchanged. Lots of phrases of endearment pursued. At last, the couple got out of the back seat and followed the skycap into the terminal, waving one last time before they were out of sight.

"You ready?" Autumn questioned as if she was bored.

"Yes, if you are." Blanche answered.

Before Blanche had a chance to lock her seatbelt again, Autumn swerved the car into the oncoming traffic and sped down the ramp towards the lane for the interstate.

"You need anything? You want to go anywhere?"

"Nothing I can think of. Do you want me to cook dinner tonight?"

"Nay... If I get hungry, I'll just eat the leftovers I still have in the fridge from last night. If you feel like cooking, we can stop at a grocery to pick up whatever you want to eat."

Blanche remembered the envelope Cole had slipped to her. She pulled it out, but when she opened it, she couldn't believe the amount of cash she held in her hand. It was easily several thousand dollars. Blanche had never held this much cash at one time. Nervously, she started glancing around hoping no one passing them had seen the large stack of bills. The envelope contained about three months' worth of her take home salary. Obviously, Colin had ignored her mother and fully intended to compensate her for the summer and cover any of her expenses. Remembering her mother's cautions about crime in the big city, especially in that French Quarter, Blanche stuffed the money into the bottom of her purse.

"Let's just go home," she replied nervously. She needed to put the money in a safe place.

"Fine," Autumn replied nonchalantly. "We have a grocery real close. I'll go home that way so you have an idea where it is."

By then, they were on the ramp of the interstate heading back to New Orleans East. After merging with the interstate traffic, Blanche wondered if the car was stuck in high gear. Autumn's driving pattern was the complete opposite of how she handled the car with Colin and Maria present. She stayed over the speed limit, stayed far too close to the car in front of them than Blanche felt she should, and kept the radio booming at full blast. What truly scared Blanche was the duration of time she would take her eyes off the road to focus on flipping between radio stations or changing discs in the player. Blanche was tempted to make the sign of the cross on her forehead when they finally screeched into the driveway.

When they entered the house, Autumn walked over to the bookcase, opened the drop leaf, and grabbed a set of keys and a small card.

"This is the extra set of keys for Colin's car and the house in case you want to go anywhere."

Autumn placed the keys on the coffee table within Blanche's reach and handed her the card.

"That's the instructions to control the house alarm. They're very simple…. I'm exhausted. I'm going take a nap. Just knock if you need anything."

Autumn stretched and yawned before heading to her bedroom. After closing the door, Blanche assumed she had climbed into bed and fallen asleep because, shortly after, the house was in complete silence.

Chapter Seven

Blanche sat in the family room unsure what to do next. The house was spotless, and Maria had told her Colin paid for a service to come in every week and clean. All Blanche needed to do in terms of housework was her own personal laundry and to keep up with the dishes. Blanche never had an afternoon totally to herself. Maybe she should call her mother. Yes, that was the thing to do. She needed to check in.

Dialing the number, Blanche grew concerned when the phone continued to ring. Her mother did have problems with arthritis in her knees so moved slowly, but she should have reached the phone by now. Placing the handset back in the cradle, Blanche tried to rationalize why her mother had failed to answer. Maybe she was taking a nap and just in a deep sleep. Maybe she was in the front yard retrieving the Sunday morning paper. Maybe she was in the bathroom and couldn't reach the phone as quickly. Though all of those scenarios made sense, Blanche was still worried so she called Colin's mother.

"Hi, Auntie Barbara, this is Blanche."

"Hi, cher. Did my son and Maria get off okay?"

"Yes..." Glancing at the clock on the wall, Blanche added, "In fact, they should be in Houston by now."

"That's wonderful. Were you calling to talk with your Mama?"

"My mother is there? ... She's by your house?"

"Yes, she drove over this morning. We went to church together and then tried that buffet brunch at that downtown hotel. It was so nice we plan to go back next weekend. We ran into two of the ladies from the rosary group at church so we invited them over. Believe it or not, we are sitting down playing pokeno. We haven't done that in years! Your mom climbed up on that foot stool I had and got it off the top shelf in the closet. Having a foursome reminds me of my younger days. I didn't remember how much fun that game was."

Blanche couldn't believe her ears as she listened to her aunt chuckling. She could hear her mother in the background laughing and talking with the two ladies.

"Let me call your Mama to the phone for you..."

"No, Auntie Barbara, don't disturb her. I just wanted to tell her everything is going well and to call if she needs me... I don't want to interrupt your afternoon. Go ahead and enjoy your game. I'll call again soon."

"Okay, cher. You take good care of Cole's stepdaughter. He loves her like she's his own child."

"I will, Auntie. You and mother take care too."

As she hung up the receiver, Blanche was trying to digest everything she had heard. Her mother acted like an invalid when Blanche was around. Rarely did she change her routine. She also kept close tabs on Blanche to ensure she had a routine as well and stuck to it. Seeing the ads on the local television channel, Blanche had tried to get her mother to go the brunch for months and she always refused complaining the price was too high. Now, the first day Blanche wasn't around, she selected it for lunch instead of the cafeteria she forced Blanche to drive to every weekend. Blanche had grown so tired of the same old fare; she had begun just getting a salad. Not only had her mother changed her routine but was also driving with her supposedly bad knee and climbing in closets pulling down pokeno games. "One thing I shouldn't feel is guilty that I left her alone," Blanche thought. It was as if her mother was glad she was gone. So, why shouldn't Blanche have some fun too?

Pulling the cable guide, Blanche looked over the movies available that afternoon and spotted another she had been dying to see. It was rated for mature audiences, and the advertisements had indicated the sex scenes were explicit. Blanche tiptoed quietly to the door of Autumn's room. She turned the handle slowly. Peeking in, she saw Autumn soundly asleep. Closing the door softly, she tiptoed back to the family room and tuned to the station where the movie was playing. At the first sound of Autumn stirring, Blanche intended to change the channel so she wouldn't expose her to inappropriate material.

Settling back against the sofa cushions, Blanche pulled the afghan around her and quickly got engrossed in the movie. When the first sex scene unfolded, she almost changed the channel. It was strange seeing another woman's body parts fill the screen. When the lover's mouth caressed the woman's breast, Blanche gasped. His tongue teasing the lady's nipple was more than Blanche was ready to see especially when the camera backed off and the male's nude buttocks were exposed.

Grabbing the remote, Blanche changed the channel before hitting the off button. She had seen advertisements that indicated parents could control what their children were watching. She wondered if Colin had that option and would be able to tell what she had viewed. What would her cousin think of her watching pornography? Would he think she had exposed Autumn to filth the first day they left town? Her stomach started turning. "This wasn't good," Blanche thought. Sitting on the sofa, she was wondering if she could call the cable company and confirm if the child protection lock, or whatever the term was, had been turned off in error. When she went to pick up the receiver to call, the phone rang.

"Hello..." Blanche replied nervously wondering if some type of cable monitor agent was on the other end.

"Blanche, this is Maria. Is everything okay?"

"Yes... Autumn is taking a nap, and I was going to watch a movie."

"We just checked into our hotel room. There's a great movie on right now. You should really watch this one if you never saw it before. Autumn and I caught it the first week it premiered."

When Maria mentioned the exact film Blanche had just turned off, Blanche nearly fainted. Maria had taken Autumn to see that?

"Blanche, I won't tell you anymore about the film because I don't want to ruin the ending for you but it is a great flick. The ending is such a surprise. I never would have guessed it. I won't keep you so you can cut it on before you miss too much. I just wanted to give you the room number we're in so you have this contact information as well as our cell numbers."

Blanche grabbed the pad and pen next to the phone and jotted down the hotel's main telephone number and the room number, but still not composed by the time she and Maria ended the call.

"Well..." She spoke aloud to the empty room. "I'm almost thirty years old. If a college student can sit through a mature movie with her mother's approval, then surely can I."

Besides, wouldn't this help her understand human relationships more so she could be better positioned to help her students with their struggles through puberty? "That's it! I need to watch this from a counselor's psychological standpoint," she reasoned. Still, her hand was shaking as she turned the movie back on. Luckily, no nude body parts were filling the screen at that point.

"That movie wasn't so great..."

Blanche was startled by Autumn's voice. She had become so engrossed in the second film she hadn't heard a sound. Autumn had not only finished her nap but dressed as well. With a purse slung over her shoulder, it was apparent she was about to go out.

"Are you going to meet a study group?" Blanche asked.

"Hmmmmm..." Autumn was thinking, "Pretty good story to tell, especially if Colin is the one that calls checking up on us... Maybe she was going to like having this Blanche around after all."

"Sounds good to me! ... Don't wait up for me." Autumn replied as she turned before walking out the front door.

"Sounds good to me?" Blanche pondered her words for a moment. People in New Orleans sure had some different ways of expressing themselves. She was glad Autumn left when she did because another sex scene was beginning to unfold. Blanche would have been embarrassed to have Autumn in the same room. She had never seen movies like this before and she needed some time to adjust to the material before she would be comfortable watching these scenes with someone she knew. The male was on top of his lover, and his bottom was bouncing in a pumping motion. At least, he was covered by the bed linens this time. Her mother had explained the facts of life to her when she reached puberty, but Blanche never envisioned what was unfolding on the screen. Watching the scenes caused her to have strange feelings, feelings she had never experienced. "It has to just be a little nervousness or maybe she was coming down with something," she thought.

Chapter Eight

The sound of the front door shutting caused Blanche to stir.

"You still watching movies?" Autumn questioned a bit irritably.

"I must have fallen asleep on the sofa," Blanche responded rubbing her eyes.

"Well, glad you're enjoying yourself... Good night," Autumn called over her shoulder as she was fighting off a yawn and walking down the hall to her bedroom.

Glancing at the clock on the wall above the television, Blanche saw it was nearly three o'clock in the morning. She was glad to see that Autumn was such a conscientious student. They must have a major test in the morning and held a cramming session. Blanche stretched, used the remote to cut off the television and retired to Aubrey's room. It was time for her to call it a night as well.

The next morning, Blanche didn't wake until ten o'clock. Glancing at the alarm clock, she panicked. How could she have slept so late? Pausing for a moment, it dawned on her, "Why not sleep in?" She didn't have anything to do, and she didn't have anywhere to go. This was like a vacation so didn't she have the right to sleep late if she wanted to? Stretching in the bed, she savored the thought, "I can sleep late."

At home, she had to be up by six o'clock the latest. Her mother needed breakfast ready by seven so she could take her morning pills. How great it was to be able to sleep in. Blanche snuggled under the covers thinking about what she would have for breakfast that morning. She wanted to try something new. Maria had several cookbooks on the baker's rack in the kitchen. It would be great to experiment with different recipes. Her mother hated it when Blanche cooked anything exotic. She usually refused to even taste it. She also complained that Blanche was wasting money buying food items they couldn't afford and knew she wouldn't eat. Blanche had just stopped trying and stuck with the traditional family meals.

Stretching one more time before rising, Blanche stepped into her slippers and grabbed her robe from the foot of the bed. As she walked down the hall, she noticed the door to Autumn's room was still closed. Assuming Autumn just kept her door shut, Blanche stopped in the bathroom to freshen up before going to the kitchen to fix breakfast. She grabbed the cookbook with the most attractive cover and sat at the kitchen table glancing through the recipes. She had often made French toast at home, but the recipe she found called for orange zest, more eggs and sugar than mother's recipe, less milk, and cinnamon instead of nutmeg. Her mother hated cinnamon so Blanche had never tasted it. She decided to put that recipe to the test.

Blanche was taking the last piece of French toast out of the frying pan when she was startled by a voice behind her.

"Morning..." Autumn said yawning. Her purse and a backpack were slung over her shoulder. Dropping them onto the kitchen floor, she walked over to the cabinet and pulled out a glass. After grabbing a carton from the refrigerator, she filled the glass with orange juice, gulped it down, and put the empty glass in the sink.

"See you tonight," she muttered as she stooped to retrieve the purse and backpack from the floor.

"Do you want some breakfast? I made French toast... It's important to have a good breakfast, especially if you're taking a test."

Autumn looked at the perfectly browned slices on the serving platter.

"It looks great but it's too early for me to eat. I'll just take one slice with me. I really need to get to class." Autumn yawned again. "Thanks, anyway. Hope you have a nice day."

Blanche watched through the kitchen window as she backed out of the drive. It must be great to have late classes. She prayed Autumn would do well on her big test. Sitting at the table, she tried a piece of the toast. She had poured melted butter over her serving and pure maple syrup she had found in the refrigerator and warmed in the microwave.

"Heavenly..." she spoke aloud. It was wonderful being able to fix whatever she wanted for breakfast.

After eating her fill, Blanche saved the leftovers in the refrigerator and cleaned the dishes. She spent most of the day going through the cookbooks Maria owned, marking the page numbers of the recipes she wanted to try and making a grocery list of items she needed. The store Autumn showed her the night before was within walking distance, but with the list of items she had, she knew she would need to use the car. After pulling some of the bills from the envelope Colin had given her, she used the card Autumn had provided the night before and practiced setting and unsetting the burglar alarm. Retrieving the set of spare keys, she set the alarm panel to the away setting and locked the wrought iron door on the front of the house.

When she sat behind the wheel of Colin's car, Blanche grew apprehensive. Riding in the car was one thing; driving it was a totally different experience. The plush leather seats, the mahogany wood trim, the superior sound system – everything about the car exuded luxury. It took her five years to pay off the Chevy Malibu she had back home. She was curious how much a car like this would cost and if Colin could ever forgive her if she wrecked it. Maybe she should walk to the grocery after all. Glancing at the list one more time, she knew she couldn't. She would have to take the car. It was impossible to carry the number of grocery bags she would end up with that far.

Blanche backed to the end of the driveway very slowly and checked for oncoming traffic at least three times before daring to back into the street. She didn't realize how slowly she was driving until an irate driver pulled past her, honking his horn, and yelling, "School zone is over!" She did try to pick up the pace a little but still maintained an air of caution. Pulling into the grocery parking lot, she chose a space at the far end so no other cars would be around. She didn't want to risk someone putting a dent in the door.

The grocery appeared to have everything she needed, even herbs Blanche considered exotic. As she walked around the store selecting fresh fruits and vegetables, another perk to her summer adventure came to mind. At home, her mother was typically sitting in the car waiting for her. No matter how fast she tried to complete the shopping, it was never fast enough for her mother.

"What took you so long? I've seen people go in the store after you and come out with more groceries than you have!"

"Mother, I went as fast as I could. It just takes time to pick out nice fruit and vegetables. You know you hate finding a single brown spot on your apples."

"It takes you a long time and you still don't do it right. I'm going to send you for my death. As slow as you are, I'll easily live to be a hundred."

Blanche often commented that her mother was more than welcome to join her so she could see why it took the time it did. That usually triggered another barrage of comments Blanche didn't need repeated causing her on most occasions to just listen. Eventually her mother would quiet down.

Thinking of ice cream, this was a perfect time to buy something other than plain old French vanilla. Blanche spent over twenty minutes in the frozen foods section. She pulled every flavor she ever wanted to try and read all the labels. She finally settled on rum raisin and pistachio almond. At home, they only had ice cream on Sundays, and her mother never wanted to be adventurous in that regard. What a brazen idea to have these tonight instead of popcorn with the movie. By the time she reached the checkout counter, Blanche was smiling so broadly that the cashier, who obviously was having a rough day, started smiling as well. Even grocery shopping had become a pleasure instead of a task.

Arriving back at the house, Blanche unpacked all of the groceries; and feeling like she needed a snack, she took the ice cream back out of the freezer section. She scooped out a serving of each, took it out to the sun room, and lay back in the lounger enjoying each creamy bite while the sun's rays poured through the sky lights above. When she finished, she slipped into a deep sleep.

A couple of hours later, Blanche woke and immediately focused on the empty ice cream dish on the side table. In less than two days, she had gone to two restaurants, watched what her mother considered sinful movies, slept late, ate exotic ice creams in the middle of the day, and taken a nap. What was becoming of her? Should she go to confession? Had she committed gluttony or broken the sixth commandment by watching those films? Recalling one of the movies she had seen about a rich woman who was bored with her life, she realized some people lived this way every day. She didn't feel as if she had done anything wrong; she had just done things differently than she normally would. Looking at the clock, she hopped up. Enough of lounging around, it was time to fix dinner. She didn't know what time to expect Autumn but she could at least have a meal prepared when she arrived.

About five o'clock, Autumn returned home.

"Would you like dinner? I made coq au vin." Blanche state proudly.

"No thanks. I had a sandwich at school so I'm not hungry, yet."

"Do you have a lot of homework for tonight?"

"I only go to classes on Monday, Wednesday, and Friday so I don't have to work on anything tonight. I could do it tomorrow... Want to do something?"

Blanche's eyes brightened. "Sure," she responded enthusiastically.

"There's a comedy show tonight... One of my friends from grammar school took a course and is performing. Want to go?"

"I've never been to a comedy show. I'd love to!"

"It starts at nine so you have plenty of time to get ready..." Autumn hesitated before eyeing Blanche from head to toe, "Blanche, what are you planning to wear?"

"What's the dress code? I could wear the outfit I had on for church yesterday. That's the best one I brought with me."

"That's the best you have?" Autumn expressed a bit of surprise.

"Is it not appropriate for a comedy show?" Blanche sensed that something about the outfit would not be quite right.

"Blanche, if you want to hang out with me, you can't go looking like that."

"Looking like what?" Blanche answered confusedly.

"I know you teach at a Catholic school so you wear a lot of conservative clothes, but Blanche, you don't have to look like a nun."

 "A... n-u-n?" Blanche was confused so she answered Autumn very slowly trying to digest Autumn's assessment of her appearance. The nuns she knew still wore habits, so her clothes didn't compare from her viewpoint.

"Yes, Blanche, a nun! Don't you have any clothes that don't look like the same kind of stuff your mother wears? You're too young to dress like that. That's the way the nuns dress at the high school I attended."

Thinking of her wardrobe, Blanche realized she had very few items she had purchased herself. Her mother routinely bought her clothes for her birthday and for Christmas so she rarely went shopping. The times she did go shopping, her mother was with her and always guided her selections. Before Blanche had a chance to look over the racks, her mother was typically screaming she had found the outfit she thought would be perfect for Blanche. Usually it was practical clothing that stood the test of time and was the best value for their limited funds.

"And, what are you going to do with your hair?"

"Is it sticking up? I'll put more hair dressing on it so it's neat."

Autumn's eyes rolled.

"That's the problem, Blanche. It's t-o-o neat."

Autumn eyed her pensively before pulling out her cell. After punching a number in, she waited impatiently, biting her nails until someone finally answered.

"Is Katherine working?"

There was a pause before Autumn continued.

"Great! May I speak with her, please?"

Autumn waited for this Katherine person to come to the phone.

"Hey, Kat? It's Autumn. My..." Autumn glanced at Blanche before continuing, "... cousin is in town, and she needs her hair done. If I bring her over in fifteen, could you work her in?"

Autumn listened intently.

"I don't know what she needs. When you see her, you decide. Just fix her... We're going out tonight to a comedy show so I need you to make her look nice."

Autumn listened again.

"Okay, we'll be right there."

Autumn hung up the line and turned back to Blanche.

"My hair stylist can take you if we get there in fifteen.... Ready? It's right down the street."

"I guess." Blanche answered hesitantly not knowing what fifteen meant but assuming minutes. She had never been to a salon. Her mother had always done her hair. She did need it pressed and rolled. She had washed it Friday night, but there wasn't time for her mother to press it for her before she left for New Orleans, so she had kept it hidden under a scarf. She quickly saved the dinner she had prepared in the refrigerator, grabbed her purse, and followed Autumn out to her car. The last thing she wanted to do was embarrass her in front of her friends by looking like some country bumpkin. Maybe she should get her hair done in a French twist. Surely that would be very fashionable.

Autumn drove over to the mall they had passed the day she arrived and parked outside a salon. Blanche had seen this salon advertised in Lafayette, so she assumed it must be part of a chain. On the drive over, Autumn asked Blanche to write her clothes and shoe sizes on a piece of paper she had grabbed. Autumn planned to shop for a new outfit for Blanche while the stylist was doing her hair.

When they entered the shop, Autumn passed up the front desk and walked straight over to the empty seats across from the station with Katherine written across the top of the mirror in lipstick.

Katherine glanced over and told them, "Will be with you in just a minute." She was combing out a customer, finishing the style with blasts of hair spray, and patting the loose hairs into place. She handed the lady a large mirror and turned her to face the wall mirrors one more time. After inspecting her hair, the customer nodded approval before walking with Katherine to the register. After ringing her up, Katherine walked back to her booth to meet Autumn. For the first time, she really looked at Blanche.

"Is this the cousin?" Kat eyed Blanche skeptically.

"Yes, what do you think?"

Kat didn't appear too receptive to take on such a challenge right before closing.

Directing the question to Blanche, she asked, "What do you normally do with your hair?"

"I wash and dry it myself, and my mother presses it for me. Then we roll it with curlers overnight. If I keep it well oiled, it usually lasts a couple of weeks."

Kat turned to Autumn who stood up and started walking towards the entrance door as she screamed over her shoulder, "She's all yours! I have shopping to get done before the stores close!"

Kat turned back to Blanche and requested she follow her to the back room. The right wall was lined with adjustable chairs and counters and the left had shampoo bowls. Kat studied Blanche again.

"Do you know what you want?"

"I'm a teacher, and I'm going to be a counselor... so conservative is appropriate. I work at a Catholic school so they don't allow anything outlandish."

Blanche felt she needed to mention that as two customers passed by. One's hair was a color Blanche had only seen in crayon boxes and another's hair was arranged to look as if spikes were emanating from her scalp.

Kat walked into a back store room and returned a short time later mixing something in a tub like container with a wooden stick. She draped Blanche with a plastic shampoo case, parted her hair into four sections, dabbed a petroleum jelly around her ears and hairline, and was about to start spreading the concoction on her hair.

"What's that?" Blanche twisted just slightly enough to keep Kat from putting the cream in.

"It's a relaxer... the same one I use on Autumn's hair."

Blanche had heard of what she called perms before but had never tried one. The ladies at school had encouraged her to get one. They told her it would make her hair so much easier to take care of, but her mother had never allowed it. She gave Blanche the impression that all of her hair would fall out if she put those chemicals in it so staying natural was in her best interest.

"How long before my hair starts falling out?" Blanched asked, the nervousness she was feeling clear in her tone.

"What?" Kat wasn't sure she had heard and understood her correctly.

"Don't perms cause your hair to fall out?"

"All a relaxer does is to loosen your natural curls a bit on a permanent basis. If you wash your hair every week and condition it properly, you shouldn't suffer any hair loss. I'll show you some items you need to buy to keep it up."

"My mother says perms make your hair fall."

"Years ago, they probably were very harsh but not the chemicals they use now. This is the same one Autumn gets. It's very mild. You have healthy hair so it shouldn't cause you any problems. Autumn has had one for years. Does it look like her hair is falling out?"

Blanche hesitated. Autumn did have a full head of hair, so it definitely didn't look like the perm had caused her any serious problems. Feeling the eyes of everyone in the salon were on her and not wanting to embarrass Autumn, Blanche sat back in the chair and let Kat proceed.

Kat worked the perm thoroughly for about twenty minutes and then signaled for Blanche to follow her to the shampoo bowl. At home, Blanche had to put her head under the bathtub faucet or in the kitchen sink and keep her eyes closed tightly so the shampoo wouldn't run into her eyes and irritate them. This was so much nicer. She understood now one of the reasons the salon in the mall back home was always packed with ladies.

Talking with her while she worked, Kat realized this was Blanche's first salon experience so she began explaining to Blanche every step she was taking. After the neutralizers and washings, the green apple scented conditioner Kat used was very soothing. Blanche fell in love with the fragrance.

"I'll let you sit under the dryer for a few minutes, then we'll rinse it out and began styling. All you have to do from now on is to wash, condition, roll your hair, sit under the dryer, and just comb it out. When the roots grow out, you just need a touch up. Come back to the salon, and we apply the perm to just the new growth. Years ago, some hairdressers would apply the relaxer to all of the hair instead of just the roots. That would cause chemical damage because the hair was over treated. The ends of the hair would tend to break off after several times. Just treating the roots shouldn't cause you to experience breakage."

Blanche sat under the dryer with her legs propped up. Comparing this experience to the hot comb her mother used made her feel pampered. She hated when the oil used to protect her hair melted from the heat and would sizzle down to her scalp. Sometimes the comb seemed to be right against her scalp. It was torture letting her mother press her hair. The perm was faster and had not burned her scalp at all, yet another myth her mother had told her. She had led Blanche to believe her scalp would be full of blisters from the chemical burns and would need treatment by a doctor.

Kat brought Blanche a selection of magazines. One told all about the lives and shenanigans of Hollywood actors and actresses. Blanche recognized some of the stars she had seen in the movies causing the stories to perk her curiosity. Before long, Kat was pushing the hood of the dryer back and motioning for her to follow to the shampoo bowl. After the final rinse, Blanche was seated at the styling booth. Her hair was sprayed with a lotion so it would be easy to remove the tangles. Then it was combed until smooth. When Blanche saw Kat pick up a scissors, she nearly shrieked.

"I'm just going to trim it and style it, nothing drastic." Kat spoke softly and calmly. "Trust me. You'll be very happy with the results. Ever had bangs before?"

"I did when I was little," Blanche replied.

Remembering that, she felt her mother would not disapprove with whatever Kat had planned. Blanche just closed her eyes. Maybe it would be better if she didn't watch. She felt Kat separate her hair into sections, comb through it again, extend, and hold the end of her locks as if measuring. Then the fatal clip would come. Each time she clipped her hair, Blanche flinched. Kat worked completely around her head, sometimes revolving the chair and sometimes adjusting the height. Finally, she stopped, sprayed it once again, and began putting the rollers in. When she completed, Blanche was under the dryer one last time.

While under the dryer, Autumn dropped in and handed a couple of bags to Kat. She saw them holding a brief conversation before Autumn was gone once again.

Blanche was able to read all the articles in the magazine that had held her attention before the timer on the dryer clicked off. Kat walked over, pushed back the hood, tested a curler, announced ten more minutes were needed, and pushed the hood back into position. This time, when Blanche came out from under the dryer, Kat handed her one of the bags Autumn had delivered.

"The rest room is large enough for you to change. It's better if you get dressed before we complete the style."

Blanche took the bag and reluctantly entered the dressing room. She gasped when she pulled out the blouse Autumn had purchased. Blanche had never worn anything so pretty. She held the blouse up against her and looked in the mirror. It was a peasant blouse in a deep, dark raspberry shade with black embroidery. Gathered at the neck and the waistline, the style was flattering to all figures. A plain long black skirt was also in the bag, as well as a pair of black high heeled sandals and sheer black stockings. She quickly changed, then rejoined Kat at the styling salon. By the look in Kat's eyes as she walked towards her, Blanche knew that she approved.

Kat pulled out another bag Autumn had delivered. This time she laid the items on the counter. It was make-ups Blanche had never used before. Her mother only allowed her to use lipstick, and it had to be pink. Kat applied a foundation, eye shadow, eyeliner, mascara, blush, and lipstick Autumn had selected. At each step, she gave Blanche instructions so she could do it herself once back home. When they had finished the make-up, Kat draped a cape around her blouse and began unrolling the curlers. She brushed her hair together into a ponytail, then began combing it down. Blanche knew they were almost done when Kat grabbed the can of hairspray. Closing her eyes, she listened as Kat misted her hair, brushed it one more time, and then sprayed it again with a finisher. When she was able to open her eyes at last she saw Autumn standing and staring at her.

"Oh, my God," Blanche thought, "What has Kat done?"

Autumn continued to stare for what seemed an eternity before stating in almost a whisper, "Blanche, you're beautiful."

Kat rotated the chair so Blanche could see herself in the mirror. At first, she thought it was the reflection of another customer. When she recognized herself, she couldn't believe the transformation either. This was the first time she looked in a mirror and saw beyond her skin tone and hair texture. Those two things had been her mother's standard of beauty. Growing up, she recalled her mother saying that skin tone was the most important because you could always straighten your hair. Maybe it was in her mother's days. After all, skin tone was the primary standard that had separated slaves from free men, and after generations, our country still had not healed from those scars.... This time, Blanche focused on her features.

The eyeliner accented the almond shape of her eyes. The mascara had brought out her naturally long lashes. The blush on her high cheekbones drew the looker's eyes to the upper part of her face. Her eyes were the best of her facial features. Her hair was no longer an oily mass pulled tightly around her head but fell softly in bouncy waves that framed her face. The deep wine colored lipstick Autumn selected perfectly accented her skin tone and complimented the color of the blouse. For the first time in her life, Blanche felt pretty.

Maybe she had learned her first lesson. She had heard the expression, "Highlight your strengths and develop your weaknesses." Now she knew that for a positive self-image, accent your best features and downplay the others.

"You're all done," Kat said smiling.

"You made me look beautiful! Thank you," she choked on the words as she glanced from Kat to Autumn.

"You are a very attractive lady, Blanche," Kat answered in a way meant to give her more confidence.

Autumn paid the bill at the register and slipped Kat a tip on the side. Turning to Blanche, she said triumphantly, "I think you're ready for your first comedy show."

As they walked out the salon, Blanche wasn't aware the back split in the simplistic black skirt Autumn selected went a lot higher than you would have imagined just holding it up in front of you. Dressing in the confined space of the restroom, she also didn't realize the fabric stretched to accent the curve of her hips. The security guard lowering the alarm gate on one of the mall entrances didn't miss the split or one inch of the legs showing through as Blanche walked passed in the high heeled sandals. In admiration, he let out a low whistle.

Chapter Nine

As they arrived at the comedy club, Autumn's friend, who was scheduled to be on the repertoire that night, met them at the door with free passes. Once inside, a guy waved them over to a table where several friends of Autumn had gathered waiting for the doors to the small theater to open.

"What are you drinking tonight?" the gentleman that waved them over said to Autumn.

"I'll just have a chartreuse."

"And you?" bending his ear towards Blanche so he could hear her order above the loud conversations and music playing.

Not sure what to say, Blanche replied, "The same is fine with me."

To ensure she didn't embarrass Autumn, Blanche planned to just follow her lead. When the gentleman returned and handed them the drinks, they each thanked him. Blanche didn't expect the liqueur to be green so was afraid to taste it until after Autumn took a sip. She guessed green was the way it was supposed to look and took a sip herself. It was unlike anything she had ever tasted before. It boasted sweetness but tasted like a blend of spices as well. It took a couple of sips lingering on her tongue before Blanche decided that she liked it. She stood next to Autumn and listened to the conversation until the doors opened, and they were allowed to enter the theatre.

Autumn's friend had reserved a table for them in the middle section along the main landing. The seats were extremely comfortable. They reminded Blanche of the oversized armchair her father use to have. As the lights began to dim, Blanche's eyes, like others in the auditorium, turned to the spotlight on the stage.

At least six comedians performed that night. If she hadn't seen the movies rated mature, she would have missed the joke in several of the stories told. Even with her newfound knowledge, there was a lot she still failed to comprehend. Several times, she wanted to crawl under the table in embarrassment since the routine was pretty raunchy. One comedian told a story of the pet dog he had as a child. After accidently eating gun shot, the family had to run for cover every time the dog lifted his leg to urinate. That one even had Blanche laughing despite the subject matter.

Her favorite comedian in the repertoire was a black, middle-aged lady. Based on the introduction, this was her first stage performance, but the audience was very receptive. Though a novice, she got a standing ovation. It was hard to determine whether it was because the lady was good or because of the number of rounds of drinks that had already been served and consumed by the time she took the stage. It seemed the audience applauded everything they heard by then.

The lady's routine consisted of a short comedy introduction before parodies of well-known songs. She had an excellent voice and imitated the original artist well. Blanche's favorite was one the lady said she titled, "All I got for Christmas was you." She said this described her Christmas seasons with her first husband. Since the song was the one Blanche liked the best, she jotted the mock words down on a napkin when the audience demanded an encore.

> I sure need a lot of things;
> I'm not talking diamond rings!
> The pipes are rusty; the lights are old;
> The heater leaves most rooms cold.
> A new house would make my dreams come true
> But all I got for Christmas was YOU!
>
> The windshield on the car is broke;
> The engine only shifts to 'choke.'
> The tire threads are down to bare;
> Driving on them is a scare.
> An S.U.V. would make my dreams come true
> But all I got for Christmas was YOU!
>
> The kids' tuition is overdue;
> I couldn't buy their books brand new.
> College costs are on the rise.
> My hopes for them are saying bye.

Savings bonds would make my dreams come true
But all I got for Christmas was YOU!

You say retro's coming back,
So it's okay the drapes have slack.
You call the furniture antiques.
Our VCR is now unique.
A DVD would make my dreams come true
But all I got for Christmas was YOU!

You say that the money's tight,
But it's always there for your beer night.
Dinner out would sure be nice,
But all I get is take out rice,
And all I got for Christmas was YOU!

I took the vow to have and hold,
When times get tough and things get old.
The winks at work make me feel new.
It's hard to keep my heart true blue,
When all I keep getting for Christmas is YOU!

When the master of ceremonies brought the house lights back up, Blanche was sorry the show had ended. She had never been so embarrassed and laughed so hard all at the same time. As she and Autumn bade goodnight to Autumn's friends, Blanche gave her a hug.

"Thank you, Autumn, for letting me join you tonight. I really had a good time."

Autumn hugged her back. She had hesitated to bring her at first but was glad now that she had. After drinking two full glasses of chartreuse, Autumn wondered if Blanche would still feel the same way in the morning.

When Blanche woke the next morning, she had a slight headache but knew a couple of aspirin would stop the throbbing. She laid in bed thinking about the day before.

"I'm attractive," she finally said it out loud. She felt good about herself. She looked at the clothes hanging on the door of Aubrey's closet. The blouse was so beautiful she wished she could wear the same thing every day. When she went to take her shower last night, Autumn had encouraged her to use Colin and Maria's bathroom instead.

"They have a whirlpool tub... Just make sure you fill it at least above the jets before you cut it on, or you'll be wiping down splashes of water on everything."

"Are you sure they won't mind?"

"Blanche, they'd be happy to know you are enjoying it. Use their bathroom anytime you want. They're not even here!"

"I've heard of those and have seen them on the television. There was one in the hotel room Colin got for us when we came to New Orleans for his wedding, but my mother said we'd get germs and infections using a public bath so we just took showers."

"Go ahead and try it. It's so relaxing. Just be careful you don't fall asleep with the jets running. I need to unpack the rest of the car."

"Do you need me to watch out for you? What if a burglar comes?"

Autumn tilted her head and replied attempting to keep the sarcasm out of voice, "Blanche, it'll just take a minute. I'll be fine. ... I promise. If I see a burglar, I will scream loud enough for you to hear me, ok?"

Blanche gathered her nightgown, underwear, and slippers. She did go into Cole and Maria's bathroom, but she didn't cut on the taps until she heard Autumn get back into the house, close the door, and the beep indicating the alarm had been set. She heard the rustling of bags as Autumn entered Aubrey's room. She heard a slight thud indicating the bags had been dropped on the floor. Then she heard Autumn's door close, and the blast of the radio was loud enough she knew she was in for the night and safe.

Cutting on the taps, she inspected the collection of bubble baths along the tub. She smelled each one but each was more enticing than the last. It was hard to select. She settled for a cucumber and melon scent and poured two capfuls into the running water. When she finally slid into the tub, she understood what Autumn meant about falling asleep. She didn't realize how tense she had been getting her hair done, wearing different clothes than she normally would, going out on the town with Autumn... so many new experiences in a single day... The waters were soothing and helped her calm down. This was a luxury she couldn't afford at home. The house only had one bathroom, so Blanche couldn't linger unless she wanted to face her mother's wrath for tying the bathroom up too long. As she relaxed in the tub, it struck her that Autumn knew she needed this tonight.

"That young lady is very mature for her age," Blanche thought and wondered if some of her insight came from the psychology classes she had taken. Blanche couldn't wait to start making her own notes.

"Bags?" Blanche sat up in bed suddenly remembering. After the long, soothing bath, she had returned to Aubrey's room and just climbed into bed. She hadn't looked at what Autumn had dumped on the floor. Sitting up, she saw about six bags in a pile next to the window bench.

"What in the world..." she spoke aloud but knew Autumn couldn't hear her.

She went over and began inspecting the contents of each. Autumn had brought to the saloon the one outfit Blanche needed for the comedy show but apparently continued her shopping. There were other outfits as well. Not just outfits but shoes with handbags to match, bras, panties, and stockings. Blanche held one of the panties mentally comparing it to the plain, white, cotton briefs her mother always purchased for her. She had never owned anything so beautiful or so exotic with the colors, the patterns, and the feel of silk. The lingerie reminded her of what the stars in the movie rated for mature audiences were wearing.

She went to Autumn's room and knocked on the door. When she didn't get a response, she knocked a second time, then a third. When there was still no response, she opened the door slowly daring to peek within.

Autumn's bed was empty. Blanche crossed the hall to the bathroom and peeked out the window. Autumn's car was gone.

"What time is it?" Blanche wondered. Walking into the living room, she saw it was past noon. She didn't believe she had slept that late. She walked back to Aubrey's room and looked at the clothes she had spread on the bed as she pulled each out of the bag. She could imagine her mother's disapproving comments but, to her, everything she touched was so beautiful and so different from what she was accustomed to wearing. Blanche picked up an item, held it in front of her, and looked at herself in the mirror. She thought about the outfit she had worn to Mass, a pinstriped pink and white seersucker jacket and angle length skirt with plain white short heeled pumps. She knew now the color pink did not compliment her complexion at all, but the items Autumn had selected did.

"I'm attractive." Tears welled in her eyes. She repeated the phrase several times trying to reinforce the words spoken to her by Kat and Autumn, trying to make herself believe them.

Lifting another outfit off the bed, she spoke aloud and in a determined tone, "I'm going to keep these! I will just pay for all of it myself even if I have to send money every month."

Glancing again at the silky underwear, she added adamantly, "Even those!"

It wasn't long before Blanche and Autumn had fallen into a routine. Blanche would split her week up. On Monday, Wednesday, and Friday, she would go to the library, read psychology books, and make her notes. At times she felt frustrated that her elementary education curriculum hadn't exposed her to more in this area of knowledge. On Tuesday, Thursday, and Saturday, she would test out recipes and cook enough to last her and Autumn two days. Sometimes Autumn would be home for dinner and sometimes not. Blanche never knew when to expect her but was happy the times they could eat together. Blanche loved most the nights and weekends she and Autumn would watch movies together or have an outing.

Every time they went out, Blanche would practice putting on her make-up, and Autumn would assist or give her hints. She finally had become somewhat of a pro though she never felt she would be able to perform as well as Autumn had that first Sunday going to church. She doubted she would ever forget Autumn juggling make-up on her lap in a moving car. Blanche needed to be able to stand or sit still and have a mirror that wasn't moving.

Since the comedy show, they had gone to the planetarium at Joe Brown Park, which was just down the street from the house. They had also gone to NOMA, the New Orleans Museum of Art, for a special exhibition. Autumn even insisted they go back to the shopping center one day. It was nice to just browse without her mother yelling at her. They walked the mall, ate in the food court, and just chatted. Blanche thought, "How nice it would have been if I had had a sister to do things with and to share my feelings." The one thing Blanche was adamant about was not going to the French Quarter.

"Autumn, it's too dangerous. My mother told me she is always hearing about muggings in that area. We can't go down there!"

Autumn had showed her a magazine that listed the museums, unique shops, and gourmet restaurants in an attempt to entice Blanche into spending a day there. Finally, she quit trying to persuade her.

"Maybe when Colin and my Mom gets back," Autumn had finally conceded.

Blanche and Autumn had developed an easy, though unpredictable, routine. Blanche felt the entire summer would be spent in this same carefree fashion until Autumn's twin, Aubrey, called one Friday to wish them a Happy Fourth of July.

Chapter Ten

Having enjoyed watching the chili cook-offs she'd seen on television, Blanche was impatient to try her own hand at making a homemade chili. What better time than the Fourth of July? Autumn had left earlier to go to the library and Blanche was busy preparing the chili so they could have lunch when Autumn returned. Their plans for the day were to have hot dogs with chili and all the fixings before heading to an afternoon movie. When the phone began ringing, Blanche cut the heat setting on the stove to simmer so the chili wouldn't stick while she answered.

"Hello..."

"Hi, Blanche? This is Aubrey. Is my sister home? I was calling to chat and wish you both a happy holiday..."

"Hi, Aubrey. Thank you so much again for letting me use your room.... Autumn is not home right now. She had to go to school to research her paper at the library, but she should be home soon. Do you want her to call you when she gets in?"

Aubrey began laughing hysterically. "Blanche, you said that so seriously that you should be an actress. If I didn't know better, I'd believe you.... So, where is she?"

Blanche took the phone away from her ear for a second and stared at it. Was the speaker broken? All seemed intact so she placed it back to her ear before responding.

"As I said, she's at the library."

"Blanche, this is a holiday. The university is closed and that includes the library."

"If the school is not open, then she must have gone to one of the public universities to use theirs."

Aubrey shrieked this time and couldn't control her laughter. Blanche was growing a bit impatient. When Aubrey couldn't seem to regain control, Blanche felt the adult thing was for her to take control of the conversation.

"Aubrey, your sister is working hard to make good grades. You should not make fun of her being conscientious. It's admirable that she chose to spend part of her holiday doing research at the library. You should be proud of that."

Aubrey finally sobered hearing the edginess in Blanche's voice.

"Blanche..... What type of holiday is the Fourth of July?"

"I'm not sure what you're asking..." Blanche's irritation was beginning to show in her voice.

"Is it a religious holiday like Christmas? Is it a government holiday?"

"Of course, it's a government holiday," Blanche responded indignantly cutting Aubrey off. What game was Aubrey playing?

"So, Blanche, ...if a private university is closed on a government holiday, what makes you think a government run, a.k.a. public university, is going to be open?"

Blanche was confounded at first as her mind stepped through the logic Aubrey just presented. It did make perfect sense that nothing would be open today so, if that was the case, then where was Autumn?

Hearing the pause and realizing Blanche had no clue as to what was going on, Aubrey blurted out, "Blanche, Autumn is probably in the French Quarter. If I had a million dollars, I'd bet it all she's at the coffee house on Decatur Street with her friends. If they rented rooms, my mother should be paying for her to stay there instead of the dorm. She should be majoring in English, not psychology. I keep trying to convince her to switch and make English her major instead of her minor. That's her real passion, especially poetry and creative writing. She says her prose is a fusion, a new literary medium."

Aubrey laughed at the idea before continuing on a more serious note, "She did start writing a novel but stopped. I read what she had written so far and it's good. I won't be surprised if my sister hits the best seller list one day. ..." Still hearing nothing but silence on the other end of the line, Aubrey wrapped up her monologue. "Look, Blanche.... Just tell her I called. I'll catch up with her some other time. I hope you have a wonderful Fourth!"

Still deciphering everything Aubrey had shared, Blanche absentmindedly responded, "I hope you have a wonderful holiday as well." It was after she hung up that she realized she hadn't been polite. She should have asked Aubrey about her plans but she was too upset to think. Out of everything Aubrey said, the only thing that truly registered in Blanche's mind was the fact Autumn could be in the French Quarter.

The smell of chili scorching turned Blanche's focus back to her cooking. She ran to the stove and turned the knob to off. Looking out the kitchen window, a nervous feeling began in her stomach. Where was Autumn? Blanche's one function was to ensure Autumn's safety and she had no idea now where the child might be. She pulled the telephone directory. Maybe Aubrey was wrong. Maybe the library was open. She looked up the listings and began to call each. Every location she tried had an announcement on their messaging system stating their hours for the holiday, and Aubrey was right. Everywhere she called was closed. The phone rang again. This time Blanche answered with a level of anticipation in her voice. Hopefully, it was Autumn checking in.

"Blanche, you sound worried. Is everything alright?"

"Oh, ... Hi, Maria. Happy Fourth of July."

"And to you. I was calling to wish you and Autumn a happy holiday. May I speak with her?"

"Oh, God," Blanche thought. The last thing she wanted was for Colin and Maria to discover how highly incompetent she was. She remembered the words Maria spoke at breakfast the Sunday morning her and Colin left, "Just keep our Autumn safe until we return." Remembering the wad of money Colin had given her she thought, "What am I going to say? How can I admit I have no clue where Autumn is. I've failed at the only thing they asked of me."

"She ran to the grocery for me. I was making chili and didn't have enough chili powder so she went to pick some up. So many places are closed today... I'm not sure where she'll be able to buy it or when she'll get back."

"No problem. Just let her know I called, and to both of you, Colin also sends his love."

"I'll tell her.... Bye, Maria!"

Blanche slammed the phone into its cradle. First, she was made to feel stupid by Aubrey. Now she just lied to Maria. It was all because of Autumn not being honest with her. She thought they had a good relationship until now... By the time Autumn did arrive home, Blanche had worked herself into a frenzy. If she could have observed her next actions, she would have known that she was imitating her mother's behavior. When she saw Autumn's vehicle pull into the driveway, she went to the front door and slung it open.

"Where have you been?" she hissed eyeing Autumn from head to toe.

Surprised by the aggressive manner Blanche greeted her, Autumn eyed her suspiciously. She wanted to reply, "It's none of your business where I go." Instead she answered curtly, "At The Library ... just as we discussed. We're not late for the movie if that's your concern. Are you ready to go?"

"That's not my concern! Your mother called to wish you a happy holiday and I had no idea where to tell her you were."

"Why didn't you tell her I was at The Library?" Autumn looked at Blanche curious as to why she hadn't recalled their conversation from the night before.

Blanche couldn't believe Autumn was holding on to the lie she had told her. Since she continued to stick to her fabricated story, she felt she had no choice but to challenge her.

"Because Aubrey also called! She happened to mention libraries should be closed today. I called every library in this city, and they all had announcements saying they were closed!"

Blanche, not realizing she was again mimicking the behavior her own mother used on her, she crossed her arms and eyed Autumn with an expression indicating Autumn had been caught lying.

Autumn looked at Blanche confused, "Blanche, I don't know what point you're trying to make so why don't you just make it because if we don't leave now, we're going to miss the movie."

Blanche was taken a little aback that Autumn was so forthright instead of playing the cat and mouse game to which she was accustomed.

"The point is," she paused a moment as Sherrie often did before dropping the hatchet, "You couldn't be at your university's library or at a public library."

"No, I wasn't at either...." Autumn looked at Blanche confused, "And, your point is?"

Since Autumn was not willing to admit her whereabouts, Blanche had to drop the hatchet, "So, young lady, are you going to tell me you were NOT in the French Quarter?"

"Yes, I was! ... Now, are you ready to go to the movie?" Autumn responded still not understanding where Blanche was going with this conversation or what she was trying to accomplish.

Blanche was not surprised that Autumn admitted it. After all, what choice did she have once Blanche stated what she suspected? Autumn was too old for a whipping but Blanche had to impose some punishment for her reckless behavior.

With an arrogant air, she announced, "We are not going to the movie today. You are grounded! ... I forbid you to go to the French Quarter ever again. Is that understood, young lady?"

Autumn paused for several moments not certain how to respond at first. When Autumn didn't answer immediately in fear as Blanche was accustomed to doing at her own home, Blanche felt the need to press her point.

With the air of someone having ultimate authority, she repeated, "I said... Is that understood, young lady? You are NOT to go to the French Quarter unaccompanied again."

Autumn looked straight into Blanche's eyes, spoke slowly, and attempted to speak calmly, "Blanche, remember why you're here. ... I'm not a baby. I'm not a minor. ... I don't need anyone to take care of me. ... I'm a college student, and I make my own decisions. ... You're not here to make rules. You're just a number. ... Remember that. You're just a number. ... If you're worried about me going to the French Quarter alone, then you can just come with me next time, okay? ... Now, are we going to the movies or not?"

Autumn folded her arms, stared at Blanche indicating that Autumn, not Blanche, held the upper hand in this war of ultimatums.

Blanche was unnerved by Autumn's response and stance. Fighting to retain her feeling of being the authoritative figure in their relationship and having no idea how to respond or handle the situation based on this turn in the conversation, she demanded, "Young lady, explain what you mean that I'm only a number."

"You have heard the saying, 'There's safety in numbers.' That's why you're here, Blanche." Autumn pointed her index finger at her. "Remember my Mom and Colin explained that to you the first weekend. You have no responsibilities this summer other than yourself. You're just here because it's less likely that a home is broken into if there's more than one person in the house. It's just a numbers game.... You're just a number! Two is better than one.... If my dorm wasn't being redone or if this rash of burglaries hadn't started, you wouldn't even be here. I'd be home alone. I got tired of arguing with my Mom and Colin that they didn't have to worry about me so, to ease their mind, I agreed to you spending the summer. If I hadn't, they'd be calling and checking on me nonstop. I'd be aggravated by now and they wouldn't be able to focus on this special project they need to complete. So you're just a number, Blanche. Nothing more! Now, are we going to the movie?"

Blanche stood trying to maintain an air of authority but not knowing what to say or do at that stage. Autumn looked at her apologetically guessing she was disheartened.

"I really want to see this movie. Aubrey told me it'll probably be up for the Best Picture Oscar and it's my last chance to catch it before midterms start so I'm going to the movie." She turned slinging her purse over her shoulder. She turned back and glared at Blanche, "Are you coming?"

When she just stood there obviously uncertain what to say or do next, Autumn shrugged, "See you tonight. ... Don't wait up for me."

Blanche just stood staring at the closed front door until she heard the engine of Autumn's compact car start. She rushed to the kitchen window and watched her pull out the driveway. Turning back around, she looked at the kitchen table decorated with the plastic red, white, and blue tablecloth she had purchased and the warmed hot dog buns sitting in the wire basket with containers of mustard, shredded cheese, sweet relish, and chopped Vidalia onions surrounding it. The plans for the day were ruined all because Blanche hadn't handled the situation well. She couldn't control the tears that began flooding down her cheeks.

Sitting on the sofa later that afternoon, she kept replaying the exchange with Autumn in her mind. Having grown up in an environment of corporal punishment, Blanche was an advocate against using that means to raise or discipline children. At her school, corporal punishment was banned and the use of denied privileges or extra homework had worked to change inappropriate behavior. In worst cases, parents had become involved. Whether corporal punishment was used in the student's home, Blanche couldn't know for certain, but at her school, just the threat of a call to a student's parent typically was all that was needed to keep the students in line. Denying privileges seemed the only option she had with Autumn, but she had failed.

Finally accepting the fact that Autumn was right, she was embarrassed by her behavior. But, what was Colin and Maria's expectations? Is she really there only to be a number as Autumn called her? She wasn't ready to accept the fact she had no other duties toward her young charge in their eyes. Disgusted with her inability to frame her purpose that summer, she dropped her head, her eyes falling on the stack of mail that had come for Colin and Maria. All bills were electronically paid using the auto draft feature their bank offered so Colin had told her not to worry about any mail they received. It all could wait until they returned. But the top letter was from Autumn's university and addressed "To the parents of Autumn Warren."

Blanche continued to eye the envelope wondering what was contained inside. Using a method she had observed from her mother whenever letters to her father arrived, she took the letter to the kitchen and laid it on the table while she boiled water. As soon as the steam started, she held the flap over the steam until the glue loosened enough for her to carefully slit the flap open without tearing the paper. She could use paste to reseal it after she had read the note. Her jaw dropped as she read the notice from Autumn's professor that Autumn was in danger of failing the adolescent psychology course because of attendance. If Autumn was not going to class, then where was she spending her days?

"I have to act on this," Blanche thought. How could Colin and Maria return home and find out the child had failed her course with Blanche, a teacher, right there in the house? First thing Monday morning, she would contact the school and make an appointment to see the professor. She had to find out what she could do to help the situation. Maybe that would also be a means of making up for what had transpired between her and Autumn today, possibly saving her from failing. Blanche was impatient for the weekend to end.

Chapter Eleven

Monday morning, Blanche woke early to bake a batch of homemade biscuits. As soon as the biscuits were in the oven, she pan fried bacon and then scrambled eggs in the grease that remained. When she heard Autumn coming out the bathroom, she knew it wouldn't be long before she entered the kitchen to drink a glass of orange juice before heading to the university. She split open a biscuit, placed a slide of cheese across it, and put it under the broiler to melt the cheese. After the cheese was bubbly, she pulled it out the broiler, added two strips of bacon and a mound of eggs before folding it back over. Pulling a strip of aluminum foil off the roll, she wrapped the biscuit shiny side in to retain the heat and placed it in a bag along with a ripened banana.

Autumn entered the kitchen and muttered, "Good morning," without really looking at Blanche. She had been cordial the entire weekend, but the relationship that had grown between them was now strained. When she finished the juice, Blanche held out the brown paper bag so she could see it out the corner of her eye as she placed her empty glass in the kitchen sink.

"A bacon, egg, and American cheese breakfast biscuit to go," she announced hesitantly.

Autumn then looked up straight into her eyes recognizing the peace offering for what it was. Though she wasn't hungry and hated cheese with eggs, she knew she couldn't refuse the gesture. Taking the bag from Blanche's hand, she placed it on the table, turned, and gave her a hug as she answered, "Thank you."

As she exited the kitchen, Autumn stopped at the door, turned, and said, "See you tonight for dinner?"

"Sure," Blanche answered enthusiastically.

"How about we order pizza and watch a movie on cable?"

"That would be great," Blanche responded happy they both were willing to put the weekend behind them and regain the rapport they had developed.

As soon as Autumn pulled out the driveway, Blanche didn't take time to eat breakfast herself. She stored the leftovers in the refrigerator, stacked the dishes and pots she had used into the dishwasher, and pulled the letter from Autumn's university out of her pocket. Dialing the number listed, she waited impatiently for someone to answer. When no one did, she glanced at the clock and realized it was probably the lunch hour. She sat in the living room watching the clock impatiently waiting for the hour to pass. As soon as the hour hand rolled around again, she re-dialed.

A young lady, obviously a student worker by the tone of her voice, answered, "Psychology... Dr. A.J.'s office."

"Hello, my name is Blanche Aubert. I'm calling to make an appointment with a Professor Brown. Is it possible for me to see him today?"

Blanche listened to the sounds of gum chewing and paper shuffling before she finally heard the response, "If you can get here for 2:00, he probably has time for you then."

Her watch had 1:05 but Blanche had no idea how to get to the university or how long it would take to drive there.

"I'm in New Orleans East off the Read Boulevard exit. Do you think I can get there on time from here?"

"Sure, if you leave now. It shouldn't take you more than thirty minutes because school zones won't be in effect."

Blanche asked for directions to the school and the building that housed Professor Brown's office as well as a suggested place to park. Stuffing the letter from the school and the directions into her purse, she ran to Aubrey's bedroom and pulled a navy blue, summer suit she had bought on one of her shopping trips with Autumn out the closet. She yanked the tags off and laid it on the bed. Changing her clothes and slipping into her new navy, short heeled sandals, she took a moment to apply a light blush and lipstick, grabbed her purse, re-set the house alarm, and headed out. Each time she got stuck at a red light, she pulled out the jotted directions and memorized the next path. It was 1:57 when she walked through the door stenciled Dr. Adam J. Brown.

Watching the young lady with hair dyed shades of pinks and purples twirling a pencil in her hand, popping gum, and seemingly bored as she studied a textbook, Blanche was certain it was the one she had spoken to on the phone. She glanced up at Blanche over her eyeglasses, straightened in the chair, and shoved the gum to the side of her mouth momentarily to speak.

"How may I help you?"

Blanche could tell the way she muttered the words, it was the script she had been told to use.

"My name is Blanche Aubert. I made an appointment to see Professor Brown for 2:00. I had called earlier and I believe you were the person who answered the phone."

"Oh, yeah."

Blanche felt she was being studied and the gum popping started again.

"He's not back from his last class yet. Have a seat. He should be here shortly."

"Thank you..." Blanche replied before turning to study the small outer office. There were two arm chairs facing a settee. A coffee table in the center of the room had stacks of magazines on psychology piled neatly on each end. A small crystal candy dish filled with peppermints was in the center of the table. A rack near the entrance door displayed the traditional informative material – class schedules, university directory, etc... At the far end of the room, a window bench had been built along the tall oak framed windows. Cushions lined each end. Blanche walked over to the window bench and sat with her back against the wall so she had the view of the courtyard below. As she watched the passersby, one gentleman in particular caught her eye.

The man was not very tall. In fact, he was probably only about three inches or so taller than Blanche. Her father had been six feet five, and the men on both sides of her family were all at least six feet two. This man would be considered short by the standards to which she was accustomed, but though he was not tall, the way he carried himself commanded attention. He had the most beautiful skin tone she had ever seen. His skin seemed to have a glow about it, a deep golden brown were the adjectives that came to her mind. His hair was thick and had just a slight wave. His broad shoulders didn't need the traditional pads added to men's sport and suit coats. Her eyes closed as she fantasized the two of them playing the roles in the latest movie love scene she had watched. A strange feeling came over her. She opened her eyes and glanced towards the student at the desk. Seeing her intent on her textbook and once again popping her gum and twirling a pen, Blanche felt more confident her inner thoughts hadn't been revealed. She looked out the window hoping to catch another glimpse of the gentleman, but he was no longer within sight as she studied the quadrangle below the window.

Blanche's attention turned back to the student as a buzzing noise came across the telephone set. The student used her pen to punch one of the buttons and a husky voice filled the air.

"Any messages, Melinda?"

"Yeah, only one…. Dr. Carmen called. She wants to talk with you about a change in the presenter for one of the topics in the lecture series."

Hearing Melinda's response and assuming the voice was Professor Brown's, Blanche shifted on the window bench into a more presentable sitting position with her back erect as she waited.

Eyeing the movement out the corner of her eye, Melinda's face turned to Blanche. She stared at her as if she had forgotten Blanche was there.

"Oh! And, you have a lady here to see you."

Blanche grew apprehensive when no response came from Professor Brown. She could hear papers shuffling through the speakerphone. Finally, he spoke.

"Melinda, I'm not seeing any appointments on my calendar?"

"She called while you were out so I told her to come on over since your calendar was empty."

Professor Brown sighed. He needed this next hour to make updates to his next lecture. Since the lady was already in the outer office and now knew he was there, he would have to make time to see her.

"Melinda, I only have about fifteen minutes to spare. If that is satisfactory, please show the lady in. If she needs more time, please set up another appointment."

"OK," Melinda responded, pressed the button to turn off the speakerphone, and turned to Blanche.

"You got fifteen. His office is through that door." Melinda gestured to the door behind her with her thumb and turned back to her book popping her gum again.

There was that phrase again, but this time Blanche knew for certain the meaning of the number. Having heard the professors' response, she hesitated to just get up and barge through the door, but Melinda had turned back to popping her gum and flipping the pages in her text book nonchalantly. Blanche started to comment that the polite thing to do was for Melinda to show her into the professor's office. Glancing at the letter in her hand and knowing this was too important to wait, she didn't want to waste time instructing the student on office protocol. If fifteen minutes was all she had today, she'd take that. Standing, she smoothed her skirt, straightened her back, took a deep breath, and walked past the outer desk to the door. Melinda glanced at her once more before studying her text book again. Blanche slowly moved her right hand to the knob, turned it, and used her left hand to help push the heavy oak door open. Taking another deep breath, she stepped into the room, turned, and closed the door softly behind her.

"Damn!" Adam thought to himself as he eyed the stretch of leg beneath the split in the back of the navy skirt. His entire career had been unblemished, unlike that of his predecessor who had been forced into early retirement due to rumors concerning how some of the female students were obtaining passing grades. There were times he had been tempted but was proud of the fact he had resisted and had a reputation for possessing high ethical standards. If this was a student standing before him, the lady presented the ultimate test of his willpower. As she turned, his eyes studied the almond shaped dark brown eyes staring back at him. He pictured himself caressing the side of her cheek with his hand before feeling the softness of his hair as he moved his hand to the base of her neck and guided her head upward so he could kiss her full lips. The top of the short matching jacket had a V-neck line, and the top button in Blanche's haste had remained undone allowing a glimpse of the curve of her breast.

He tilted his head downward remembering he and another professor were in the pool being considered for the position of dean of the department. Not knowing the nature of the appointment due to Melinda's typical lack of details and wondering if the lady might be a plant to set him up by his adversary, he spoke in a voice terser than normal, "How may I help you?"

Shocked that the man sitting behind the desk was the same one she had admired as she peered out the window into the quadrangle, Blanche's voice broke as she stumbled over her words holding the letter forward like a young student in the principal's office bringing in a note from her parents.

"This letter came in the mail regarding Autumn Warren. I'm here to discuss it."

Adam placed an elbow on the desk, lifting his fist to his lips. He typically stood, walked over and greeted his guest with a handshake, but his reaction to this lady's attractiveness forced him to remain seated. He eyed her for a few minutes before taking his fist from his lips and, with an open palm, gestured she should come forward and take one of the arm chairs opposite his desk.

Nervously, Blanche stumbled forward on the high heels, placed the letter on the desk in front of him, and took the seat he had he had designated. Facing downward, Adam took the letter into his hands and read the memo. This opening gave him time to shift gears and, when he spoke, his voice came across in his typical professional, polite manner.

"This is the standard letter notifying parents when a student may be in danger of failing a course. What would you like to discuss?"

"What can I do to help turn the situation around? I don't want Autumn to fail this course. I feel personally responsible."

The lady's words and her appearance raised a red flag. Adam thought about the privacy laws so had to question her further.

"I'm sorry but you seem far too young to have a daughter Autumn Warren's age."

"She's not my daughter. Autumn is in a parent/step-parent home environment."

Adam's attraction to the lady diminished slightly as he imagined the meaning of what Blanche had shared. So the lady across from him had married the student's father. He wondered how old the guy was and if he fit the stereotype, older man going through a mid-life crisis and falling for the first young thing that came along willing to give him the time of day.

"The guy must have money," he thought. She hadn't struck him as a gold digger when he first saw her but that impression had probably worked in her favor with this older man as well. He wondered if she had been the cause of his marriage to Autumn's mother breaking up. She was certainly tempting enough. No wonder the student may be having difficulties. Her father had married someone that could be her peer. Despite the negative thoughts, he found himself still attracted to her. Isn't that typical for a siren? He focused on the legal aspects of their meeting.

"I'm sorry Miss....." Adam purposely didn't finish his sentence tilting his head indicating she should introduce herself.

"Blanche Aubert," Blanche responded embarrassed she had not stated her name when she first entered.

"Ms. Aubert, if I have Melinda pull Autumn Warren's files, would your name be listed as having privy to her personal records?"

Blanche's head dropped slightly, her eyes focused on the letter in his hands. Further embarrassed, she answered in a monotone voice, "No..."

Just as he thought, Adam surmised, "Only her father and mother would be listed, not this younger jezebel of a step mom."

"I'm sorry, Ms. Aubert. I can't discuss the student's record with you."

Blanche's eyes filled with tears. She had failed again. Being a teacher herself, she should have known she couldn't just barge into Autumn's life without any authorization from Colin and Maria. Disgustedly, she lifted the letter Adam had placed back in front of her on the desk and shoved it into her purse. She was about to thank the professor for his time and take her leave when her eyes fell on a flyer on the corner of his desk.

The gloomy look on the lady's face had Adam feeling sorry for her. He knew what her home life must be like. He pictured the student's father in an office tower somewhere working long hours to keep his young bride in the manner he was sure he had promised her while also keeping up his child support and possibly alimony payments. The young bride was stuck at home trying to play the role of mother to a peer who most likely resented her breaking up her parents' marriage. Adam wondered what consequences the young bride faced if she failed guiding the step daughter. As crazy as the situation seemed, he wanted an excuse to see her again. He had never had an affair with a married woman and was proud of that fact as well but, before he could stop himself, the words had spilled.

"Are you interested in psychology?" He picked up one of the flyers and handed it to Blanche.

"Yes, I am," she answered enthusiastically.

Seeing her face brighten, he explained the flyer's content, "We're hosting a lecture series for the first time this summer for incoming Freshmen. Visiting professors from around the country that are acknowledged experts are presenting seminars in their field of expertise. We're hoping the exposure this summer will help the incoming students pinpoint their interest timely and avoid changes in their major when they become upper classmen. ... I can give you a free pass if you would like to attend any of the lectures. You've only missed one so far."

Blanche looked up excitedly, "Could I? I'd love to attend them all. I have been a fourth grade teacher, but this coming year, I'll be the counselor at our elementary school. This would be so helpful to me. I would be so grateful, Professor Brown."

"Odd," Adam thought, "The lady works instead of just enjoying a life of leisure." She seemed sincere, and her comments perked his interest in her even more.

"The students call me Dr. A.J. but please call me Adam."

Blanche smiled at him shyly before answering, "I'd be eternally grateful, ... Adam."

He smiled back and found it difficult to take his eyes off her but turned and punched the button on the speakerphone. When the ring was answered, he barked instructions, "Melinda, would you please print a lecture series pass in the name of Ms. Blanche Aubert and bring it in?"

"OK," came across the speakerphone followed by the pop of gum.

Hitting the button again to turn the speakerphone off, Adam turned to Blanche, "It should only take a few minutes."

Blanche looked up with obvious disappointment on her face. "One is today and starting in a few minutes. I have no idea where this building is."

Adam glanced at his watch. They had gone well beyond the fifteen minutes he had granted. It was time for him to go to his next lecture.

He would have to do his best to incorporate the changes he intended to add in on the fly instead of typing them into his lecture notes as he usually did.

"I have a class in that same hall. We can walk over together and I can show you where the auditorium is."

"Professor Br…" Blanche caught herself, "I mean, Adam. Thank you for being so kind."

As Melinda walked in with a pass in a clear clip-on name holder, Blanche quickly attached it to her blouse, grabbed her purse, and stood waiting for Adam to lead the way. They walked quickly and in silence across the quadrangle, went through the building opposite the one that housed his office, crossed a public street, and entered a newly built five story construction. Blanche held the railing following Adam as quickly as the high heeled shoes allowed as he bounded up the stairs to the second floor. When she caught up with him, he pointed to the door on the floor above.

"When you get to the top of the next flight, that door on the right leads to the back of the auditorium. You'll find yourself looking down towards the stage so, even if the lecture has started, you won't disturb anything by entering. My class is down this hall. I hope you enjoy it."

"I'm sure I will. Thank you again," Blanche called over her shoulder as she climbed the next flight of stairs.

Adam stood a few moments watching her shapely legs through the slit in the skirt before a student called to him, "We're having class today, Doctor A.J.?"

He turned and faced the inquiring student, "Of course." He took a final glance at Blanche's ascent on the stairs before turning to walk with the student to his classroom.

Chapter Twelve

Having finished his last lecture for the day, Adam slipped into the back door of the auditorium. Glancing among the students, he spotted Blanche on the edge of her seat writing notes. The majority of the students present seemed to have drifted to sleep. Many that were still awake seemed extremely bored. Blanche raised her hand to ask a question. Based on the professor's responsiveness towards her, Adam knew she had been an asset in the seminar. Some of those nodding away even perked up hearing a voice other than the humdrum voice of the elderly gentleman. Adam took a seat in the back row and observed. The lecture was scheduled to go on for another fifteen minutes. He was impressed by the examples Blanche shared and the students present appeared to finally grasp the subject matter once Blanche had interjected providing real life examples to which they could relate. Adam didn't regret having given her the pass.

When the class ended, he waited for Blanche at the rear of the auditorium. As she passed his aisle, she appeared even more disheartened than she did in his office when he advised he would not discuss Autumn's records with her.

"Blanche," he called her name, and she turned as he rose from his seat and started walking towards her. "Based on the little I was able to see, I would have thought you were enjoying the lecture but not based on your expression."

"Oh, Adam," she tilted her head downward and shook it slowly from side to side.

Adam could tell something beyond Autumn Warren's notification letter had caused her to become upset. Without thinking, he placed a hand on each side of her upper arms. Speaking as softly and gently as he could, he offered, "There's a coffee house only a block up the street. Would you like to go there and talk about it?"

Blanche nodded in affirmation. To keep them from being separated in the crowd of students exiting the building, he took her hand into his and led her out of the building. When they stepped out the front of the building, Adam became conscious he was still holding Blanche's hand.

Releasing it, he used the same hand to point out the location of the coffee house.

"You can see it from here." They walked silently together.

When they entered the establishment, Adam led the way to the counter.

"Would you care for a snack? I missed lunch today so I'm planning on getting something light."

Realizing she hadn't eaten breakfast or lunch, Blanche turned to the display case. Adam watched as her face lit up like a toddler in a candy store for the first time. She came across as having a childlike wonder and appreciation of the things around her instead of the bored expression he would expect from a lady who should be cosmopolitan based on her home circumstances.

Blanche's mother had baked cupcakes when she was a child, and she often got a raisin bran muffin when they went to the cafeteria after mass on Sunday. She had never seen the exotic selection of pastries on display in the case before her. Though it was the end of the day and several pans were completely empty, the coffee shop still had seven different muffins to choose from – wedding cake, red velvet cake, carrot cake, pistachio almond, chocolate lava, mango peach, and lemon supreme. They were also several pastries unlike any Blanche had ever seen – an almond cream croissant, a cherry cheese tart, baklava, and a white chocolate chip and pecan cookie. It was hard for her to decide. Sensing she wanted to sample more than one item, Adam indicated the coffee shop also had mini versions in the case beyond the counter. After admitting he often got a half dozen of the minis, Blanche commented she'd do the same. Adam pulled out a credit card, and it was swiped before Blanche had a chance to protest and pay her share of the bill.

As they sat in the rear of the coffee shop, Adam smiled at the tiny moans of pleasure as Blanche tasted each of the minis she had selected. Sipping his coffee as he watched her sigh over each heavenly concoction, Blanche remained oblivious to the fact he had been so closing observing her pleasure until she took the last bit and reached for a napkin to wipe her lips.

"I guess I was hungrier than I thought," she stated and smiled embarrassingly. "Thank you for the treats."

"You're most welcome. It's good to see someone truly enjoying themselves for a change.... So, tell me about the lecture. This is a pilot I recommended to the former dean. If we don't get positive feedback, we don't plan to offer the series next summer. It didn't appear you were satisfied with the lecture overall. Was it worth your time?"

"Oh, no! I was more than satisfied with everything I learned. It was definitely worth my time." Blanche pulled the handouts from her purse and showed Adam the notes she had taken on the importance of nutrition to adolescents during their growth spurt. "It was very informative."

Adam glanced through the notes she had jotted down from the second of the lectures in the biosocial development series. It didn't appear she had been bored and her reaction indicated genuine interest in the topic.

"You appeared upset when I saw you at the end of the lecture."

Blanche turned her head to one side scared to raise the topic. Remembering Adam was a professor and his job was to teach, she knew she should be as comfortable discussing issues with him as she did with the other teachers at her grammar school. Turning her face towards him, she confided.

"Adam, I was upset because I feel so stupid, so ignorant. There's a student at our school that we should have been helping and haven't been just because we didn't recognize the symptoms."

Interested in this real life application of what she had learned over the past two hours, Adam leaned in indicating his willingness to hear the story and encouraging her to continue.

"When I had her in the fourth grade, this little girl was one of my best students. Her name was Sharon. She was attentive in class, never a disciplinary problem. Her parents volunteered as chaperones for field trips. They were always willing to help her with her assignments. The child was a joy, the type teachers wished they could clone. When she went to fifth grade, things seemed to change. One day in the teacher's lounge, I overheard the fifth grade teacher complaining that I must have just given her those grades because I liked her. She was saying the child was apathetic and just plain lazy. Now, I know the change is because of her iron level."

Adam looked at Blanche questioningly, "Why do you feel so certain about that diagnosis without knowledge of the girl's medical history?"

Blanche glanced around to ensure no one would overhear what she said next. Speaking softly, she began whispering to Adam, "Last year, one of her friends came and got me because she had locked herself in the bathroom and was crying. I went to talk to her to find out what was wrong. She was in there scared to death because her panties had spots of blood. She thought she was bleeding to death. Since she was only ten, her mother hadn't explained to her about a menstrual period yet. After today's lecture, I feel she started menstruating so early because of stress. Her father lost his job and he's now working two minimal wage jobs. Her mother had to go to work as well to help him keep things going. At only ten, she was responsible for taking her five and seven year old brothers home from school, fixing them a snack, helping them with their homework, and taking care of them until one of her parents got home. That's a lot of responsibility for someone not yet eleven. It also meant she wasn't as physically active as she used to be. Her parents instructed her to go straight home and for the three of them to stay behind the locked doors as a safety precaution. So, she wasn't out playing after school like other kids her age. After hearing this lecture, I feel adamant that the stress combined with the inactivity caused her menarche."

Blanche pointed to those points from the lecture.

"I'd have to agree with your assessment," Adam nodded as he glanced through the passages Blanche had highlighted.

"Also, being in a lower income bracket, I bet her mother is bringing home fried foods she can buy cheap from the fast food chains. She probably doesn't have the time to cook like she did as an at home mom. So instead of the fruits and vegetables they're accustomed to eating, she's eating fad foods. Between her period and poor diet, her iron level may be depleted. She's not lazy or apathetic, she just has low iron. As soon as I get home tonight, I'm going to call her mother and ask her to have her hemoglobin checked… even if I have to pay for the test myself. We need to get her back on track before the new school year starts."

Adam read through the passages on diet Blanche pointed out. Laying the papers on the table, he looked at Blanche with a serious expression before commenting, "Everything you said is making sense, and I agree it wouldn't hurt to share this information with her mother. It's a simple, inexpensive test, and it's definitely worth checking out. … You're going to be a good counselor, Blanche."

Blanche beamed at the compliment, especially coming from someone of Adam's status.

"Thank you. I can't wait until Thursday. It's the first on cognitive development."

The cashier approached and asked if they wanted anything else since they were scheduled to close in fifteen minutes.

Glancing at his watch, Adam offered, "Would you like to continue this discussion over dinner? There's a restaurant not too far from here that is open late."

"Dinner? Oh, Adam, I didn't realize it was that late. Autumn wanted pizza tonight. I need to go. "

Adam folded his hands together and leaned them against his lips frustrated as he recalled Blanche's home situation. He thought it slightly ironic that dinner would be pizza after she had heard a lecture that touched on the nutritional aspects of one's diet but surmised it was a feeble attempt to gain points in her stepdaughter's eyes.

Blanche gathered her papers off the table, stuffed then in her purse, and rose extending her hand to thank him once again.

Adam rose before taking her hand in his.

"Then, I'll see you around campus?"

"Definitely! Good night...." Blanche smiled across her shoulder as she walked away from the table.

After she turned to push the exit door open, Adam took one last admiring glance at the length of leg showing through the back split in her skirt.

Chapter Thirteen

Sitting at his desk Thursday afternoon, Adam couldn't focus on the budgetary spreadsheets before him. His eyes kept turning to the wall clock, and he spent more time counting the seconds tick away than counting the columns of numbers he needed to confirm for the psychology department. When the tone came across the intercom system indicating the end of a class period, he glanced at the clock once again. In fifteen minutes, the lecture Blanche planned to attend would be finishing.

"She's married, Adam. Let it go." He hoped that speaking the words aloud would force a reality check and help his concentration. When he got another different sum after adding the same column of figures for the third time, he stood, tossed the pencil on his desk, walked over to the coat rack, and donned his sport jacket. He still had roughly five minutes to make it to the lecture hall.

Entering the rear of the auditorium, the seats were already empty. The lecture must have completed earlier than scheduled. However, Blanche and the visiting professor were down on the stage in an intense conversation. He walked down the stairs to the bottom level, turned to the left, and leaped up the short set of steps leading to the podium on the stage. Seeing his approach, the visiting professor acknowledged his presence.

"Professor Brown, it's so good you are here to join in our conversation. We were discussing the merit of adolescents being given the opportunity to fantasize so they could begin to think in terms of possibility rather than only in terms of reality."

Blanche seemed frustrated at the concept. She turned to Adam hoping he would take her side.

"I know I've been working in a Catholic school environment, and our classrooms are very disciplined compared to, for example, a Montessori method; but school is to learn your lessons, not to speculate and hypothesize. Isn't that more for a high school environment, like chemistry or geometry classes? Even then, students are going through exercises to demonstrate known hypotheses, not being asked to develop new ones."

The visiting professor pressed his point, "Adolescents must be free to develop their own personal style. They need to become more capable of drawing their own logical conclusions, and teachers must find ways to develop their deductive reasoning skills."

Blanche could only think of her own adolescent period. Her mother had always dictated what she was to think and feel. The elderly nuns didn't hesitate using a ruler on the palms of their students' hands if they couldn't recite the proper facts when called upon to answer questions posed from the previous night's homework assignment. What the professor proposed was the opposite of everything she had ever experienced or the current culture at their school. Learning facts was their norm. Thinking of English classes where students were free to write anything they wished to help them master language rather than the typical book reports or essays on dictated subject matters was a stretch. Blanche cringed at the thought of introducing the concept at her school. She fell silent, her head throbbing from the new ideas she had heard that afternoon.

Throwing his arms open into the air, the professor continued, "Students must be free to express themselves. Education should not be about regurgitating facts. A student truly understands when he demonstrates he can relate new ideas to old." He glanced at Blanche's troubled face and said softly, "Empower them... Don't restrict them from finding their destiny."

Her face became more sullen as she recalled her mother's words over her decision to take a psychology course, "What you're in is a waste of time. Drop out that nonsense..."

She looked up to the professor and repeated, "Don't restrict them from finding their destiny."

Satisfied that part of his message seemed to be getting through, the professor turned to Adam and shook his hand enthusiastically, "Thank you for the invitation. It has been most enjoyable. I look forward to returning next summer."

With that, he gave Blanche one final glance before retrieving his brief case on the side of the podium and exiting the auditorium.

"Could I interest you in joining me for a glass of wine? It looks like you could use a little help relaxing right now."

"Oh, Adam, his ideas are so fresh, so new to me."

He placed his arm around her shoulder and guided her from the auditorium. Once outside, they walked together a short distance to a neighborhood lounge. Taking a table on the upper balcony, Adam ordered a bottle of Pinot Grigio. They sat in silence sipping the wine and watching the sunset with Blanche deep in thought about the new concepts and Adam deep in thought about Blanche.

Chapter Fourteen

So engrossed on learning as much as she could that summer, Blanche didn't recognize the routine that had developed between her and Adam. He always seemed to appear at the end of each lecture, and she looked forward to having the chance to discuss her newfound knowledge with someone that could clarify concepts and debate the topics with her. They would walk over to the coffee shop, the lounge, or a neighborhood restaurant that served po-boy sandwiches. They openly discussed a variety of subjects that impacted adolescents: peer pressure and the merits of role-playing to encourage positive rather than destructive behavior; the physical changes experienced and the need for increased hygiene; growth spurts and the need for school lunch programs to adjust the intake of calcium, iron, and zinc which impacts proper bone and muscle development; how experimenting with smoking could decrease food consumption, interfere with nutrient absorption and limit growth spurts; striving for emotional maturity during their awakening sexuality; the need to begin moving towards economic independence along with the pros and cons of part-time employment; and the influence of family and culture.

It was the last topic that hit the closest to home for Blanche. The topic was the final in the psychosocial development series and dealt with identity. There were times she started to walk out the lecture because too many painful memories were coming to mind. It seemed her life was the case study for everything she was hearing. She sank further into her chair as she listened to the fact self-loathing could arise from parental rejection, causing an adolescent to feel worthless and even trigger depression. The adolescent might often fall into a role of always trying to please others to gain acceptance and increase their self-esteem. She thought about all the things she would try to do to get a kind word from her mother since those occasions were few and far between. At the end of the lecture, she remained in her seat waiting for and needing the silence of an empty auditorium. She closed her eyes as memories flooded her mind and she realized how strongly her mother had controlled her destiny. Though she didn't regret the path she now had taken, her interest had been in nursing ever since her father died. Her mother had said that medicine wasn't for Blanche and that all nurses did were become mistresses to the doctors they met. After asking her if she wanted to become a whore, she had stood above her

and waited until Blanche wrote on her college application form that she
wanted to major in elementary education.

When she heard footsteps descending to her row of seats, Blanche
didn't have to look to know it was Adam. He sat next to her but didn't
speak. Instead he took her left hand in his right and squeezed it softly.
They sat together in silence until the clean-up crew came in with
brooms and trash cans to tidy the auditorium.

"Was this a 'heal thyself' moment?"

Blanche smiled at his insightfulness and laid her head on his shoulder.
She had come to value the friendship they had developed, and she felt
as comfortable around Adam as she did in Colin's presence.

"Doctor, how about dinner to celebrate your new beginning?" he
whispered softly.

"I'd like that," she answered and lifted her head from her shoulder and
began gathering her things.

"Since this is the last in the lecture series, let's do something special to
celebrate. There's a restaurant not far from my condo I think you'd
enjoy. Game?"

Knowing tonight was one she wouldn't see Autumn, Blanche couldn't
think of any reason to turn down his offer. Besides, she didn't want to
be alone with her negative thoughts.

"I'd love to," she smiled up at Adam.

"Where are you parked?"

"In the garage across the street from this hall."

"When you pull out, just park on the side street…. I'll drive around to
meet you so you can follow me, okay?"

Blanche nodded in agreement.

"When we get to my place, you'll need to punch in this code to activate the gate again after I drive through." Adam took a note pad out his jacket pocket and jotted down a four digit number before handing the slip to Blanche. "You can park in any spot marked for visitors. I'll walk over and meet you in that area."

Blanche nodded again that she understood. After they left the auditorium, she retrieved Colin's Lexus from the garage and stayed park in the area she understood based on Adam's instructions until a black sedan pulled alongside her. Honking once to indicate his arrival, Blanche waved, turned on the ignition, and pulled into the street to follow him. Adam took every precaution to make it easy for Blanche to keep up with him during the rush hour traffic. A half hour later, she was pulling into a parking lot behind Adam. After parking in a designated visitor's spot and stepping from Colin's car, the sounds of a calliope could be heard.

"Where's the music coming from?" she questioned as Adam approached.

"One of the paddle wheelers on the river," Adam answered. "Let's walk that way so you can see it. The river is right across the railroad track here."

Taking her hand in his, Adam led her through a passenger gate from the parking lot, across a railroad track, and onto a walkway. They found an empty bench and took a seat in the riverfront park to enjoy the views of the Mississippi River: the ferry crossing from the end of Canal St. to Algiers Point and back, the paddle wheeler loading tourists for the evening dinner cruise to the Chalmette national cemetery, tugboats guiding cargo ships through the river's channel, parents playing with their children, and residents of the area walking their dogs.

"Adam, the river current looks so strong. It looks menacing, but yet, it's so peaceful here."

"Yes, I love living here. There's always something going on, and you meet folks from all over the world… Sometimes, instead of driving to the university, I walk down to Canal Street and take the streetcar. It takes a lot longer, but it gives me time to think."

"What do you call this area of the city where you live?"

Adam looked at Blanche inquiringly. "Are you not from here in New Orleans?"

"No, I grew up in Lafayette."

Adam found it odd that her husband hadn't brought her down to the area. He wondered how they had met, how long she had been living in the city, and how long they had been married. "Too busy making money," he thought.

"This is the French Quarter," Adam replied nonchalantly.

"The French Quarter!" Blanche replied in an agitated tone glancing about as if she needed to reassess her surroundings.

"Blanche, is something wrong?"

"This isn't what I pictured of the French Quarter at all. I thought it was more ... seedy," she said in a lower tone embarrassed by her mistaken impression of what the area would be like.

"The area is old and some of the streets are narrow similar to European cities, but it's not seedy," Adam chuckled. "Ready for dinner? We can walk along the river towards the French Market. The restaurant is at the end of this path."

Blanche rose and they walked side by side along the riverfront. Adam pointed out Jackson Square, St. Louis Cathedral, the Cabildo, and the Presbytere. When they got to the end of the path, Adam offered his hand once again as they stepped down the short stairway and crossed the railroad tracks. The restaurant he chose wasn't far from the gilded St. Joan of Arc statue and he provided a short history lesson on the monument.

When Adam checked in at the hostess station, they were led up a flight of stairs to the main floor. The restaurant also had a view of the river. Since the sun was setting, the hostess lit the candle on their table before placing menus in front of them.

"Adam, please. Let me pay the bill tonight. You've been too kind this summer. Giving me the free pass to the lecture series and the amount of time you've spent with me after the lectures discussing and debating issues... Let me do something to repay you. Please..." Blanche gave him her most pleading look as she impatiently waited for his response.

"It's you that has done me the favor. Blanche, you've made me realize that I was in a rut. I've taught the same classes for over five years now. I've been parroting the lessons, and that's been an injustice to my students. Your enthusiasm and interest has re-energized me. Thanks to you and seeing other professors' techniques through this lecture series, I'm going to be a better instructor this coming semester. You have made the teacher into a student. I'll be researching and learning new methods to get the ideas and points across in the future. So, NO, you're not paying tonight." Adam smiled as the waiter approached, introduced himself, and laid a basket of hot rolls and pats of butter in the center of the table.

After they had completed the main course, the waiter handed each of them the dessert menu. When Blanche turned to ask about the house special, Adam quickly interjected.

"There's a coffee house I think you'd love to see. We could have dessert there."

Turning to face Adam, Blanche laid the dessert menu down and agreed to retire to their next stop. After exiting the restaurant, Adam began filling her in on the establishment. His enthusiasm was contagious, and their steps quickened as they walked along a slate covered sidewalk.

"You won't believe this place when you see it. The owner of the coffee shop is a former English professor from the university. He was forced to retire and take over the family business when his father passed. After his mother died, he converted the business into a coffee shop so he can pursue his true passion, literature, once again." Adam paused as they waited for the traffic on Decatur Street to come to a stop. After crossing safely, he gave Blanche a quick glance assessing her interest before continuing.

"His parents had an import business here in the French Quarter, so as a child, he met and conversed with people from all over the world. His father's business colleagues would give him books from their country of origin as Christmas and birthday gifts. That's how his passion for worldwide literature was sparked. Between his books, his parents' collection, textbooks being discarded from schools, books from library sales, and donations, he has a literary collection that rivals any library or university in town. What is most impressive is that he keeps the place open twenty-four hours a day, seven days a week. He gives jobs to the students so they have a place to work, and when he's not sleeping, he walks around answering the students' questions, holding discussions, and even edits their papers for them. I believe they learn more here than at school. It's fascinating. He told me he gets to enjoy all the positive aspects of teaching without the politics of the learning institutions. Tonight is poetry night. He converted the building they used as a storage area into a small auditorium. Any student is welcome to come and read their original works or perform. A lot of the music majors come as here as well."

As they turned a corner onto a site street from Decatur Street, Adam announced, "Here it is!"

Looking up, Blanche saw the name of the coffee shop was The Library. Recalling her argument with Autumn over the Fourth of July weekend, a strange feeling came over her. Before Autumn left that morning, she had said, "I'm going to The Library to research a paper I have due..." Blanche had assumed she meant at the university but this had to be the place Autumn had gone. She hadn't lied at all. She was in the French Quarter, and she was also at The Library. As Blanche entered, Adam explained the layout of the structure to her.

"This was built typical of the French Quarter buildings. The bottom floor was the family's business. The second story was living area, and the third floor was used for bedrooms. The import business had expanded, and the professor's father also purchased the three storied property on the right and, for storage, the Creole cottage on the left. This middle section where we're standing is the original house. He converted the bottom floor to the coffee shop and lives in the two stories above."

Pointing to the left, Adam continued, "See the curtain in the corner. He cut a doorway to lead into the Creole cottage. That's where the poetry readings will be held."

Taking Blanche's hand, they walked to the right through another doorway. As Blanche looked up, there was a spiral staircase circling all three floors, and everywhere were shelves lined with books. Students were along the landings perusing titles, leaning against the railings reading, or sitting on settees in little alcoves making notes on petite tables. Blanche stared in awe at the stained glass ceiling at the top of the third floor.

"Impressive, isn't it?" Adam whispered as he admired the rays from back lights illuminating the glass so visitors could enjoy the beauty of the ceiling even after the sun set.

Taking Blanche's hand once again, he led her back through the coffee shop into the Creole cottage. The seating was not what Blanche expected. Instead of auditorium style seats anchored in uniform rows, odd chairs, tables, and old sofas were strategically placed around the room. Adam led her to a love seat in the rear. A copy of the menu for the day was in the center of the table. The menu had a wider variety of items than Blanche had anticipated. It was an extensive list of imported wines and beers, international coffees, cakes, pies, croissants, pastries, salads, soups and sandwiches.

When the waiter approached, Blanche looked at Adam, "I've never had an Irish coffee. I thought coffee was grown only in warmer climates, like South America... I'd like to try that. Have you ever tasted it?"

Adam smiled at Blanche's joke as he responded, "It's excellent here. They don't skimp on the ingredients like other establishments." Looking to the student waiter, he placed their order, "Two Irish coffees and two slices of the amaretto cheesecake."

"Do you want to pay now or run a tab?"

"Start a tab for now," Adam responded as he leaned back against the love seat, his arm lying along the back of the area where Blanche was sitting. About fifteen minutes after receiving their order, an elderly gentleman walked from behind the curtain, placed a high stool in the front of the curtain, turned on a spotlight, and dimmed the lights in the audience.

"Attention, ladies and gentlemen. We have quite a repertoire for you tonight. The students presenting have worked long and hard on these original works, and having read or listened to each, I think you will find this evening most enjoyable. Please... Don't skimp on the applause!"

He smiled before taking his seat in the armchair on the far left of the curtain.

Adam whispered to Blanche, "The students come out from behind the curtain one at a time, introduce their selection themselves. There is only one rule the professor enforces. They are not allowed to state their names. The professor insists they keep their identities private since the shows are open to the public."

Blanche leaned back with her coffee as the first student entered, climbed onto the stool, and recited. An hour into the program, Blanche was holding her empty cup up as the waiter refilled her Irish coffee. Adam leaned towards her and whispered into her ear as the next student emerged from behind the curtain, "I know this girl. She's one of my best students. Her name is Danielle. She raises questions I would expect from a Senior. If it wasn't for her level of participation, I'm not sure how I would reach some of the kids in that class. She's a godsend. I hope I get to teach her again in the fall... "

Looking up towards the stage, Blanche's hand started trembling as she worked to balance the full cup. She splattered coffee onto the table before she was able to lay the cup securely onto the saucer again.

"That's not a Danielle," she looked at Adam confused. "That's Autumn Warren, the student I came to see you about. How can you claim she's one of your best students when you sent a letter saying she might fail due to lack of attendance?"

Equally confused, Adam turned, and they were face to face as they whispered back and forth to each other.

"That is your stepdaughter? She's on my role as Danielle." Though he was still facing Blanche, he was obviously struggling to recall the roster from his classes.

"Stepdaughter? She's not my stepdaughter. Where did you get that idea?"

"The first time you came to my office. You inquired about Autumn Warren." Adam's eyes shifted as he tried to recall the exact works Blanche had used. "You said she weren't her mother and then you added that she was in a parent/step-parent situation. I got the impression you came to see me because you were her stepmother."

Blanche shook her head staring at Adam in disbelief. "I was only giving you information about her based on your questions. Her mother's name was Maria Warren based on her first marriage. She's married now to my cousin. My cousin Colin Laurent is her stepfather. They are away on business so I'm here just spending the summer with her. I came to see you because they're out of town and not returning for two more weeks. I was there on their behalf."

Adam stared into Blanche's eyes, "You're … not married?"

"Married? … Me? … No," Blanche answered him in an adamant tone. Out the corner of his eye, Adam caught the professor standing up and glaring at the couple in the rear whose whispers were becoming a distraction. Settling backwards in the loveseat, Adam and Blanche fell silent once again as Autumn climbed onto the stool to recite. Adam was watching Blanche more than he was watching Danielle/Autumn, something he would have to get to the bottom of when he got back to his office the next day.

Blanche listened intently as Autumn announced the title of her poem, "Willows and Oaks." When she began to recite, Blanche leaned forward straining to hear Autumn's soft voice.

The strength of a man is not contrived.
A man's demeanor, individually defined.
His emotions hidden, open, or repressed.
His wealth not determined by his dress.

A woman is sweet and emotional,
Sometimes distant but devotional.
Some may forget to be a lady.
The rest are proper and not shady.

They say men are like oaks, solid and strong,
Head of the household and never wrong.
Bending to no one's will but their own,
And never relinquishing their throne.

Women are gentle and bend with the wind,
There from the day their families begin.
Bending and twisting to everyone's needs
And never collapsing to their knees.

Autumn had recited the poem with such emotion the audience applauded loudly as she slipped from the stool and gave a short bow indicating the end of her first performance. Blanche's eyes had welled as she listened to the words. She wondered if Autumn had written the poem based on her personal experience. How hard it must have been when Maria and her father had separated. Then to adjust to Colin stepping in... Colin, like Blanche's own father until the end, was a tower of strength but sometimes unyielding. Blanche had noticed how the struggle through his divorce had changed her cousin. Though he was kind and very understanding, she didn't doubt there were times he laid down the law with Autumn. She remembered the difference in Autumn's driving to and from the airport. Because of the personal tragedy he had suffered, Autumn would not have had a choice in her driving technique when Colin was in the car. She recalled the difference in the tone between Colin and Maria that morning trying to get Autumn out of bed so they could get to church. Having spent the summer with her and the transition she had helped Blanche through, Blanche knew Autumn was insightful. Though young, she had observed her mother's struggles after the divorce as a single mom dedicated only to her daughters and doing everything for them. Blanche's heart went out to her. She nodded yes when the waitress offered her a third Irish coffee. She didn't notice the questioning glance Adam tossed her way when she began gulping the warm liquid down.

By the time Autumn took the stool for her final performance that night, Blanche was on her fifth Irish coffee. The warm liquid was soothing as was the arm Adam had slipped around her shoulder as her mind focused on memories of her father triggered by Autumn's first poem. Autumn confidently announced the title of her work, "You Went Away," before reciting:

> Long ago, you were my life.
> I wanted you to make me your wife.
> But, far apart we had to grow
> Learning life we didn't know.
>
> Then came along a few guys
> Whose names I won't even disguise.
> And, yes, each one hurt me
> But never could usurp me…
>
> Forgiving people, I can do
> But not forgetting what they do.
> I can never change this me
> As I struggle with who I am to be.
>
> Never again is what I swore
> Even with those I adored.
> Giving in is what will kill me
> As I fight wars I don't see.
>
> I know you had to go
> Far away to places I don't know.
> You went away when I needed you.
> You can't come back now; our love is through.

Several ladies in the audience wiped tears from their eyes but stood and applauded Autumn as she slipped down from the stool and took her final bow. This poem bothered Blanche. Autumn was too young to have known such sorrow. Was this also from experience? Had she been hurt at such a young age? Though Blanche had never dated, some of her peers in school had gone on dates as early as the eighth grade. She said a silent prayer that Autumn would never experience the pains of her mother going through a divorce or herself having a broken, disappointing relationship again. Little did Blanche know that parts of Autumn's poem would be an omen of what was to come in her own life.

Two more students followed Autumn's last performance. When the final recitation concluded, the professor stood and pulled a cord attached to the wall next to his armchair. The curtains opened and all the students were standing together holding hands. They took a final bow in unison to the applause of the audience. Then the professor drew the curtains closed once again and took the stool himself to recite one of his favorite passages before thanking the audience for their attendance and support.

"How did you like it?" Adam whispered into Blanche's ear as the professor closed the show.

"Adam, I can't describe the experience. I'm so glad I had the chance to come. Thank you for suggesting this."

He took his arm from around her shoulder to pull his wallet from his back pocket as the waiter approached with the final bill. Blanche leaned down, her face resting on the soft pillows piled against the arm of the love seat.

As Adam signed the credit card receipt and slipped several bills to the grateful waiter, he turned to Blanche, "Ready?"

Nodding yes, Blanche rubbed her eyes and rose from the love seat. When Blanche stood, she felt dizzy so placed a hand on Adam's arm to steady herself. Watching her, Adam quickly placed his arm around her waist encouraging her to lean against him for support.

"You're not ready to drive home yet…"

"I think you're right," Blanche responded acknowledging she didn't have her full faculties.

"I have a guest room. You can lie down for a while…"

Not thinking of an alternative choice in the matter, Blanche nodded in agreement. They slipped out the door of the coffee house and walked the few short blocks to Adam's condo. Though the walk and the night breeze blowing off the Mississippi River was refreshing and made her feel slightly better, Blanche knew she was still not ready to risk driving Colin's car by the time they reached the complex. At the elevator, Adam swiped his security card which permitted access to the residential elevators. By the time the elevator reached his floor, Blanche's head was resting on Adam's shoulder. He walked slowly, both of his arms encircling her waist, until they reached the front door. Punching his access code into the security pad, they entered, and he led her to the guest room. By then, everything was a blur to Blanche. She kept her head on Adam's shoulder, her eyes slightly closed and allowing him to take the lead.

Leading her to the side of the bed, his arms guided her to a sitting position. As soon as she felt the bed beneath her, Blanche laid just her upper body down, but when her head hit the pillow, she moaned. Instead of feeling better, reclining made her feel worse. Adam gently lifted her legs onto the bed. When she moaned again, he reached across her for a second pillow. Using his left hand, he slid his arm around her upper back lifting her just enough to slide the second pillow beneath her head. Being not as flat helped her feel better. She thought about her father tucking her in at night when she was a little girl and planting a kiss on her forehead before leaving her bedroom. She always kissed him on the cheek in return. Instinctively, she turned to kiss Adam on the cheek to thank him for being so kind. He was lifting away from her as she did, and the feathery kiss fell in the slight curve of his neck arousing a sensual reaction in him she hadn't intended. She lay back against the pillows in a dream-like state.

Adam stood at the side of the bed watching her. He had fallen in love with her over these past weeks but had kept his distance thinking she was married. But tonight, he had found out differently, and now, the woman he loved, the woman he wanted to marry and felt was his soul mate, was in his apartment and in one of his beds. He eyed her from head to toe with longing. She was so beautiful, so intelligent, so mature and yet seemed childlike in her appreciation and expressions of wonder at the simplest pleasures they had experienced together: the time they went to a coffee shop and she picked what she termed an exotic muffin, trying barbecued shrimp oozing with a buttery sauce and giggling over using her hands to eat in a restaurant, eating a hot beignet with extra powdered sugar dusting her blouse, biting into a warm praline recently spooned from the huge copper pots at the candy shop next to campus.... He recalled every moment they had spent together and surmised she was just a woman that enjoyed life and didn't take even simple pleasures for granted.

He couldn't resist reaching down and planting a kiss on her lips. In her dream-like state, Blanche imagined she was one of the leading ladies in the movies she had seen. In response, she circled her arms around Adam's neck and kissed him softly in return, then exhaled slowly. Adam kissed her again, this time harder and longer. When she didn't resist, he used his tongue to tease the tip of hers before deepening his kisses. When Blanche eagerly responded, his right hand began unbuttoning her blouse. Pushing the material in layers on each side of her, he began planting soft kisses on the curve of her left breast. When her breathing became more rapid and she thrust her chest upwards towards him, he used a single finger to slowly slide her bra strap down her arm and then eased the cup of the bra lower exposing her nipple.

Using his tongue, he teased her gently at first. Blanche moaned in pleasure and arched her breast upward towards him aching for more. When he suckled her, she began mimicking the behavior she had seen in the movies gasping as pleasurable sensations flowed. Her responsiveness urged Adam to continue. Still suckling her nipple, he slipped his hand under her skirt and used a finger to massage her clitoris. Blanche went weak in his arms, tossing her head backwards. When Adam felt the telltale shudder of her body indicating she had climaxed, it was his undoing. He stood, pushed her skirt up, and used both of his hands to slide her panties off. Unbuttoning his slacks, he lowered his pants and briefs just enough to expose his manhood. Mounting her impatiently, he slid inside of her.

Blanche tensed and grimaced. Adam heard her hiss right at the point he detected the resistance, but it was too late to control his ejaculation. Stunned, he pulled out from her, stood, and quickly put his own clothing back in order. Then, out of respect for her, he pulled her skirt down, slipped her bra back into place, and clumsily re-buttoned her blouse. He stood for a few minutes watching her drift off to sleep before leaving the guest bedroom, closing the door gently behind him.

Chapter Fifteen

Standing on the balcony of his own bedroom, Adam leaned on the railing chiding himself. The woman he wanted to marry had been a virgin, and he had desecrated her. Her initial reactions led him to believe she was experienced, but he realized now the affect the night of drinking had on her response. She wasn't experienced; she was drunk. Hell, she wasn't even experienced at drinking. What he thought had been a joke about the Irish coffee wasn't a joke after all.

"Damn, Adam, how could you?" he spoke aloud condemning himself as memories of the last conversation he had with his mother came to mind.

He was twelve years old at the time. It was the first day of school and three of his seventh grade friends had come home with him. They were working on their homework assignments together in his bedroom before pairing up in his backyard to shoot hoops. His mother had walked in with a plate of homemade oatmeal cookies and caught part of their conversation about the changed appearance of their female classmates. They all went quiet and were trying to muffle their laughter until she left the room.

That night, after his friends were gone, she had called him into the den. She patted the cushion next to hers indicating he was to sit down. Knowing her son loved her, she questioned how he would feel if someone would make fun of her. Adam had grown angry, stood, and said he would fight them until their nose bled. When she explained, those girls would be someone's mother one day and their bodies were changing to prepare them for motherhood, she could tell the analogy hit home. His expression became sorrowful that they were poking fun at his classmates. His mother made him promise he would never be disrespectful to the girls or to ladies. From that day on, he became their champion instead.

Having become one of the leaders among his classmates at an early age, he glared disapprovingly at any snide remark about the girls his peers made. His friends and others began following his example. They began holding the doors for the girls, quickly picking up items they had dropped for them, and helping them by carrying their books. The shy glances and giggles they received in return made them feel grown and a new respectful environment began to form. A few months later, his mother passed after losing her battle with breast cancer. As he laid a rose on her coffin at the gravesite, he had vowed, in her memory, he would always show respect for women and be their champion. And now, he had failed at the time it meant the most……

"In the morning," thought Adam, "he and Blanche needed to talk." He would first apologize for taking advantage of her and then express his love and desire to enter into a more permanent relationship. As he exited from the balcony and moved towards his own bed, he thought of her in the guest room next to his. He wanted to go back to her, take her into his arms, and spend the night caressing her, kissing her, wanting to make-up for what he had done. He held back. They needed to talk first. He needed to know she felt the same way. They needed to discuss their dreams and their future. No, he needed to wait until morning. He needed to know his presence was her choosing and not the effect of the Irish coffees she had consumed. He tossed in his bed agitated for hours before finally falling to sleep.

Blanche stirred, shifted her position, blinked her eyes then opened them widely as the realization she was not in Aubrey's room struck. Sitting up on the bed, she glanced around the room in a panic wondering where she was. Events of the night before came back to her. Had she and Adam made love? She looked at her clothes. Her blouse was buttoned one off. She cupped her hands over her mouth tightly stifling her cries. She got off the bed, slipped on her sandals, walked to the door of the bedroom, and opened it slowly. Peeking out, Adam was not in sight. Glancing at her watch, the time was 4:00 A.M. She tiptoed from the room, grabbed her purse from the coffee table in the living room, and padded to the front door. She took one glance back to ensure she had not woken Adam before slipping out the front door. She stood by the elevator pumping the down button and nervously praying for it to come before Adam discovered her running away. Finally the door opened. She jumped inside, quickly touched the button for the ground floor, and then began hitting the close door symbol repeatedly trying to get the door to close faster. As the door began to shut, she glanced one more time down the hall to the front door of Adam's condo. Luckily, the door was still shut. She sighed in relief.

As she walked past the security guard station, the guard on duty called out, "Do you need a cab, miss?"

"No, thank you," Blanche responded shyly and hastened her steps to the entrance door. Stepping out the building into the parking lot, a breeze blowing off the river made Blanche realize she wasn't wearing panties. She stopped in her tracks and pulled her skirt tightly around her. Her vaginal area felt sticky and cool from the breeze attempting to lift her skirt. Though no area of her body was exposed to anyone watching her, she felt nude. She glanced back towards Adam's condo. She wondered if he was still asleep. Even if his was, what was she to do? Ask the security guard to let he sneak in and look for her panties? Even if she could create some excuse to convince them to admit her, how could she face Adam if he woke and caught her? Shaking her head disgustedly at the thought, she pulled her skirt tightly around her legs and quickly walked to her car holding onto the makeshift folds. Getting in, she turned the ignition and sped out the parking lot. She had to get home as quickly as possible.

Her chest muscles were tightening, and she was taking short breaths at the thought of being in public not properly attired. What if a policeman stopped her? What if she had to get out and stand on the side of the car? Would the brightness of the head beams show she was not wearing undies? Could she be arrested for indecent exposure? She glanced at the speedometer and slowed to five miles under the speed limit as a precaution. It seemed the trip to New Orleans East took twice as long as usual.

When she arrived at Colin and Maria's, Autumn's car was parked in the driveway. She sat in Colin's car for what seemed an eternity before mustering the courage to go into the house. She punched in the code to disable the alarm system as quickly as she could and praying the buzzing sound would not wake Autumn. The house was in dead silence. Tiptoeing to Aubrey's room, she slipped off the blouse and skirt she had been wearing, pulled a pair of panties out the drawer, and pulled her nightgown on. She slipped into bed and tried to sleep. Maybe things won't seem so bad in the morning....

When Adam's alarm buzzed, he tossed aside the covers, grabbed his robe, and pulled it on as he walked to the guest bedroom. He took several deep breaths before having the courage to knock softly on the door. When he didn't hear a response, he knocked harder waiting for Blanche to respond. When still no response, he turned the knob, opened the door a crack, then pushed it hard when he spotted the empty bed. Walking into the room, he stood at the foot of the bed looking at the impression her body had made in the coverlet. As he moved to the side of the bed to straighten the coverlet, the toe of his bare foot caught on an object. He glanced down to the carpet and saw the black, satiny bikini panties he had slipped off of Blanche. He reached down and lifted the panties to his nose inhaling the scent of her. As he slipped the panties into his robe pocket, he made another vow for the second time in his life. He vowed he would win her forgiveness, and he would get her back.

Chapter Sixteen

As the sun's rays beamed through the open blinds in Aubrey's room, Blanche pulled the crocheted afghan over her head wishing for darkness again. She tossed into different positions in the bed trying to force herself to go back to sleep. Her head was aching from the Irish coffees she had consumed the night before. The ache in her pelvic region reminded her of her sinful actions at Adam's. She moaned and pulled the pillow alongside her face and buried her face in the softness. When sleep failed to come, she began berating herself. How could you drink yourself into a stupor? How could you embarrass Adam holding onto his arm to keep from stumbling as he helped you walk out the coffee house? Did his students see them leaving? If so, what would they say around campus? Had she ruined his reputation? Had Autumn seen her? They were sitting all the way in the back, and the lights were dimmed. If she had seen her, had she told her friends that she knew Blanche? If so, had Autumn had to endure snide comments because of her? She punched the pillow in anger then pulled it back across her face.

She couldn't bear to think of her behavior at Adam's place. She tried to remember as much as she could of the night before, but everything was a blur. She remembered feeling nauseated as she fell down onto the bed. She remembered Adam lifting her and placing a second pillow under her head. The rest of the night wasn't clear in her mind. She had felt the weight of his body on top of hers and the discomfort as he took her virginity. Then nothing else came to her until the point she woke and slipped out of his condo.

Why had he left her alone in the room? Could he tell she was a virgin? What if he didn't realize it? She had no idea what the male might experience or feel. She concluded he had assumed she wasn't and left her disgusted by the wanton way she had acted that night. Blanche pulled the pillow tighter over her face. Though the lecture series was over, he had invited her to sit in his last classes. She couldn't go back to the campus. She couldn't ever face him again.

"Oh, God," she thought. Face him? What about facing Autumn? Would Autumn be able to tell Blanche had lost her virginity? She should have been here for the summer as a role model. Some role model she turned out to be. Colin and Maria would be coming home weekend after next. Would Colin be able to tell? She couldn't bear to see the look of disappointment on his face, his little princess having sex with a man she barely knew. What about her mother when she got home? Blanche couldn't imagine her mother's reaction. One of her mother's first lectures to her once her period started had been, "Men don't buy the cow when they can get the milk free." She and Adam weren't even dating, and she had thrown herself at him. Now she was ruined. She had hoped she would meet the right person one day, but even if she did, she could never date them or offer herself to them in marriage if she got a proposal. What was she to do? Admit she wasn't a virgin and hope the man would still want her. Not tell him, wait until her wedding night and hope he didn't detect it? No, she was ruined. Now she could never date or hope to marry. Now that dream was gone. She turned her face into the pillow and cried until her eyes were swollen. After her tears were spent, she drifted into a light sleep.

Blanche heard the house alarm beeping and turned to eye the alarm clock on the nightstand in Aubrey's room. Was it really four in the afternoon? Had she stayed in bed all day? She blinked her eyes and listened to the steps coming down the hallway. When she heard the knock on the door, she knew she had to answer. She couldn't spend the rest of her life hiding in Aubrey's bedroom. She had to start facing the repercussions of her actions.

"Come in" she managed to choke out as she sat upright in the bed.

"Hi," Autumn called out as she opened the door, entered the room, walked over to the bottom of the bed, and took a seat on the edge of the mattress. "Hiding?" she questioned and tossed a smile at Blanche. "I know why!"

She can tell what happened, Blanche thought. She lowered her head in disgust.

"You don't have to feel bad about what you did."

How could she tell Blanche thought? Was there something different in your appearance once you became a woman?

"Come on, Blanche, talk to me. I know you're embarrassed about going down to the French Quarter after refusing to go with me all the times I begged you. That's okay. After all, you did say you wouldn't go unescorted, and you were there with Doctor A.J., right? I just hope you had a good time."

Blanche couldn't believe what she just heard. So, Autumn couldn't tell? Was Autumn only there to acknowledge she had seen Blanche at the coffee house?

"So, now that you've gone, do you intend to go back and see some of the sights? Do you feel there's nothing scary about being down there?"

Blanche finally got the courage to speak, "It was a nice experience. I enjoyed the park along the river, the restaurant we went to, and seeing your library... Oh, Autumn, I'm so sorry for the way I acted the Fourth of July weekend. It's a wonderful place for students to hang out. I can understand now why you go there... I feel so foolish!"

Blanche hung her head again in disgust. Autumn got up from the foot of the bed, walked over to the head, and sat next to Blanche. She threw her arms around her and gave her a firm hug.

"All is forgiven and forgotten. I'm just glad you finally experienced some of what the French Quarter has to offer and I hope you do go back. You still have almost two weeks to play tourist before my Mom and Colin return."

"Maybe...." Blanche answered in a non-committing tone placing her hands over Autumn's arms and placing a kiss on her cheek. She needed a hug right now more than Autumn could imagine. It felt good and she was beginning to feel more confident that no one would be able to tell she was no longer a virgin until Autumn spoke the next words.

"I know the other reason you're in here hiding as well."

Blanche kept her hands on Autumn's arm but stiffened thinking, "She can tell."

"You're embarrassed because you're dating my professor. I don't know how you two met and something is telling me that I won't be happy if I ask so I'll just let that stay a mystery. But, Blanche, I'm so happy for you. You're a great person, and everyone loves Doctor A.J. The students that have had him as an instructor were saying backstage that it's the first time they ever saw him come to the performances with someone. They all were saying, 'It's about time!' They were so happy to see him on a date."

Autumn turned so Blanche had to face her before continuing.

"And, they all were saying how attractive you were. The guys said he waited until he got a good-looking lady before he brought someone around."

Autumn laughed and gave Blanche a kiss on the cheek.

"Blanche, I'm so happy for you. You two make a great couple. You're both in education. You probably have a lot in common. I hope it works out. I'll be back in the dorm soon, and Aubrey will be here only about a week before she goes back to school in Texas. Whenever you want to come down for the weekend, you're welcome to stay in either of our rooms. I have a private dorm room. You can even stay with me on campus if you like."

As Autumn stood and walked to the door, it dawned on Blanche her fear was over. Autumn couldn't tell what had happened. It was Blanche's secret. Her face brightened at the knowledge.

"Glad to see you smiling again," Autumn said as she turned at the doorway. "I'm starving. I guess you didn't have time to cook. Are you hungry? How about Chinese? We could go over to the food court or to the restaurant on Chef Menteur Highway?"

"I'd love to try that restaurant on the highway again. Their shrimp egg foo young was great when we went last week, and I really like the crab and cream cheese appetizer you ordered."

"Crab Rangoons..." Autumn supplied the name of the dish.

"Can we get an order of those again?"

"Sure. Whatever you like. If we have leftovers, we can have them for lunch tomorrow."

"I'll hurry and get dressed," Blanche answered excitedly.

"I'll go check the movie listing for tonight while waiting," Autumn called out as she walked down the hall to the living room.

As Blanche stood, she felt the slight ache in her vaginal region. She had to get to confession. She was certain what had happened between her and Adam counted as a mortal sin. If she died before she had God's forgiveness, she would burn in hell for eternity. Her mother insisted she go to confession weekly. "Even if you don't have a grave sin, Blanche, you need the blessings," she had told her often as a child, so Autumn seeing her stand in the confessional line at church that Sunday would not appear odd based on her normal routine. "Maybe I'll get through this," she thought. As she showered, the hint of blood flowing down the drain dampened her spirits again. She had to keep reminding herself it was her secret. When she dressed, she slipped a sanitary pad into her panties in case she had any more discharge.

Chapter Seventeen

Over dinner, they talked about Autumn's poetry. Blanche shared the comments Aubrey had made to her and encouraged her to consider changing her major or declaring a double major.

"May I read your book?"

This time it was Autumn who hung her head in embarrassment.

"Aubrey promised she wouldn't tell anyone about it. It's not finished yet," Autumn shrugged her shoulders and took a bite of sweet and sour shrimp.

"Then I'll read it when it's published," Blanche announced, "And I know I will get an autographed copy since I know the author."

Autumn smiled and stabbed another shrimp.

"Autumn, why does Professor Brown think your name is Danielle?"

Autumn started laughing hysterically. She took a sip of wine to calm down before she explained.

"That's one bad thing that happened as a result of you coming last night."

"It's not the only one," Blanche thought but kept the comment to herself.

"Danielle is my friend from high school. In class today, when I answered to her name when he called the role, he told me to please see him after class. When I walked up to his desk, he had the most serious expression I've ever seen. He looked at me sternly and said, 'Can you tell me about this charade, Ms. Warren? You're listed officially for my 8:00 class.' After I explained to him what Danielle and I did, I could tell he was not happy with it, but he's going to let it go even though he gave me a firm warning. He said we should have come to him in the first place and let him help us get the records straight. Doctor A. J. is cool like that. He really tries to help the students work through all the stupid rules and regulations the university has. That's why so many of them like him."

"But, what did you do that he thinks you're this Danielle?"

"I can't deal with those early classes. By the time I registered, the only spot left was his 8:00 A.M. session. Danielle had gotten a part time job and had to work afternoons, but she was stuck in the 1:30 session. We went to the registrar's office, and they wouldn't let us swap places. They wanted us to first officially drop the course we were in and to re-register. But, if we did that, we were both afraid that someone on the waiting list might have got the slots so we decided to just swap places on our own instead. Danielle went to my class, and I went to hers."

Realizing she still had the warning letter that had come in the mail in her purse, Blanche pulled it out and showed it to Autumn.

"So, you've been going to class but not getting credit for being in attendance?"

Autumn read the letter then stared at Blanche.

"So, this is how you met him," she stated knowing Blanche had not only opened the notice but had chosen to act on it despite their heated discussion the Fourth of July weekend that she was not there to take charge.

Blanche focused on the crab rangoons, "These are so good." She promptly filled her mouth making it impolite for her to speak.

Knowing she was trying to avoid the topic and a possible continuation of that discussion, Autumn continued explaining her and Danielle's plan.

"When he called Danielle's name from the roll of the afternoon session, I answered. Danielle isn't the smartest friend I have. She's not dumb, just clueless sometimes. I called her on her cell when Doctor A.J. requested I come to his office. She didn't understand she should have answered when he called my name from the morning class' roll. She never missed a class but was sitting in class scared to speak up because she knew she didn't belong there officially.... She sat in the back of the class behind one of the football players so Doctor A.J. wouldn't even notice her."

"I'm just so happy Adam is working with you, and everything will be fine."

"He's even letting us take the final in the class we've been attending. That's great. Instead of fighting rush hour traffic to get uptown for 8:00, I can go to The Library the night before, get some more studying in, and wake up fresh."

A thought struck Blanche, "So, when you took tests, you took them under Danielle's name? She's getting your grades."

"We got the idea because he never picked up any tests he gave. He told us in the first class the only grade that counted was the final exam. He felt this course was one that challenged us to grow so all that mattered is where we ended up, not the little bumps on the road we traveled to get there. He would give out pop quizzes and tests, but we graded them ourselves based on class discussions, then kept them as study guides. If he hadn't said that in the first session, I would have never thought of the swap."

Blanche eyed Autumn in wonder. She would never have been brave enough to try to pull off such a shenanigan. The only thought that came to her mind was one of the main lessons she had learned that summer, "Don't restrict them from finding their destiny." It seems both of Colin's stepdaughters were well on their way in that regard. Glancing at the smirk on Autumn's face that she had pulled this off, she imagined Autumn was the cause of the patches of grey hair Colin now had at his temples.

"So, when do you see him again?" Autumn questioned with a sheepish look on her face.

Blanche glanced down at her plate and re-arranged the remaining morsels with her fork.

"We'll see..."

"Don't you like him?"

Blanche didn't know how to respond. She had only thought of Adam as an instructor until last night. Could she dare to think of him in another way? What did he think of her? Could he ever have serious thoughts about her? Her mother had said one time, "A man is like a dog. He'll lie with anything." If that was true, last night meant nothing to Adam. Blanche was only a convenient one night stand. Her forehead furrowed as she struggled with these flitting thoughts.

"Seems like the verdict is still out?" Autumn giggled at Blanche's expression.

Blanche was glad that ended any more talk about Adam. It's all in her past now. She had to try to forget him and what had happened between them.

The students could tell Doctor A.J. was distracted. Though he was reviewing all the material for the final, he kept glancing towards the rear of the classroom as if he was expecting something. Only Autumn knew it was not something but someone he was hoping to see. At the end of class, disappointment was obvious in his expression as he laid the chalk down for the last time. Autumn started to approach him, but her gut feeling was not to interfere unless she detected a trigger from either him or Blanche. She picked up her belongings and turned to leave the room feeling his eyes watching her and confident the right trigger would come soon.

Chapter Eighteen

Blanche sat in the seat closest to the security station of terminal D in the Louis Armstrong International airport. She had worn the outfit Autumn first selected for her when they went to the comedy show. She had also washed her hair the night before, rolled it, and sat under the dryer as Kat and Autumn had taught her so it was bouncy and fell perfectly framing her face. She used the same make-up Autumn had purchased that first afternoon and took extra care applying it. She'd be going home the next weekend and the reaction from Colin and Maria would be the test. Should she wear one of her old things to go back to her life in Lafayette or her new outfit? Her stomach was getting queasy, and she began tapping her right foot in anticipation. Glancing at the board, the plane was marked as in range so it wouldn't be long before Colin and Maria would arrive. She waited until the board changed to indicate the plane had landed and a crowd began exiting from terminal D into the main terminal of the airport. Taking several deep breaths to try to calm her nervousness, she stood, patted her hair to ensure all the strands were in place, and walked over to a spot on the right side of the exit gate where Colin and Maria would be sure to see her. She spotted Colin first. He was walking with Maria on his left side and seemingly deep in conversation. Blanche put her arms behind her back, crossed her fingers, and prayed.

As they walked towards the main terminal, Colin glanced at the crowd waiting to find their loved ones among the arriving passengers. An attractive lady caught his eye, but he didn't dare focus on her. He was proud he had never wavered from keeping his marriage vows. He still let his eyes admire a pretty woman but not with his wife at his side. To avoid temptation, he looked past the lady searching the crowd for Blanche. Based on their conversation from the night before, she planned to meet them in the main terminal with a luggage cart.

When Colin passed her up without speaking, Blanche just stood there stunned. Was he that upset with the change in her hair and clothes? Maria had stopped walking and was also staring at him. He had taken only a few steps before turning to see why his wife wasn't keeping up with his pace.

"Colin!" Maria scolded.

"What?" he looked at Maria trying to assess the source of her reaction.

"Are you just going to ignore poor Blanche?" Agitated, Maria turned from him, walked over to Blanche, put her arms around her, and gave her a hug. "Thank you for coming to pick us up. You look great. I love your hair."

Maria flicked a lock with her fingers, and Blanche's hair fell softly back in place along the left side of her cheek.

"Blanche?" Colin was caught off guard by the fact the woman he had admired from a distance and had purposely chosen to avoid turned out to be the cousin for whom he was searching the crowds. "Damn!"

"Colin," Maria muttered disgustedly before turning to Blanche, "Please forgive my clueless husband. What your dear, sweet cousin is trying to say is man talk for 'you look good.' When he gets over it, he'll follow us." Turning to her husband and laughing at the expression on his face, Maria ordered, "Bring the cart, sweetheart," as she laid the case she had been carrying on the top shelf before taking Blanche's arm in hers, and they walked together towards the baggage claim chatting about her transformation.

"Wow!" Colin spoke aloud to no one in particular as he watched the now proud, erect manner in which Blanche walked away conversing with Maria. He shook his head, tossed his own luggage on the bottom shelf, and followed at a quickened pace to catch up.

After collecting the luggage, they walked to the short term parking garage. Blanche had become so accustomed to driving Colin's car that, after she clicked the trunk open for him to load the various bags, she climbed into the driver's seat. Maria instinctively took her normal seat on the passenger side across from Blanche, and the two continued chatting about everything Blanche and Autumn had done together. Blanche relaying her embarrassment over her first salon experience had Maria laughing to the point she had to hold her side. Colin took a place in the back seat and watched as Blanche expertly backed the car out the spot, drove to the self-service exit gate, swiped both the ticket and the credit card Autumn had given her, and took the side road to the interstate. She maneuvered the car confidently through the rush hour traffic laughing and talking with Maria until they pulled into the drive behind Autumn's car. Colin studied his young cousin the entire time surprised at her transformation in such a short time frame.

"Autumn is already home from taking her last final. I know she did well. Adam said she is one of his best students." Turning to face Maria first, then Colin, she continued talking, "Are the two of you too tired from the trip? If not, can we go out and celebrate with her?"

Colin's first reaction was "Who the hell is Adam?"

"We're not too tired," Maria answered before Colin spoke his mind. "That's a great idea..." she offered and turned the handle of the sedan to exit the car. Blanche did likewise, and the two ladies grabbed their purses and walked to the house still chattering away leaving Colin to handle the luggage. Colin laid his head against the back seat cushion and thought about Maria, his two stepdaughters, and Blanche, the four women besides his mother that meant the most to him. He had broken the reins of control completely from his mother after his disastrous first marriage. The three in his life based on this second marriage were a different story. He doubted he would ever break the reins they had woven around him.

"Autumn has created a fourth one," he laughed at the thought before exiting the car to bring the luggage into the house wondering if he'd get to drive to whichever restaurant destination the ladies had chosen. By the time they left for dinner, the three were still chattering away so Blanche did take the back seat to sit next to Autumn, allowing Colin the honor of driving them again. Listening to the three ladies, he felt like their chauffeur as he pulled out the driveway.

Chapter Nineteen

The morning Colin, Maria, and Autumn were to drive Blanche back to Lafayette, she was sitting on the bed in Aubrey's room staring at the packed luggage. Maria had surprised her with a set of luggage as another thank you for staying the summer so she had plenty of room for her new wardrobe. Two outfits remained, one she would wear and one she had to pack. Her stomach was in knots, and she was sucking a mint to fight back the nausea she had been experiencing. The thought of going home and back to the environment she had grown up in sickened Blanche. She wasn't ready to face her mother and see her reaction to the change. After all the three had done for her, she was also scared to not wear something from her new wardrobe in front of Autumn, Maria, and Colin. She couldn't just give away all the clothes they had bought for her to charity. That would be an insult, and she would be wasting Colin's money. If he would allow her to pay him for the items, she wouldn't hesitate to give them away as soon as she got home, but he remained adamant he would not accept a penny.

Still undecided, she stood in front of the dresser mirror to apply her make-up. Disgustedly, she reached for the pink lipstick her mother always bought for her and applied it to her lips. Now that she had learned about make-up and how best to complement your skin tone, Blanche knew the pink made her complexion look sallow. The shade was all wrong for her. Thinking of the students at the school and knowing she was a role model, she knew she couldn't go back to what Autumn had described as nun's wear. Pulling several tissues out the box on Aubrey's nightstand, she quickly wiped the pale pink from her lips and applied the make-up she had become accustomed to wearing. After closing her make-up kit and packing it in the last suitcase still opened, she tossed the pink seersucker suit on top and zipped it shut before she changed her mind. She slipped on the V-necked royal blue sailor top and the black knit slacks and slipped her manicured toes into the sandals she had purchased herself the week before. This was the most conservative outfit of her new wardrobe. Taking a deep breath, she looked around Aubrey's room one more time before opening the door and calling to Colin she was ready.

The closer they got to Lafayette, the more restless Blanche became. When they pulled in front of her house, her mother and Colin's were sitting on the porch drinking pink lemonade and waiting for their arrival. They stood and waved as the car pulled to a halt. When Blanche got out the car, her mother's happy expression changed. She stared at her with a solemn look on her face. Blanche cringed and nervously rubbed her hands together. Colin and Maria had ascended the steps. He placed a kiss on his mother's cheek, and Maria then gave her a hug. Autumn had stayed back with Blanche and picked up on the silent exchange between mother and daughter.

Autumn remembered that look well. The last time she had seen it was on her grandmother's face when Maria announced Aubrey was going to attend college in Texas. The shouting match that followed was the worst argument Autumn had ever witnessed. Her grandmother was screaming all the reasons that she shouldn't let a young girl go off to some god-forsaken place Maria didn't know anything about with no family close by to keep an eye on her, especially when there were fine colleges right there in New Orleans. Trying to explain the colleges in town offered only a general communications curriculum and Aubrey wanted to focus on print journalism did nothing to persuade her grandmother but Maria had stood her ground. It wasn't the first time her mother and grandmother clashed over liberties Maria was granting her daughters. Recognizing that Blanche needed a champion at that moment, Autumn took control.

"You look good. Don't go back to being a nun. Think of your students." Autumn whispered orders before walking away from Blanche, ascending the short steps, and giving Blanche's mother a huge hug and kiss to distract her gaze from Blanche's. Speaking loudly so Blanche and Colin would hear, she kicked off the conversation she knew had to happen.

"Hi, Aunt Sherrie! Doesn't Blanche look great? I brought her to have her hair done and taught her some make-up tips. We also shopped for some new clothes. We can't have her not looking her best in her new role as counselor, can we?"

Colin picked up on what was playing out before them immediately, and his eyes locked with Autumn's. She nodded towards him, and he became Blanche's champion as well.

"Mom, what do you think? Doesn't Blanche look great?"

"She looks like a movie star. Cher, come up here and let your old aunt's eyes see you better."

Encouraged, Blanche slowly walked up the sidewalk, ascended the steps carefully in her high-heeled sandals, and stood before her Aunt Barbara.

"Yes, indeed! She looks beautiful, doesn't she, Sherrie? You all come in and have some lunch. The two of us have been cooking all morning waiting for your arrival."

Blanche kept her eyes averted away from her mother's and walked with her aunt's arm around her waist to their small dining room. Colin and Autumn noticed Sherrie remained silent during the entire meal but sustained a disdainful stare at Blanche. Blanche kept her head down eating as if she had to force each bite down. Autumn looked at Colin appealingly.

"Labor Day weekend, we are planning a barbecue."

Maria looked at Colin indicating, "We are?"

"Why don't I drive down Friday night and pick the three of you up and you spend the weekend with us? Then we'll have the whole family together for the holiday."

Barbara quickly chimed in, "We'd love to. Since Blanche's been away, we've been doing new things. Us two old gals have some new breath in us. I haven't been to New Orleans since you got married. It would be nice to get away for a weekend. Won't that be nice, Sherrie?"

Forcing a smile, Sherrie looked at her sister and finally broke her silence, "If you wish, dear."

Blanche got the courage to speak at that point, "Cole, you don't have to come all this way. There's no reason I can't drive the three of us down."

Surprised but glad to see Blanche being assertive, he answered, "We'll hold the barbecue at the house in Lacombe. I had promised you a weekend there, and we never got around to it. I'll draw you a map before we go."

Barbara kept talking about how much she was looking forward to that weekend, "Don't you all plan any desserts. Me and Sherrie will bake home-made cakes and bring them down with us. Won't we, Sherrie?"

"Yes, dear," she answered her sister shortly and continued staring at her daughter.

By the time Colin, Maria, and Autumn were ready to drive back to New Orleans, no word had yet passed between Blanche and her mother.

"Auntie, I'll drop my mom home on our way out. Thanks for a lovely meal and thanks again for letting us borrow Blanche for the summer."

Autumn quickly walked up, gave Sherrie a big hug and kiss, and stated, "Aunt Sherrie, please don't let Blanche go back to dressing how she used to. She looked like a nun. She's far too pretty for that. Promise me. Please..."

Autumn gave Sherrie her sweetest smile and wouldn't let go of her until she spoke.

"Don't you worry none.... Blanche will be just fine."

Knowing that's the best response she'd be able to muster, Autumn reluctantly followed her mother and stepfather down the path to the car whispering to Blanche as she passed, "Stand up for yourself. You have the right to choose your own things. You're not a kid anymore. Your mother needs to let go."

Unable to speak, Blanche just nodded in response.

As she and Sherrie were waving good-bye to Colin's family, a gentleman approached from across the street.

"Blanche?"

"Tony..." Blanche responded nonchalantly.

"You remember me... Great."

Blanche remembered him all too well. She and Tony had started first grade together. Back then, he had blond curly hair which eventually turned to a dark brown by the time they were in seventh grade. Though they spent eight years taking the same classes in grammar school and lived in the same neighborhood, he had never spoken to her a single time. He only had eyes for the light skinned girls. He had married Kathleen, the fairest girl in their eighth grade class. The rumor was she had left him for a white man she met at her job. Blanche laughed at the thought that, even with his blond hair and hazel eyes, Tony still hadn't been fair enough. His birth certificate still said black.

"How's your wife and kids?" She had no idea why he had crossed the street and struck up a conversation. Maybe she had learned a little this summer and had grown more confident. Knowing the rumor mill, she purposely posed the question. It was a chance to get back at him for all the years he had shunned her.

"The kids are fine. Kathleen and I are divorced."

"So sorry to hear..." Blanche forced her face into a frown feigning pity.

"Hey. You look great. ... Maybe we could go to dinner sometimes."

Her mother quickly responded, "She'd love to, Tony."

Blanche calmed the anger she was feeling that her mother was taking the decision away from her. "Tony, school is about to start, and I have this new job as a counselor. Things are going to be pretty busy. ... Maybe after things settle in. Have a good day."

As she turned to walk into the house leaving her mother and Tony at the gate staring in shock at her back, Blanche thought, "You're nothing of a man compared to Adam, and you never will be. All you can offer a woman is fair skin, and that's not the main thing that matters anymore. In school, you were as dumb as a doorknob and so was Kathleen. The two of you deserved each other. Why was I ever envious of them?" She shook her head in disbelief of how things looked back then as a young teen compared to now.

"She's just tired, Tony. They just drove in from New Orleans. She'll be happy to go out with you anytime. "

She heard her mother's words right before she closed the front door behind her. Walking over to the living room curtain, she peeked through the Austrian shades at her mother and Tony conversing. She could tell her mother was trying to salvage the moment so glad to have someone fair skinned taking an interest in her daughter. Tony's mother and hers had been best friends in school but Tony's mother quit speaking to Sherrie once she married Blanche's father. Tony glanced towards the house one more time before turning to cross the street and finish the visit with his aging parents.

Though she would never date a person so shallow, gaining Tony's attention helped Blanche feel more confident about her appearance until Sherrie stormed in slamming the door behind her.

"You stupid, simple little country bumpkin! How dare you turn that boy down?"

"That's the problem, mother... He's still a boy." After spending time with Adam this past summer, Blanche recalled the characteristics of a true man, characteristics she recalled her father and Colin demonstrating. After eight years attending classes and school functions with Tony, she knew Tony would never demonstrate those attributes but the sentence flooded out before she realized it. Having spent the summer debating both in class and with Adam and Autumn, it seemed natural to speak her mind. Seeing her mother's face pale at the words Blanche had spat her way, she cowered knowing she had disrespected her and stopped short of saying, "I know what it's like to be in the company of a real man."

"You should be glad someone like him wants to give you the time of day! With all that dark make-up on your face, you look like a whore." Haughtily, Sherrie stood close to her and announced, "Maybe that's why he walked over here. Seeing a whore, he needs someone to pass the time with... to have a little fun with until he finds someone decent to marry. ... You were supposed to go to New Orleans and be an example for that child. Instead, you let a young girl take you by the nose and lead your foolish, simple mind. Nothing I taught you all these years sank in? You go to New Orleans and forget everything you learned. What did you think you were there for? To be that child's toy? You just let her comb your hair, put make-up on you and dress you like you were her doll? Is that what you did? Just sit in New Orleans like a limp rag doll? Any dumb thing she wanted to do to you, you just let her? You have about as much sense as those make-up heads they sell for young girls at Christmas. You just sat there like those bodiless heads and let the girl play with you like you were her toy doll?"

Blanche turned away, not wanting to hear anymore of her mother's criticism.

"I need to unpack," she whispered as she walked down the short hall to her room.

"I hope you kept the decent things I bought for you. I know you don't plan to go to school or church looking like that."

Her mother was still screaming at her as Blanche closed the door. She looked at the stark bedroom and thought about the life she had experienced this past summer. She sat silently on the foot of the bed, tears rolling down her cheeks.

Chapter Twenty

It was the first day the staff was to report to school, and Blanche stood in front of her closet debating what to wear. Her mother had continued the verbal abuse berating her hair, her clothes, and, especially, her make-up. With the constant harassment, Blanche had begun doubting whether she should continue wearing her new things. The worst moment so far had occurred when her mother dug through the laundry. Though Blanche typically did all the washing, her mother had gone into the dryer the first time she washed clothes, pulled a black satin bra and bikini panties out, and stormed into Blanche's room shoving them into her face.

"Didn't I teach you colors cause yeast infections? Didn't I teach you that cotton is the best fabric for undergarments? Why did you buy this trash? Did you let that young, foolish girl waste Colin's good money on this whore underwear? I know you didn't spend the little you have on this trash when you had all the under clothes you needed when you went out there. You had perfectly good, decent underwear, not these whore clothes. What did you do? Spend the summer on Bourbon Street with the other prostitutes? Why else would you need to buy this kind of trash? What's become of you, you simple minded fool?"

Every word her mother had spoken since she returned played through her mind, especially the fact that Tony had finally talked to her, after all these years, because she looked like a prostitute. She hadn't felt out of place when she was on the university's campus in New Orleans but New Orleans is a unique city, unlike any other in the world. It was also a very tolerant, open-minded city. Nothing that they saw and nothing that happened seemed to shock New Orleanians. They were accustomed to visitors from all around the world, accustomed to being the birthplace for new ideas, accustomed to letting each person show their uniqueness. Maybe what worked there wasn't for her home town. As she stared into the closet, moving hangars slowly back and forth on the rod, the elderly professor's words came to her, "Don't restrict them from finding their destiny."

The words helped her to recall the positive things she had observed and experienced not only on campus but at the coffee shop called The Library. She remembered the students' eagerness to learn, to debate, and to test their original works and ideas on an audience. It's what she wanted for her own students. She didn't want them to just regurgitate facts but to think on their own, to explore new worlds, to follow their destiny. Without hesitation, she grabbed one of the new outfits from the closet, applied the make-up Autumn had purchased for her, pulled on her silk stockings, and slipped into the four inched heels. Grabbing a briefcase she had purchased on one of her shopping trips, she shoved her notes into it, and walked confidently out her bedroom door.

Her mother's voice shrilled when she saw her. Blanche continued past her ignoring the negative comments until she closed the car door and turned the volume up on the radio drowning out he mother's screams and taunts until she was out of ear range. She knew she had made the right decision by the looks of approval she got from the other teachers and the principal when she entered the meeting room. It gave her the confidence she needed to present her proposed agenda for the coming school year as the counselor. After presenting her agenda, she sat nervously waiting for comments.

The principal finally looked up from the notes he had taken and stated, "I can't think of a single thing I would change. This is an excellent presentation, Blanche, and I look forward to you implementing these ideas this school year. This took a lot of effort on your part to prepare such a detailed proposal over the summer. Thank you for your hard work and dedication... Does anyone else have anything you'd like to add?"

He glanced around the table giving the other teachers and staff members a chance for input. The only thing Blanche heard were murmurs of approval, how great a job she had done, and how thankful they all were to have her in this position supporting their efforts in the classroom. Blanche released a sigh of relief as they turned to the next agenda item. When the meeting ended, she tossed her papers into the briefcase, rose, and exited quietly out the door as was her norm. One of the teachers about the same age as Blanche rushed to catch up with her.

"Blanche, I love your new hairstyle, and that suit is sharp. Maybe we could eat lunch together sometimes?"

Blanche fought back the tears. She turned to her, "I'd love to, Melanie."

"See you tomorrow then," the teacher smiled before walking in the opposite direction to her parked car.

For the first time in her life, Blanche knew this was the start of a life-long friendship, the first true friendship she ever had, and it felt good. As she turned the car onto the street where her parents' house stood, the butterflies in her stomach started again. As soon as she hit the door, she knew she would be subjected to her mother's taunts. The criticism and sarcasm hadn't slowed, and she didn't know how much more she could bear.

Chapter Twenty-One

Standing over the commode in the teacher's lounge, Blanche thought her stomach had finally settled. The nausea she felt when she woke that morning hadn't eased. Attributing it to nervousness because she had to make her first address at a parent-teacher conference, she was glad it was all over, and her now empty stomach made her feel better. She stepped out the stall, walked over to the sink, dampened a paper towel with cold water, patted her forehead, and then held the cool towel against her eyelids.

"When's your baby due?"

She turned toward the voice and saw the janitor's wife sitting on the sofa.

"Honey, it's going to get better. Wait until you're about three months. All that nausea will go away. That's when it happened for me. Yes, for each one of my babies, I was sick to my stomach until I passed those first three months. Then I was fine. Mark my words..."

After pointing her finger at Blanche to emphasize the advice she had just shared, she stood to leave the lounge. Blanche went to call after her, "I'm not married," but the words stuck in her throat as she remembered the night she spent with Adam. Instead, what came out was, "No! Oh my God, no! Please, no!"

Feeling weak, she stumbled to the sofa and sat down. She tried to clear her mind and remember her last period. It had ended a little over two weeks before she spent the night at Adam's condo. The night she had got drunk, relied on his strong arms to guide her safely, and ended up losing her virginity was probably the height of her fertile period, and now she was overdue. She had attributed her period's lateness to the stress she had been under, dealing with her mother, starting a new job, giving speeches for the first time. She had to know for certain. But how? If she went to the family doctor, she wasn't confident her mother would not find out. Blanche remembered seeing pregnancy tests that were supposed to be error proof advertised on television. But where could she buy one without someone seeing her and telling her mother? She knew what she would do. She would wait until they went to New

Orleans that weekend for the Labor Day party at Colin's. Somehow she would manage to purchase a test out there where no one knew her. It would be easier to dispose of it as well. Her mother wouldn't dig through Colin and Maria's trash. Feeling good about her plan, she dabbed her forehead one more time impatient for the weekend to come.

Friday night, Blanche rushed home to pack her things. Her mother was already packed by the time she arrived. She started immediately on Blanche as soon as she entered the door.
"So, the whore is home… Your aunt has been waiting for you to pick her up for over an hour now. I already packed a case for you with appropriate clothes so we can leave now."

Blanche looked at the suitcase her mother pointed to on the floor of the living room. She picked it up, walked to her bedroom, tossed it on the bed, opened the lid, and pulled all the old things out. She walked to the kitchen, grabbed a clean garbage bag from under the counter, went back to her room, stuffed the items into the bag, and shoved it onto the top shelf of her closet. Then she pulled some of her new casual outfits out the closet and began folding them to pack instead.

Bursting through the door without knocking, Sherrie looked angrily at the new clothes being folded and packed into the case.

"You always were an ungrateful child, Blanche. Here I took time out of my day to pack your suitcase for you so we could leave as soon as you got home and not be on this highway, three women alone, with night falling and here you are, totally inconsiderate of the danger you could be putting your mother and your aunt in, wasting time to pack things you shouldn't have bought in the first place. I never thought you would grow up to be such a stubborn, mule-headed woman. You're insisting on wearing that trash. I should have burned all that junk when you left for work this morning. Then you'll have to dress and act sensibly again."

The thought her mother would destroy her things hadn't crossed Blanche's mind, but remembering her thirteenth birthday party, she would not have been surprised if she had. She had loved the outfit her father's sister, her Aunt Nora, had given her as a present but never had a chance to wear it. After everyone had gone home that day, her mother went to Blanche's room, picked up the box holding the clothes from Aunt Nora, walked it to the back yard, tossed it onto the still hot barbecue pit, poured the lighter fluid on top of it, struck a match, and tossed it on top. Blanche watched helplessly as the beautiful suit went up in flames. Her father had run out into the yard when he saw the flames through the window and heard Blanche sobbing and screaming for her mother to please stop.

"Sherrie, what are you doing?"

"I don't want anything from Nora in my house!" she had responded angrily, and satisfied the clothes couldn't be salvaged, she turned and stomped away. Her father had grabbed a hose and doused the flames but the suit was ruined.

"I'm sorry, baby girl. Daddy will get you an outfit to replace it, okay?"

Blanche's tears couldn't stop flowing. Though her father was trying to make things right again, it was not going to be the same. It was not the gift from Aunt Nora. That's what had made it so special.

Remembering that, Blanche thought of the only thing that might prevent her mother from destroying her possessions.

"Mother, Colin bought these things, and he expects me to wear them. Like you always tell me, how can we disappoint him when he's done so much for us?"

By the look on her mother's face, Blanche knew she had chosen the right words. Her mother would not want Colin to know she had ruined everything he had bought. However, her tirade started again and continued the entire time Blanche was packing, they were setting the lights to appear someone was home, they walked to the car to load cakes and suitcases, and they drove over to pick up Aunt Barbara. After that, her mother stopped focusing as much on Blanche and started her typical gossiping with her sister, making the three hour trek to the New Orleans area more bearable.

Night was falling as they crossed the Causeway toward the north shore. At a red light on the north shore, Blanche pulled out the directions to Colin's and read them one more time. As they pulled into the drive bearing the numbers of the address Colin had given her, her heart lightened when she saw Autumn open the front door and run out to meet them. As Blanche stepped from the car, they flung their arms around each other and exchanged a welcoming hug. At that moment, Blanche knew everything would somehow work out just fine.

Chapter Twenty-Two

Maria showed Sherrie and her mother-in-law to two downstairs bedrooms on the opposite side of the den from the master suite she and Colin shared. She told Blanche she, Autumn, and Aubrey would be sharing the upstairs suite. Blanche sighed with relief once she entered the quarters. There was no way her mother would make it up the high stairway with her bad knees. She also knew she would not intrude into the bedroom knowing Autumn and Aubrey were also present. The suite had a private bath so Blanche felt more at ease. She would be able to take the pregnancy test and keep it a secret. Now, she only needed the opportunity to get to a drug store and purchase a kit.

Saturday morning, they all gathered into the dining room for breakfast. Her mother was acting civil even to Blanche in front of Colin's family. After breakfast, Colin escorted his mother and his Aunt Sherrie onto the lanai while Maria, her daughters, and Blanche went to the kitchen to begin preparing for the barbecue the next day. The four worked together so well, Blanche felt she had known the twins and Maria for years. As they worked, Aubrey told them about her experiences that summer in New York. At one point, Maria was searching frantically through the pantry.

"Girls, it seems we are out of parsley flakes and black pepper. I thought I had bought some the last time we were here but that was before we left for the summer. I must have left them at the other house instead."

She stood glancing at the different shelves of the pantry trying to see where else the two items could possibly be.

"Maria, my car is the last one in the drive way. I saw the store when we were coming in. I can run and pick it up for you."

"You don't mind, Blanche?"

"After what you all did for me this summer, I'd be insulted if you didn't let me do something so simple for you. … I'll be right back."

Blanche jumped off the stool where she was chopping onions, pulled off her apron, and walked from the kitchen before Maria could change her mind. She peeked through the patio doors. Colin was waiting on the two elderly ladies as if they were queens visiting from Europe. They were sitting in lounge chairs sipping lemonade while he played their favorite songs on the sound system. Satisfied her mother would remain occupied, Blanche ran up the stairs, grabbed her purse, and rushed back down and out the door before anyone would stop her.

On the way to the grocery, she stopped at a pharmacy that was part of a nationwide chain. She walked up and down the aisle that stocked all the over the counter medications twice as her frustration and apprehension heightened over not locating a pregnancy test kit. She walked down a center aisle reading the signs hanging from the ceiling trying to determine where they might be stocked. When she got to the section that listed baby items, she walked slowly down that aisle hoping something might give her a clue. At the end of the aisle, she spotted the pregnancy tests on the top shelf above condoms. Blanche hung her head for a minute embarrassed before quickly looking from side to side to ensure no one she knew was watching. Thinking of how long she had been gone, she forced her eyes upward to focus on the selection of pregnancy tests only for it to register they were behind a locked acrylic door. She couldn't dare be so bold as to go to the counter and request someone with a key pull one for her. Disappointed, she marched quickly out the pharmacy and headed to the grocery store.

When she arrived at the grocery, she quickly grabbed the two items Maria needed and then walked over to the pharmacy section. She glanced around assessing the other patrons until she felt confident everyone around were strangers. Grateful to be in an area where no one should recognize her, she searched for the pregnancy test section, and the tightness in her chest eased when she found them stocked on an open shelf.

She wanted to make the right selection, but they all seemed to read the same way. The percent accuracy was 99% on each. They all said they tested for evidence of the pregnancy hormone in the urine stream. The length of time you had to hold the testing device strip in your urine seemed consistent. One said that after five seconds, it would turn pink to indicate it was working. One said it was accurate one day before your missed period. One used a plus and minus sign to indicate pregnancy. Another used bars. Blanche shied away from the one showing bars being scared she might misread the number of bars. She finally settled on one that said to lay the test flat while waiting. It was a brand she had seen advertised on television.

Using the same caution, glancing down aisles and around the store to make sure she didn't recognize anyone, she rushed to an express register as soon as the line cleared. She first pulled the pregnancy test out the hand basket where she had hidden it under a scarf she had grabbed from a rack she passed.

"I need that in a separate bag," she smiled at the girl trying to hide her embarrassment.

The girl dropped it into the bag, then placed the bag on the counter opening another for Blanche's other items. As the cashier scanned the other items, Blanche took the pregnancy test and wrapped the bag around it several times before stuffing it into her purse hoping no one noticed it. Paying for the items with cash, she hastened her steps out the store, sat in the car, closed her eyes, and sighed with relief she had completed the first step of her mission. When she arrived back at the house, she opened the front door and peeked in first. Seeing no one in the foyer, she scooted up the steps, placed her purse within her suitcase, and went back down the stairs holding only the grocery bag with the pepper and parsley flakes. Peeking through the patio doors, her mother, aunt, and Colin were the same as when she had left. Smiling, her mission hadn't been detected, she proceeded to the kitchen where Maria, Autumn, and Aubrey were so intent on playing catch-up, it didn't seemed they had missed Blanche. She dropped the bag onto the counter saying she'd be back as soon as used the restroom.

Pulling her purse from the suitcase, she glanced down the stair checking if anyone else was coming up before slipping into the upstairs bathroom and locking the door. After pulling the bag from her purse, she dropped it onto the vanity seat and began unwrapping the box. Blanche pulled the directions out and read them carefully. Once confident she knew the right steps, she sat on the commode peeking between her legs to ensure where the urine was flowing. After, she placed the test on a paper towel on the side of the tub and started monitoring the time on her watch. When the designated minutes had passed, she grabbed the test and held it under the lights of the vanity mirror. Seeing the positive indication, she kept staring at the test praying the results might change. Not seeing any other indication appearing and the positive not changing, she wrapped the test inside the bag once again and stuffed it back into her purse.

Blanche sat on the side of the bath tub. Now that she knew there was a high probability she was pregnant, she had no idea what she would do. It was bad enough to be an unwed mother, but to present her mother with a grandbaby that would not have fair skin would be even worse. If she had gotten pregnant for Tony, she was sure her mother would have accepted that situation easier, perhaps even be happy over it. But, a baby for Adam? There was no way she could present her mother with a baby Blanche's own skin tone, let alone Adam's. She thought about her thirteenth birthday party, the incident that had caused her mother to ostracize her Aunt Nora.

For her thirteenth birthday party, her father had planned a summer afternoon barbeque in their backyard. Before the guests arrived, he had spent the morning grilling chicken quarters, pork ribs, smoked sausage, hot sausage, hot dogs, and boudin. Her mother had been busy in the kitchen preparing the side dishes - potato salad, rice dressing, macaroni and cheese, and green peas. Blanche couldn't remember seeing such a quantity of food in their kitchen at one time as she helped her mother by gathering fresh parsley and green onions from their small herb garden and chopping the hard boiled eggs for the potato salad. Her father had invited relatives from both sides of the family. Having been raised on different sides of the track, bringing them all together was a rare occasion, but her father had wanted everyone to share the joy of his only child becoming a teenager.

After they sang "Happy Birthday," her mother began cutting the homemade lemon cake with a raspberry filling and cream cheese icing. The children had each taken a turn hand cranking the family's recipe for peach almond ice cream. A large dollop of ice cream was placed aside each cake slice as her mother served the dessert. When Blanche took her first bite, she couldn't imagine a more perfect day. Even the weather had cooperated as she looked up at the overcast sky which granted welcome relief from the humidity of a southern Louisiana summer. Continuing to eat her birthday cake and ice cream, Blanche smiled as she glanced at all of the family members that had gathered to share a meal of her favorite things in celebration of this milestone in her life.

The picnic table her father had made was covered with a plastic table cloth and her gifts had been piled in the center. After the cake and ice cream was consumed, it was time to open her presents. Her closest classmates from school and her first cousins gathered around the picnic table to watch as Blanche excitedly tore the wrappings off each gift. The girls present gasped at the outfit Nora, one of her paternal aunts, had given her. Glad Blanche loved her present and her girlfriends approved, her Aunt Nora commented, "It won't be long before the boys will be coming around so you need to look your best." The comment had Blanche and her girlfriends giggling until Blanche's maternal grandmother blurted, "And when they do, Blanche, remember you need to add cream to your coffee."

All conversations in the yard stopped as her paternal relatives all turned to stare at her grandmother. Blanche wanted to die of embarrassment. She didn't believe her grandmother had said that in front of their guests. In the Creole culture, that phrase was the so-called polite way to remind Blanche her complexion was too dark for her grandmother's standards. To offset her gene pool, she needed to select a spouse of fairer skin so her children would have a better chance of coming out with a more acceptable appearance.

Her Aunt Nora had responded cattily, "At least she passes your brown bag and blue vein tests!"

In response, her grandmother had stood up from her comfortable position under an umbrella in the lounge chair, glared at Blanche's aunt stone-faced for what seemed an eternity to Blanche, turned, and walked haughtily into the house, never rejoining the festivities.

Aunt Nora had watched her grandmother's retreat and Blanche's mother, Sherrie, walking alongside her trying to calm her down. As the screened door to the kitchen closed behind them, Aunt Nora had uttered aloud, "You old, prejudice, ignorant bitch!"

Blanche's father had quickly yelled in a scolding tone to her aunt, "Nora!"

As Aunt Nora turned to face him, it was obvious her anger was not yet contained, and she rambled on.

"I warned you not to marry into that family. You know we were too dark for the likes of them. The only reason they gave you the time of day was because you had the most successful black owned small business in town, and they needed money."

Turning to face the closed door that led to the kitchen, Nora continued speaking louder hoping her brother's wife and mother-in-law would hear, "She ain't no better than the rest of us.... Always acting all 'huffy puffy' proud just because she has that fair skin, straight hair, and blue eyes but her birth certificate still says she's black. She ain't nothing but a nigger just like the rest of us.... She's just a WHITE nigger!"

"Nora, PLEASE," Blanche's father spoke pleadingly as he tilted his head towards Blanche and her friends.

Turning and seeing the tears rolling down Blanche's face, her Aunt Nora walked over, took her into her arms and gave her a hug.

"I'm sorry, baby. Let's finish opening these presents. When those boys do start coming around, you just remember this... the blacker the berry; the sweeter its juice."

Blanche's paternal relatives burst into laughter over Nora's attempt at philosophy, and Blanche's friends quickly joined in the laughter, vowing to remember that piece of advice. Blanche couldn't help but laugh as well at those words of wisdom. As she continued to open presents, the tension in the yard waned as the guests ooh'd and aah'd over each gift. The scene was quickly forgotten but not by Blanche as she lay in bed that night listening to her parents arguing over whether Nora would ever be invited to their house again.

On a later visit with her father to Aunt Nora's house, Blanche asked her about the comments, and her aunt had educated her. One or both of the two tests Nora had alluded to had been used among the elite of the black Creole society during her grandmother's youth to determine whether a person would be admitted to social functions. Her paternal relatives would never have been invited to functions given by the lighter skinned blacks in the community unless they had a high social standing or wealth.

Glancing at her arm, Blanche knew her skin was not darker than a brown paper bag. Studying the back of her hands and rotating her left arm to view the underside, she knew her skin tone was also light enough that you could see the blue veins beneath it. With her complexion being a café au lait, coffee with cream added, as her grandmother had commented, she would, though barely, pass both tests.

No, she hadn't added cream to her coffee. She had added stronger, blacker coffee to the little cream her own coffee already had. What was she going to do?

Recalling her mother assuring Tony she was just tired, she thought about going back to Lafayette and dating him. If she gave in to the sexual attempts he had a reputation for and was sure to try on their first date, could she pass off the pregnancy to him? If her mother thought it was Tony's baby, she wouldn't be as upset. But, what if he offered to marry her? To let him touch her once would be hard enough, but to be stuck in a marriage with someone so shallow would be hell to Blanche. Besides, when the baby was born, what then? Would he say the child can't be his and accuse her of having used him?

Through the generations, the gene pool for those of African descent in southern Louisiana had become so diluted with French, Indian, Spanish, and German blood lines, you never knew what the child would look like until it was born. Darker skinned couples could have a blond, blue-eyed child, and lighter skinned couples could have a child with a complexion darker than either parent. Even if she decided to choose that option, what about the baby's features? She thought of her features, Tony's, and Adam's. Could she pass the baby off if it resembled neither parent? No, there was no way she could consider doing something so deceitful. Even though her time with Adam had only been a one night stand, she still did not want his child to carry Tony's name or be raised by him if a marriage resulted and did last. That was not an option she could choose.

Could she possibly slip into New Orleans one weekend alone and have an abortion? Reaching into her purse, she pulled out the prayer card she had picked up the first weekend she spent in New Orleans when she had attended mass with Colin's family.

Her heart went out to the picture of the infant under the caption, "Speak up for those who cannot speak for themselves." She held the prayer card tightly as she took a moment to read the prayer to end abortion.

A soft knock on the bathroom door startled Blanche.

"Blanche, are you okay?"

Aubrey's soft voice whispered from the other side of the closed door.

"I'm fine!" she called out, but hearing the tremor in her voice, she knew it didn't come across that way. Hopefully, Aubrey wouldn't detect it.

"My mom sent me to check on you because we thought you'd be back downstairs by now. No problem! Don't rush. We just wanted to be sure you were okay."

Blanche knew Autumn would have detected something was wrong based on the length of time they had spent together that summer so was thankful Aubrey was the one that had been sent instead.

"Thanks for checking. I'll be down shortly!" Blanche called back feeling relieved her voice sounded more normal.

After she heard Aubrey's footsteps on the stair, she exited the bathroom, took her purse and hid it under the clothes in her suitcase before rejoining the trio in the kitchen. Autumn had finished chopping the onions she had been working on earlier. Maria was pulling two bunches of carrots out the refrigerator.

"I'll clean those for you," Blanche offered.

"Thank you, Blanche," Maria replied as she handed the two bunches over to her. She pulled a knife and vegetable peeler out of a drawer and handed those to her as well.

Blanche was grateful to be at the sink with her back turned to the others. She needed time to adjust to this new knowledge and was thankful for being able to hide her face from the others.

Shortly, Colin walked into the kitchen. He took one of the carrot sticks Blanche had cut for the vegetable platter they were making and bit into it, the crunching sound testifying to the freshness of the vegetable.

"These are great," he spoke to Maria.

"I got them from the organic store. It seems the ones they sell there are sweeter than what the supermarket carries."

"The ladies outside are getting hungry. What do you four say to taking a break and going out for lunch?"

"I hate to stop at this point. I can just fix some sandwiches, and we go out for dinner tonight instead," Maria offered.

Maria and Colin looked towards Autumn and Aubrey for concurrence. Each of the twins nodded in agreement.

"Blanche, is that okay with you?" Maria questioned.

Not turning around, Blanche responded, "Could we take them to the Creole restaurant on the service road tonight? I think my mother would love the menu there. Their food is just like home made, and they serve such generous portions."

"That's a good idea. Their gumbo is great. With the jumbo shrimp and hot sausage they put in it, I know my mom would love a bowl of that," Colin replied and, though her back was still towards them, Blanche sensed the other three were in agreement.

"Then we'll get busy making a platter of sandwiches and a salad. We'll bring them out to the lanai."

Satisfied with the plan, Colin swiped another carrot from the platter and rejoined the elderly ladies.

Sighing with relief, Blanche tossed the peelings from the first bunch into the trash before starting on the second. She had quickly suggested the restaurant because she knew they didn't have a liquor license. Since Colin's family enjoyed wine with meals when they were celebrating special events, she didn't want to make excuses why she didn't want to enjoy a glass with them. They may have thought it was out of fear because her mother was present and may have pushed the subject. Blanche couldn't think of any excuse to continue turning down the offer, and she had to protect her baby, Adam's baby. She thought about the time they had celebrated Autumn's grades. She had a glass of champagne that night, and she also had a glass of plum wine at the Chinese restaurant she and Autumn had gone too the night after she was with Adam. She said a silent prayer those occasions hadn't done major harm to the life growing inside of her.

Life was growing inside of her. At six weeks, it was possible to hear the baby's heartbeat using a vaginal ultrasound. She placed her hands on her abdomen and thought about a tiny heart beating inside of her, and for the first time since knowing, she felt excited about the idea that she, Blanche Aubert, would be bringing a new life into the world.

By the time they were leaving for dinner at the Creole restaurant, Sherrie seemed content. Whenever she was the center of attention, her manner seemed milder. Colin, Maria, the twins, and Blanche had waited on her hand and foot the entire day. The bedroom she stayed in was decorated so luxuriously, and the bathroom she shared with her sister was as fine as any hotel. It seems Sherrie was actually enjoying herself and not focusing on Blanche for a change.

At the restaurant, Colin sat Sherrie at the head of one end of the table. Maria sat on her left with Aubrey on her other side. Barbara was on her right and Colin was on his mother's other side. Autumn sat on Colin's right so Blanche was the farthest she could get from her mother. Colin took charge explaining the menu. When the waitress appeared with hot, buttered French bread slices spread with garlic, Sherrie was moaning with pleasure. Her focus became the meal instead of her daughter. Blanche settled back and was able to enjoy the meal herself. Blanche, Autumn, and Aubrey conversed and laughed while Colin and Maria entertained the other end of the table. By the time they got home, everyone was ready to call it a night. Colin would be up by dawn starting the barbecue before their guests began arriving at noon for the picnic. Sherrie even gave Blanche a smile when she kissed her good night before going up the stairs to join Autumn and Aubrey.

When she finally entered the bedroom, Autumn gave her a strange look but didn't make any comments. Blanche tried to focus on what Aubrey was saying though Autumn's reaction had her curious. "Was she jealous?" Blanche thought because she had to share the attention Blanche usually gave only to her with her sister. Attributing her look to that, Blanche turned her attention to a photograph album Aubrey had pulled from her suitcase and focused on the photos from her summer in New York City as Aubrey excitedly pointed to a new friend she had met there who lived in Baton Rouge.

Chapter Twenty-Three

Sunday morning was buzzing in the Laurent household. After a light breakfast of croissants and fresh fruit, Maria, the twins, and Blanche were preparing the last menu items while Colin, though experienced, was barbecuing under the continued direction of his mother and aunt. Guests began arriving around 11:30, and Maria left the three to finish up the last items in the kitchen while she played hostess. About 11:45, Maria called for Autumn. Apparently, a guest had arrived Autumn invited that Maria didn't know. Autumn gave Blanche the same odd glaring look she had the night before as she pulled off her apron and then exited from the kitchen.

By the time Autumn approached the guest, her mother was beaming.

"Doctor Brown was telling me how well you did in his class this summer and how much he enjoyed having you as a student."

Autumn could tell the pride her mother was feeling hearing such a good report. She also knew it meant a sense of relief for her as well, and she felt less as if she had abandoned her daughter for her work duties, an issue with which all working mothers seem to struggle.

"Hi, Doctor A.J., I'm so glad you could come."

"I wouldn't have passed up this invitation for the world," he smiled at Autumn knowing the secret they shared.

When the fall session began and Autumn met with him as her assigned advisor for the year, she could tell he was struggling not to ask about Blanche as she stood to leave his office.

"Doctor A.J., do you have any plans for the Labor Day weekend? We're having a barbecue. All of our family from Lafayette will be in town. Would you like to join us?"

Adam had smiled knowing she was opening a door for him. Though he had planned to spend the weekend back home with his cousin in New York City, he had to seize this chance to talk with Blanche and convince her to consider a relationship with him. It may be the last opportunity he had. He gladly accepted the invitation, and Autumn had jotted down the time, date, and directions to the house across the lake.

"Thank you," was the only response he dared to give her as she turned and left his office. Once her back was to him, he couldn't see the wide grin that had spread across Autumn's face.

"Autumn, why don't you escort Doctor Brown out to the lanai and introduce him to Colin? Colin can introduce him to the other guests."

"Sure! Right this way, Doctor A.J."

As they stepped away from her mom, Autumn whispered, "Blanche is in the kitchen. I'll be sure you get to sit together at the picnic tables."

Adam nodded his head in acknowledgement.

As they approached Colin, Autumn made the introductions.

"Colin, this is my advisor for this year, Doctor A.J. ... Doctor A.J., this is my stepdad, Colin Laurent."

"Please call me Adam. You have a lovely home." Doctor A.J. extended his hand to greet Colin.

Before taking his hand and shaking it warmly, Colin glanced towards the house searching for Blanche as he recalled her mentioning the name on the ride from the airport. Taking the lead, he began introducing Adam to the other guests as Autumn returned to the kitchen to help finish the set-up. As she stepped through the door, she eyed Blanche busily adding the last of the dips to the vegetable and fruit platters. She felt a slight twinge of guilt that she had set her up but the feeling didn't last for very long.

Blanche looked up and announced, "This is it. These two platters are the last items your mom had on the list. Once we bring these out to the serving tables, lunch is ready. Want to help me carry them out?"
"Sure!" Autumn answered her so enthusiastically that it was Blanche donning the odd expression this time. As each gathered one of the

huge crystal platters in their arms, Autumn led the way through the kitchen door into the den and out through the patio doors to the lanai.

Focusing on not dropping her platter, Blanche hadn't noticed the number of guests that had gathered and were sipping drinks as they mingled on the well-manicured lawn. After she and Autumn placed the platters in the last open spots on the serving table, she turned to Autumn.

"Everything looks great. I'm so glad we were able to come. We're having such a nice time. Even my mom seems happy. So, what do we do now?"

"Grab a glass of lemonade ourselves and mingle 'til my mom and Colin announce that it's time to eat."

Blanche gave Autumn another odd glance. Maria had prepared a huge punch bowl of Sangria with fresh fruit floating on top and a second fruity punch spiked with rum. She thought, for certain, that Autumn would head straight for a rum punch. As they turned to walk over to the outdoor bar, Blanche grabbed Autumn's wrist and squeezed it tightly. Her face paled as she spotted Adam talking with one of Colin's work partners she had met earlier.

"You invited him?" Blanche stared at Autumn accusingly.

"Let's go upstairs," Autumn demanded pulling Blanche's clenched hand from around her wrist.

By the time they reached the upstairs guest suite, Blanche was furious.

"Autumn, how could you and not tell me?"

"You know well why I didn't tell you. If I had, you'd make up some stupid excuse not to come! He wants to see you."

Blanche stood breathing hard, knowing Autumn was right. She was shocked when Autumn walked over to the suitcase, swung the cover open, and pushed her clothes aside, opened the purse, and extracted the pregnancy test stick.

"And, if you don't tell him, I will! He has a right to know. It's his baby too!"

"How did you know?"

"You're not exactly adept at hiding things, Blanche. You were never in a bathroom that long the entire summer, even when you took a bath in the whirlpool tub and should have been relaxing. Then you spend over five minutes saving your purse when we came back from the restaurant. A purse that normally sits on the dresser gets stuffed in your suitcase, and you're shoving clothes around on top of it to hide it? Come on! … Really, Blanche! … Really! … Maybe Aubrey thinks you're just weird like that because she was gone all summer, but did you think I wouldn't suspect something was up?"

"I can't believe you went through my personal things."

"Oh! … You dare to throw that at me?" Autumn's face grew stern and reddened. She spoke in a louder voice, "I recall you opening a letter addressed to my parents… Remember that one?"

"Okay, so we're even," Blanche whispered trying to get Autumn to lower her voice which was raising louder and louder in volume with each word she spoke.

They both turned as Aubrey's voice called from the bottom of the stair, "Autumn, are you and Blanche up there? Mom says it's time to eat."

"We'll be right down!" Autumn yelled before whispering to Blanche, "Have you seen a doctor yet?"

Blanche shook her head side to side indicating, "No."

"I can make you an appointment with my mom's gynecologist. He has Saturday hours."

"Thank you," she whispered to Autumn relieved and grateful someone she could confide in now knew.

"We better get back downstairs, but remember, if you don't tell him, I will."

Blanche pouted at the face of the determined girl standing in front of her. She remembered she didn't win the battle of wills the Fourth of July weekend, and she doubted she would win this one either. She followed Autumn reluctantly down the stairs where they met Aubrey and crossed the den to join the other guests outside.

Chapter Twenty-Four

By the time the trio prepared their plates and walked to where the picnic and other tables had been set up, the only empty seats left were across from Sherrie. The three open spots where they could sit together were between Adam and Colin. Nausea rose in Blanche's throat, and she gasped trying to control the emotions running through her and clouding her head. Turning, Autumn grabbed her arm and whispered, "Get a grip." As they approached the tables, Autumn released Blanche's arm and shoved Aubrey toward the seat next to Colin, nearly knocking her plate out her hand. She quickly took the seat next to her leaving Blanche no choice but to sit next to Adam.

As Aubrey eyed Autumn, upset she almost knocked her food to the ground, and Blanche eyed Autumn upset she was making decisions affecting her life, Autumn sat in the middle empty chair at the table pleasantly smiling and biting into a honey glazed pork rib.

Blanche placed her plate and lemonade on the table. Adam immediately stood and pulled out the chair for her. Ignoring him, she sat and dove into her food.

"Blanche, don't be so impolite. Tell the gentleman 'thank you'," Sherrie whispered embarrassed her daughter had ignored the gesture offered by Autumn's professor. Having met him earlier and pleased by the amount of attention Adam had lavished on her, Sherrie was eager to impress him as well.

Without looking Adam's way, Blanche whispered, "Thank you," as her mother ordered.

"Please excuse my daughter, Adam. She's not accustomed to big social events like I am."

Ignoring the slight, Adam seized the opening, "Ms. Sherrie, you have a beautiful daughter."

"You think my daughter's pretty?" Sherrie's mother giggled at the compliment.

"I think she's beautiful," Adam replied turning to stare at Blanche who turned her head away from him and towards Autumn.

"Her name is Blanche... Are you from here, Adam?"

"No, Ma'am. I grew up in New York City. I came to New Orleans because there was a position open that promised tenure. Those are getting hard to come by these days. New York is a wonderful place to live. I'm glad I made the move though. I have grown to love New Orleans just as much as some of the people I've met here."

Adam's voice grew huskier at the last words as his eyes didn't move from Blanche's face.

"Let me share some of our Creole culture with you...."

Colin choked on a bite of rib that got caught in his throat and eyed his aunt with concern. He thought, "Thank God Maria has set up the picnic tables as individual units, and the only people sitting at theirs was the family and Adam. His business associates were at a table of their own talking shop as usual.

"Did you know blanche is French for white?"

"I don't speak French, but I've heard students talk about a department store that is closed now but was quite popular with the locals here in New Orleans. It was called Maison Blanche and had a mascot called Mr. Bingle. The students were saying they hang a Mr. Bingle in the City Park carousel area for the Celebration in the Oaks now. I think the ones from New Orleans go to the festivities just to see Mr. Bingle. It sounds like it's just as much a tradition here as going to tell Santa Claus what you want for Christmas. Based on those stories I've heard, I assumed it translates to white house and because of the white façade of the building that's now a hotel?"

Sherrie was pleased with what Adam shared.

"You're right, young man. Maison Blanche does mean white house. We are Creoles. We have strong French ancestry. My father's people were from northern France, and my mother's people were from

Belgium, but it was a French speaking country at the time they immigrated to America. We're mixed up down here so, when our babies are born, we're not sure how they're going to look because they don't get their color right away."

Blanche cringed knowing what was coming next. She turned her face away from Adam's and took a bite of the fruity cole slaw she had helped Maria prepare. She wished she could block out the next words her mother spoke.

"When Blanche was born, her skin was as fair as mine. By the time she was six months old, she had turned the color she is now. If I knew she was going to turn that dark, I wouldn't have named her something that means white. Isn't that funny? Someone brown skinned named white."

Sherrie started laughing at the story. Being the longest time she had spent around Colin's aunt, Aubrey sat staring with her mouth open stunned at what she had heard. Autumn looked at the lady with disdain, feeling sorry she would embarrass Blanche that way. Colin rubbed his chin eyeing his aunt and thinking of the years of verbal abuse Blanche had suffered and hoping she would eventually leave from the toxic home environment and move to New Orleans with them. Maria struggled to introduce a different topic. Adam acted as if it was no big deal. He turned from Blanche to Sherrie, then back to Blanche before shocking all of them with his response.

"I guess that does seem ironic, but I know you must be proud of the beautiful skin tone she has. She has a glow about her. White people spend hours in the sun risking skin cancer to get the exact skin tone she has naturally. Nothing from a bottle can be as beautiful."

Turning his attention from Blanche to her mother, Adam continued.

"How often do you sun bathe, Ms. Sherrie? Seems you haven't in sometime, and that's not healthy. You need sunlight. It helps the body produce vitamin D … Didn't you get any sun this summer? I guess they don't have beaches in this area, do they? I hear of families going to Biloxi for the weekend if they want to bring their kids to the beach. Maybe you ladies will give me the pleasure of your company and allow me to drive you down there one day. "

Sherrie focused on her food again since the conversation hadn't turned in the direction she wanted. Colin took a huge bite out a chicken leg satisfied his aunt seemed to finally have met her match with Autumn's professor. As Maria introduced other topics, the tension that had built at the table eased. When the guests had finished the main course, Maria stood and announced Sherrie and her mother-in-law had brought a selection of home-made cakes that were laid on the dining room table and requested the guests help themselves to the desserts. Her and Colin stepped away momentarily to put out a variety of ice cream from the freezer and to get the serving line moving.

"If you like pound cake, I made an almond flavored one," Sherrie told Adam proudly.

"Ma'am, that sounds delicious. I hope there's some left by the time I get there because I definitely want to sample your cake. I haven't had a homemade cake since my grandmother passed. May I serve the two of you?"

Barbara looked at her walking cane and the distance back to the house. "Thank you, young man. I'd like a scoop of my bread pudding with a little vanilla ice cream on top."

"Did you make that bread pudding? If so, I need to try that too."

Barbara beamed, "My secret is I let the raisins soak overnight in bourbon before I add them in and bake it. I add a bit of brown sugar too." She winked at Adam, and he graced her with a smile.

Eager to not let her sister outdo her and to turn the attention back to herself, Sherrie interrupted the conversation, "I made a rum cake. It's the bundt cake with all the pecans on top."

"Ladies, please don't describe another dessert to me. I don't see a wheelbarrow in this yard so there's no way to roll me to my car. Let me get your desserts, and then I'll serve the other ladies here."

Adam glanced at Aubrey and Autumn but stared at Blanche for a moment before standing from the table to act as a waiter.

After Sherrie and Barbara were busy enjoying their desserts, he took Aubrey and Autumn's orders. When Blanche remained silent, he spoke directly to her.

"And Blanche, what do you desire?"

Blanche couldn't help but look into his eyes when he addressed her directly, catching the double meaning to his words, "Just a slice of the almond pound cake. That's my favorite of all the desserts my mom made."

Their eyes locked for a brief moment before Adam returned to his waiter's duties.

As the festivities were drawing to a close, Adam turned to Sherrie, and the next words he spoke caused Blanche to pale.

"Ms. Sherrie, there's a banquet at the university next weekend. I'd be embarrassed to show up by myself. I don't have anyone to go with me. Would you mind if your daughter would do me the honor?"

Blanche looked pleadingly at her mother and opened her mouth but no words came out. Sherrie started laughing hysterically.

"She'd love to go with you, Adam. Wouldn't you, Blanche?"

Blanche stared at her mother in disbelief. Did her mother just agree for Blanche to go out with someone with a skin tone as dark as Adam's? Watching her mother's smile turn into a sneer, Blanche guessed what was going through her mother's mind. She took Blanche's reaction not as shock at Adam's boldness but as horror that she would have to be seen in public with a dark skinned man. Her mother thought it was amusing that Blanche would get stuck going out with someone she felt was inferior because of his skin tone. This was one of her mother's ways of punishing Blanche for changing her clothes, hair, and make-up without her permission. Realizing her intent, she grew a little angry that Adam was the brunt of her mother's hostility. Seeing Blanche's face, Sherrie sat back smugly smiling that she had gotten the upper hand.

Autumn broke the tension building, "What does she have to wear, Doctor A.J.?"

Too excited that he would have an evening with Blanche alone and not understanding the exchange taking place between mother and daughter, Adam answered Autumn's questions enthusiastically stating the day, time, and place of the event and advising it was semi-formal.

"Blanche, we'll get you an outfit. I know all your sizes. And, Aubrey is leaving Monday to go back to school in Texas so you can use her room again." Autumn rapidly uttered solutions to every objection Blanche planned to use. When Maria returned to the table and joined in the plans, Blanche was soon cornered into not being able to deny such a simple request from Adam.

As Adam bade everyone good-bye, his eyes stared into Blanche's, "Until the weekend, then." He tucked the address for the house in New Orleans that Autumn gave him into his wallet before turning one last time to Blanche and stating, "I'll pick you up for 5:00."

"She'll be ready," Autumn responded on Blanche's behalf, "She's driving down the night before as soon as school lets out."

Blanche gave Autumn a scolding look. Autumn clenched her jaw and stared back at her daring Blanche to contradict what she had said. When Blanche's eyes shifted under Autumn's stare, Autumn leaned over and whispered to her, "Remember, my mom's gynecologist has Saturday office hours. I'll make you an appointment for Saturday morning so you can find out for certain before you talk to Adam that night."

Blanche nodded her head slightly in agreement then turned back to Autumn and mouthed a silent, "Thank you."

On the drive back to Lafayette the next day, Sherrie confirmed what Blanche had surmised.
"That poor boy! Who would ever go out with something that short and dark?" Turning to her sister in the back seat, Sherrie continued, "No wonder he begged me to let Blanche go to that school banquet with

him." Turning back to face the windshield, she continued her commentary.

"I know you're upset, Blanche, but think of this as your Christian duty to help that poor little monkey man out. How could I turn him down? He was so pitiful. It would have been embarrassing to Colin and Autumn to act ugly towards their guest. It won't hurt you to go with the poor man to a banquet. It's just one night. And, besides, it might be an opportunity for you to meet somebody nice when you get there. .. Since you acted so ugly with Tony, he might not ask you out again."

Blanche was visibly upset as she thought to herself, "And it wasn't embarrassing to me for you to tell him the story behind my name?"

Satisfied, her daughter was stuck in an unwanted situation, Sherrie turned to gossiping with Barbara for the rest of the ride home as Blanche focused on the ultimatum Autumn reminded her of when she gave her a spare set of keys to the house, "Remember, if you don't tell him, I will!"

Chapter Twenty-Five

When Blanche arrived at Maria's old house Friday night, it was in total darkness. Maria and Colin were spending the weekend in Lacombe having the extra picnic tables and chairs they had rented for the Labor Day event picked up and tidying up other loose ends from the previous weekend. Autumn had moved back into the dormitory. Blanche couldn't believe she had the entire house to herself for the weekend. When she entered Aubrey's bedroom and turned on the light, she gasped. Hanging on a hook on the closet door was the most beautiful dress she had ever seen. She walked over to the closet, reached her hand under the plastic covering, and smoothed it over the fine fabric. She had never worn anything so elegant. The black halter style mid length gown shimmered with silver threads. It was an empire style flowing softly from below the high bodice. A pair of silver low-heeled sandals sat in a shoe box on the window bench as well as the right bra to complement the dress' style, two pairs of silky, sheer toed, black stockings, and a lacey black wrap for her shoulders. When she pulled the plastic back down to cover the dress, she heard a thump against the closet. Shifting the dress forward, she saw a silver evening bag with a rhinestone buckle had been hung on the hangar as well.

"I guess Cinderella is going to the ball," she said aloud. As she went to drop her purse on the bottom shelf of the night stand, she saw an envelope with her name scribbled across it in Autumn's handwriting. She slit the envelope open and removed a note slip. The doctor's name, address, directions to the office, and the time she needed to be there were all noted. There was also a caution not to be late since the receptionist was working Blanche in between other appointments. Blanche's eyes brimmed as her excitement waned remembering her situation. She stuffed the note into her purse and set the alarm before retiring to Maria and Colin's whirlpool tub. She didn't cut on the jets afraid the waves might not be good for the baby but filled the tub with bubble bath and took a long soak. She needed to relax her nerves and hoped the warm water would help her figure out the best way to break the news to Adam.

The next day, she woke early. She took a quick shower so her body would be at its freshest for the doctor's examination. After dressing, she took the note Autumn had left for her and studied the directions to the doctor's office. After setting the house alarm, she got into her car and drove to the interstate taking the west ramp towards uptown New Orleans. Taking the Saint Charles Avenue exit, she drove as slow as the traffic permitted studying the milestones Autumn had listed. Finally, she saw signs of a hospital complex on her left. Maneuvering to the left lane, she crossed the last large intersection and took a left turn searching for a parking spot on the side street. Walking towards the complex, she was only a half block from the medical building where the doctor's office should be located. Entering the lobby, she confirmed the suite number on the directory and took the elevator to the floor. The receptionist greeted her, asked if it was her first visit, and handed her a medical history form and a billing form to fill out. Taking a clipboard, the form, and pen, Blanche sat in a corner where she hoped her presence would not be as noticeable.

Glancing around the reception area, she didn't notice anyone that seemed familiar. She was grateful Autumn had arranged this for her. The atmosphere was calming, soft instrumental music was playing through the sound system, the walls were painted a soothing aqua, aquariums with exotic fishes were positioned in several key spots in the room, an assortment of magazines were available on various tables, and an information display held pamphlets on topics of importance to women. Blanche had read once that she could come to a doctor's visit informed with a list of issues you wanted to discuss. It would ensure you got the most out of the visit, and when the doctor saw you were prepared, they wouldn't hesitate to spend as much time as needed with you. As soon as she finished the forms, she would pull a pamphlet on pregnancy and prepare her list of questions.

It didn't take any time for her to complete her medical history. Blanche had been healthy her entire life. She ran down the list of medical problems and checked no to each, no to any medications she was on, wrote none to past surgeries, then hesitated when it asked for the reason for today's visit. She put in annual physical just in case someone would walk up to the counter and see her form before the receptionist moved it. She'd tell the doctor once she was in a private exam room the real reason for her coming.

When it was time to fill out the billing information, she hesitated again. She had health insurance from her job at school, but her home address was on file. She didn't want anything from the doctor's going to the house. Her mother opened all the mail even if it was addressed to Blanche. Her work address was on file as well, but she didn't want to raise questions at the school. She filled out the home address field but squeezed in a mailing address field as well and listed Maria's house. She could get Autumn to pull any correspondence for her that way.

Feeling apprehensive but satisfied she had taken all the precautionary steps she could, she brought the forms back to the receptionist, gave her the medical card and her driver's license to make copies, then pulled a couple of pamphlets from the rack before returning to her seat to make a list of questions for the doctor.

When a nurse emerged from behind a set of closed doors to the left of the receptionist desk and called Blanche's name, the nausea she typically felt intensified. She raised her hand to indicate she was coming, pulled a mint from her purse, and prayed the sweet taste would keep her from vomiting in front of the ladies seated in the area.

As she walked past the waiting nurse, the nurse motioned to a scale beyond the door. Blanche dropped her purse on the chair next to the scale then stood as still as she could while the nurse recorded her weight and height. She followed her to an exam room where she also took Blanche's blood pressure and temperature. After reviewing her forms, she turned to Blanche.

"So, you're here for your annual physical?"

"Yes, I haven't had a physical since I started work, and I also think I'm pregnant."

Blanche choked on the words as she pulled at a broken nail instead of facing the nurse. The nurse stood, pulled a gown from a cabinet under the exam table, and responded in a nonchalant but professional tone, "You need to undress and put this gown on so it opens to the front." She opened another cabinet on the wall and took out a package that held a plastic cup and wipes similar to what Blanche had seen in restaurants.

"Do you know how to do a clean urine sample?" When Blanche shook her head indicating no, the nurse explained to use the wipes and put a mid-stream urine sample in the cup. She pointed to a shelf that rotated in the wall next to the door and told Blanche to place the urine cup on that once she finished and then get on the exam table. She pointed to an area behind a curtain and advised there was a commode and rack where she could hang her clothes.

Blanche nodded and waited until the nurse had left the room to do as instructed. After completing the urine sample and placing it on the shelf, she rotated it outward to get picked up. Then she stepped behind the curtain, put on the gown before taking the sheet that was laying on the exam table, and wrapping it around her before sitting on the edge. When the nurse came in to check if she was ready, she unwrapped the sheet and placed it loosely draping Blanche's waist and legs and instructed Blanche to lie back on the table while she positioned her feet into two steel cups she had pulled out from the sides of the table. Blanche's apprehension grew as she heard the nurse pulling items out for the doctor.

Before today, her visits to the doctor had only been to take her temperature, listen to her heart, check her ears and nose, and maybe take a blood test. She had no idea what to expect and was growing more nervous each minute. The nurse stood, announced the doctor would be in shortly, and left the room. Blanche pushed the sheet down in between her legs to restore some sense of modesty.

When the doctor entered, he stood above her on the table, introduced himself, then sat at a small writing table reviewing her medical form. He then stood above her once again, undid the front of her exam gown, moved her right arm above her head, and began pressing her breast with his fingers even pressing the area around her nipple. Blanche grew tense as he finished and repeated the process on her left breast. She wondered if this was normal or if the doctor just enjoyed feeling his patients. Seeing the nurse eyeing the entire procedure and not acting as if this was outside of the norm, she assumed this was the standard examination. When he finished and pulled the gown closed, Blanche tied the strings tightly to keep her breast from being exposed again. When the doctor sat on a stool at the base of the exam table and asked her to scoot her butt closer to the edge, Blanche wanted to get off the table and walk out. That was more than she was prepared to handle. She had heard some of the elderly teachers at the school comment there was no dignity when you're having a baby, but to have two complete strangers staring at her vagina was not what she ever envisioned.

When the doctor pushed her legs gently apart and ordered her to relax, Blanche's breathing started coming in short gasps, and she began trembling. The doctor spoke gently again and tried to soothe her. When she felt steel sliding into her vagina, she went to close her legs but tried hard to follow his instructions. When Blanche commented how uncomfortable the instrument felt, the doctor did nothing to adjust the pinching sensation but responded he was almost done.

When the steel clamp was eased out, Blanche thought her ordeal was over. When the doctor stood above her, put one hand on her abdomen and slid fingers inside of her, she was so startled she closed her legs slightly and her breathing again came in short gasps again. He finally stopped pressing her abdomen in different spots and told her she could sit up. Blanche quickly took her heels out the cups, pushed into a seating position, and pulled the sheet tightly around her body. The doctor sat at the small writing desk making notes while the nurse sprayed a slide, cleaned up the area, and then walked out the room. When the doctor completed his notes, he turned to Blanche.

"Ms. Aubert, you are indeed pregnant based on the results of the urine test and my examination. You noted the first day of your last period as July 23 so your estimated delivery date is April 24. We typically count 40 weeks from that date but keep in mind that only approximately five percent of babies arrive on their estimated date. Do you have any questions?"

"It was only once," Blanche whispered so softly the doctor barely heard her. Hearing the pregnancy confirmed, she completely forgot about the list of questions she had prepared. When the doctor advised he was no longer practicing obstetrics, only gynecology, Blanche questioned what she should be doing to have a healthy baby until she made another appointment. In response, the doctor jotted down some suggested over the counter vitamins she could purchase emphasizing the folic acid content and explaining to Blanche it could prevent most serious birth defects of the baby's brain and spine. It was then that Blanche remembered her list. She asked the doctor if she could pull it, and he sat down as they discussed other concerns she had. After her list was exhausted and she had no further questions, he gave her a sheet with obstetricians he recommended and his best wishes before leaving her to dress.

At the reception desk, Blanche paid cash for the visit, took the receipt, and walked stone-faced from the doctor's office to the elevator. On the first floor, she exited the elevator and then just stood at the directory seeing a couple of the names of obstetricians from the list she was given had offices in the same building. How long she stood staring blankly at the directory, she didn't know.

"May I help you, miss?"

Blanche turned her head and saw the security guard had walked over.

"No, sir, but thank you…"

She turned to leave and return to her car. The car seemed to be on auto pilot as she pulled into the drive at Maria's. She went to Aubrey's room, dropped her purse on the night stand, and sat on the window bench. What now? What was to become of her and the baby? She remembered one of the eighth grade girls at school getting pregnant. Rumor was the girl's mother had beaten the child so severely when she found out, it was surprising she hadn't lost the baby. Blanche cringed remembering the beatings she had endured as a child. She couldn't imagine her mother's reaction at the news. The phone ringing broke her train of thought. Robotically, she rose, walked to the nightstand, and lifted the receiver but words just couldn't come out.

"Blanche?"

Hearing Autumn's voice on the other end, she finally answered, "I am pregnant."

An audible sigh was heard on the other end.

"Did you like the doctor? How did everything go?"

"It was so embarrassing getting examined. I felt dirty... But, he was kind. Thank you, Autumn, for making the appointment."

"When's the baby due?"

"The end of April..."

Hearing the disappointment in Blanche's voice, Autumn tried to reassure her.

"Blanche, you're not the first unwed mother in this world. Adam is a great guy. I just know he's going to stand by you through this. Even if he doesn't, you still have me, my mom, and Colin. Everything is going to be fine! You and the baby won't lack for anything. We'll be there for you."

"Thanks, Autumn...."

"Tell Adam tonight!"

Blanche gazed towards the outfit on the closet, then at her stomach. Based on the doctor's calculations and informing her forty weeks from when her last period was due is how they calculated the due date, Blanche was roughly seven weeks so almost two months already. She hadn't started showing yet so the gown should still fit. Knowing her possible condition, Autumn had guided her mother into selecting a style that would work even if her middle had expanded. She grimaced at the thought of blurting the news to Adam.

Hearing silence, Autumn spoke sternly, "Blanche, I need to go. The professor is out of town, and I'm playing emcee for him at The Library for the poetry session today. But, remember, if you don't tell Doctor A.J., I will. Promise me!"

"I promise," she answered Autumn with a lack of conviction in her voice.

"I'll check back with you to see how everything went."

"Ok… Thanks again, Autumn."

As Autumn hung up on her end, Blanche glanced at the clock and pondered what she could do to occupy herself and keep the negative thoughts from clouding her mind. Going to the briefcase she had brought with her, she went out to the sun room, dropped the case on the wrought iron table, and took a seat.

She tried to focus on the work for next week's school activities but her mind kept watching the clock in the living room instead. She finally gave up and tried to view a movie. When a sex scene unfolded, it reminded her of the night she had lost her virginity. Disgusted with herself, she turned the movie off and headed to the library. Maybe she could find something that would give her an idea of how to approach Adam since she was failing to draft the right words on her own. She would search the psychology books praying for a way to break the news. Instead of taking her car, she walked the short distance down Read Boulevard to the East New Orleans Regional branch. She reasoned the exercise would be good for the baby, would help calm her nerves, and the fresh hair might help clear her mind. At the library, she sat in the psychology section in a lounge chair isolated from the main flow of traffic.

When her watch chimed three times, Blanche closed the psychology magazines and books she had been perusing and headed back to Maria's old house. She took another soak in the whirlpool tub before dressing and sitting on the sofa in the den nervously watching the clock. At 4:45, she heard a car backing into the driveway. Grabbing the evening bag off the coffee table, she stood, walked to the front door, reset the alarm, and stepped out to meet Adam before he had a chance to ring the bell. At least by not inviting him in, she avoided immediately having conversation with him that might lead to her announcing her pregnancy.

"Blanche, you look beautiful," Adam stated as he stared at her from head to toe. Walking to the passenger side of the car, he opened the door for her.

She wanted to respond how particularly handsome he looked in the black tuxedo he was wearing but couldn't bring herself to say anything. As she sat on the seat of the car and swung her legs inside, the flounced skirt caught Adam's attention as he eyed her shapely legs covered by the sheer black stockings. Remembering the night at his condo, he took a deep breath trying to gain control and thinking , "This is going to be a long night," as he walked around the back of the car and took his place in the driver's seat.

As the car turned onto Interstate-10 west, Adam broke the silence.

"I've missed you. I enjoyed the time we spent together this summer. You never came to any of my lectures. Did you feel they wouldn't compare to those from the visiting professors?"

Surprised he thought Blanche hadn't attended because she felt him inferior, she immediately broke her silence.

"Oh, Adam, no! Please don't think that. I would have loved to attend your lectures."

"I watched for you but I never saw you."

Blanche fell silent again. Remembering Autumn's threat, she ventured, "I was embarrassed by the way I behaved at The Library. You had your students there and I was so tipsy from Irish coffees, I had to lean on you to leave. I thought Irish was a type of coffee bean. My cousin keeps Colombian coffee beans at the house, and they freshly grind them whenever they brew a pot. I didn't know it meant the coffee was laced with Irish whiskey. I couldn't face you again after that."

Blanche didn't dare bring up what had happened at the condo so sought safer territory to discuss what had occurred between them that fateful night.

Adam chuckled remembering her dousing one after another, "I started to comment on it when you ordered a third but thought you had read the card."

"What card?"

"The card on the table describing the various coffees they served. The ones that have alcohol are starred, and there's a note saying they won't serve those to any of the students regardless of their age."

"I didn't notice the card. I just read off the menu."

Adam laughed aloud as he shifted lanes and gunned the motor to cross the high rise.

"We should go back there before you leave tomorrow. How about meeting me for breakfast?"

"That would be nice," Blanche answered glad he had also avoided what had happened later that evening.

They sat in silence the rest of the drive to the university enjoying the jazz music from a radio station Adam selected.

"Move slowly, Adam, you have all night. Take it slowly. Don't push too hard too fast or you may not see her again." He kept reminding himself of those words as the evening progressed. When they got off the elevator and entered the sports arena which had been converted to a banquet hall, the stares from other faculty members admiring the lady at his side filled Adam with pride. His chest stood out as he introduced Blanche to his peers, the university president, and others in attendance before taking their reserved seats. The admiring glances from his nemesis made Adam feel especially proud as he glanced at the homely (but rich) lady he had married in hopes her family's wealth and position would further his career.

Seeing the way Blanche easily interacted with those seated at their table and held her own amid the variety of topics that were raised, Adam knew she was the right person for her. He had fallen in love with her beauty, her intelligence, her kind ways, soft voice, and dedication to the students at a small, inner city school. Watching her tonight, he knew she could hold her own in his world, as well. She was the perfect wife. She may have slipped away once, but thanks to Autumn, she was back in his life, and he wouldn't let her slip away again.

The banquet went longer than he anticipated and he could tell Blanche was tired by the time it ended and managed to get through all the conversations that followed before they could escape to the garage and retrieve his car. Knowing they would meet for breakfast the next morning, he didn't push for further conversation when they returned to the house where she was staying. He did push for one thing though. He wasn't going to take the risk of her not showing up and not knowing how to contact her again.

"We're still meeting for breakfast?" he inquired when he walked her to the door.

"Yes, I'll be there in the morning."

"About ten? Is that ok"

"That's fine," Blanche spoke softly, pulling the key from her bag, and turning to open the door.

"Let's swap numbers. You can call when you turn onto Decatur Street, and I'll come down and open the gate to the parking lot for you. You can park for free there and not have to go to the pay lot."

It sounded perfectly reasonable so Blanche entered Adam's number into the cell phone Colin had bought her when she said she would drive them down for Labor Day. "As a precaution, cous. If you break down on the highway, you can just call instead of being at the mercy of who knows might stop." It made sense so she had accepted the gift knowing he was concerned with all of their safety.

"And yours?" Adam questioned.

"I don't recall it," Blanche blushed with embarrassment.

"You can pull it out the phone," he stated and reached over to show her how to punch up the number.

She watched as he hit menu, settings, phone, and own number. He memorized the numbers on the screen then quickly punched the digits into his own cellular set. His hand brushing against hers set Blanche's nerves on edge. It triggered the same feelings she had that night before her mind blacked out from the alcohol. She had missed him as well but hadn't realized it until that moment. Since she had returned home, her only thoughts were of the tragic event that had happened between them, her mother's chiding, and the predicament she was now in.

"Until the morning then," he whispered to her, his lips so close to Blanche's, they were almost touching.

"Until the morning," she answered.

He stood staring into her eyes before forcing himself to turn and leave her.

"Damn, Adam!" he cursed all the way on the drive back to the condo. He wanted her so much.

Two people tossed restlessly in their beds that night and woke red-eyed from lack of sleep the next morning.

Chapter Twenty-Six

Blanche woke to the sound of the house alarm going off. Soon steps were heard in the hallway and a knock on the door followed.

"Who is it?"

Opening the door, Autumn entered, "Who do you think it is? How many people have keys to this house? ... Who else were you expecting? Adam?" Autumn sat on the edge at the foot of the bed crossing her leg so the mattress supported her thigh, and she could face Blanche.

"No, we're meeting for breakfast at The Library at ten. What time is it now?"

"It's only 8:30. So, what did he say?"

Blanche looked at Autumn confused.

"What did he say about the baby? ... You didn't tell him, did you?"

"Not yet," Blanche admitted and turned her head from Autumn seeing the menacing stare Autumn was giving her.

"I will tell him. I promise. It just wasn't the right timing. Even if I scream it at him out the window as I'm driving off, I WILL TELL HIM." Seeing Autumn's doubtful face, Blanche emphasized again, "I PROMISE!"

Autumn snickered at the thought thinking that was probably the only way Blanche would have the nerve to announce it, yelling down the street as she sped away.

"How did the dress fit?" Autumn turned and eyed the short gown on the hook on the closet door.

"Oh, Autumn, I've never had anything so beautiful." Blanche sat up in bed also admiring the gown again.

"What did you wear to your high school proms?"

"Gowns a lady my mom knows who sews for a living made up for me. My mom picked the patterns and the material. All I did was show up for the fittings."

"Who did you go with?"

"A guy from school whose mother my mom knew. He didn't have a date either so we went together."

Blanche smiled remembering the overweight guy and her sitting in the corner of a hotel ballroom watching the other couples dance. What a difference compared to the evening she had the night before with Adam.

"I'm glad you liked the outfit. My mom and I went shopping before her and Colin headed across the lake, and she picked it out for you."

"I don't know how I'll ever repay all of you for all you've done for me."

"Marry Adam so I get all A's," Autumn laughed.

Blanche did as well.

"I'll let you sleep some more. I'm going hang out in my room until you leave. Keep the keys for your next visit. That's an extra set I made up. Call me when you're coming down if you ever want company, and I'll come over."

"Okay," Blanche smiled as she laid her head back down against the pillow. She was grateful to have her extended family in her life. She didn't know how she would get through all of this without Autumn's support. She knew Autumn was right. She would have to tell Adam, and they needed to make a decision together. Even if they didn't marry, eventually she wanted her child to know his father.

Around nine, the alarm on Aubrey's nightstand went off. Blanche rose, dressed, packed her suitcase, and knocked on Autumn's door to announce she was leaving. Autumn walked out to her car with her.

"Wish me luck," Blanche begged as she buckled her seat beat.

Autumn hung on the window, "You don't need luck. The guy is crazy about you. I know you can't talk once you get home so call me on your cell here at the house after and tell me everything. I won't leave here until I hear from you!"

"Okay," Blanche blushed, then started the motor, and pulled out the drive.

Her stomach was in knots by the time she reached the French Quarter. Stopped at a light on Decatur Street, she called Adam from the cell and announced she was a few blocks away. As promised, he was at the gate and swiped his access card the minute he saw her allowing her to enter the parking lot and select a spot in the visitor's section. He ran over and was at the side of the car opening the door for her as she unbuckled her seat belt. When she got out the car, he took her hand in his hand as they walked down Decatur together towards the coffee shop. The scene reminded her of that fateful night. They selected a table by the glass windows where they could watch the tourist walking by, ordered from the menu, and ate in silence after their pastries and coffee were delivered. Adam finally broke the silence.

"Was the decaf you ordered as good as the Irish coffee?"

Blanche giggled before answering, "Decaf Colombian is all I need from now on. No more Irish coffees for me."

Adam reached across the table and took her hands into his. When he did, Blanche knew the discussion was about to change. She kept her eyes looking downward counting the breakfast muffin crumbs, scared to hear what Adam would say next.

"Blanche, this isn't easy for me, and I know it's even harder for you, but please hear me out."

She kept her eyes down but swallowed hard sensing Adam was about to bring up that night at his condo.

"You left before I could apologize for what I did that night."

Blanche pulled her hands from his, crossed her arms, and stared out the window.

"Blanche, I know you were a virgin... I'm so sorry your first time was that way... I know I can never make it up to you, but Blanche, I love you. Could you find it in your heart to forgive me and agree to have a relationship with me? I want to see you again... I need to see you again. I have missed you so much... I didn't realize how I looked forward to seeing you after the lectures until you didn't come to mine. I felt so empty, so lonely. Please consider what I've said... I know you need time to think this over so I promise that I won't call until I hear from you, but I DO need to hear from you. If your answer is no, I understand. I don't blame you for not forgiving me for what I did that night, but I'm praying you'll agree to see me again... I don't expect you to drive on the highway each weekend. I know that would be tiring. I'll gladly come to Lafayette."

Adam fell silent waiting for Blanche's response. She thought about everything he had said and blurted out the only thing that came to her mind.

"Adam, I'm pregnant... Do you still want to date me now?"

"ARE YOU SURE?" Adam's voice was strong and had a slight quiver. Could it be the woman he loved was also carrying his child? He tried to contain his excitement at the thought of a baby, of him becoming a father. He felt as if he had played a father role often when his students came to him for advice. He enjoyed guiding them, reassuring them, helping them through decision processes. And now... The thought of having a child of his own? It was difficult to contain his excitement... Blanche had still not responded. Adam touched his hand to her arm and repeated the question.

Those were the last words Blanche wanted to hear, especially a second time.

"Are you sure?" She didn't know what he would say but that response was not what she expected.
"He's hoping and praying I'm not," she thought to herself, "He's not ready to be tied down to a child. All he wanted was to continue in a

non-committed relationship having free sex." Not changing her stance, she pulled slightly away from Adam breaking his touch and spoke loud enough for only Adam to hear, "I'm sure... I saw a gynecologist yesterday morning... Autumn felt you had the right to know."

Still staring out the window as she spoke the words, Blanche didn't see the look of joy that crossed Adam's face as he said, "NO, I DON"T WANT TO DATE YOU!"

Before he could say anything else, Blanche blurted, "Since we won't be seeing each other, I'll have Autumn call you after the baby's born. She'll let you know if you have a son or daughter. If you ever want to see it, you can always contact us through her."

Blanche rose, grabbed her purse, and started to leave, but Adam rose as well and stood before her blocking her path towards the door. He grabbed the purse from her hands and tossed it back onto her chair. His index finger caught the opening between the bones under her chin and lifted her tear-filled eyes toward his as his other arm pulled her against him.

"I want to marry you," he whispered before planting a deepening kiss on her lips and molding her body against his.

Blanche couldn't believe her good fortune. Unlike the stories her mother had told her when she was growing up, she felt Adam was marrying her because he really wanted to, not because he had to. She doubted he would ever throw the issue at her that he had to marry her because she got pregnant. The rest of the day seemed like a Cinderella story. After kissing her, he dropped to his knee with the other patrons now staring at them, and asked in a loud voice, "Blanche Aubert, will you marry me?" Students who knew him came running, made a circle around them, and watched in anticipation waiting for her response. Not accustomed to the attention, Blanche had quickly answered, "Yes." After the students congratulated them, Adam paid the bill, and they walked back to his condo.

They stood by the railing on the lanai outside his den watching the traffic on the river, her head leaning on his shoulder as he hugged her tightly against him. Blanche felt more content than she had in a long time. Her spirits lightened as Adam's strength seemed to fill her. She felt less like her future was doomed. Every so often, he would turn and place a light kiss on her forehead. At one point, he placed a hand on her abdomen and whispered, "Thank you for the gift of our child." His words were soothing, and she felt more confident things would work out well for her, Adam, and their baby.

As the bells at St. Louis Cathedral signaled the five minute warning for mass to begin, Blanche pulled back from Adam's arms, "I need to head back. It's nearly a three hour drive, and I don't want to be alone on the highway once it gets too dark."

"Will you come down next weekend so we can make plans, or should I come there?"

Thinking of her mother, Blanche responded abruptly, "I'll come here. I don't want anything big, Adam. Can we have a small ceremony? After all, I am already pregnant. Did you want to invite a lot of people?"

"My parents are both dead... My family isn't very large, and everyone lives out of the state. The person that's most important to me is a first cousin on my father's side. I'd like him to be my best man. I'm hoping my mother's youngest sister will be able to come. She's the only one of my mother's relatives who keeps in touch with me... This is your day, Blanche. Plan whatever makes you happy. Just tell me when and where, and I promise I won't be a second late."

He pulled her towards him and held her tightly against him one more time before escorting her to her car in the parking lot. When they passed the security desk, Adam stopped and registered Blanche for access to the condo, introducing her to the guards as his fiancée.

"They'll have a parking card and elevator access card ready by next weekend."

After she took her seat behind the wheel, Adam closed the door then reached through the window to kiss her one more time.

"Until next weekend... I love you, Blanche."

"Until next weekend," she responded before backing out her spot.

Before taking the on-ramp to Interstate-10 west, Blanche pulled onto the side of the road and parked. She dialed the home number for Maria's house on Read to share the news with Autumn.
"Hello!"

Blanche could sense the anticipation in Autumn's voice.

"Yes, I told him."

"What did he say?"

"He had already said he loved me before I told him. When I broke the news, he asked me to marry him. I accepted, so I'm coming back next weekend so we can talk about plans."

"Are you going to tell your mom?"

"Not yet. Not until after next weekend. I'd like to tell Colin and your mom first."

Autumn understood what she was feeling. Telling Colin would be the practice session. If she could get through announcing it to him, she would then have built up enough courage to tell her mother.

"I'll let them know you're coming back. I know they'll be across the lake next weekend again so let's meet there for lunch on Saturday. It's okay if Adam comes with you. As you saw, we have plenty of room at Colin's. You're both welcome to spend the entire weekend there if you want."

"Thank you, Autumn, but we'll see you all just for lunch Saturday."

"Blanche?"

Autumn's voice had an odd tone to it.

"Do you love him or are you marrying him just because you're pregnant? Please don't do that to him... He's a nice guy. He doesn't deserve that."

Autumn's words echoed in her mind as she drove back to Lafayette. Adam had professed his love to her several times but not once had she said, "I love you," back to him. Even as she drove out the parking lot, all she had replied was, "Until next weekend." Did she love him, or was she marrying him only because of the baby? She had some soul searching to do before she returned. Autumn was right. She had to be fair to Adam as well. He did deserve more.

Chapter Twenty-Seven

When Blanche pulled into the driveway at her house, it was dark and there weren't any lights on in the house or on the porch. Though she was worried, she was also grateful her mother wasn't home when she arrived. She took her things out the car and went to her bedroom to unpack. When she finished, she went to the kitchen, poured herself a glass of lemonade, and walked out to sit on the front porch sipping the cool liquid, an activity that was always relaxing to her. Plus, the fresh air would be good for both her and the baby.

Her heart tightened in her chest when Tony pulled his car into the driveway across the street and she watched him open the left rear passenger seat for her mother to step out. Opening doors for elderly women was the only gentlemanly gesture Blanche had ever observed in Tony. Sherrie patted his arm and he leaned down and gave her a kiss on the cheek before rushing to the right passenger side and opening the door for his own mother and holding the walking cane she handed him.

As Sherrie crossed the street and walked up the steps to the porch, she announced that she had invited Tony and his mother to dinner Wednesday night. Looking across the street, Tony waved excitedly to Blanche before supporting his mother's arm as he helped her up the steps to their front door. Fearing he may cross the street to talk with her, Blanche hurried back into the house followed closely by her mother.

"I had such a lovely day today. I was sitting out on the front porch when Tony and Ethel were leaving to go to lunch. Tony crossed the street and asked if you and I would like to join them. When I told him you had gone to New Orleans for the weekend, he insisted I come along. Wasn't that sweet of him to show such concern for me?" Her mother gave Blanche a look that said it all, "Unlike you."

Blanche's face was indicating obvious worry over what had transpired among the three but Sherrie seemed oblivious to her daughter's expression and rattled on.

"Ethel and I talked just like we use to in the old days, just like we did when we were in school together. I can't wait to tell sister all the gossip

I learned today. In fact, I better call her now before she calls it a night and takes that hearing aid out."

Turning and focusing on Blanche, Sherrie continued, "I need you to help me in the kitchen when you come from school on Wednesday so don't stay late dealing with those tee-negs. I bragged about your cooking skills to Tony so he's expecting to have one of your home cooked meals. I'll make a grocery list of items you need to pick up Tuesday night. His first wife didn't know how to cook at all so, though you're dark, that's one thing he can brag about if he ever asks you out again. At least you can cook a decent meal."

Though disconcerted at the thought of having to entertain Tony and his mother, Blanche just nodded her head in agreement thankful her mother was distracted and not asking about the weekend. Knowing she had discounted Adam based on his appearance, it shouldn't have been a surprise to Blanche her mother didn't inquire about the university event. Sherrie had no interest in anything regarding Adam and the perceived Christian duty Blanche performed by attending a banquet.

When Blanche got home Wednesday night, the table in their small dining room had been set with the best dishes and linens they had, the ones her mother only took out for special occasions. When Sherrie caught her eyeing the linens and picking up one of the crystal glasses that typically stayed only in the buffet cabinet, she spoke harshly.

"Don't just stand there gawking, girl. Get yourself in the kitchen and start fixing a decent meal. I made a cake already. You need to make the chicken stew and potato salad. I found out that is Tony's favorite meal. Don't forget to put a little country sausage in the gravy and a pinch of thyme."

Blanche laid the glass down and went to her bedroom to remove the suit she had worn to school that day so she could slip on a tunic top and a pair of slacks. When she crossed through the living room where her mother was polishing the last of the silver, Sherrie cursed at her, "When you finish cooking, don't leave on those tight whore pants. Ethel wouldn't want anyone that dresses like that for her son. You'll need to change into that nice skirt I got you for Christmas so you look decent instead of like you just walked off Bourbon Street."

Blanche ignored the criticism and went into the kitchen where she began preparing the stew. After frying the chicken pieces just until they browned on each side, she dumped the chopped Vidalia onions and a diced orange bell pepper in the pan, stirred the seasonings until the scraps of chicken that had stuck to the bottom loosened, then set the fire to simmer until the onions were translucent. At that stage, she added diced garlic and simmered the seasonings another five minutes. As the scents wafted to her nose, she wished it was Adam, not Tony, for whom she was preparing the meal. While the seasonings sautéed in the pan, she chopped the fresh parsley, green onions, and celery she would use in the potato salad. Her mother had already boiled the eggs so she separated the yolks to make Creole mayonnaise for the salad. The cooking reminded her of the days at Colin's that past summer, and her nerves began to relax. By the time Tony and his mother crossed the street and rang the doorbell, the meal was complete. As her mother met the guest at the door and escorted them to the dining room, Blanche transferred the food into serving dishes and began bringing the dishes to the table.

When she brought the chicken stew out and placed it in the center of the table, Tony opened the tureen and started dishing out his plate. Blanche watched disgustedly before returning to the kitchen to bring out the other items. She thought about her father, Colin, and Adam, the three men she admired in her life. They would never have served themselves first. Colin and her father would have been helping her bring the food out, held her chair for her to be seated, and ensured the ladies served themselves before they dished out their own plate. She remembered Adam playing waiter at the Labor Day event at Colin's and how often he had catered to her at the coffee shop and other outings they had. Tony seemed uncouth in comparison as she entered with the potato salad and saw the pleased look on her mother's and Miss Ethel's face as Tony slurped the last of the meat from a chicken thigh.

"Hurry up, Blanche," her mother scolded. "Poor Tony is almost finished with his stew, and you haven't even brought the lima bean casserole out."

By the time Blanche sat down to join the trio at the table, Tony was dishing out a second helping, ignoring the fact that Blanche hadn't had her first yet. Watching his self-indulgent actions reminded Blanche of the spoiled child Tony had been, and it seemed he had not changed. He was still self-centered and came across as having that same air of entitlement he had developed as a pampered child held on a pedestal just because of his fair appearance. He had grown up thinking only of himself. Tony was the first thing in Tony's life. Anyone else got the leftovers if there were any. It was obvious tonight the Tony first attitude was the way things would always be.

When Tony finally sat back in his chair patting his stomach and letting out an unapologetic belch, Sherrie looked at Blanche irritated once again and said, feigning a polite way, "Blanche, Tony is ready for dessert."

Blanche glanced down at her half eaten plate of food getting cold and rose going back to the kitchen to get the cake. Before she could turn with the cake plate in her hands, she felt a presence behind her. Suddenly Tony's hands were on her sides, his fingers caressing the sides of her breast nearly touching her nipples and pulling her back towards him as he rubbed his penis against her backside.

"That was a great stew you cooked," he whispered into her right ear before kissing her neck.

Maybe he thought he was being sexy, but his actions and the sloppy, wet mouth on her skin made Blanche cringe. She grabbed the cake and turned forcing it between them. Trying to remain civil, she shoved the cake into him forcing him to step back a couple of steps.

"Would you please carry this for me?" she said in the sweetest voice she could muster, "I need to get the ice cream."

Having no choice, Tony turned to deliver it to the living room. Blanche quickly pulled the ice cream out the box and followed before he could return to the kitchen.

Throughout the dessert, Tony gave her lewd glances. Whenever Ethel wouldn't see her expression, Sherrie would make gestures at Blanche to smile and be more attentive to Tony. After his third slice of cake and second dish of ice cream, it appeared the bottomless pit finally had his fill. Blanche could see why his middle was already beginning to spread. She had noticed a gym bag on the floor at Adam's so knew he took advantage of the exercise equipment available for the residents of the condominium complex. Looking at the flabby arms on Tony, she doubted he ever stepped foot inside a gym.

It was close to ten before Miss Ethel and Tony finally rose to leave. As Blanche followed them to the door, Tony turned, pulled her close to him, and gave her a sloppy kiss on the cheek.

"That stew was great. I can't wait until next time."

Blanche stopped short and managed to keep the response she was thinking to herself, "Who said there will be a next time?"

Instead she smiled as her mother poked her hard in the side with her elbow and gave Miss Ethel a hug and kiss thanking her for coming. She kept the plastered smile on her face until they had turned to cross the street. As she went back into the dining room and began collecting the dishes she would have to hand wash, Sherrie bragged about how well she thought the dinner had gone and that she was sure Tony would be asking Blanche to go out with him soon. When Sherrie started making plans for the weekend that would include Ethel and Tony, Blanche blurted out a sentence before she thought of the repercussions.

"Mother, I have to go back to New Orleans this weekend." When Sherrie turned with a questioning look on her face, Blanche hurriedly added, "Autumn has a paper that's due and she needs me to review it and help her edit it."

Accepting the explanation, Sherrie's expression softened. Blanche couldn't believe how easily she had just lied to her mother. She had learned at an early age not to lie because the repercussions would be worse. Then she thought of the things she was still hiding from her and realized what she had just done was minor in comparison. Blanche listened as her mother gave instructions on how she expected her to handle the good china. She breathed a sigh of relief when Sherrie finally retired to her bedroom and quit acting as an overseer, but it was close

to midnight before Blanche had everything clean and saved back in the
china cabinet the way her mother wanted.

Chapter Twenty-Eight

Friday afternoon, Blanche's cell rang as she was walking out the school building with Melanie.

"Hello?" she greeted curiously since she didn't recognize the calling number immediately.

"Hi, my love. Are you still driving down tonight?"

Hearing Adam's voice, Blanche smiled excited at the thought of getting to see him again. Seeing her expression, Melanie mouthed the word boyfriend questioningly at Blanche. When Blanche nodded, Melanie whispered, "Have a good weekend," before turning towards her car. Once Melanie was out of ear range, Blanche spoke more openly to Adam.

"Hi," she whispered in a tone that sounded sexy even to her own ears. "I packed last night and loaded the car this morning so I'm about to get on the highway now."

"How about going to dinner here in the French Quarter and getting dessert at The Library afterwards?"

"That sounds great."

"You should be here by 6:30 so would a 7:00 reservation be ok?"

"That should be perfect."

"I'll you see then. Just call when you pull onto Decatur. I picked up your parking pass yesterday so I'll meet you, and we can test it out."

"Ok," Blanche responded and was smiling as she hung up the line. She felt giddy as she walked to her car and headed towards New Orleans instead of home. When she took the Elysian Fields exit off of the Interstate 6-10 bypass of I-10 and turned south towards the Mississippi River, she pulled out her cell and called Adam to tell him where she was. As they had discussed, he was at the gate with a new parking pass. He first reached through the car window and gave her a light kiss on the lips before swiping the pass. As the gate slowly opened, he handed the card to Blanche then followed her to a visitor's spot. He waited at the trunk of the car for her to exit. She rolled up the windows, and when she got out the driver's side, Adam called for her to pop the trunk open. Walking to the rear of the car, Blanche looked at him curiously.

"Why?"

"I'm not going to let you carry your suitcase. I'll take it."

Realizing Adam was expecting her to spend the weekend at his condo, Blanche wasn't sure how to react or to respond. She stood staring at him wondering what to do or say. Adam walked past her, opened the door on the driver's side, reached in, and pulled the handle that popped open the trunk. He grabbed the suitcase, closed the trunk, and glanced in the car for any additional items. Turning to Blanche, he questioned, "Do you need your briefcase?"

Still stunned, she managed to utter, "Yes, please."

He lifted her briefcase off the back seat, locked the car, kissed her again on the lips, and began walking towards the building entrance. Blanche reluctantly followed. When they reached the elevator, Adam pulled out the building pass that would allow access to the elevators and into his condo. He swiped the card and a green arrow lit. At the door to the condo, he swiped the card again, put in a code, and Blanche heard the click that indicated the door could be open. He pushed open the door, handed the tested card to Blanche, then stepped to the side allowing her to enter before him. She stood in the foyer waiting for Adam to enter. He dropped her brief case on the dining room table and proceeded to his master suite with her suitcase. Placing it on the bench at the foot of his bed, he glanced at his watch and turned to Blanche.

"We still have about fifteen minutes before we need to leave for dinner. May I get you anything?"

Still shocked that Adam expected them to sleep in the same bed that night, Blanche opened her mouth but no words came out. She stood, swallowing hard, trying to think of how to broach the subject. Adam eyed her for a moment and his face turned into an expression that indicated he was not satisfied with his actions. Thinking he would take her suitcase and move it to the guest bedroom instead, Blanche smiled shyly. Instead of moving her case, Adam walked to his dresser, opened the top drawer, and removed an object before returning to Blanche. He slipped the ring onto her finger and smiled satisfied with himself.

"I was forgetting to make it official."

Blanche looked down at the diamond ring that was sparkling back at her. It had two tiers above the band. The top tier highlighted a round solitaire diamond that had to be at least a carat and a half. The second tier had four emerald shaped diamonds about one fourth of a carat each, two on each side of the solitaire. Within the band were smaller diamonds set as baguettes. Based on the weight on her finger, the metal had to be platinum. Blanche could not have selected anything more beautiful.

"I know we may need to get it sized, but do you like it? If not, we could shop in the morning for something different..."

Adam was staring at her in apprehension waiting to hear if she was satisfied with the ring.

"Adam, it's gorgeous," she whispered before he took her hand and led her to the front door so they could take the short walk to the restaurant.

Adam watched Blanche nibble at her food, spending more time shifting it around on her plate than eating it. She had accepted the ring and seemed pleased with the style he had chosen, but something was obviously bothering her.

"Have you changed your mind?"

Blanche eyed Adam questioningly, "About what?"

"About marrying me..."

Confused, she searched his face for signs he was hoping she might be backing out of the proposal but saw only genuine worry instead.

"Oh... No, Adam," she eyed the ring again, "I love the ring. It's beautiful, and I'm not changing my mind." Blanche emphasized the not as she thought about the caveman behavior she had observed in Tony earlier that week.

"So, what's wrong? This summer, we discussed every topic imaginable, but tonight, you seem distant. You don't have your usual appetite. Is everything alright with the baby?"

Again, Blanche was quick to reassure him the baby was fine.

"Then, what is it, Blanche? We need to be able to talk things out when we're married."

Knowing he was right and had opened the door, Blanche alluded to the issue that was bothering her.

"Until we are married, I wasn't expecting to stay at your apartment..." Blanche swallowed hard and took a deep breath exhaling slowly before continuing, "I thought I would be staying at the house in New Orleans east until we were married."

Adam observed her behavior the entire time she spoke. Her eyes stayed focused on the food left on her plate as she pushed it from one side to the other as she had all evening. "So, that's what's bothering her," he thought. He had an inexperienced, shy lady on the other side of the table. Because of the baby, alcohol couldn't be used to calm her nerves. She was feeling spending the night with him was totally inappropriate and was dreading what he expected of her. Considering she was already pregnant, she was also feeling foolish about stating her objections to his presumption she'd be okay with the arrangement.

Adam took the fork out of her hand and laid it on the side of the plate. Taking both of her hands in his, he gently pulled them towards his mouth and planted a soft kiss on the top of her fingers. Capturing her eyes, he spoke in the kindest tone he could muster.

"Blanche, this weekend is whatever you want it to be. If you don't want to have sex, that's fine. I just want you near me…. I need your presence. I need us to be close…. I just want to circle my arms around you, enjoy the warmth of your body next to mine, and feel I'm protecting you and our baby…. I need you with me."

Adam kissed her hands again before releasing them and continuing, "If you're not comfortable with that, it's okay too… But, I'm hoping you stay. I just want to hold you."
Blanche thought about the afternoon she spent in his arms watching the ships traverse the Mighty Mississippi. It was so comforting, and after dealing with Tony, his mother, and her own this past week, it was a feeling she longed for and needed.

"I'd like that," she finally looked in Adam's eyes as she spoke, smiled, then turned to her plate and devoured the last of her meal.

"An old-fashioned girl… My mom would approve," Adam thought and pondered on the fact Blanche was a rarity, one that would be difficult to find again.

As they exited the restaurant, he placed his hand on her waist and pulled her close to him. They walked slowly, not hurrying towards The Library. After enjoying two blood orange custard cups, they repeated the leisurely walk taking the Moonwalk along the river back to Adam's condo. Once there, Adam gave her a detailed tour of the condo showing her where everything was stored in the kitchen, the master bathroom, and the closets, making it clear he expected her to feel as though his place was now hers as well.

"Tired?"

"It was a long day at school, and after the drive, I am feeling exhausted. It seems I get wiped out faster these days."

Knowing she needed him to be discrete, Adam responded, "I have to post this week's grades, so I'll be working on the computer in the office. Just call when you're ready for bed."

Giving her a soft kiss on the cheek, he turned and went into the office allowing her the freedom to prepare for bed without his eyes watching. Grateful for his tactfulness, Blanche scurried to the master suite, opened her suitcase, removed her nightgown and toiletries, and walked quickly into the master bath taking a moment to lock the door behind her. After a quick shower, she dressed, took the matching robe out the suitcase, and walked to the office to tell Adam she was retiring for the night.

When he only gave her a quick glance and stated he'd join her shortly, Blanche rushed back to the master bedroom. Seeing his watch on the nightstand on the right side of the bed, she took off her robe, laid it on top of her suitcase, climbed into the king sized bed on the left side, pulled the covers up, and pretended to be asleep.

When the mattress finally shifted under Adam's weight as he climbed into bed, her body stiffened. Still pretending to sleep, she tried not to react when he kissed her softly on the cheek but knew the short breath she exhaled indicated to him she was not sleeping. As he promised at the restaurant, he laid his arm across her middle, and molded his body around hers. She could tell when he finally had fallen asleep. His breathing was even and shallow, and his arm was limp. At that point, Blanche relaxed against his body and also fell into a deep sleep.

The smell of croissants baking, bacon frying, and coffee percolating woke Blanche. Sensing she was alone in the bed, she stretched her arms above her head and yawned. At that moment, the door to the bedroom opened, and Adam entered carrying a breakfast tray. He placed it on the bed between them, sat back against the headboard, and turned the television channel to a Saturday morning news program. Leaning across to Blanche, he gave her a quick kiss on the cheek.

"Good morning. I made breakfast. I think I piled enough on the tray for both of us, but there's more in the kitchen if you're still hungry."

He sat back upright, took one of the napkins from the tray and covered his lap before stuffing a croissant with bacon and scrambled eggs. He leaned the sandwich over to Blanche's mouth and she took a bite.

"Excellent," she turned and smiled at him. Sitting upright in the bed, she made herself a breakfast sandwich. They ate together in silence, watching breaking world news stories. When they had finished eating, Adam took the tray and laid it on the floor on his side of the bed before pulling Blanche into his arms. Hugging her tightly against him, he planted a kiss on her forehead.

"So, what's the plan for today? I picked up brochures that describe the venues and menu offerings of places I've heard are nice for weddings. Did you want to get married here in New Orleans, in Lafayette, or fly to somewhere exotic? What have you decided? "

Blanche was embarrassed to admit she hadn't given it any thought. The first hurdle in her mind was telling her family.

"Actually, we're expected for lunch at Colin's today. I need to break the news to them. Right now, Autumn is the only person in my family that knows."

Feeling her body stiffen slightly and having observed the interaction between her and Colin at the Labor Day picnic, Adam offered, "Why don't I talk to Colin, and you and Autumn can break the news to Maria?"

When her body eased, he knew his suspicions were on target. Blanche was apprehensive about admitting to her family she was having what they called a shotgun wedding. When she leaned her head against him and crossed her arms over his, he gave her another tight squeeze and kiss. No other words had to be spoken between them. She needed his support, and now she also knew she could count on it.

As they pulled into the drive at the house across the lake, Autumn opened the front door and walked out to greet them.

"Hi, Doctor A.J. and congratulations," she smiled at her former professor and current advisor before giving Blanche a bear hug.

When they separated, Blanche lifted her left hand to show Autumn the ring. In response, Autumn nodded in approval.

"My mom's in the kitchen tossing a salad, and Colin's out on the patio grilling steaks."

Blanche looked towards Adam who took the lead, "Why don't you two go to the kitchen and do your lady things?" He held out his arms, made two fists, and flexed his muscles before continuing, "I'm going out to the grill and offer to help with the men's work."

So grateful he was assuming the tough job of telling Colin, Blanche reached over and gave Adam a kiss on the cheek before following Autumn to the kitchen. As they disappeared and he soon heard a squeal from Maria, Adam smiled and touched his finger to the spot where Blanche had kissed him. "Progress," he spoke aloud before taking a deep breath and going out to speak with Colin on the patio.

"Hey, man! Good to see you again," Colin greeted Adam enthusiastically before pulling a beer from the patio refrigerator and handing it to him.

"Thank you. And, thanks for having me over, but this isn't just a casual lunch. I need to talk with you, and I'm letting you know upfront that you probably are not going to like what I'm here to say."

Colin became stone faced as he glanced towards Autumn through the bay window of the kitchen before giving Adam a look that clearly said, "If you touched my stepdaughter, you signed your own death warrant."

"This isn't about Autumn!" Adam lifted his empty hand quickly, his palm facing Colin indicating he should calm down and hear him out. Colin's expression softened slightly, then turned to one of curiosity as Adam said, "It's about Blanche."

Colin set a dial on the grill and motioned to two seats on the far side of the patio. A few minutes later, Blanche's face peered through the bay window eyeing the two men in a deep discussion. She turned to Autumn and nodded indicating the three inside needed to sit down so she could break the other news to Maria. Autumn took the lead inside telling her mom to join them at the breakfast table in the alcove. As soon as Blanche sat at the table, she blurted out, "Maria, I'm pregnant."

She waited to hear the lecture she knew would follow, especially the part about being a disappointment instead of a role model to Autumn.

Instead, Maria simply stated, "Then, we're not going for a Catholic ceremony. We need to plan this wedding faster than I thought and the two of you can get your marriage blessed in the church afterwards." She stood, walked over to the stand beneath the telephone, pulled out a telephone directory, a pen, and a writing pad, and rejoined the two at the table. "So, what would you like?" Seeing the blank stare on Blanche's face, Maria turned to Autumn, "Go get those old bridal magazines out the study. I think Blanche needs to glance through those before we make any plans."

While Autumn ran off to pull the magazines and a wedding guide from the stacks on the library type shelves in the room that was used as a study and home office, Maria started questioning Blanche on her favorite color, flowers, food, guest lists, venue, etc... Blanche sat in silence, nodding to some of the questions, her head spinning as she tried to think of a response and still not understanding how easily Maria had accepted the news and moved on.

"My mother's favorite color is blue," she finally got the nerve to speak instead of simply nodding her head when she heard something she liked.

Not wanting to sound ugly and to point out the fact that this was Blanche's wedding and not her mother's, Maria said instead, "Blue isn't exactly a fall color. We might be able to make that work, but what is your favorite color, Blanche?"

"I always liked orange," Blanche said enthusiastically.

"Orange?" Maria nodded in acknowledgement and tried to sound positive, "That is a fall color!"

When Autumn returned, she separated the stack she had pulled into three piles between them.

"Autumn, would you be my maid of honor?"

Autumn walked over to Blanche and gave her a hug before answering, "I'd be honored."

"Blanche's favorite color is orange," Maria announced.

Glad her face was behind Blanche's, Autumn stood and mouthed, "ORANGE!," to her mother thinking of her reddish hair contrasting with an orange gown. She continued to mouth, "I'll look like a clown." She stuck her finger in her mouth and pretended to gag before forcing a smile on her face and taking her seat back at the table.

Autumn and Maria began browsing through magazines pointing out various things to Blanche, waiting for her nod of approval, and jotting down notes. Finally adjusting to the idea there would be no negative repercussions from Maria, Blanche began looking through her stack as well and was heavily into the plans for her wedding when a deep voice boomed behind her.

"Blanche, please join me in the study."

Turning, she saw Colin walking from the kitchen. Her breathing started in short gasps and her eyes welled. Maria patted her hand and whispered, "Everything is going to be fine." She squeezed her hand tightly before releasing it. Blanche smiled at her grateful for the assurance. Looking at Autumn, Autumn shrugged her shoulders and sighed before admitting, "I survived the lecture in his study after wrecking his Mercedes." She grinned and Blanche's breathing returned to normal. She managed a smile, chuckling at the expression on Autumn's face. She stood, and before turning to join Colin in the study, she told them, "Wish me the same luck."

As she walked across the den to the study, she spotted Adam on one of the patio chairs sipping a beer, his back towards her. By the time she reached the study, Colin was sitting in the chair behind the desk, staring at the book shelves, his arms crossed, his expression obviously in deep thought. As she sat in the chair opposite him, he turned to face her, and the first words he spoke were not the words she expected to hear.

"Will you be happy?"

Blanche felt the same way she had when Autumn asked her on the phone call if she loved Adam. She started soul searching again. She wasn't accustomed to choices in her life. She had always followed the dictates of her mother. Being faced with having to make decisions was too new to her. Having to tell Maria something as simple as the colors she wanted for the wedding, rather than have her mother immediately meddle in and state what Blanche liked and wanted, was a major step. Sitting here in the study with Colin pondering her future and feeling she could take these types of life changing steps was mind boggling.

Colin broke the silence.

"Blanche, I know your mother raised you with very strict discipline. I know things haven't been easy for you, especially after your father passed. But, this is a major step! When you marry someone, it should be for life…" Colin hung his head before continuing, and he stammered over his next words. "I know what you're thinking. Who am I to lecture on marriage?" He paused and took several deep breaths before continuing. Blanche's heart went out to him sorry her situation was causing him to remember the painful circumstances that ended his first marriage. He coughed before continuing. "Let's just say I'm speaking from experience… I want it to be right for you." Colin started choking on his words again. He stood, went over to a stand, and poured bourbon out of the decanter into one of the gold trimmed glasses. He took a couple of sips and more deep breaths and stood looking out the window before continuing.

"Adam told me you're pregnant. He also made it clear it was a situation where he took advantage of you. He wants to make things right. Based on information he's shared, I don't doubt he loves you and that he is positioned financially to take care of you and the baby. But this isn't our grandparents' or even our parents' generation anymore, Blanche. Don't feel you have to marry him because you're pregnant. He's the type of man that will stand by you if you marry him or not. … Blanche, I haven't been around much since I left for college, and I apologize to you for that. But I do know my aunt well so I know your life is going to be hell back at home. The key is you don't have to stay there."

Colin finally turned from the window and faced her.

"You're welcome to move in here." He waved his hand to the two bedrooms where Sherrie and his mother had stayed. "I will have those two rooms renovated for you anyway you want so you have your own space and a nursery for the baby. We can add on if you like and need more space. You don't have to suffer through your mother's bull anymore. You're an adult, and you're not alone. We'll help you through this."

He walked over and knelt before her. Taking her hands into his, he looked into her eyes and held her gaze, "He's a good man, Blanche. Your father would have approved. I approve, but will you be happy? I don't want you to feel forced into a situation because of what happened one night. You don't have to marry him unless you really want to."

Colin stood, walked back to the window, and swallowed the rest of the bourbon in one gulp. He rubbed his right hand through his hair and stayed looking out the window as he continued.

"I know you spent a lot of time together this summer, but damn, you've known the guy for less than four months! I feel responsible... dragging you here for the summer, dumping the responsibility of chaperoning my stepdaughter on you in a strange city, an environment you're not familiar with..."

Colin's voice began to choke, and he couldn't continue. Blanche sat disturbed by the fact Colin was blaming himself for her predicament. A memory flooded back to her at that moment, the memory of her sitting on the window bench in the waiting room outside of Adam's office and capturing a glimpse of him walking across the quadrangle. She remembered her feelings that first time and all the times that summer she had looked forward to their conversations and seeing him. Her mind finally cleared of all the negatives, and her eyes filled with tears at the realization. She could now answer both Autumn's and Colin's questions. She stood and walked the short distance to Colin. Standing beside him, she put her arm around his waist and looked into his eyes.

"Cole, none of this is your fault. I thank you for changing my life. Autumn told me one time I dressed like a nun. It wasn't just my dress. I was living the life of a nun. I was just as secluded as if I was in a convent. I fell in love with Adam the first time I saw him." She spoke the words in a strong, unwavering voice now knowing they were true and from her heart. "Every time I saw him, I just fell in love with him more. He is a good man. I know we've know each other for just a short time but we have so much in common, and we're both so excited about this baby." She thought about the first time she knew and the joy she soon felt at knowing a life was growing inside of her. She thought about that Sunday standing with Adam watching the ships on the river and hearing him say, "Thank you for the gift of our child." She thought about gross Tony in comparison, and the image made her treasure the man Adam was more. How ironic that Adam was the first man in the bible and the first man in her life as well. She smiled at the thought. "I do want to marry him, Cole. I know he will make me happy. I wouldn't change anything from this past summer. I love him!"

Satisfied, Colin turned, hugged her, and kissed her on the forehead. They stood in silence hugging until Maria barged into the study, a furious look on her face.

"I'm not lecturing her!" Colin stated immediately in his defense trying to calm the angry look his wife was shooting his way.

Blanche smiled seeing Autumn at Maria's heels with the same threatening expression.

"Why don't we all go get poor Adam stuck on the patio and just have lunch?" Colin stated as he glanced among the three women looking determinedly at him in his study. The three glanced at each other before responding in almost perfect unison, "We agree." Shaking his head, Colin poured another shot of bourbon for himself and a second for Adam stating, "The poor guy doesn't know what he's getting into."

That night at Adam's was a repeat of the night before except for one thing. When he came to bed that evening, instead of pretending to be asleep, Blanche turned towards him and kissed him hesitantly on the lips. After all, she was already pregnant.

Chapter Twenty-Nine

As Blanche pulled into the driveway at home, Tony crossed the street smiling, leaned against the window, and announced his mother had invited them to dinner again that Wednesday.

"What are you cooking for me this time?"

He reached inside of the car and placed his left hand on her left thigh and massaged her inner thigh with his fingers staring at her with his lewd expression again. When his hand continued the massage but began drifting slowly upward, Blanche roughly pulled his hand up off her thigh and pushed it back out the window. She shoved her left hand upward to his face and yelled, "I'm engaged to be married, Tony, so me and my fiancé would appreciate it if you keep your hands off me. And if my mother invited you to dinner, then ask her what she's cooking."

Blanche stepped out the car, slammed the door shut, and walked toward the front door. She could get her suitcase later. Her mother was in the dining room digging through the drawers of the china cabinet selecting linens. Blanche assumed this was preparation for the Wednesday event. When the phone rang, Blanche knew who was on the other line. She ran to answer it before her mother stood.

"Hello..."

Just as she guessed, it was Miss Ethel, Tony's mother.

"My mother is busy right now. May she call you back?"

"Who is it, Blanche?" Her mother stood and stared towards the phone.

Ignoring the question, Blanche listened to the words being spoken on the other line turning slightly away from her mother so Miss Ethel wouldn't hear her mother's words. Finally answering, "Thank you," to the congratulations from her neighbor, Blanche hung up the receiver.

"I asked, 'Who is it, Blanche?'" Her mother's voice was a notch higher as she spoke the words angrily to Blanche because she hadn't answered her the first time.

"It was only Miss Ethel. She said she'll call back."

"Nonsense, stupid girl! I'll call her now."

Blanche retired to her room, her stomach turning and nauseated knowing what was coming next. It wasn't planned to happen this way. Adam was going to drive down and spend the day in Lafayette next Saturday. They were going to bring her mother out to lunch and tell her at the restaurant together. Blanche was going to hide the engagement ring until then. Because she lost her patience due to Tony's obscene behavior, everything was coming to a head. She knew she'd have to face her mother alone.

When her mother burst through the bedroom door without knocking, Blanche almost vomited on the spot. She stuck a mint in her mouth trying to control the sudden onset of nausea.

Sherrie walked over to her, grabbed her hand, and stared at the ring on her finger.

"What nonsense is this I'm hearing from Ethel? I told her this is all a lie! You're not even dating anyone. How can you be engaged? Where did you get this ring? Did you borrow it from Maria to play games with Tony? Are you trying to fool the poor boy? If so, that's the second time you did something stupid to blow your chances. What's wrong with you, foolish girl, that you're not acting like you should toward that boy? Answer me!" Sherrie demanded slamming Blanche's hand down hard toward the bed.

Blanche tried to remain calm and remember the words Colin had spoken to her, "You don't have to suffer through your mother's bull anymore. You're an adult." It sounded good with Colin there protecting her, but somehow she didn't feel as confident with her mother standing over her as she sat on the bed. Images of her holding the belt and striking her as a child returned, especially that last beating when her father had come in. She cowered away from her, and her voice was meek as she answered.

"But I am dating, mother. Remember, you selected the man for me."

"What are you talking about, you simpleton?"

"Adam... Remember, Labor Day weekend? You volunteered me to go to the banquet with him. You told me it was my Christian duty to date the man."

Sherrie looked at Blanche in amusement and started laughing hysterically.

"Are you telling me you went out one time with that little monkey man, and he gave you an engagement ring? The only way that would happen is if you were pregnant."

Sherrie continued laughing but seeing Blanche turn her head in embarrassment, she reached and grabbed her chin and yanked her face upward towards her.

"You had sex with that man? Are you pregnant? When was your last period?"

Blanche's eyes closed under her mother's stare so she didn't see it coming as she released her chin, swung her hand back, and slapped her as hard as she could across her face. The force sent Blanche falling against the pillow. Sherrie slapped her face again and again until Blanche managed to cover her face with her hands. Even then, she continued beating her about her head as hard as she could and yelling at her the entire time, "You stupid, ignorant, little country bitch. The first time a man tells you that you're pretty, you open your legs. How dumb can you be? Didn't I raise you to wait until you're married? You go open your legs for a short, black monkey like that just because he says he admired you. You stupid, stupid, stupid girl!" Her mother hit her harder with each word. "You think Tony will want the likes of you now? You're not even a virgin, and that's all you had to offer him besides being able to cook."

Finally exhausted, the blows stopped. Blanche stayed cowered on the bed, her hands protecting her face until she heard her mother retreat down the hallway. She heard her dialing the phone and talking to Ethel. Her mother spoke convincingly explaining it was just someone Blanche had done a favor for, and that he was so enamored, he gave her the ring as a gift. Blanche cringed as she heard her state, "It's not anything serious." When she finished the conversation, she stormed back into Blanche's room.

"I'll make arrangements tomorrow for you to get rid of that thing." She pointed to Blanche's stomach as she spoke the words. "You will date Tony, and let's pray the first time you lay with him, he won't be able to tell. There's ways to tighten you up again."

Blanche put her arms protectively around her abdomen. Shaking her head and tears rolling down her face, she stated, "I'm not killing my baby. I want it, and I want to marry Adam."

Her mother came in and slapped her hard across the face again, "You'll do what I say or else? Where do you think you'll be without me? You're not having a bastard, especially a black one."

Keeping her face lowered, Blanche spoke softly, "The baby won't be a bastard. Maria and Autumn are already making plans for our wedding. We're getting married in New Orleans as soon as the arrangements can be finalized."

Sherrie slapped Blanche hard again across the face again and stormed out her bedroom. Blanche knew it wasn't over, but she couldn't envision what her mother would do next.

Chapter Thirty

The next day, Blanche dressed for school as usual. When she went to button the skirt of the suit she had selected, she noticed the skirt was not as loose around her waist as it had been. She probably had gained about five pounds these first two months. She knew she would have to tell the principal at the school. Thinking of walking out to face her mother and to have the conversation at work increased the nausea she was feeling. She ran to the bathroom just in time. Afterwards, she rinsed her mouth with the minty mouthwash and placed a cool towel on her face. She hoped the morning sickness would end soon but feared it was something more than that. One of the summer lectures had covered issues that could have impacted a child's development. Blanche knew that stress during pregnancy produced hormones in the mother's body that could affect the baby's brain development.

"I'm sorry, little one," she whispered as she looked down at her abdomen, "You don't have the greatest mommy, but I'm trying to do better."

As she walked past her mother drinking coffee at the dining room, her mother screamed at her,

"WHORE! You wanted to pull your drawers down, and now you're going to have a drawers full!"

She didn't respond as she walked out the door, got into her car, and drove towards school. She immediately went to the principal's office and made an appointment to see him with the secretary for when the school day ended. Then she went to her own office but couldn't concentrate on reviewing the high school scholarship applications the eighth grade students had submitted. Her mind was only on the altercation with her mother the night before, wondering what her mother was going to do next, and fearing having to tell the principal that afternoon of her predicament. She was still on the same form when Melanie popped her head into the office.

"Free for lunch today? How about the soup and salad buffet?"

Blanche looked up and started to say she wasn't free, but remembering the life inside of her and that she had skipped breakfast wanting to get away from her mother as quickly as possible, she knew she had to get something nutritious inside of her for the baby's sake."

"That sounds good, Melanie. I just need to grab my purse."

As Blanche leaned to the right to pull her purse out the bottom desk drawer, she balanced with her left hand against the desk.

"Wow! That diamond is a beauty!" Melanie stepped forward, pulled Blanche's hand upward so she could examine the ring closer. "So you got engaged? I knew you had a boyfriend but didn't realize it was that serious."

Blanche and Melanie hadn't discussed a lot of personal issues. Their conversations focused on topics related to the school so she felt she could fudge the truth just a little.

"It's a professor I met in New Orleans one summer. I've been seeing him for a while. He gave me the ring this weekend."

She didn't want to lie to Melanie, but in her mind, "Last summer was one summer and 'a while' was a relative term."

"Let me know the date. I will throw you the best bridal shower this school has ever seen. I know all the teachers will want to come and wish you well."

"I rather not," Blanche answered as she dropped her purse on the desk and stood to leave.

Surprised, Melanie gave her a curious stare. Knowing it would come out sooner than later, Blanche decided to share the news.

"Melanie, I'm pregnant. I'm meeting with the principal to tell him this afternoon. The baby is due the end of April."

Blanche watched Melanie's face for her reaction the entire time. The confused look remained, and Melanie looked at Blanche and replied, "So, that means I'm going to plan two showers... A bridal and a baby!"

She smiled, walked over, threw her arms around Blanche, gave her a hug, and said, "Double congratulations."

Blanche's eyes filled with tears. She knew at that moment that she had found a true friend. "Just the one shower... for the baby! ... I do appreciate that, Melanie. If only you knew how much your friendship means to me right now." Blanche thought, "You're the only bright light to keep my sanity when I'm home."

Melanie patted her on the arm and whispered, "I'm hungry. Let's go. If you're not hungry, I know that baby is. Grab your purse. I have a class right after the lunch hour so we need to get moving. ... Do you have a doctor yet? If not, we can talk about it over lunch. The lady my sister goes to is great. She delivered both of her kids. I think you'd be very pleased with her. She is on our insurance so you don't have to be concerned with that. Her office isn't far from here so you could make appointments for right after school. After we order, I'll call my sister from my cell and get the contact info because all I know is she calls her Doctor Sarah."

"Okay," Blanche smiled relieved her friend had taken the news so well. It gave her courage to face the principal later that day.

At the end of the school day, Blanche reluctantly walked to the principal's office and waited outside by the school's secretary until she was given permission to enter. When she did, she felt a wave of nausea coming over her. Knowing it was due to stress, she popped a mint into her mouth and took a couple of deep breaths trying to calm her nerves. As she entered, the principal greeted her enthusiastically.

"Blanche, I'm so proud of the job you're doing this year as our counselor. I just got off the phone with Sharon's mother. She is so happy that you told her to bring Sharon for that simple blood test. She is being treated for the anemia, and her mother can see the difference in her energy level and her grades. She had nothing but praise for you. I've already drawn up your contract for next year, and I have no doubts it will be approved."

Blanche turned her head to the side, embarrassed to receive praise based on the reason for her visit. Seeing her reaction, the principal grew apprehensive.

"Do you not want to renew your contract as counselor?"

Blanche looked at the gentleman and stated, "I do love my position and all I've been able to do to help the students and the teachers, but I won't be able to renew next year." She showed the principal the ring before continuing, "I'm getting married, and I'll be moving to New Orleans this summer."

The statement shocked Blanche. She and Adam had discussed if he would seek a position at the university in Lafayette so Blanche could continue her contract. She knew Adam sensed she was apprehensive about leaving home and was also feeling she was abandoning her mother. They had discussed Blanche giving up her career temporarily and becoming a stay at home mother until the baby was older. That was one of several scenarios they had tossed around on Sunday before she headed back home, but Blanche had not made a final decision yet, at least not consciously. Her mother's reaction had shown Blanche she would always have the upper hand in their relationship, and Blanche couldn't and wouldn't allow her child to grow up in the same negative environment she had experienced.

"Congratulations! Under those circumstances, I don't mind loosing you on our staff. I'll post a vacancy in the local newspapers in this area. I'd like you to help me interview the candidates so we can select someone who will continue with the work you have started."

Blanche turned her head once again.

"Blanche, are you not comfortable assisting with the interviews?"

Looking up at the principal again, she fought to find the right words to share her situation, "I'm not sure if you want to wait until next year to replace me. You may want to replace me now. I don't feel I'm an acceptable role model for the students."

"Blanche, the students love you. I can't think of a better role model."

Not knowing how else to state it, she blurted out the other reason for her visit, "I'm pregnant," and then watched for the principal's reaction.

The elderly gentleman leaned forward, placed his elbows on the desk, and crossed his hands together, eyeing Blanche for several minutes before he spoke. She grew more and more uncomfortable under his stare.

"Tell me, Blanche. How did you feel when you first discovered you were pregnant?"

Blanche recalled that moment and tears flooded her eyes, "Scared... Alone... Worried what was to become of me and the baby... Unsure if I should tell the father or not and wondering what his reaction to the news would be. And worst of all was how to go home and tell my mother and see the disappointment on her face. I couldn't sleep well and couldn't' focus not knowing what was going to happen."

"And, how did you feel when you did tell the father?"

"He's a good man! When I realized how much he truly loved me and that he wanted to marry me and support me through all of this, it was such a relief." Blanche gasped the last words out.

"And did you ever consider an abortion?"

Shocked by the question, Blanche stared at the principal before admitting.

"I did, but because of my Catholic upbringing, I could never destroy this life growing inside of me."

The principal unlocked his hands, sat back in the chair, and stated, "Blanche, I can't think of a more appropriate role model for our students to have."

"I got pregnant outside of marriage!" Blanche raised her voice in confusion over the statement.

"So did our Blessed Mother..."

Blanche frowned not feeling the birth of the infant Jesus compared to her situation but realized she had never thought of things in that light before.

"Blanche, you have the unique ability to now speak from experience. You're lucky to have a college degree and to be financially independent. Even if you hadn't been fortunate enough to have a good man to stand beside you, you could have your baby and support the two of you. What about these young thirteen year olds who would be ruining their future if they got pregnant now? Their hormones are raging, and they're not thinking of any consequences... only that they're in love for the first time in their lives. You can reach them... You can describe to them your feelings of fear even for someone in your position. And you can also tell them you chose to do the right thing and not abort the baby regardless of what the father chose to do. People listen more to those who have been there than to those who preach about it but haven't walked in the same shoes. Don't you agree?"

Blanche nodded her head reluctantly as she fought to understand the perspective the principal was making.

"When is your baby due?"

"April 24 is the date the gynecologist gave me."

"Then, I'll try to get your replacement on staff by the beginning of April so you have time to transition the files and plans before the baby comes. I think we can afford to have you both on payroll for the two months."

Blanche smiled and nodded her thanks to the principal.

"Is there anything else you wanted to discuss?"

"No, that's all for now. Thank you for being so understanding."

"We're all human, Blanche. We all make mistakes from time to time, but I have never considered a baby a mistake. I'm happy for you that everything is working out well. If there is anything you need, don't hesitate to ask."

"Thank you, again."

Blanche rose and shook the principal's hand before exiting his office. She walked back to her own office feeling a sense of relief that she had this behind her and the discussion had gone so well. As she gathered her belongings, Melanie knocked softly on the door.

"How did it go?"

"Far better than I ever imagined it would. I remember when the days going to the principal's office meant smacks on your knuckles with a ruler. Things have definitely changed."

"Thank God for that," Melanie stated in an exaggerated tone.

They both laughed as Blanche flicked off the lights in her office. They walked towards their cars discussing Blanche's phone conversation with the receptionist at Doctor Sarah's. As she approached her Malibu, she knew her day had gone far too well. Eyeing the flat, she dropped her purse from her shoulder and pulled out her cell to call for the car service.

"I'll wait with you," Melanie offered.

After hanging up, Blanche announced, "They're willing to come out, but it'll be over an hour before they get here and another hour before they can return with the repaired tire."

"Why don't I just drop you off home and pick you up in the morning instead of you sitting around here for that long."

"You don't mind, Melanie?"

"Of course not! I believe you're on my way anyway. Call them and let them know, and then you can get home and rest. However, if you're on the highway to New Orleans on weekends, I think you should tell them to just put on a new tire. I've not had a lot of success with repairs, and it's not worth getting stuck on the Atchafalaya."

"You're right."

Blanche made the quick call giving the service the new instructions before following Melanie to her car. She started stepping her through the directions to her house. When Melanie pulled up, Blanche noticed the car of one of her mother's pokeno partners parked in front of the house. After thanking Melanie for the ride, she walked along the side of the house to enter through the back door hoping not to disturb their pokeno game. As she passed the dining room window and heard the sounds of voices speaking with animation inside, Blanche grew quiet. Something told her to stop and listen to the conversation. She could make out her mother's voice, her aunt's, and the two friends they invited over for pokeno.

Chapter Thirty-One

Barbara's voice was argumentative as she spoke, "You know why I didn't have another baby. It was a struggle for me to finally get pregnant for Colin. That endometriosis ruined by uterus, but I don't know why you didn't have more. You had a good man, Sherrie. That man wanted children and he deserved for you to treat him better."

"Sister, you knew who I really loved."

"Yes, we all know you were crazy about Sonny." The ladies at the table nodded in agreement, their faces breaking into wide smiles as they recalled their younger days and the boys they use to date. "But when that boy came back from the service having lost a leg, you dropped him like he was a hot potato. I never understood that, Sherrie. If you love someone, it shouldn't stop just because he lost his leg. Unless you knew, you couldn't even tell. He was walking just fine with that artificial one they gave him in the service. And, my, my, my! That boy had the bluest eyes I'd ever seen in a Creole. He was good looking. If I hadn't already married Colin's father, I would have grabbed him myself even though he had one leg."

"There was no way I was going to start out in life with a burden."

"But he had a pension from the service, and he still could work."

"After waiting for him all those years and for him to come back half a man was too disappointing. That's how I got stuck marrying that black fool. All the good ones were gone by then, and with Daddy sick, our family needed the money."

"I don't know why you talked about that man like that and why you kept visiting old Miss Celine. That was wrong, Sherrie. It was just wrong. And you were together over ten years before you had Blanche."

"I only finally kept that one because Mother said I had to have one child for him if I was going to hold onto him and to keep the money flowing. She said to stick it out at least until Daddy's farm was paid off, and they had some money in the bank. Then she got sick and I needed the fool to pay her medical bills so I had to stay with him longer."

"At the end before he died, things were different between you two. What made the man go down so fast?"

"That stupid Blanche!"

"What did she have to do it with it?"

"That simple girl never did catch on to anything. You had to explain everything to her. She came home one day and told him I was seeing old Miss Celine. That's when all hell broke loose. Before Blanche opened her mouth, the fool was talking about paying for me to go to a specialist in Houston to see why we didn't have more babies. He hadn't suspected anything until then."

"Remember Miss Ida?" one of the ladies spoke up. "She was cheaper, but her concoctions didn't always work. I know a lady that went to her three times, and her period still didn't come down. Her baby was born deaf. All she did was mess the child up."

"That's why I stuck with Miss Celine. She was higher than any of the other ones around, but she knew what she was doing. If old Miss Celine was still alive, that lil' black bastard Blanche is carrying now would be flushed down the toilet by this weekend. If you brewed the tea she gave you like she said, sometimes your period would come down overnight. If I was late one day, I'd go and get my tea."

"Sherrie, don't talk like that. That man Blanche is marrying is gorgeous. Ladies, just wait until you see him.... If he was from here, I'd swear he was a mulatto. Sherrie is always calling the man black just because his skin is a little darker than Blanche's, but the only time you see a skin tone like that is the first time the races mix. And he has light brown eyes. It's something about the man that just glows. He has fine features, a perfect set of lips, not too big and not too thin, and a gorgeous head of hair like Omar Sharif. And, as pretty as Blanche is, that baby is going to be beautiful... I can't wait to hold that little rascal in my arms."

"Sister, Mother used to say it's like we weren't raised in the same house. I can't believe you're saying that monkey man she got pregnant for looks good. And you're making over that man's skin tone? It's the same as an orangutan's."

"Sherrie, you need to give up on all those old time ideas. All you see is the man's skin tone and it's not fair enough for your taste. People don't be lookin' at color like they used to. You're still in the dark ages. If I was younger, I'd sure open my legs to him."

"I was surprised mother let you marry Colin's father. He was too dark for my taste. That showed you weren't picky about who you were willing to open your legs too."

"Look how beautiful my baby is. Colin came out looking like he was Spanish. He has the perfect tan to his skin and that black, wavy hair of his is just beautiful. I loved combing his hair when he was little..."

"Sister, don't be so stupid. Colin is over six feet in height. You ever saw a tall Mexican? How could you say Colin looks Spanish?"

Ignoring the slight, Barbara whimpered, "I wish I could have had more babies."

"You might not have been that lucky with all of them... Well, I was lucky with Blanche. She wasn't as dark as her father, and she did have a cute face, but I wasn't taking a chance on having another one. Mother said to have at least one so I did my duty. I wasn't going to keep popping out jungle bunnies for that black fool.... And, if this stupid girl goes through with this marriage, her name will be Blanche Brown."

"Sherrie, what's wrong with that?"

"What's wrong with it? Her name will be two colors. It'll mean white brown. It doesn't even make sense. Whoever heard of a color white brown? That's too much."

"Sherrie, you're the only person that would think of something like that. Stop all this stupid talk, and let's just play the game."

Blanche stepped back as silently as she could towards the street and stayed hidden at the corner of the house. She repeated the words her mother had spoken, "She came home one day and told him I was seeing old Miss Celine. That's when all hell broke loose. ..."

Blanche gasped when the memory returned. It was when she was thirteen and the last time her mother had beaten her unmercifully. Blanche's father had come into the room and stopped her mother by grabbing her arm. She remembered everything now, and with her new knowledge, she finally understood.

Chapter Thirty-Two

In eighth grade, Blanche's class had taken the traditional day trip on a hired bus to Baton Rouge. As part of their Louisiana history class, the eighth graders always went to Baton Rouge to visit the capitol and to observe the state legislature in action. Blanche had volunteered to assist the teacher by collecting all the permission slips for the field trip. By the time she boarded the bus, the only seat left was next to Margaret, the girl the entire class was required to shun as ordered by their parents. The rumor going around the church parish was that after Margaret's father died, her mother started seeing a married man who paid the bills for her. Instead of going to work, she was able to remain at home with her children. Because of the scandal, none of the ladies in the parish spoke to Margaret's mother, and the children were forbidden to socialize with her children.

Being the only seat left on the bus, Blanche had no choice but to sit there. When she told her hello, Blanche smiled but didn't respond. She didn't dare answer. If one of the kids told her mother that Blanche was talking to her, she knew her mother would find out, and Blanche was sure to get a beating as a result.

On the way back from Baton Rouge, Margaret turned to Blanche as they passed old Miss Celine's house.

"Isn't that your mama?"

Blanche stood up slightly so she could see out the window. She didn't speak but nodded in affirmation.

"No wonder you're an only child. Your mama goes by old Miss Celine."

Not understanding what Margaret meant and knowing she couldn't speak to her and request an explanation, Blanche turned away and kept her eyes focused on the front window of the bus. That night at dinner, her father asked her about the trip. Blanche gladly told him about all the sites they had visited. She was especially excited about the students being able to see the front rooms of the Governor's mansion, but remembering Margaret's comment, she frowned.

"What's wrong, baby girl? It sounds like you had a nice day. Why are you frowning?"

"A girl on the bus said something I don't understand."

"What was that? Maybe Daddy can explain it to you."

"She said I'm an only child because Mother goes by old Miss Celine."

Her father's eyes turned red as he turned to Sherrie. Her mother looked at Blanche and scolded, "Get to your room now."

"But, mother, I'm not finished eating my dinner."

"There will be no dinner for you tonight. You're punished. Go to your room now!"

Blanche had immediately got up from her chair and ran to her room seeing the look on her mother's face. She could hear her parents arguing, and then there was a deafening silence in the house. The silence remained until the next morning…

Thinking her father had already left for work, her mother had come to her bedroom screaming, "I'm going to teach you to stay out of grown-up people's business." She had begun beating her unmercifully. Blanche had coiled into a fetal position to protect her body from some of the lashes she was enduring. Her skin grew more and more tender as welts formed under the blows from the strap. Her mother's sudden screech caused her to turn her head slightly, peeking to see what had happened.

Her father was standing in the room. He apparently had grabbed her mother's arm when she went to swing at Blanche again. He was holding her arm midair in a fierce grip. Blanche's mother fair skin had grown even paler as she cowered under his glare. Blanche had never seen her father look so furious. His expression scared Blanche as well as he warned her mother, "Don't ever hit my child again!"

It seemed an eternity before he finally released her mother's arm. Blanche's mother rubbed her arm feverishly as she backed out Blanche's bedroom maintaining a watchful eye on her father.

Once she left, her father had closed his eyes, his teeth clenched. When he opened his eyes again, he had the calm demeanor Blanche knew. He sat on the side of her bed and placed his hand on her shoulder.

"Are you okay, baby girl?"

Her back, buttocks, and thighs were still stinging but she sensed she had to ensure her father that all was well.

"I'll be fine, Daddy."

He looked at the door, then back at Blanche. "I need to go to work now, but if your Mama even looks at you cross, you call me, and Daddy will be right back home. Ok, baby girl?"

"Ok, Daddy," she whispered as he bent over and kissed her softly on her forehead.

After that incident, things were different in their house. The next night, she found her father sitting in the third bedroom which was used only when they had visitors staying overnight.

"Daddy, is everything ok?" She sat beside him on the bed concerned. It looked as if her father had been crying. His eyes were bloodshot. Blanche had never seen her father cry. He always came across as a pillar of strength, but tonight, it seemed his spirit was broken. He seemed vulnerable to her.

"You know, Blanche. When I bought this house, I felt we had to have three bedrooms... a room for me and your mother, a room for our baby girls, and a room for our sons." Her father glanced around the empty room before continuing.... "Baby girl, I want you to promise your Daddy something."

He seemed to be hurting so bad that Blanche wanted to do anything to lift his spirits.

"What's that, Daddy?" She placed her hand on his arm. He covered her hand with his patting it gently.

"Promise me that you'll never give up on your dreams. It's a sad day when a person's dreams are shattered... It's a sad day, Blanche." Her father's voice broke, and he had to stop speaking. He hung his head. Blanche knew he needed to be alone.

She rose, kissed him on the cheek, and left the room. Before leaving, she whispered, "I promise, Daddy...." But she spoke so low, she doubted her father heard.

From then on, her father had slept in the empty third bedroom. Not understanding what had happened between her parents, Blanche thought it was her father's way of trying to find his dream again.

Now Blanche understood why her mother had been so brutal. Without knowing it, she had told her father that her mother had been taking an old-fashioned, home brewed birth control method to keep from becoming pregnant. And now she also knew why her father's health had suddenly gone down... He had given up on life. He had died of a broken heart. He was a beaten man married to a wife who didn't want to bear his children in fear their complexions would be too dark.

Tears rolled down Blanche's face as she thought of the conversation she had with her father about giving up on his dreams. All he ever wanted was to be loved. She crossed her hands across her abdomen and whispered to the life growing inside of her, "I love you, my little baby. Mommy will always love you, and you will have brothers and sisters."

She remembered her grandmother's words, "You need to put a little cream in your coffee." "Black coffee tastes good too," she thought, "for those strong enough to handle it."

Seeing Tony pull up in his car, Blanche wiped her eyes, walked hurriedly down the alley to the back door and entered through the wash room. She purposely let the screen door slam hard before locking it.

"Who's that?" her mother called out.

Blanche walked into the dining room where the pokeno boards had been spread on the table. Seeing her, Sherrie grew nervous.

"I didn't hear your car pull up. Why didn't you come through the kitchen door like you usually do?"

"I had a flat. My friend Melanie, one of the teachers at school, gave me a ride home."

"How long have you been here?" Sherrie demanded.

"Long enough," Blanche replied and lifter her chin indicating she had heard the conversation. With a new air of confidence as their eyes locked, she walked past her mother to her bedroom. Blanche realized she was the one that now had the upper hand in their relationship. Knowledge was power. The pokeno game ended shortly after.

When Blanche emerged from her room at dinner time, the table was already set. A cup of hot tea was by Blanche's place. She rose, took the cup, and went to the kitchen and poured it down the drain. When she returned to the table, Sherrie didn't look up from her plate but commented.

"That was a perfectly good cup of tea."

"I won't be drinking tea in this house unless I prepare it myself," Blanche emphasized each word she spoke. "I am marrying Adam and I am giving birth to his child. And if you want to entertain Tony and Miss Ethel Wednesday night, you'll have to cook the meal yourself. Cook it only for three. I don't enjoy his company so I'm eating out that night and going to a movie. I'll be home after they're gone."

The rest of the meal was eaten in silence. Maybe it was a perfectly good cup of the orange pekoe and pekoe cut black tea blend they kept as a staple in the house. Maybe her mother was trying to make amends. Maybe she should have acknowledged the gesture and drank the hot tea, but Blanche wouldn't take the risk for her baby's sake and for Adam's.

Surprisingly, the next morning when Blanche woke, she had no trace of morning sickness.

Chapter Thirty-Three

Saturday morning, Blanche woke her usual time and went into the kitchen to prepare breakfast for herself and her mother. They ate in silence until Blanche announced that she expected Adam for lunch. Sherrie didn't reply but began stabbing her food and eating it faster to quickly finish her breakfast. She then stepped out to the front porch to enjoy the fresh air before the sun shifted, and she had to retire back inside the house to protect her fair skin.

Blanche watched her mother exit to the porch, cleared the table, and went into the kitchen to clean the dishes before starting the lunch preparations. The night before she had picked up Vidalia onions, fresh garlic, parsley, celery, an orange bell pepper, cream of mushroom soup, and cream of chicken soup as well as two pounds of peeled crawfish tails, all the ingredients she needed to make an easy etoufée for Adam. All she had to do was sautés the seasonings in margarine, add the soups and the crawfish tails, and let it all simmer for fifteen minutes. Though Blanche loved it best over angel hair pasta, she would serve it over steamed rice with green peas and potato salad. It was a typical Creole meal, and she knew Adam would love the seafood based on entrées he had ordered in restaurants.

Busy preparing lunch and with the sound of the overhead stove vent blocking out the noise from the street, Adam was already entering the front gate of their house by the time Blanche saw him. She quickly washed her hands, but Adam had already approached the bottom step of the porch. She could hear the conversation as she walked hurriedly to the front door.

"Good morning, Ms. Sherrie."

"Don't greet me acting all innocent! You begged me to let my daughter go to that banquet with you, and you repaid me by taking advantage of her? You think you're welcome to set foot in my house? Walking up here as if nothing happened when you got her pregnant that night? How dare you bring your short, black ass here?"

Blanche couldn't believe her mother had been that forthright with Adam. Her stomach had a sinking feeling. She closed her eyes and hung her head shaking it slightly from one side to the other. All these days she had suffered her mother's mental abuse over getting pregnant outside of marriage. She knew her mother was upset and not ready to let go of the subject, but she never anticipated her mother would attack Adam so viciously when he arrived.

Spying Blanche's reaction through the screen door, Adam surmised what had been happening. When he last saw her, Blanche appeared depressed and downtrodden. Adam knew, based on his conversation with Colin, that his future mother-in-law had a strong prejudicial streak and would be difficult to win over, especially under the circumstances. No matter what facts were presented to her, she would hold steadfastly to her opinions. Remembering his vow to always respect women the day he laid the single red rose on his mother's coffin, he fought to control the anger he felt at the abuse he knew Blanche had been suffering and fought to find words that would silence his future mother-in-law without being disrespectful under the circumstances. Looking up at Sherrie, he felt being open and honest was his only option.

"No, Ms. Sherrie…. I didn't take advantage of her that night…. But I did this past summer. She trusted me and came to my apartment counting on my friendship, and I betrayed that trust. The weekend of the banquet is when I proposed. I asked her to marry me because I love your daughter, and I want to make things right."

As Blanche was stepping onto the porch, she stopped where she stood frozen by Adam's confession. She looked first at him, then to her mother. Sherrie was staring at him her chest heaving in anger. She stood and walked towards Blanche hissing, "You went to New Orleans to be there for Colin's stepdaughter, and instead, you were spending your time at a man's place? Didn't I teach you a single woman doesn't go to a man's apartment unchaperoned? Didn't I teach you what it would do to your reputation? You had to bring shame on this family? And, for that?" She tossed her head in Adam's direction.

When Blanche didn't respond, she pushed her aside haughtily and gave her an icy stare as she entered the house.

Blanche glanced towards Adam, crossed the width of the porch to where he stood at the top of the steps, and whispered, "Adam, now she knows we were together over the summer. Now she knows we had met before the Labor Day barbecue by Colin's."

"And the point is? … When the baby's born, she'll know then. … Anyway, since she now knows you are pregnant, does it matter when you got pregnant? It's best to get everything out in the open at one time and put this behind us."

"I guess you're right," Blanche answered despondingly.

Adam stepped gingerly up the last step, pulled her up into his arms, and kissed her passionately before noticing the slight bruising on her cheek. He caressed her cheek gently with his hand before kissing her again.

"I'm sorry I wasn't here to break the news with you. Are you alright?"

"That won't be happening ever again."

Adam was surprised at the assertive manner Blanche answered him. He leaned back and looked into her face. The shyness seemed to be gone. She spoke and looked as if she knew her rights and intended to demand them. There was a sense of self confidence about her. Not knowing if the change was permanent or just because he was there to provide support, Adam continued.

"I don't want you feeling sad about this. It's not good for you or the baby. I'm happy you're carrying my child, and I can't wait to hold that child in my arms. I love you, Blanche. Remember that the days I'm not here, and please call me whenever you need to talk, especially if you start feeling down. Okay?"

"Okay…" Blanche looked up, and Adam kissed her soundly on the lips again. She laid her head on his shoulder.

"Everything feels so right when I'm with you, and it seems such a challenge when you're not around. Sometimes I start doubting myself, doubting everything…."

"I know, but hang in there. It won't be long before we're together permanently. I picked up the marriage license application from the Department of Public Health. It lists the documents I'll need you need to bring me. Only one of us needs to file so you won't need to take off and come to New Orleans on a week day. Once we have all the documents, I can file it. We can go through the rules. That's one of the things we need to discuss today regarding our future plans."

Blanche couldn't wait to tell him over lunch that she had already made her final decision and had worked out everything with the principal at her school.

They hugged tightly not knowing Sherrie was watching and listening from beyond the doorway. When Sherrie saw Tony and Ethel observing Blanche and Adam from across the street, she became even more determined to stop the marriage. How dare Blanche embarrass her by kissing and hugging that dark man in front of their neighbors. As the couple turned to enter the house, she slipped down the hallway and went to her bedroom. She stayed there until Adam drove off to head back to New Orleans.

Chapter Thirty-Four

The next morning at breakfast Blanche announced that, since Adam was not welcome at the house, she would be spending the weekends in New Orleans from now on and would be moving there once she had finished the contract at her school and was discharged from having the baby. Sherrie acted as if she hadn't heard her and continued eating her breakfast as if Blanche wasn't present. Blanche wasn't sure if the silent treatment was more welcome than the abuse she had suffered in the past. By the end of breakfast, the unnerving silence had caused her stomach to be just as upset as the verbal abuse that had been ongoing. She looked forward to Friday afternoon when she could join Adam and finalize the wedding plans with Maria and Autumn.

Pulling into the parking lot at Adam's complex, Blanche felt a sigh of relief. She couldn't wait to live here permanently. The atmosphere in the French Quarter felt as if you had stepped back in time. It was like being in a different world. Seeing the wrought iron laced balconies hung with flowers in bloom, smelling the scent of beignets frying and coffee brewing, hearing the calliope playing on the river boats, and being able to watch the Mississippi flowing from your own balcony was such a soothing atmosphere.

Stepping from the car, she popped the latch for the trunk and retrieved her luggage. The only thing that was firm for the weekend was to meet with Maria and Autumn tomorrow for lunch and finalize the wedding plans. Maybe she and Adam could just stay in tonight, watch a movie, and order pizza. She didn't feel up to going out; she longed only to sit on the sofa and feel his arms around her. As she stepped through the entrance door of the building and passed the security desk, one of the guards hailed her down. Walking over, she opened her purse to retrieve her identification card.

"No, Mrs. Brown, you don't need to show your I.D. Your husband said you are to meet him at this condo instead."

Blanche smiled at the reference of Adam as her husband. She felt important being referred to as Mrs. Brown although the salutation was premature. Confused, she took the note from the guard, entered the elevator, and pushed the button for a floor three stories higher than Adam's condo. As she exited, she noted the signs and turned left towards the condo's number. She knocked softly on the door only to realize it was slightly ajar. Afraid to just enter on her own, she peeked in and called softly, "Hello.. Is anyone here?"

In response, Adam came rushing to the front door to greet her. He took her case from her and dropped it along the wall inside the front door before pulling her into his arms and kissing her soundly.

"I'm glad you had a safe trip. Stepping back and taking her by the hand, he tugged her along excitedly exclaiming, "Let me show you the place! This was two condos, but they were renovated into a single apartment. I have seen the owner in the building before, and I know he travels often, but this past Monday he had excessive luggage with him on the elevator. He was telling someone that his company closed their New Orleans branch, and he had to relocate to Dallas to keep his job. He already has an apartment there, and his family is already moved so his kids could start in their new school on time. He had to stay behind to close the office and wrap up a few business issues. I stopped him after we exited from the elevator and offered to assist him with his luggage. I found out he was about to list this place on the market. I convinced him not to list it until you saw it. If you love it, we can just do a private sale. That way, we split the commission a real estate agent would get saving him and me the extra fees. His relocation is due to a merger I read about in the newspaper. He had to get there fast, or he may not have had a job. He's willing to let the place go for the balance of his mortgage plus enough to put a down payment on a new home."

Blanche looked at Adam confused.

"Don't worry. He'll have all the furniture out within two weeks. He's putting it in storage in Dallas until he finds a home there. They're living in a furnished apartment for now."

To clarify the confused look wasn't about the living room furniture filling the space where they stood, Blanche spoke softly, "But Adam, your place is fine. Won't this be a lot more expensive?"

"My place is fine for now, but it's only a two bedroom. This one has four, and we'll need the extra space once we have another kid. Let me show you around."

Blanche followed reluctantly. They had discussed having at least two children, but it seems Adam already had a time table set in that regard. Her life seemed to be a whirlwind these past few months.

Adam escorted her to the right side of the condo first to a master suite and announced it would be theirs. The room also had a private balcony, like Adam's, with a view of the river and two separate walk-in closets lined with cedar. He showed her a second bedroom on the same side that could be converted to the baby's nursery. This bedroom had a half bath that was also accessible from the living room. Entering the living room again, Adam stepped her through it to the kitchen. The kitchen was as huge as the one at Colin's house across the lake and equipped with appliances unlike any Blanche had seen. They were two refrigerators and a separate, upright deep freezer. The stove had eight burners as well as a grill. Adam slid a door into the wall and there was a pantry Blanche could walk into with shelves of varying heights lining both sides. As they walked back into the hallway and through an arched doorway, they entered a room on the opposite side of the kitchen that was used for dining. The outer wall was solid glass from ceiling to floor and faced the river. Blanche stood mesmerized looking, down at the lights of the city, watching the ferry cross the river while tourists walked along the river bank. It was a scene she only imagined for vacation areas, not for one's home. To think that she, Blanche Aubert, could actually live in a place so luxurious seemed like a dream. Adam let her take in the view for a short while before stepping away and pressing a button. A set of curtains slowly closed granting privacy if needed.

"This way," he announced as they stepped left to another hallway. Pointing to the door on the right, Adam announced, "This room is used as a study or home office. They peeked in to see the office before continuing down the hall. Opening a set of louvered doors on the left, Adam noted, "Here is the laundry area."

Continuing down the hall, Adam opened a second door on the right stating, "When the baby gets older, this can be his next bedroom."

The room was slightly larger than the nursery to be but more than adequate for a teenager. After Blanche checked out the third bedroom, Adam led her through a door that was not accessible from the hallway.

"The bedrooms on this side each have a private area with a commode and sink but share the bath and shower."

They walked through the bathing area and through the other private area entering the fourth bedroom. The last bedroom was nearly as large as the master suite. It was furnished with a queen sized bed, dresser, two night stands, chest, and a sitting area. The sitting area had a lounge chair, table, and lamp. It was next to a sliding door that led to a small balcony where two wrought iron chairs and a small table were situated. It was a perfect place to sit and have your morning coffee or to take an afternoon tea break. From the balcony, you could see both the river and into the French Quarter. Adam's condo only had a view of the river. Being a corner suite, this condo was fortunate to have views of both sides.

As she stepped back into the bedroom, Blanche's jaw dropped when Adam announced, "I thought this would be perfect for your mother's bedroom."

"My mother's?" Blanche stared at Adam flabbergasted. Adam hung his head momentarily before raising it and trying to be more animated about his revelation.

"I know you don't like these tan walls for her. It does seem more like a man's room. But, I'm planning to have the room redone. You told Maria your mother's favorite color is blue. I asked her to pick up some wallpaper sample books from one of the paint stores. What do you think? A pale blue or something more of a medium shade? I took the liberty of inviting Colin, Maria, and Autumn over for lunch tomorrow. We can show them this place and work on the wedding plans."

Blanche's expression didn't change. Adam walked over and placed his hands lightly on her upper arms massaging them gently.

"I'm sorry. I'm making too many assumptions without consulting you first. Nothing is final. I haven't signed any papers. If you don't agree with this move, all I need to do is turn the keys over to the realtor the guy intended to use and let him know we're not interested in the place after all... Regarding lunch, I don't expect you to cook. After the drive, I know you need to rest. I'm handling everything in that regard."

Adam continued to watch Blanche's expression hoping the apology would return the smile he had grown to love to her face. When she continued to frown, he apologized again.

"I'm sorry. What can I do to make this up to you?"

"Adam, it's not about the lunch plans. I think it's a great idea to offer Colin's family over here for a change. I'm happy I'll get to entertain them in return for all they've done for me... It's also not about the apartment."

Blanche stepped into the living room. With the furniture still in place, she could see the full potential of the condo. Something about it said family to her instead of the bachelor pad feel to Adam's current condo.

"Blanche, I was going to mention it later tonight, but I'll break the news now. I was offered the position to be dean for the psychology department. Since you told me last week you were okay with moving to New Orleans, I accepted. I'll be getting a raise, and after selling my place, this is affordable on just my salary. You won't have to go back to work unless you want to."

Blanche turned, and her facial expression had finally changed. She seemed so happy as she congratulated Adam.

"My darling, I'm so happy for you! Based on my experience with you this past summer, things Autumn has shared with me, and seeing how your students react to you, I know you've worked hard and are so deserving of this."

She walked over and took Adam's hands into her own. Glancing about the condo once again, she looked into his eyes so he could see how sincere she was.

"The place is gorgeous. I love it. It's more than I ever dreamed of." She let go of his hands and walked through the fourth bedroom out to the balcony again. Adam followed. Pointing to the play area across from their building, she continued, "There's even a convenient place to bring the kids down to play, and we're right next to the riverfront park." Blanche thought about the families she'd seen out roller skating, playing ball, or just sitting on a blanket enjoying the view and having a light picnic lunch together. Stepping past Adam into the bedroom, her frown returned.

Walking over to face Blanche, Adam questioned, "Then, what's bothering you? Something is wrong."

Blanche waved her hand around the room, "My mother's?"

"Colin and I have been talking. He's been trying to get his mother to move to New Orleans for over a year now. She's getting up there in age, and he doesn't want to wait until she's ill and has to make the move. He rather her come now while they can enjoy quality time together. After her visit for the Labor Day barbecue, he thinks she's finally going to agree to the move. If you're coming here too, your mother would be alone. She's getting up there in age as well, and being her only child, you'll be her primary caregiver. With the baby, it'll be hard for you to handle things in Lafayette. Won't it be better for her to move here and to help you out with the baby? After all, this is your first..."

Everything Adam said made logical sense to her. She was totally in agreement except that Blanche knew that logic didn't rule when it came to her mother. Blanche didn't believe the man Adam was, and she was grateful that she had found someone so forgiving, so thoughtful, so understanding, and so in command and in control. After handling so many things since her father passed, it was nice to know she had someone in her life she could lean on, someone with a solid head on his shoulders, someone who was proactive and always planning for their future. Knowing Adam didn't understand still why she was uncomfortable, she spoke her mind although raising the subject was embarrassing to her.

"My mother's room," she said the words again as she walked around the bedroom. "Adam, after the way she spoke to you last week? ... After the way she treated you, you're still willing to do this for her?"

"Baby, she's your mother so she's part of the package. I know she may never respect me. I'm not what she had in mind for her daughter, but I accept that. We'll work through it. Once the baby is born, things will change. I love you. It's important for me that you're happy. You won't be if you're worried about how she's getting along all by herself with no family nearby. I'm okay with her living here as well."

As Adam took her into his arms, tears rose in Blanche's eyes. She thought to herself, "Things won't change once the baby's born. They'll only get worse because the baby's skin tone will be too dark. She'll never accept our child. I doubt she'll ever even hold it." Not wanting to ruin Adam's excitement further, she kept her dark thoughts to herself. Later that night, Adam called the owner and told him they were keeping the keys. They discussed a date to meet with a lawyer to begin the process of transferring the title into Adam and Blanche's name. Adam would meet with the movers and oversee the furniture being removed on the owner's behalf. Since the place would be theirs, they planned to cook the meal in their own place but to serve the lunch with Colin's family in the new condo the next day. Blanche would be busy making trips between the two condos setting the dining room table with their own linens, dishes, and flatware while Adam was preparing the meal. They would fix drinks in their condo and let each guest carry their own glass up the new apartment. It seems their plans were beginning to fall easily into place.

Chapter Thirty-Five

When Autumn called on her cell and said they were in front of The Library so would arrive shortly, Blanche went down to meet the trio while Adam finished tossing the salad he had prepared and delivered it to the new apartment. They met in Adam's former bachelor pad (as Blanche had begun to think of it) and prepared drinks. Walking to the doors off the den that led to a view of the river, Maria gasped.

"Oh, Adam, this is a magnificent view."

Colin walked over and joined his wife, "It reminds me of my cousin's place. I like this view better though because you can see further down river." Calling over his shoulder, he continued, "Blanche, I don't think you ever met my second cousin Clark since he's related on my father's side. His wife Bernadette is about your age if I'm remembering correctly. It might be nice to have another couple the two of you can socialize with that's close by. May I add them to the guest list so you get to meet them? "

Blanche glanced at Adam who nodded and answered for both of them, "My main associates are my colleagues, and our social contact is primarily limited to university related events. With Blanche being from out of town, it would be nice to meet another couple. That's a great idea, Colin."

Colin smiled at the affirmation of his suggestion, noticing the way Adam and Blanche were beginning to communicate silently with their eyes. It appeared they were already an old, married couple. He smiled at the thought as he turned, put his arm around Maria, and continued to enjoy the view of the river. Autumn broke the silence.

"May I help set the table? I'm hungry."

Colin glanced at his stepdaughter shaking his head. Having spent the summer with Autumn, Blanche knew exactly how the morning had started in the Laurent household. Autumn had slept in and probably not waken until Colin banged on her door saying they needed to get over to Adam's. Having missed breakfast, she probably was starving by now. Colin noticed the silent look that went between Adam and Blanche, but it was Blanche that spoke this time.

"We're not eating here because we're moving."

Maria turned and exclaimed, "You two are giving up this great condo?"

Blanche laughed as Adam said, "Bring your drinks and follow us." Looking directly at Autumn, he added, "Lunch is served."

The trio exchanged glances before following Adam and Blanche out the condo, onto the elevators, and up three floors. Adam unlocked the door, and Blanche stated as she guided the trio in, "This isn't our furniture. It's the former owner's, but this will soon be our new condo. Adam felt we needed more room with the baby coming."

"Feel free to explore it," Adam announced. "All the family's personal belongings have been removed. Only the furniture needs to be picked up, and the moving company should be here Friday to take care of that. We should close the following week. Then Blanche and I can begin redecorating the place."

Colin and Adam did a quick walk through on their own, letting the three ladies spent more leisurely time inspecting the new surroundings as Blanche explained how they planned to utilize each bedroom. By the time the ladies joined the men in the dining room, Adam and Colin had been discussing the price tag on the place, and they heard Colin agreeing with Adam that the place was a steal, far too good a deal to pass up. They sat down for lunch with the curtains drawn so they could all enjoy the scenery. After lunch, the trio helped Adam and Blanche bring everything back down to Adam's and tidy up. Back in Adam's condo, Colin and Adam sat on one side of the den as they reviewed a standard real estate contract together while the ladies discussed the wedding attire. Maria glanced at Autumn indicating she'd take the lead.

"Blanche, I know your favorite color is orange, but since it's fall, how about this color scheme?"

Maria pulled out ribbon samples and showed Blanche.

"Autumn's gown would be Hunter's green, and her bouquet would consist of a mix of valeria and ivory roses with white baby's breath. We could also have valeria and ivory colored ribbons flowing down from the bouquet to contrast against the dark green of her dress. We'd add the ivory because your bouquet would be ivory roses with white baby's breath... I know valerian is a Eurasian plant having pinkish flower clusters so I don't know why the florist calls this color valeria, but it is a deep orange. We know you like orange, and it's a color that complements the Hunter's green well. Do you like this combination? If so, how about bird of paradise floral arrangements for the tables? We stopped at the florist and picked up one of each of the flowers for you to see."

As Maria dug into the duffle they had brought and handed the flowers to Blanche, Blanche held them as tenderly as she would hold a fine china tea cup. She was glad Maria had brought samples of the flowers because the only flowers Blanche knew were roses and carnations. Roses and azaleas were the typical garden flowers in the area where she was raised, and carnations were the standard corsage the boys brought the girls for prom night. She would have been embarrassed to admit she had never heard of a valerian and had no clue what a bird of paradise looked like.

"Oh, Maria, all of these are so beautiful. And Autumn, won't this color complement your hair well?"

Autumn's eyes opened wide as she nodded in agreement. As Blanche turned back to admiring the flowers, she mouthed, "Thank you," to her mother and breathed a sigh of relief grateful the gown she would have to wear would not be orange. Maria pulled images of gowns she and Autumn had printed from the internet and laid them out for Blanche to see.

"Oh..." Blanche exhaled as she saw the gown Maria and Autumn had selected for her. "And the style is perfect for the occasion considering my condition."

She smiled before turning back to the photo of the ivory colored strapless gown. The front fell just below the knee flowing gradually to an ankle length in the back. The faille fabric was made of silk, and the draped sweetheart bodice ended at the waist with a flower made of the same fabric. Autumn's gown would be similar but plain. Autumn's would be made of chiffon, the ruched bust would not be adorned at the waist, and the hemline of the short gown would fall right below her knee, not the high and low design of the bride's.

"If you're okay with these, I'll order the gowns Monday morning. They should be here within a few weeks."

Blanche got up and gave Maria a hug. As she sat back down in her seat at the table, she questioned, "The gown is beautiful, but before you order it, I need to know how much will the gown cost? I have been saving money since I graduated from college, but I need to allow for the other wedding costs as well."

Maria shook her head and said, "No. Colin is adamant he is taking care of the total costs for your wedding. You and your mother won't have to spend a penny."

Blanche turned toward Colin to voice her protest, but before she could speak, Maria added, "You know how Colin is when he makes his mind up on a subject. You're the closest thing to a sister he's ever had, and this is not an argument you'll win, Blanche, so let's just keep the subject of the cost closed."

Maria used a firm voice on the last sentence. Knowing she was right, Blanche turned back to the table and picked up the photo of the wedding gown again.

"It is beautiful," she said as she glanced from Maria to Autumn and back to the dress. Opening another folder, Maria showed Blanche a photo of pair of short heeled, peep toe, silk pumps with a ruched knot face. Blanche's shoes would be ivory, but Autumn's would be a fabric that could be dyed to match her gown. As Blanche nodded consent, Maria went into the duffle and pulled out a box. She handed it to Blanche saying, "Colin picked this out for you."

Blanche opened the box, pushed the tissue aside, and pulled out a jewelry case. Opening it, she took a short, gasping breath seeing the crystal and pearl necklace with a matching bracelet and earrings.

"There's more," Maria coaxed her to dig further.

Laying the jewelry case on the table, Blanche pushed more tissue aside and pulled out a tiara. The band was not the ornamental style of royalty but a small band set with fine crystals that shimmered like diamonds.

"We could pull your hair back into a bun at the base of your neck so the tiara falls right above it. We can add a veil if you like, nothing too long. Colin said it's for his little princess."

At that Blanche couldn't hold back the tears. Her thoughts went back to her childhood, the days when Colin called her the little princess and the first time she heard the words tee-neg.

Chapter Thirty-Six

It was a Saturday afternoon. Her maternal grandmother, Aunt Barbara, and Colin had come for a visit. Her mother was playing their favorite records in the living room while they all dined on cinnamon teacakes and drank lemonade. Blanche was about seven years old at the time. Colin walked over to her, took the saucer of teacakes from her, and laid it on the coffee table. He then held out his hand gesturing for her to join him in a dance.

Colin was fifteen years her senior and the closest thing to a brother she ever had. He was always kind, gentle, and attentive when he came to visit. Cole often brought her some little token, if only her favorite candy bar. He didn't mind playing her board games with her even if she wanted to play the same one over and over again. He would tell her about the things he had been doing and show her pictures of places he had been. Most importantly, Cole would ask her about school and give her the opportunity to tell him all about what was happening in her life. He even listened to her dreams. He never poked fun at the things she wanted to do and encouraged her to do well in school so she could achieve her goals. In fact, Blanche realized that Colin's visits were the only time she ever got to talk about herself or her life with anyone after her father passed. With Cole, she could share everything. She felt like a little princess whenever he came around, and it was his nickname for her.

"I've never danced before, Cole." Blanche was smiling at him shyly as she stood and began twisting her body slightly from side to side.

Colin smiled kindly at her and said, "I know.... That's why I want to teach you."

Hesitantly, she put her hand in his, and her heart sang as he stooped slightly to adjust his height to a comfortable position for her. He guided her left hand atop his right shoulder; then he slipped his right hand to rest on her left side.

"Just let me lead you..." he whispered.

He started out with very slow movements until Blanche was getting the feel for the steps. Then he glided her across the living room floor to a song whose words she couldn't quite remember now.

The next song was rock type music. Colin separated from her and told her to match his movements. The beat was very quick.

"Listen to the music, and let the rhythm move you..." Colin instructed.

Soon Blanche could feel the beat as well. Colin smiled in approval. The afternoon was beginning to be the most wonderful Blanche had ever spent. She felt she was soaring as high as a kite until she heard her grandmother murmur to her mother and aunt, "Tee-neg."

When Blanche heard the words, she turned and stared at them. Her grandmother was seated in the rocking chair, and her two daughters had stood and went to stand behind her. They had been whispering among themselves before her grandmother's voice rang out. Though only seven years old, she understood exactly what her grandmother meant. Her dance movements were not appropriate for a Creole child. She had demonstrated too much rhythm which, to her grandmother, meant her gene pool contained too much African blood. She was eyeing Blanche as if she was a stranger instead of her own flesh and blood.

Blanche stopped dancing immediately, her eyes brimming with tears. She ran to her bedroom and closed the door. She was so embarrassed she couldn't stand to let Colin see her again on that visit. She wasn't a little princess. In both her grandmother's and her own mother's eyes, she was just a tee-neg.

Even from behind her bedroom door, Blanche could tell that Colin was angry over what had happened. Blanche could hear him spewing harsh words before storming out the house purposely banging the front door closed as hard as he could. He waited for his mother in the car but Blanche could still hear his comments as they drove off, and her aunt was trying to no avail to calm him down.

As she placed the tiara back in the gift box, she wondered if Colin remembered that day as well. The tears kept overflowing and went streaming down her face.

Autumn grabbed her purse, pulled out a pack of tissues, and handed them to Blanche.

Colin turned their way and called, "A wedding day should be a happy occasion. What's going on over there?"

"Tears of happiness," Autumn snapped back at her stepfather. As Maria shoved the photos back into the folder, Autumn announced, "I think we're ready to discuss the guest list. We're done with the gowns and flowers."

The men rose to join them as Blanche dabbed her eyes dry. Adam walked over to the small desk adjacent to the front door where he usually dropped his mail, pulled out the drawer, and removed a slip of paper. Placing it on the table for the three ladies to see he stated, "I know Blanche doesn't want a large wedding so I only listed colleagues that are a must to invite and my closest relatives."

Colin glanced at the list and turned to Blanche after seeing only fifteen names were listed with addresses. "Blanche, how many total guests were you thinking of?"

Eyeing Colin sheepishly, Blanche picked up her purse and pulled out her list, "With those I have listed, it shouldn't go over forty people total." She put her head down and said in such a low voice that Colin barely heard her, "I included my Auntie Nora. I'd like her to be there."

Colin reached down, put his hand under Blanche's chin, and lifted her face upward before stating, "My mother has already contacted her and told her she's invited."

Blanche eyed Colin confused, "How did she know where to find her? After my father died, my mother forbade me to have any contact with that side of the family. I don't know where Auntie Nora is. How does Auntie Barbara know?"

"Blanche, my mother and your Aunt Nora were class mates in high school. They were best friends. It's through that friendship that your mother met your father. My mom never agreed with the passé blanc attitude of your mother and our grandmother. She's kept in touch with Nora all these years. She has given her pictures of you and invited her to all your major events. At your high school graduation, she was sitting in the last seat in the balcony to make sure your mother didn't see her there. She was there when you graduated from college as well. My mom feels it time to stop the passé blanc attitude, and Nora needs to sit in the front for a change."

"I never knew," Blanche said shaking her head as the knowledge Colin shared sunk in.

"For your birthday and Christmas, my mom always brought you two presents, remember?"

Blanche looked up and said, "Yes."

"Do you also remember that one box never had a name on it, and it was always a new outfit?"

"Yes," Blanched nodded enthusiastically as she recalled always getting the two gifts.

"The unmarked box with the clothes was from your Aunt Nora. My mom just delivered it for her."

"My mother always thought Auntie Barbara was just spoiling me by giving me two gifts..."

"That was the intent. Your Aunt Nora said it gave her great pleasure having forbidden things from her in Sherrie's house."

Blanche recalled her thirteenth birthday when her mother had set the first set of clothes Aunt Nora had given her on fire in the barbecue pit and said nothing of Nora's would ever be in her house again.

"All these years..." Blanche said as the irony of it all hit her.

Things fell silent for a short time as Adam also pondered what Colin had shared. He wasn't familiar with all the customs and phrases used by Creoles but he had assumed correctly that passé blanc was Creole for 'passing for white.' If his future mother-in-law's family had done that on occasion in the past, he had a harder uphill battle to win over his mother-in-law than he had previously estimated. He wondered if he should share his family's background with Blanche and her mother. He wondered if that would make a difference to Sherrie and help Blanche understand why he could so easily empathize with the situation he was facing. He didn't know a lot about what had happened with his parents other than the little his maternal aunt had shared with him. What difference did it really make? It didn't change his skin tone, and it won't change their baby's. Adam shrugged the thought off....

Colin broke the silence, "If we're only looking at forty guests, we could have the wedding at the house across the lake. Did you all pick a date yet?"

Adam and Blanche both nodded, "No."

"How about the Saturday before Thanksgiving? Blanche, won't the school be closed then for the annual teacher's convention?"

"Yes," she replied thinking the timing would be perfect.

Adam added, "The university is closed Wednesday through Friday. I could take off the other two days, and we'd have the entire week free."

Colin looked at Autumn, "You've been wanting me to put a gazebo in the yard at the house across the lake. If that's the date of the wedding, we could get one installed in time for the wedding ceremony." He looked towards Maria as he continued, "We could rent chairs for the guests to sit in front of the gazebo for the ceremony and set up a tent on the other side of the yard with tables and chairs for the reception afterwards."

Maria nodded enthusiastically at the idea and turned to Blanche, "Blanche, your thoughts?"

She looked at Adam and said, "It sounds perfect. Would that be okay with you?"

Adam looked at Colin and the two guys punched their right fists together indicating the plans were a lock.

Adam added, "I'll apply for the marriage license the first week in November. It has a seventy two hour waiting period, but then it's good for thirty days so the date will fall just fine. I won't put this condo on the market until after the wedding. That way I'll have plenty of space for my relatives coming in town instead of booking hotel rooms."

Colin inquired, "What about the time? Would 2:00 P.M. be okay? Blanche, I see your friend Melanie is on the list and recognize the names of some of the folks from your school. 2:00 P.M. would allow folks driving in from Lafayette plenty of time to get here, and the reception would end early enough for them to drive home the same day. What do you think?"

"That sounds fine," Blanche replied as she looked to Adam who nodded in agreement.

Adam gave Colin a look indicating there was something more the two guys needed to discuss. Picking up on the clue, Colin wrapped up the conversation "Ladies, pull those menus out and select a caterer. We have a date. We have a place. We have a time. Now we need food because at 2:00 P.M. Autumn is going to be hungry."

Autumn glanced up at her stepfather with a smirk on her face.

"We guys are going back over there to look over this contract one more time."

As Autumn and Blanche looked over the menus from caterers Maria had spread on the table, Maria glanced at the two men in serious conversation. She surmised correctly that something else was being planned, and Maria knew that she and Autumn would eventually have a hand in it. Late that night as the trio was ready to leave, Blanche and Adam escorted them to Colin's car so they could pick up the wallpaper sample books Adam had asked Maria to get for them. As Maria handed the books over to Blanche, she told her, "You can keep them for two weeks so there's no rush. Hold the pieces up against the walls in your new place. That'll give you a better feel for what it will look like."

"Thank you, Maria. Autumn…" Blanche gave Colin a hug, and her eyes welled with tears as she thought about the tiara he had selected once again.

That night, Blanche had no inhibitions as she and Adam made love. After all, the security guard had called her Mrs. Brown.

Chapter Thirty-Seven

When she arrived home Sunday night, Blanche's mother was sitting at the table in their dining room reading the Sunday newspaper. Blanche laid one of the wallpaper sample books on the table and spoke in a soft voice.

"Mother, Adam is buying a new place for us to live. It has four bedrooms. One is for you. He wants you to move to New Orleans as well and live with us. He is completely redoing the room for you. Even if you decide not to move in, it'll be your room whenever you come to visit, and we are hoping you would at least visit from time to time. Your bedroom is very large. It even has a sitting area and a balcony that has a nice view. I put paper clips on the wallpaper I thought you would like. We also went on websites and printed pictures of furniture. I marked the one Adam wants to buy for you. If you don't like the furniture, we could go to the library and look at websites so you can pick something else. Look through the wallpaper sample book. Look at what I selected, and let me know what you like. I'll show it to Adam next weekend so he can start getting your bedroom ready. He took pictures with his digital camera and printed them. It shows what your room looks like now and the view from your balcony."

Sherrie continued reading the paper acting as if Blanche hadn't said a word. Blanche sighed, left the book on the table, and went back to her car to unload her luggage.

She spent another week getting the silent treatment from her mother. Friday morning, Blanche packed her case for her weekend trip to New Orleans. As she passed her mother sitting at the dining room table drinking a cup of coffee, Sherrie remained silent. After loading everything in the car, Blanche returned to the dining room and looked at the wallpaper sample book sitting exactly where she had first left it.

"Mother, did you look at the two wallpaper samples I picked out? Maria agreed those would be very nice for a bedroom, especially since your favorite color is blue."

Sherrie continued sipping her coffee and didn't look up at Blanche. Sighing, Blanche picked up the book and turned to walk out the house.

"I'll be back Sunday night. You have a good weekend, mother."

As she was about to close the door, her mother said in a rough tone, "You don't put those large flowers in a bedroom, simpleton, unless you're trying to make my place look like a whore house. Just because you're one doesn't mean I'll break down and become one too. Of course, the smaller floral print would be better. Not that I'd ever set foot in the black bastard's place. I'm just giving you advice so the stupid man doesn't spend all that money, and the house doesn't look presentable. You never did have any kind of taste. That's why I had to pick all your clothes."

Blanche turned and eyed her mother looking at the newspaper and still pretending she wasn't there. Smiling she called out, "Thank you, mother, for keeping me from making a wrong decision."

Without looking up, Sherrie uttered one word, "Whore."

Blanche smiled as she closed the door behind her. At least her mother was talking to her again.

The week before the wedding came faster than Blanche imagined it would. She went to work that morning but took the afternoon off so they could leave by 1:00 P.M. She was going to first stop by Adam's and show her mother her new home, then drive across the lake to spend the night at Colin's. When she arrived at the house, her Aunt Barbara was already there fussing with her sister. She must have taken a cab over to save Blanche the time it would take to pick her up.

"Sherrie, you need to pack more clothes. Colin says it doesn't make sense for us to come home right after the wedding. We may as well stay for the week and have Thanksgiving there at his house. He wants all of us together. Won't that be nice?"

Blanche listened but was confused. They hadn't discussed post wedding plans so all she had packed was a weekend bag since her wedding attire would be at Colin's. Glancing at the clock, they had to get on the highway soon, or she'd be late for her own rehearsal. She made up her mind that she would just wash what she had packed over and over if they did end up spending the week.

"Hi, Auntie. Hi, mother. Are you both ready for us to go?"

Her mother snapped the suitcase closed, picked up her purse, walked out her bedroom, through the house, out the front door, and got into the front passenger seat of the car.

"I guess she's ready, Auntie," Blanche said softly as she lifted her mother's heavy case and struggled to get it out the house and into her trunk. Her aunt followed with her luggage. After Blanche went back into the house, closed the windows, and locked the front door, she turned and saw Tony and Miss Ethel at her mother's side of the car.

As Blanche walked around the car and sat in the driver's seat, Ethel said, "Congratulations, Blanche. We'll see you tomorrow. Tony is off from work so he'll be able to drive me to your wedding after all."

After Tony escorted his mother back across the street, Blanche turned and stared at her mother with an expression saying, "How dare you invite those people to my wedding?" Blanche had given her mother four invitations. She knew her mother would give two to the ladies they played pokeno with and took for granted the other two would be for the two ladies she'd been in the sodality with at church for years. Now Blanche realized she should have asked her intent.

Sherrie kept her head focused at the windshield but the smirk on her face showed Blanche she knew Blanche was not happy about this turn of events. The angrier Blanche seemed as she drove away, the happier Sherrie seemed to get.

Arriving in New Orleans, Blanche drove into the French Quarter to the building where the condo was. As she swiped her access card to enter the parking lot, her mother spoke in an angry tone, "Where is this? This isn't Colin's place."

"It's Adam's place, mother. I want you to see your new bedroom. Then we'll drive over to Colin's."

"I don't care to see that black bastard!"

"Adam's not home. He's at the airport picking up relatives. You won't see him until we go to the rehearsal tonight."

"Sherrie, quit being stubborn and get out the car! Even if you don't want to see the place, I do." Barbara opened the door and stepped out yelling at her sister, "You know you always say how high crime is in New Orleans. You sit in this car by yourself, and someone might come along and mug you. Worse than that... Seeing white meat all alone, one of those young black bucks might rape you. They say older women are easy prey."

 As her aunt stood, Blanche stared at her across the hood of the car shocked that she made such untrue, stereotypical accusations. Her mother quickly opened the car door and came to join them. Behind her mother's back, Barbara winked at Blanche. First Colin had shared with Blanche the story about his mother keeping in touch with Nora all these years. Now she had observed firsthand how her aunt used her mother's own perverted perception of reality against her to manipulate her into seeing the condo. Blanche smiled back realizing she had been severely underestimating who was really the one controlling the relationship between the two sisters.

As Blanche opened the front door of the condo and the security guard spotted the two elderly ladies with her, one rushed to hold the door and offer his arm for her mother and aunt to come up the short steps. Blanche introduced her mother and aunt to the guard, and he continued to hold Sherrie's arm until they entered the elevator. Her mother was obviously pleased by the attention. As Blanche opened the door of the new condo, the smell of fresh paint and new furniture filled the air. Blanche first showed them the baby's room.

"Neither Adam nor I want to know the baby's sex. We rather be surprised so I picked out a Noah's ark theme for the baby's room. I liked the baby animals, and it'll fit for either a boy or a girl. Adam liked the red accent. He said that baby's see red easier so it increases their IQ faster."

"This is precious," her aunt said as she walked into the nursery eyeing the wallpaper border closer. She opened the closet and checked out the California styled shelving created especially to organize baby items. Blanche's mother stood in the room seeming indifferent to it all. As they left from the nursery, Blanche just mentioned that the next suite was her and Adam's. She walked quickly past the door of the master suite and pointed to the kitchen on the left.

Barbara exclaimed, "My, my, my! This kitchen is fancier than Colin's. Look at all these gadgets. I don't even know what some of these appliances are for."

"Neither do I, Auntie, but being around Colin, Maria, and Autumn, I'm learning fast," Blanche chuckled.

When they entered the dining room, the curtain was closed. Blanche walked over to the wall and pressed the button that drew the curtains slowly open.

"This is my favorite room. I love the view."

"Lordy!" Barbara's tone clearly indicated how impressed she was, "You ever saw anything like this, Sherrie?"

Her mother looked at the view through the wall of glass but still made no comment. Blanche pushed the button to close the curtains back and led the way down the other hallway. Not stopping in each room, she called out the study, the third bedroom, pointed to the washing facilities, and then stopped at the fourth bedroom.

"This is the room Adam had prepared for you, mother."

Blanche opened the door and walked across the room, pulling the draperies open, and sliding the door that led to the balcony.

"Sherrie!" Barbara exclaimed, "This room is fit for a queen."

The room had turned out beautiful. The wallpaper Sherrie implied she selected was from the satin and bows collection and covered three of the four walls. Pink tea roses gathered with satiny white ribbons were against panels of a pale blue with pearled satin borders separating the panels. The French Provincial style furniture was white, and the canopied bedposts contrasted against the accent wall painted Wedgewood blue. A border of the same wallpaper style was along the top of the accent wall. The sitting area had both a lounge chair in a pale, powder blue fabric and a white high back rocker with cushions the same print as the wallpaper. The bed coverlet was a white eyelet material. A crystal lamp was positioned on a glass topped table between the two chairs. Stepping onto the balcony, the owner had agreed to leave the wrought iron set. Adam had contracted to add an awning over the balcony so the area would be shaded. It was made of a material advertised to keep the temperature at a cooler setting.

Though her mother stood stoically at a point in the room where she could see everything, even a glimpse of the view from the balcony, Blanche saw her eyes flitting around eyeing every item in the bedroom. Her eyes studied the porcelain statue of the blessed mother in the middle of the dresser as well as the other accent pieces Blanche and Maria had selected to decorate the room. Seeing she was taking it all in, Blanche demonstrated (supposedly for her aunt's benefit) the walk in closet and the bathroom arrangements.

"Sherrie, you can't ask for anything more than you have here."

Blanche closed the sliding doors to the balcony and locked them before leading the way back to the front door announcing, "We need to get moving, or we'll be late for the rehearsal. It's close to rush hour so the traffic across the lake to Colin's will be backing up."

As she locked the front door of the condo, Sherrie finally spoke, "It was stupid to waste that man's money on all those dust catchers. How will you have time to keep up that kind of housework with a baby coming?"

"I don't have to, mother. The condo fee comes with an option for maid service. Adam had it for his other condo, and he insisted on keeping it for this place as well so he's paying the extra costs. The only thing I'd be responsible for is light daily cleaning like doing the dishes, and we have a dishwasher to help with that. The apartment won't be a burden."

Barbara slapped her sister on the arm and whispered, "You old passé blanc. You're even gonna have a maid.... You gonna think you're white for sure now!"

At that, Blanche noticed her mother fighting it, but a wide grin finally crossed her face.

As the elevator opened and an elderly, well-dressed, white gentleman tipped his hat and greeted them with, "Good afternoon, ladies," Sherrie's smile broadened even more.

Chapter Thirty-Eight

Arriving at Colin's, Autumn rushed out to greet them.

"You're just in time. The pastor from the local church just arrived. Adam and his cousin got here about a half hour ago. Everything is ready for the rehearsal."

The ladies followed Autumn into the house and out to the back garden where the yard was beginning to be transformed for the wedding the next day. A tent had been erected on the left side of the yard, and workers were busy setting up tables and chairs beneath it. The gazebo had been installed as Colin promised, and the men were standing by the gazebo discussing their duties with the pastor.

Maria walked up and greeted her mother-in-law and Sherrie.

"I know it's a long ride. Would you like to join me in the kitchen for a glass of iced tea? As soon as the rehearsal is over, we'll be having dinner in the dining room."

Sherrie glanced at Adam who waved in greeting. She turned ignoring the gesture.

"Maria, that would be lovely. Blanche didn't stop anywhere along the highway. She's so inconsiderate, that girl is. I'm dying of thirst."

Seeing Sherrie was avoiding having to acknowledge Adam, Maria led the two ladies to the kitchen where Aubrey was taking hot rolls out of the oven. Once the rehearsal was over, the wedding party gathered in the dining room with the men on one side of the table and the ladies on the other. Adam attempted to include his future mother-in-law in the conversations, but grunts or single word responses were the most he managed to muster from her. His cousin finally leaned over and whispered something in Adam's ear.

Embarrassed by her mother's behavior towards her fiancé, Blanche was certain he was asking Adam if he was sure he wanted to go through with the marriage. She began getting anxious wondering if Adam would change his mind because of her mother and not come the next day. As her expression grew sadder, she felt Adam's toe tickle her ankle under the table. Shocked, she looked up and faced him. When he winked at her, a smile crossed her face, and she blushed. Eyeing the looks between them, Sherrie got up, announced she was tired, and retired to the room at Colin's where she had slept before. After her exit, the atmosphere in the room lightened and even grew more boisterous after Colin refilled the men's drinks. When it was time for Adam and his cousin Kelvin to leave, Adam pulled Blanche into his arms and kissed her passionately.

"I love you. Tomorrow will be the happiest day of my life."

He kissed her one more time before thanking Colin and Maria for hosting the events and exiting with his cousin. Blanche breathed a sigh of relief feeling more confident Adam would return the next day.

Autumn looked at her and assuming correctly the ride from Lafayette had been an ordeal with her mother suggested, "Go on up and get to bed. You and the baby need to rest, and you don't want bags under your eyes tomorrow. Colin hired a photographer so you need to look your best. As soon as I help my mom and Aubrey clean-up the kitchen, I'll be right up."

Giving Autumn a hug, Blanche kissed her on the cheek and slowly ascended the stairway to the attic bedroom.

The next morning, Colin and Maria were busy in the kitchen preparing breakfast for the family. The scent of bacon frying and sausages browning soon had Autumn, Aubrey, Blanche, and Barbara gathering in the breakfast nook. When Maria began placing platters of the bacon, sausage, banana fritters, scrambled eggs, and hot biscuits on the serving table, Blanche glanced up at the kitchen clock and noted the time.

"My mother should be up by now. I'm going to check on her."

As she moved her napkin from her lap and went to stand, Sherrie entered the kitchen holding one hand to her head. Blanche ran to her side.

"Mother, are you okay?"

"I'm not feeling well. I just want a cup of lemon tea, please."

Blanche put her left hand on her mother's left arm and her right arm around her waist before escorting her to the seat next to Blanche's. Having heard Sherrie's request, Maria had already poured hot water from the kettle on the stove over a tea bag. She walked over and placed the cup between Blanche and Sherrie. Blanche dipped the tea bag up and down until it was the strength her mother liked, squeezed fresh lemon juice into the cup and added two packets of artificial sweetener. She handed the cup to her mother.

"Thank you, Blanche."

Everyone was watching Sherrie with concern except for Autumn. Her face indicated, "What game are you playing today?"

As Sherrie took the hot cup of tea from Blanche, her hand began trembling and the tea began spilling onto the table.

"Mother, what's wrong?" Blanche looked into her mother's face and saw her eyes had glazed over.

"Oh, my God! Colin, please call for an ambulance," she called out to her cousin in desperation.

"No!" Autumn said adamantly. She rose and began walking from the room yelling over her shoulder, "Aubrey, get some orange juice in her."

Blanche looked at Autumn in dismay, "We shouldn't give her anything to eat or drink until we get her to an emergency room, and they approve it."

Autumn turned and eyed Blanche with her teeth clenched. "You're not spending your wedding day in an emergency room." Turning to Aubrey, she ordered, "Aubrey, think about Maw Maw! Get the juice. I'll be right back."

Colin was at the phone wall about to dial 911 but hesitated based on the adamant way Autumn had taken charged and referenced Maria's mother. Aubrey nodded, got up, poured a glass of juice, came over to Sherrie, held her head, and slowly started pouring the cool liquid into her mouth. The trembling stopped, and Sherrie was soon fussing at Aubrey to let go of her. By the time Autumn returned, Sherrie seemed herself again.

Blanche choked the words out, "Mother, Aubrey was only trying to help. I'm so worried about you."

"Worried about me? Why?" Sherrie answered in an angry tone.

Blanche began explaining, "Your hand started trembling. Your eyes seemed to just be staring. I think we need to get you to an emergency room and have a doctor check you."

Sherrie looked at Blanche with the saddest expression she could manage and responded, "If you insist, Blanche.... As long as you stay with me.... You know I hate hospitals, and those forms are so confusing. I need you to deal with all of that for me, Blanche."

Blanche was almost in tears as she answered, "Mother, you know I won't leave you."

"She doesn't need to go to an emergency room!" Autumn stated emphatically.

Blanche's voice grew angry, "Autumn, how could you say that? My mother could be dying!" Blanche broke down and tears began flowing.

As Autumn held up a prescription bottle, Colin and Maria glanced at each other, then to Sherrie, and then to Blanche listening to Autumn's words.

"She's not dying. She's diabetic!"

"What?" Blanche rose, walked towards Autumn, took the prescription from her hand and read the label.

"I pick up all my mother's prescriptions. I've never seen one to treat diabetes."

Autumn pointed to the top of the label that indicated it was from the insurance company's mail order supplier. To ensure Blanche knew she was speaking with authority, she told her it was the same company her grandmother used to get her diabetic supplies delivered.

Autumn turned to face Sherrie as she spoke and continued, "I bet the medicine was arriving while you were at school, and she was hiding the prescription before you came home... And, based on the date that prescription was filled and the amount of pills missing, she purposely took an overdose to drop her sugar level. That's why she only ate a salad at the rehearsal dinner last night. It's not that she wasn't hungry, she was being certain her sugar level would drop."

Colin and Maria remained silent, but the look exchanged between them indicated they were confident Autumn had uncovered the truth. Colin moved from the wall phone and stood by the island in the center of the kitchen.

Barbara looked at Sherrie and yelled, "You never told Blanche you were diabetic?"

With an angry expression, Sherrie hissed at her sister, "As I told you before, you always had to explain everything to that stupid girl." Turning to Blanche, she scolded, "Why do you think I told you I have to take my medicine on time? That's what diabetics have to do." Turning to Autumn, she continued, "You red haired little witch, what gave you the right to go through my things?"

Autumn didn't back down, "What gives you the right to try to ruin your daughter's wedding day? You did this on purpose to stop this wedding. If Blanche wants you to go to an emergency room, Aubrey will be happy to take you. But Blanche is getting married today to Doctor A.J. and I'm not going to let you stop it!"

"Autumn," Colin said in a soft but firm voice indicating that was enough.

Having counted the pills, Blanche looked at her mother, "You might have died. Are you that against me marrying Adam that you would risk killing yourself? Mother, what if your sugar level had dropped during the night, you'd be in a coma." She eyed her mother in disbelief that she had taken such a risk.

"She didn't take the pills last night. When she retired to her room, she didn't take anything with her when she left the dinner table, but I found a glass of water on the nightstand in her bedroom. She got up during the night and timed when she would take the pills knowing when they would kick in."

"Autumn," Colin gave his stepdaughter a sterner glance indicating, "Don't say anything more. This is between Blanche and her mother."

"Mother, how could you?" Blanche dropped the prescription onto the center island, ran from the room, and up the stairs to the loft bedroom. Before following her, Autumn called to Aubrey, "Make her eat before she succeeds in ruining this day! She needs carbs. And don't let her take any more pills!"

Nodding in agreement, Aubrey got up, went to the serving table, and began preparing a plate.

Barbara shook her head and looked at her sister disgustedly, "Sherrie, you've done some awful things through the years, but I never thought that even you would do something this scornful. And after seeing what that boy went through to invite you into his home and make you comfortable... How could you, Sherrie? She's marrying a fine man. How could you try to ruin this day for Blanche? I'm ashamed to admit you're my sister."

As Aubrey placed a breakfast plate in front of Sherrie, she angrily stabbed a link of sausage and began chewing it. Colin let out a sigh and sat back at the table to finish his own breakfast. The kitchen area was in deadly silence, but the sound of voices could be heard in the upstairs loft.

An hour later, the Laurent household was buzzing. A truck had backed into the driveway, and the catering staff began unloading linens for the tables, china, silverware, and glasses. The florist had also arrived, and as soon as the linens were laid, the bird of paradise floral arrangements were placed as centerpieces. Blanche watched the buzz of activity from the upstairs window. She admired the garland of white and ivory flowers that was carefully pulled from the florist's van to surround the railings on the gazebo. Instead of excitement, tears continued to roll down her cheeks. Autumn sat by her side offering words of encouragement but nothing seemed to lift the depression Blanche had fallen into. Finally, Autumn went down the stairs and found her stepfather.

"She's still crying. Go upstairs and talk to her."

Colin looked at Maria with an expression that said, "What am I going to do with your daughter?" Maria gave him a glance back indicating, "You knew what you were getting into before you married me."
Colin shook his head. After glancing between mother and daughter, he obeyed the orders his stepdaughter spat at him knowing she was right.

Chapter Thirty-Nine

Reaching the top of the stairs, Colin knocked softly on the door. When no response came, he opened the door and peeked in. Blanche was sitting on the window bench wiping her eyes. He walked over, sat behind her, pulled her into his arms, and kissed her on the top of the head. They sat in silence as she lay back against him, tears flowing once again. He knew she was doubting whether she should go through with the marriage. As he held her, he tried to think of the right words to calm her and convince her she was not making a mistake. When her chest stopped heaving, he spoke softly.

"Princess, growing up, we depend so heavily on our parents. We follow their rules blindly thinking they have our best interest at heart, but there comes a time when we realize that parents aren't perfect. They may have done the best they could do but they're not perfect. Your mother will never change her ways, but her ways are not always the right way. I know it's hard to feel that way about a parent and to see that in them. That doesn't stop you from loving them. You're just seeing things as an adult instead of a child... Blanche, this day isn't about you. It isn't about Adam. It's about the child growing inside of you. You know where your mother went wrong. You know what to do differently to raise your own child. Adam's a good man, and he'll make a great father... Princess, what kind of life do you want for your baby? The same one you had or something better?"

Colin kissed her one more time on the top of her head, then rose from the window bench and left the room. He closed the door softly behind him. When he arrived back in the yard to continue helping Maria project manage the preparations, Autumn stuck her chin out at him, her teeth clenched.

"I did the best I could," he announced before walking to the sound system and going over the music with D.J. they had hired.

Glancing at her watch, Maria looked up at Autumn and announced, "Two hours and counting."

Maria, Autumn, and Aubrey reviewed the seating plan for the luncheon and began placing the name cards on the tables. Round tables had been set up to seat only five people so the folks had plenty of elbow room. A long table faced the round tables. The bridal party would be seated there. Though there was only Autumn acting as the maid of honor and Adam's cousin Kelvin serving as the best man, Colin would escort Blanche to the gazebo and also sign the marriage license since three signatures were required. Then the bridal party would lead the guests to the tent for the buffet and dancing. The bride's family and guests would be seated on the side closest to the house and the groom's family and guest would be seated on the other. Once the meal began, Autumn would plan a toast with sparkling white grape juice (considering Blanche's condition) for the bride and Kelvin would follow with a toast for the groom.

As Autumn laid the last of the mini name cards from her stack on the table, she glanced upwards to the loft bedroom. Whispering softly to no one but herself, she said, "Don't blow this, Blanche. It's time for you to stand up for yourself and your baby. You have to make your own life."

When it was time to dress, Autumn took the bridal bouquet the florist had left. Aubrey carried the bridesmaid's bouquet for her as they ascended the stairway. At the top of the stair, the twins paused, glanced at each other, and took deep breaths before opening the door. Blanche was already dressed in her wedding gown and standing in front of the full length oval mirror. Turning, she nervously spoke, "How do I look?"

The twins smiled at each other before rushing towards her speaking in unison, "You look beautiful. You are the prettiest bride we've ever seen!"

Looking at Autumn, Blanche requested, "Will you do my make-up for me?"

"Gladly," Autumn announced as she and Aubrey exchanged a high five.

The day proved that Barbara did have the upper hand in the relationship between the two sisters. Sherrie was not only dressed on time in the outfit Maria had purchased for her, but she was also smiling when she emerged from her bedroom followed by her sister who stayed closely by her side, a stern look on her face. After Maria pinned corsages on them, Colin escorted them to the front row of chairs in front of the gazebo. Adam approached and greeted the two ladies.

"Congratulations, young man, on winning my daughter," Sherrie said under her sister's watchful eye.

Colin leaned down and whispered in his mother's ear, "Thank you, Mom." He gave her a kiss on the cheek. She looked up and gave her son a wink before he walked back down the center aisle to the den where, as soon as the final guests were seated, he would signal the D.J. to play the traditional music as Autumn first walked to the gazebo and he then followed escorting Blanche.

The last of the guests were finally seated. Colin paced the den impatiently glancing at his watch. Hearing steps, he rushed to the bottom of the stairway and saw Aubrey coming down.

"They're ready," she announced as the doorbell rang. She looked at her stepfather curiously and replied she'd answer the door as he watched Autumn followed by Blanche coming down the stairway. As Blanche stepped below the support beam and saw who Aubrey had admitted into the foyer, she quickened her steps. Handing her bridal bouquet to Aubrey, she opened her arms and the lady rushed to her hugging her tightly.

"Auntie Nora, it's been so long!"

After a bear hug, the elderly lady released her grip and slanted her backwards to see Blanche's face.

"Don't let those eyes fill with tears! You'll mess up that beautiful make-up. I had to give you this before the wedding. I'd be honored if you carried it today. It was your grandmother's. She got it as her First Communion present." Nora dug into her purse and pulled out a blue crystal rosary. As Aubrey held it, she took time winding it around the base of Blanche's bridal bouquet. Once Blanche held the bouquet, you couldn't even detect the rosary was there. Taking it from Aubrey and handing it back to Blanche, she continued, "It ain't nothing fancy, and it's cheap.... But a bride needs to have something old, something new, something borrowed, and something blue. I see you got plenty new things on. This will cover the other three because I do want my mother's rosary back, young lady."

Autumn glanced at Aubrey and grimaced, "We thought of everything but that old tradition."

Nora's eyes welled and her voice was filled with emotion as she said, "I'm going take a seat. We can talk more later at the reception."

As she passed Colin, Nora gave him a kiss on the cheek. "Thank you for inviting me into your home. It takes a lot of stamina for you and your mama to butt heads with my crazy sister-in-law. I appreciate it. And thank you for putting on such a beautiful wedding for my niece. I know my brother would be proud." Nora began wiping her eyes.

"I'll show you to a seat," Aubrey offered.

"Thank you, sweetheart."

As she and Nora walked across the den towards the patio doors, she called over her shoulder to her stepfather, "I'll tell the D.J. to change the music."

Colin looked at Blanche, "Are you ready, princess?"

"She's ready," Autumn answered on Blanche's behalf and led the way through the patio doors.

When the pastor finally pronounced Adam and Blanche as husband and wife, Colin's left hand released the grip that had Maria's right nearly aching. Maria patted the back of her husband's hand and watched as he exhaled a slow, deep breath. She smiled wondering if he had been holding his breath though the entire ceremony. As the bride and groom led the way down the center aisle followed first by their maid of honor and best man, then to be followed by their immediate families and friends, Sherrie spotted Nora sitting in the last row on the bride's side.

"Who invited her?" she sneered at her sister.

Barbara jabbed her in the ribs with her elbow, "Remember our discussion and smile!"

Sherrie plastered a fake smile back on her face as she followed the bridal party to the tent where the reception would be held.

Chapter Forty

After every guest had been served, Autumn walked over to a microphone that had been set up by the head table to deliver her toast to the couple. With her back to the house, she was the only one that didn't stare at the tall, slim, elegantly dressed white lady with platinum blond hair and striking blue eyes being escorted towards the tent. The waiter pointed out to the lady the last empty chair at the front round table on Adam's side of the tent. She whispered something to him and he ran back towards the house, brought another chair over, and set it at the edge of the tent on Blanche's side. Barbara signaled the waiter to put the chair at their table, and she began moving her own chair over to accommodate another place. The waiter quickly responded, and the lady approached their table.

She whispered, "You don't mind if I join you?"

"No indeed, cher. We'd be happy for you to join us," Barbara patted the seat of the empty chair that had been set next to her.

Leaning towards Barbara, the lady continued whispering, "I should be sitting over there on the groom's side, but I don't want to disrupt the toasting. I'm already embarrassed my connection was delayed in Atlanta, and I missed the ceremony. I don't want to embarrass myself further so thank you for allowing me to join your circle."

"Nonsense," Barbara assured her and signaled for the waiter to come over. She had him bring the lady a plate of food and a champagne glass filled with the sparkling white grape juice. They sat quietly as Autumn finished her toast and Kelvin went to the microphone to deliver his. Though the guests stayed focus on the speeches, eyes still wandered for a glance at the lady wondering who she was.

As Kelvin completed his toast, Colin approached the microphone, thanked the guests for being present, and announced the couple would be cutting their wedding cake shortly in the dining room. He pointed out the dance floor that had been set-up between the tent and the gazebo, and added that the buffet line had been replenished. He also announced that the waiters would be coming around to take drink orders. Colin signaled the D.J., and the music changed from instrumental to popular dance classics.

Adam stood and walked towards the front, round table on Blanche's side as several pairs of eyes followed him. As he approached, the lady stood and opened her arms welcoming him.

Adam greeted the lady enthusiastically, "Aunt Elaine, I'm so glad you made it."

They hugged warmly and exchanged kisses.

"I warned you not to wait for me at the airport. My connection was delayed over two hours. You would have missed your own wedding. Thank you for arranging a car for me." Glancing back to Barbara, she continued, "This if my first trip to the New Orleans area. I do have a driver's license, but I have no sense of direction. In New York, we take cabs everywhere. If I had to follow a map or attempt to use one of those newfangled GPS things, I probably would have missed the reception as well."

Adam broke in, "I see you've already met my mother-in-law and Blanche's Aunt Barbara. Come! Let me introduce you to my wife."

Adam took his aunt's hand and led her to the head table.

Turning to her sister, Barbara said, "You can close your mouth now, Sherrie." Then turning to their pokeno partners, she continued, "Didn't I tell ya'll that boy looked like a mulatto? Now we know... His maw was white."

Finally composing herself at the news and seeing Elaine hug Blanche, Sherrie lifted her head proudly and turned to the table where her neighbors Ethel and Tony were sitting announcing, "That's Blanche's husband's aunt. Poor thing... Her plane got delayed so she's just arriving from New York City."

As she turned back to stab one of the hot fried oysters the waiters were delivering to the tables, Barbara looked at her sister and shook her head. "Some things never change," she stated and started laughing at her sister now bragging about Blanche's husband.

As the reception drew to a close and the last of the guests left, the immediate family gathered into the dining room while the catering staff dismantled the tent and dance floor and began packing the china and loading the rented tables and chairs into moving vans. Elaine turned to Adam and asked if there was a private place they could talk. Colin showed them to his office and rejoined the family as Nora and his mother were laughing about one of their high school escapades to Sherrie's growing displeasure.

Glancing at the clock, Colin looked at Blanche and said, "If they talk too long, you'll miss your flight."

"Colin," Maria admonished, and Blanche saw her cousin grimace.

"Well, we may as well tell her now," Autumn stated as she stuck her chin out at her stepfather. "Adam's taking you to New York for your honeymoon. He wants to show you where he grew up."

"Honeymoon? It's a little late for that," Sherrie spoke loud enough for all to hear, "I thought we were spending the week here in New Orleans and having Thanksgiving dinner together."

Barbara jabbed her in the side to shut her up and leaned towards her before speaking, "I said you and I needed to pack for the week. You and I are spending Thanksgiving by my son's. I didn't say anything about Blanche. She's going to New York." Turning to face Kelvin, she continued, "If you don't have other plans, you and Adam's aunt should join us for Thanksgiving Day dinner. You're all family now so you're more than welcome."

As Kelvin thanked her, Blanche looked at Autumn growing apprehensive, "I didn't pack for a trip to New York. I only brought a weekend bag. We're leaving tonight?"

Standing, Autumn walked to the hall closet, opened the door, and rolled her own large suitcase out.

"You're using my luggage. Me, my mom, and my sister have it already packed for you."

Confused Blanche glanced from Autumn to Aubrey and then to Maria, "Packed with what?"

Maria laughed at that point, and as Blanche turned to face her, she explained, "Your cousin here felt you needed a trousseau, and I agreed. You're at the stage you need to start wearing maternity clothes. Things are looking tight on you so he bought you a new wardrobe. Everything you need is in Autumn's suitcases. You only have to change out your wedding dress, move your toiletries over, and you're ready to go."

"And I'd advise you to do that now. The two of you need to head to the airport. You have to check your cases at least an hour before the plane takes off," Colin spoke adamantly.

Autumn grabbed Blanche's hand and pulled her towards the stair, "I'll pack your toiletries while you change. You're going to have a blast in New York!"

As Sherrie sat seething at the table, Barbara jabbed her sister again, "I said, 'SMILE'!"

Colin tapped Maria's shoe under the table, and the two of them grinned, fighting to contain their laughter.

As Blanche and Autumn descended the stair, a solemn Adam emerged from the study accompanied by his aunt. Excited over Blanche's first plane ride, Autumn didn't notice the changed expression on the groom's face and announced excitedly, "She's all packed." Glancing at the clock, Adam retreated to the guest bedroom where the men had changed and slipped into more casual clothes. Returning to the foyer, he kissed his Aunt Elaine one more time and said, "We'll be back Saturday around 4:00 so we'll have a day for you and Blanche to get to know each other better before she has to drive home. I bought a new condo but kept the old for now, and the master suite is ready for you. Kelvin isn't leaving until we return so he'll drive you anywhere you need to go... I love you, Aunt Elaine."

"I love you.... Have a wonderful time, and Adam, remember what I said. You're entitled to this! Handle it while you're in New York.... I'll see you Saturday."

Adam's face turned solemn again as he turned to leave.

As Colin helped load Blanche's case in Adam's car, Kelvin approached Elaine, "You must be tired after flying all morning. Ready to head back across the lake? Adam's place is a good forty five minute drive from here."

"Thank you, Kelvin. It's so nice of you to look after me until my nephew returns."

"More than look after you. Adam has already planned every minute of your day while he's gone and charged me with being your tour guide. We start in the morning with beignets and café au lait for breakfast. I'll share the schedule with you then."

"He inherited that from his mother... My sister was always the most organized of the three siblings."

As they bid the other relatives good night, Kelvin turned to Nora and asked if she needed a ride anywhere. When Barbara announced Nora was also spending the week and sharing her room, Sherrie rose from the table in a huff and retired for the night.

Nora whispered, "You sure about this?"

"My sister never did run my life, and I'm hoping it's now at a point she's not running our niece's anymore. Nora, it's past time for that child to be happy."

"I agree, but you know Sherrie... I hope that boy has patience. She's sure gonna work on his last nerve."

That night in bed as Colin pulled his wife into his arms and thanked her for all her efforts to make the day a success, Maria questioned, "Do you think Adam's mix heritage will make a difference to Aunt Sherrie? Do you think she'll finally accept him? I pray he and Blanche can have a happy marriage, but I'm worried she'll put an unnecessary strain on things."

"Sweetheart, you know Creoles. It's not that they want to be white. They just don't want to be treated as inferior to whites. Creoles ruled south Louisiana and were considered a race until this area became Americanized. The census listed a black Creole as mulatto because they were neither black nor white. Remember Canal Street was the neutral ground trying to keep the peace between the Creoles and the Americans coming into the area. Even then, not everything changed down here. We're the only state with parishes instead of counties... It's a proud and unique heritage we have... But there's a lot of Creoles that still oppose interracial marriages as strong as some bigots. We're a culture that tends to stick to ourselves and typically marry only others with Creole ancestry... Heaven knows what's going through Aunt Sherrie's head now... In her mind, it might be a worse situation because she may view herself as competing with Adam's aunt for stature... We've done everything we can to help them get started. All we can do now is pray and try to keep that red headed daughter of yours from declaring civil war on my aunt."

"My mother's been diabetic for years and I didn't make the connection. Autumn's so close to her grandmother. She watches her like a hawk whenever she visits looking for any signs of changes in her health. Still, it was sharp of her to realize what was happening. I was panicking just like Blanche."

"Autumn did save the day, didn't she? I'm proud of her in that regard. I'm proud of everything she's done to get Blanche out from under her mother's claws."

"Me too...." Maria snuggled closer to her husband laying her head on his bare chest and wrapping an arm around his midriff.

"Mrs. Laurent, what do you say we renew our vows?"

In response, Maria placed a kiss on his chest as Colin used a single finger to begin sliding the lacy strap of the gown off her shoulder.

Chapter Forty-One

As Blanche sat in the gate area waiting for the announcement that the plane would start boarding, her excitement grew. It was not only her first airplane ride, but she would be visiting a city as fascinating as New York. As a child she had spent every Thanksgiving morning in front of the television watching the Macy's parade, and this week she would be able to see it in person. It would be so different from the Mardi Gras parade they had in Lafayette each year.

She studied the other passengers in the waiting area: the business crowd reading E-mails on hand held devices or typing on their laptops, families feeding their children snacks trying to keep them content as they waited impatiently to board the plane, avid readers hoping to complete another chapter in a best-selling novel, teens playing on various game devices... She wondered about each person's destination and the reason for their travel that day. She wondered if New York was home for them or if the families were bringing the children to experience the parade, one of the unique American traditions.

When the call was made for the first class passengers to board, Adam announced, "That's us!" He pulled the tickets from his pocket and escorted Blanche to the gate where Blanche saw their names pop up on the screen as the lady scanned their boarding passes. As soon as they were seated, a stewardess appeared and offered them something to drink. Blanche ordered orange juice, and Adam ordered a double scotch on the rocks. When the stewardess delivered the drinks, Adam downed half the glass in one gulp. It was then Blanche noticed he wasn't himself. He did order drinks when they went out but always sipped. Often, one drink would last Adam the entire night. There was an aura of sadness about him, and she was curious if the parting words from his Aunt Elaine had anything to do with his mood.

"Adam, you seem despondent. Is it because of what your aunt wants you to do in New York?"

"We may have to mix a little business with pleasure while we're there."

"I don't mind. She seems so kind. Is there anything I can do to assist? I'd be happy to."

"Well, one thing she did make me realize is I need to add your name to some accounts I have. It's good we're going to New York after all. You can sign the papers in person."

"What type of business does she want you to handle?"

"This. I told her I don't want it…. She's adamant I take it and deposit it immediately," Adam said disgustedly as he handed Blanche an envelope.

"It's not open," Blanche stated after turning the envelope over and examining the logo of a New York legal firm embellished in the upper right corner. She turned to face Adam not sure what he expected her to do with the envelope.

"You're my wife now…. You open it," Adam's voice broke as he spoke, and he took another swallow of the scotch emptying the glass. The stewardess immediately appeared among the passengers still boarding and replaced the empty glass with a full one.

"Adam!" Blanche gasped as she pulled the check out the envelope. "Am I reading this correctly?" She held the check in front of him.

"That's about what I would estimate…. Seems our new condo, its renovation cost, and the new furniture will be paid off, and we'll also have a college fund for our kids…. I won't have to rush to sell the old place now. I can hold out for the best price."

Blanche couldn't believe the nonchalant way Adam was reacting to the seven figure dollar sum in front of her eyes. He took another long swallow of the scotch. It appeared he wasn't happy over the check at all.

"Adam, this is more money than I'd earn in a lifetime as a teacher or a counselor… Are you upset because you don't feel your Aunt Elaine can afford this?"

He took Blanche's right hand in his left and squeezed it tightly.

"That's not from her even though she was instrumental in me getting it... I know I haven't talked about my family much..."

"You haven't talked about them at all, and I definitely hadn't anticipated this," Blanche thought to herself as she counted the zeros in the check amount once again confirming what her eyes were seeing.

"That check is my mother's share of her inheritance from her father's estate. He only had three kids so, based on the little knowledge I have of his business and his home, he should have been worth at least three times that sum."

"This is bringing back sad memories for you? You're missing him?" Blanche spoke softly remembering her paternal grandparents and how special Christmas dinners were because all of the Aubert descendants, no matter how far they had gone, would come home for that one day.

He choked on the words as he began sharing a part of his past with his wife, "Missing him? Quite the contrary! My grandfather disowned my mother when he found out she was dating my father. He cut her off from everything.... My parents didn't care. They got married anyway. They were so in love. If they could have pitched a tent in Central Park, they would have been happy living as hippies.... About three years after my mother died of cancer, I was coming home from high school, and I was missing her terribly. Instead of walking home, I went to the cemetery where she was buried.... As I approached, I noticed an elderly, white gentleman kneeling by her grave as if he was saying a prayer. I stopped where I was and just watched him wondering what he was doing there.... He finally stood, and as he turned, our eyes locked. They stayed locked as he approached me. When he got close, he opened his mouth as if he was going to speak, but the expression on his face suddenly changed as if he had second thoughts.... Instead of speaking, he averted his eyes and walked right pass me. I watched him leave the graveyard and get into a limousine that was waiting for him.... I told my Dad that night what happened. He asked me to describe the man, and when I did, he said, 'You finally met your grandfather.' We never talked about it again, and that's the only time I ever saw the man.... Aunt Elaine said he changed at the end. He was sorry he hadn't made peace with my mother before she died so he updated his will the week before he passed."

Adam took another swallow of scotch before continuing.

"Based on what my aunt said, he didn't reform his prejudicial ways completely. He specified I was not to know the terms of his will. He set it up that I didn't inherit anything unless I first demonstrated I was going to be a success in life on my own. Apparently he felt enough of his taxes were going to support welfare recipients, and he didn't want any more of his hard earned money being wasted that way.... The other stipulation is that I was married. I had to show I was settling down and not going to waste my inheritance living the life of a playboy.... When I called Aunt Elaine, told her I was getting married, and invited her to the wedding, she contacted the family's lawyer and got things in motion.... She's the only one on my mother's side of the family that had any contact with us. At the end, she was great. She'd come over every day and help care for my mother. After my Dad died, she stepped in and gave me a lot of guidance and stayed in touch. She tried her best to look after me despite the pressure from her family to cut all ties."

Blanche squeezed her husband's hand, "He regretted not being a part of your life and was trying to make up for it." Blanche thought about her mother forbidding her to see or have any contact with her father's family after he passed. "Adam, I know it was hard growing up without your mother's relatives in your life, but doesn't it make you feel better he did change at the end?"

Adam glanced at the check one more time.

"When I look at that money, there's only thing I can think of... If we had access to those kinds of funds when my mother was first diagnosed with cancer, she could have received the best medical care no matter where in the world she had to travel to get it... She may have been able to celebrate with us today... All I can see when I look at that check is that it's too late for what's most important in life... life itself."

Blanche's eyes filled with tears as she empathized with her husband's feelings. She began thinking of her father and how proud he would have been to escort her down the aisle on her wedding day. She stuffed the check into her purse. It was a bittersweet day indeed. As the plane lifted off the runway and broke through the clouds, Blanche's spirit lifted slightly. She looked out on the sea of white clouds below them and imagined what heaven must be like for their loved ones. She whispered with her head against the window, "I love you, Daddy. I pray every day you're at peace."

And now, she added Adam's parents to her prayers.

Chapter Forty-Two

As the airplane circled for its final descent into the LaGuardia airport, Blanche could tell Adam was feeling more upbeat.

"I love New Orleans, but it always feels good to come home to Queens." He leaned over and kissed his wife as he looked out the window pointing out landmarks to Blanche.

"Queens?" Blanche turned from the window and inquired, "I thought we were flying into New York City. How far will we be from New York?"

Smiling, Adam began educating his wife on his home town, "If you're not from here, your impression is the one most people have. They associate only the most recognizable landmarks of lower Manhattan with New York City when, actually, the city consists of five boroughs: Manhattan, Queens, the Bronx, Brooklyn, and Staten Island. Some people think Harlem is also a borough, but it's not. It's part of Manhattan and is the geographic area north of Central Park. Even within the boroughs are neighborhoods as populated as most cities. We're going to Woodside, one of the neighborhoods in Queens. LaGuardia is the domestic airport, and it's the closest to where we'll be staying so we'll be there soon.... Kelvin should have everything ready for us at the house."

After retrieving their luggage and stepping out to the area where cabs and limousines were waiting hoping to win a fare, a middle-aged gentleman waved excitedly to Adam. Waving back, Adam led the way to the limo where he was standing. While the luggage was being loaded, he and the gentleman shook hands, and Adam then pulled Blanche next to him.

"Stephan, this is my wife Blanche."

The man responded in a language Blanche had never heard; but when Adam smiled, she followed his lead and smiled as well offering her hand to shake his.

Blanche told him shyly, "Thanks for picking us up."

Adam tipped the man who had assisted with their luggage as Stephan opened the rear passenger door of the limo for Blanche to take a seat. After she sat on the bench type seat in the rear, Stephan slid a drawer open and showed her a variety of drinks and, with a show of his hand, indicated she was to help herself. Blanche took a bottle of raspberry infused spring water and, shortly, Adam was on the seat beside her. Stephan began maneuvering the long vehicle through the pile-up of cars dropping and picking up passengers. It wasn't long before they were sailing down Queens Boulevard and in roughly twenty minutes, Stephan took a left off of Queens Boulevard and then a right into a driveway.

As Stephan and Adam unloaded the luggage, Blanche took notice of the neighborhood. It was unlike anything she had ever imagined New York City would be. Tall trees lined both sides of the street. The buildings were at most four stories high, not the skyscrapers that made up the skyline she associated with New York. Flowers were blooming in the beds in front. She could feel what Adam described. The street where Kelvin lived seemed like home. It was nothing like the hustle and bustle of huge masses along steel, stone, and concrete she'd seen on television.

After Adam opened the front door of the apartment in the building to their left and Stephan helped him get their luggage upstairs to their master suite, they shook hands again. As Stephan tipped his cap towards her, he must have bid Blanche a good night though, once again, it was spoken in the language he had used at the airport. Instead of getting into the limo and driving off, Stephan took out a key and entered the apartment on the second floor of the building to the right of where they were standing. Adam came down the steps to meet Blanche.

"It's already after midnight. Are you ready to retire, Mrs. Brown?"

Blanche blushed at the reference. Looking one more time up and down the street, she commented, "Adam, it seems so peaceful here." Glancing back to where the cars were speeding down Queens Boulevard, she continued, "I wouldn't have believed that being just a half block off a major thoroughfare like that would make such a difference. With the trees lining the street and the homes slightly back from the sidewalk, this feels like a haven. It's so nice of Kelvin to let us stay here while we're in New York."

"The opposite, my love. It's nice of us to let Kelvin live in our place."

Blanche looked at his in a questioning tone.

"Stephan and my father worked for the same limousine line. My father taught school in the daytime and drove cabs and limousines at night to make extra money. When my mother got seriously ill and the medical bills were piling up, Stephan and his wife Adriana told my parents about an efficiency apartment that was about to be available in the building next to theirs." Adam pointed to an iron, security door a few steps below the street level. "We moved in at a ridiculously low price for rent considering New York standards. After my father passed, I stayed… When I received the proceeds from his life insurance, Aunt Elaine helped me invest it with a financial advisor so I could stay in college and only work part time. Since I was young, the guy convinced both of us I could take higher risks and those investments paid off well… At the point the building's owner changed it to a co-op, I bought the right side of the building. So I own the last apartment where I lived with my parents and the upper apartment here. Stephan and Adriana own the entire building where you saw him enter. Their entire Greek family lives in the rest."

Adam began pointing out the various entrance doors. "They have Stephan's cousin's family in the right upper, a daughter that just got married a year ago in the lower right apartment, and Stephan's brother in the lower left. Their youngest daughter and Stephan's mother live in the upper left with Stephan and Adriana, the door where you saw Stephan enter. They have always treated me like family. Adriana would bring us dinner sometimes when my mother's illness began progressing… They looked after me after my father passed."

Adam paused for a moment staring at the window of the basement efficiency in his own building as he reminisced before continuing. Taking Blanche's hand, he began leading her up the steep steps to the entrance door of the upper right apartment.

"When I got the position in New Orleans, I wasn't sure how things would work out and if I'd like living there so I didn't sell this place just in case I had to move back home. Kelvin moved in and, in exchange for rent, he keeps it up for me, makes sure any taxes are paid, and covers the insurance on the building."

"Do you use the basement efficiency at all?"

"At first, I didn't. I kept it like a shrine and would go down and just sit for a while when I wanted to feel close to my parents. One day when I was in the apartment, it was as if they spoke to me. Why waste a place that could help others? So I partnered with the housing director at the university I attended. I rent the place furnished as it was to low income students entering college. It helps kids that may not be able to afford to come to New York and attend school get a start in life. I only charge a minimum amount to help cover their utilities... Ready to see your other home?"

Blanche nodded as Adam opened the lead crystal entrance door and began giving her a tour of the floor plan. The first floor consisted of a living room, dining room, kitchen, half bath, washroom, and a large pantry. There was a second stairway beyond the pantry that led to the second floor. Adam used the back stairway to lead Blanche upstairs. In the rear of the house on the second floor was the bedroom Kelvin used. Adam showed her a bath and the second bedroom as well as a smaller bedroom he and Kelvin used as an office. At the front of the house was the master suite. When they reached the master suite, Adam opened the door before lifting Blanche into his arms. As he carried his new bride across the threshold, their eyes locked... The light switch remained in the off position...

Adam's arm shifted against Blanche's midriff at the sound of the doorbell ringing. He reached across her to the nightstand, picked up the alarm clock, and checked the time.

"I have no idea who that could be," he grumbled as he pushed the covers aside, walked across to an open suitcase, took out and slid a pajama bottom on his nude body, and donned a T-shirt to go and answer the door. Blanche heard an animated conversation, and when the house fell into silence again, Adam's footsteps began ascending the stairway though slower than his norm.

Using his foot, he kicked open the bedroom door and entered carrying a tray, "From Adriana... She wanted to fix breakfast for the bride and groom."

"How lovely!" Blanche exclaimed as Adam laid a bed tray in the empty space where he had been sleeping alongside his wife and removed a towel displaying two plates. One was filled with fritters sprinkled with cinnamon sugar and two mini bowls of warm honey. The other had triangles of Spanakopita. A pot of hot coffee was in one corner of the tray.

Though everything smelled appetizing, Blanche reached across the tray to pick up the vase with a single rose tied with a narrow ribbon. She sniffed in the sweet scent before placing the vase back on the tray.

Adam lifted a fritter ad held it for her to take a bite. Blanche moaned with pleasure, "What are these?"

"They're called Loukoumades. They're typically used as a dessert so this isn't a traditional Greek breakfast. Usually, it's a light meal of coffee or tea and bread or a baked good. Adriana knows how much I love these and her spinach pies so she made all of this just for us."

After eating one of the fritters plain and then trying one dipped in honey, Blanche tasted one of the spinach pies.

"Oh, Adam, it's so flaky. It's like biting into a zillion sheets of crunch, and the spinach makes me feel like I'm eating something healthy for the baby."

"It's made with phyllo dough. I've never tried making anything with it myself, but I love it. When we get into Manhattan, we'll stop at this pastry shop that's one of my favorites so you can sample baklava. It's made with phyllo dough too and is flaky, nutty, and syrupy all at once."

As Blanche ate another of the Loukoumades, a drip of honey fell onto her chin. Reaching over with his finger, Adam lightly wiped the spot from her chin. His touch was so soft and delicate, Blanche took a sharp breath. Watching her reaction, Adam's leaned over and kissed her deeply. Shortly after the breakfast tray was moved to the floor alongside the bed...

Several hours later, Blanche woke to Adam in the bed next to her reading a novel. He leaned and kissed her on the forehead.

"What would you like to do today, my love? All that is firm for today is a play tonight because Kelvin already purchased the tickets for us. Tomorrow, we need to meet with my financial advisor, deposit the check, and get your signature on my accounts. I know you want to see the Macy's parade Thursday. The rest of the time depends on what you'd like to see first."

Adam walked across to the dresser, picked up a folder, returned to the bed and began showing Blanche some of the things he thought she would enjoy doing. Kelvin had printed out an itinerary for them highlighting in bold font the adventures that were firm and in regular font the activities that were optional. Blanche could see the time slots where they had theater tickets. Kelvin had purchased tickets for three plays: Rent, 42nd St., and The Book of Mormon. Two of the plays were at night, and one was a matinee. He also purchased tickets for a comedy club and Blanche noted those tickets were for Tuesday night. Kelvin had listed the address on Broadway. He had listed MOMA, the Museum of Modern Art, as one of the sites Blanche shouldn't miss. He had included the schedule for the ferry that would leave from around Battery Park heading to New Jersey for visitors desiring to see the Statue of Liberty on Liberty Island and the museum on Ellis Island. He had marked off a spot on a map where he thought would be the best location to catch the Thanksgiving Day Parade. Of all the plans made, Adam could tell the thought of seeing the parade excited his bride the most. He commented they would just take the 7 line, the purple line, from Queens into Manhattan and connect to the red line and the spot Kelvin noted was not far from the Lincoln Center stop. Adam told his bride, though it wasn't New Years' Eve, he intended to kiss her every time they crossed Times Square. Blanche blushed in response.

Pointing to one of the theater addresses, she questioned, "Kelvin noted this as an Off Broadway production but he listed the address as on Broadway?"

"Tourists do get confused by the terminology but not all the theaters are on Broadway, and the designations have nothing to do with the theater's physical location. It's associated with the number of seats in the theater. If you go to what's considered a Broadway production, the theater can seat at least five hundred. 'Off Broadway' implies the theater size is at least one hundred seats but less than five hundred. 'Off Off Broadway' productions are in smaller theaters with less than a hundred seats. For example, though Rent started out as a Broadway production, it has had such a long run that it's moved to a smaller theater now."

Blanche nodded she understood. Considering it was nearly late afternoon and they were still recuperating from the wedding and airplane ride the day before, they both opted for a leisurely day. They settled on going to mass at Saint Sebastian's Roman Catholic church and then taking the seven line into Manhattan for an early dinner at one of Adam's favorite restaurants in Central Park before heading into lower Manhattan for the play. After the play, they would stop by the pastry shop for baklava and coffee as a late night snack before heading back to the apartment.

Each time that week when Adam and Blanche left the apartment and walked the short distance to the seven line, Blanche's anticipation grew as she learned the city and experienced all the sites New York had to offer. By the time Saturday morning came and Stephan rang the doorbell to assist with the luggage and drive them back to LaGuardia, Blanche was happy to be going home but also sad as Adam locked the front door of his New York apartment. In such a short time, she had fallen in love with the city. Riding the subways was a little scary to her, and she had clung close to Adam. When they walked the streets of Manhattan shopping and stopping at the various florist stands to select a fresh bouquet for their dining room table, she had felt like a celebrity. She enjoyed eating lunch at a quaint sidewalk café that was one of Adam's favorites in an area he called Chelsea. The café reminded Blanche of a postcard one of the teachers at school had sent her when she took a vacation to Paris, France. It also reminded Blanche of the

French Quarter in New Orleans with its wrought iron railings and overhead awnings. It made her long for the day when she and the baby would join Adam in the new condo on a permanent basis.

There was so much they had done but still so much more to do. She sighed as Adam took her arm to support her going down the steep steps. Hearing her reaction and studying her face, Adam stopped on the steps, put his hand on her chin and turned her face towards his.

"I know this wasn't the fanciest of honeymoons, but did you enjoy your time here?"

"Oh, Adam, it was wonderful."

"Most couples head to the beaches of the Caribbean or places more exotic."

"Why sit on a beach for a week when you can experience the excitement of a city like New York? I couldn't imagine a more splendid way to celebrate the start of our new life together. It meant so much to me to learn more about your childhood and to see some of the places that meant the most to you when you were growing up.... I only sighed because I hate to leave."

"All it costs us is the price of a plane ticket. We can visit as often as you like. This is now your home, too. I like your friend Melanie. After the baby's born and you're discharged, maybe the two of you or you and Autumn could escape for a weekend getaway. Fly up, see a play, do some shopping, whatever you like, my love.... "

Blanche smiled at the thought and also the potential for their future lives together, "I don't want to rush the baby's childhood years, but I can't wait until he or she's old enough to experience their first Thanksgiving Day Parade." She leaned her head on her husband's shoulder as they continued down the remainder of the steps to the waiting limo.

As Stephan held the door open for her, he looked at Adam, "Did you want to stop?"

This time Adam sighed before answering, "Yes..."

As Stephan pulled away from the curb, to Blanche's surprise, he turned in the opposite direction from LaGuardia when he reached the corner. After driving a short distance, they pulled in front of a cemetery, and Adam squeezed her hand tightly. She understood why he had responded to Stephan that way. They were stopping to pay respect to his parents before heading back to New Orleans. Blanche wrapped her arm around her husband's and patted it lightly trying to offer him support as they said a short prayer together at the gravesite.

As the plane lowered its altitude over Lake Pontchartrain and circled towards the spillway for an eastern runway approach, a knot in Blanche's stomach made her flinch. Adam put his hand on her arm, and the concern in his voice scared Blanche as well, "Is the baby alright?"

Blanche paused before answering, unsure herself at first what had caused her reaction. Realizing it was the thought of facing her mother and returning to Lafayette, her eyes filled with tears. "Only six more months," she thought. She patted Adam's hands and looked out the window so he couldn't see how depressed she was growing at the idea of having to leave him. She whispered quietly, "The baby is fine." She kept her other thought to herself, "Mommy is not."

Chapter Forty-Three

Arriving at the condo in the French Quarter did nothing to lift Blanche's spirits. After the wedding and a week in New York, it was hard to go back to her old life. So much had changed since her summer in New Orleans. As Adam pulled into the parking lot and she heard the sign of the calliope, she thought about what Colin had said the morning of her wedding, "What kind of life do you want for your baby? The same one you had or something better?" Her spirits lifted a little knowing she had made the right choice by marrying Adam. Other than her eighth grade field trip to Baton Rouge and their previous trip to New Orleans when Colin had married Maria, Blanche had not been anywhere else outside of Lafayette. Adam was so cosmopolitan. She thought about the future her child would have under Adam's tutelage. She thought about the new condo. She thought about her loving husband. She thought about weekend trips to New York with Melanie, Autumn, or Adam. Knowing the key was to focus on the wonderful things in her life rather than the past, Blanche was smiling by the time Adam walked to the passenger side of the car to open the door for her.

When they reached the floor of the new condo, Adam brought the suitcases into their master bedroom and dialed the number of his old place. Kelvin answered and told Adam that, knowing they would be tired from their trip, he and Elaine were preparing dinner. Adam and Blanche should come down about eight that night to join them. He had also spoken to Colin. Instead of Blanche having to cross the lake and pick up her mother and two aunts, Colin would drive them over the next day after breakfast. Hanging up the line, Adam filled Blanche in on the weekend plans. In response, she walked over, placed her arms around her husband's waist, and hugged him tightly. Adam put his arms around her, leaned down, and kissed her softly on the cheek.

"I'm going to miss you. The week seems so long now. On Fridays, I'm watching the clock at work impatient for the day to end so I can come to New Orleans."

"Blanche, we need to talk about that." Adam pulled slightly away from her and led her to the two chairs in the sitting area of their master suite. As Blanche sat down, he knelt before her as he continued. "As soon as school closes for the Christmas holidays, I want you to spend all the time you're off here. Is that okay with you?"

Blanche nodded enthusiastically.

"And after, I don't want you driving on that highway every weekend anymore. Even if the doctor says it's not a problem, I'm worried about you and the baby making a round trip like that so often. I'm especially worried about something going wrong. I'd hate to have you stranded on that stretch over the Atchafalaya. I will start coming there instead."

Adam spoke the last words firmly indicating he expected no argument regarding his decision. Blanche lowered her head thinking of the last time Adam visited and her mother's reaction and words. She would have to ask her mother if it was alright for Adam to spend the weekend. After all, it was her mother's house. She wondered how receptive she would be.

"I can tell something is on your mind. Are you feeling I won't be welcome even though we're married now?"

She nodded indicating Adam had guessed her thoughts correctly.

"What about us staying by Colin's mother or your Aunt Nora's for the weekends? If that isn't feasible, maybe I can do a short term, six month lease and get an apartment in Lafayette until May. When you get back home, check out apartment complexes, and I'll also do some research on the internet. Ok?"

Blanche nodded in response. She hadn't thought about other options for Adam coming to Lafayette but felt all of the ones he outlined were doable.

That night, as the four of them ate dinner together in Adam's old condo, Kelvin entertained both Blanche and Elaine with stories of Adam as a child. Elaine shared stories about Adam's mother when they were growing up. The only thing that upset Blanche was the realization that during their time together she had been focused on her own situation and the baby. Listening to the stories, she knew she had been selfish in a way. She reached across the table, placed her hand on top of Adam's, and squeezed it gently. Her husband deserved equal time, and from that moment on, she vowed in her heart not to continue neglecting him.

The next morning, the four of them walked to one of New Orleans' oldest and well known restaurants for brunch. The four of them gathered afterwards in Adam's new condo to review the proofs from their wedding day that the photographer had dropped off while they were in New York. When the doorbell rang indicating Colin had arrived with her mother and two aunts, Blanche felt nauseated. Adam noticed her reaction and made a mental note to take time off from work and be in Lafayette for her next appointment. He wanted to discuss with her doctor how her home situation could be affecting the pregnancy. Barbara and Nora entered the condo chatting away.

"Where's my mother and Colin?" Blanche asked.

Nora and Barbara exchanged glances, each changing their animated smiles into frowns. Nora was the one that responded, "She's adamant she's going to wait out in the parking lot for you so Colin is sitting with her. Barbara insisted I come up and see your new place... Do you mind?"

"No, Aunt Nora. Of course not! Let me show you around. Then I'll grab my bag, and we'll head home."

Blanche glanced at Adam, her expression solemn. His expression changed as well knowing Sherrie's actions were the first sign he was still not welcome in his mother-in-law's home. As Barbara sat down to look at the wedding pictures with Elaine and Kelvin, Adam volunteered to take Nora on a tour of the condo while Blanche packed the few things she had taken out the suitcase for last night. When they reached a room where he knew the others could not hear them, he approached her on the possibility of spending weekends at her place. Nora's eyes filled with tears.

"Cher, I'd love to have the two of you over. I've missed that child so much; the two of you can move in if you like. We have too many years to make up. Since all my kids are grown and gone and my husband and I split up, I'm staying in my parents' home right now. It's one of those old farm houses with three bedrooms and the high ceilings. I'm there by myself so I have two empty bedrooms most days. You two lay claim to the one you like best, and it's yours for as long as you want it.... Blanche remembers where her grandparents lived because we had Christmas dinner there every year. I'll get keys made for both of you."

"Thank you, Aunt Nora."

"I'll see you Friday then?"

"Yes," Adam said. He sighed with relief. His mind would be more at ease knowing that he, rather than his pregnant wife, would be making those six hour round trips every weekend.

As they reached the bedroom that would be a guest room for now, Adam made Nora promise that she would be coming to spend Christmas with them and that bedroom would be hers.

After they rejoined the others in the living room, Barbara brought the album with the proofs over to Blanche, "You need to pack this as well. The folks at your school will want to see your pictures. Everything turned out beautiful. You need to show these off."

Blanche smiled and tucked the album into her suitcase. As they bid Kelvin and Elaine adieu, Adam took the luggage down for his wife. Seeing them enter the parking lot, Colin got out his car and began transferring the luggage for his mother, his Aunt Sherrie, and Blanche's Aunt Nora into Blanche's trunk. Barbara and Nora got into the back seat of Blanche's car continuing their animated conversation. After squeezing the last of the luggage in, Colin returned to his vehicle and opened the door for his aunt. Sherrie sat there seething. She didn't move until Colin put his hand out to assist and reminded her it was dangerous for them to be on the highway too late. Knowing she had no other choice, she finally took his hand, exited the car, walked the short distance to Blanche's, and got in on the front passenger side. Blanche hugged Colin once again thanking him for everything he had done and then got embarrassed as Adam kissed her passionately not caring who was watching. Waving as they pulled out the parking lot, an eerie silence fell among the four ladies.

It wasn't long before Barbara broke the stillness. She tried to tell a story from their past that would have all of them laughing and all of them did except for Sherrie. She maintained her stance the entire ride from New Orleans to Lafayette.

Blanche first dropped her Aunt Nora home. Under the pretense of needing assistance with her luggage, Nora got Blanche to get out the car and come around to help her extract her case.

"I'll see you Friday afternoon."

Looking at her questioningly, Nora whispered, "Adam is coming here for the weekend. Call him and give him the directions and address to your grandparents' house. Y'all be spending the weekends here for as long as you need to."

"Thank you, Auntie Nora," Blanche smiled and sighed with relief as she hugged her aunt in gratitude.

As soon as she got back in the car and pulled away from the curb, all the frustration her mother had been holding in since her botched attempt at stopping the wedding was released. Turning to her sister in the back seat, her tirade began.

"How dare you invite that woman to the wedding? You had no right!"

Barbara didn't back down. "The only person who can tell me who to invite or not invite to my son's house is my son! You're the one that had no right to act the way you did, Sherrie!"

The arguments continued until Blanche pulled up in front of Colin's mother's house and popped the trunk. Seeing Blanche about to retrieve her luggage, Barbara stepped out the car quickly pointing her finger at Sherrie and shouting warnings to her until she slammed the car door shut. As she approached Blanche, she admonished her as well.

"Don't you be doing any heavy lifting from now on! The baby is getting too far along now. " Her voice softened as she continued, "You had a beautiful wedding, and you married a wonderful man. Be happy." Then, speaking louder so she knew Sherrie could hear, "And have as many babies as he's willing to give you and he can take care of."

Thinking of the check they deposited with Adam's financial advisor in New York, Blanche thought, "I don't know about having as many as he can take care of. Even the new condo doesn't have that many bedrooms."

Blanche kissed her aunt and whispered, "Thank you for coming and especially for all you did for Auntie Nora."

"Though Nora and I were best friends in high school, I was never allowed to bring her home. I would have been welcome at Nora's house, but I wasn't allowed to step a foot in there either.... You know, Blanche, I've been stuck in that old mode of my childhood and never thought about the fact that I have my own house now, and I can do whatever I want here."

Speaking louder so she knew her sister would hear, "And you remember that when you move to New Orleans. That place is yours, not your mother's. If she does agree to move in, she does as you say. She has no rights to set any rules for you, Adam, or your children!"

Her voice softened to a whisper as she continued, "Nora hinted to me that you and Adam may be staying with her on weekends. Why don't the three of you come over for Sunday dinner at noon? I'd love to have you all. And, Blanche, you and Adam are welcome to stay by me as well anytime you need to."

"Thank you, Auntie. We'll be there on Sunday."

She hugged her tightly before going around and taking her place in the driver's seat. As they pulled away from the curb, Barbara could hear her sister turning her anger on Blanche.

Before leaning down to pick up her suitcase and walk the short distance to her front door, Barbara spoke aloud, "Careful, Sherrie, or you'll lose that girl forever and she's all you have...."

Before she left from school Friday afternoon, Blanche called Adam and gave him the directions to her Aunt Nora's. Realizing she had forgot the album with the proofs at home and needed to give it to Adam to return her selections to the photographer, she swung back home, parked on the curb, and ran up the steps to enter the house. As she opened the front door, she heard the sound of voices. Blanche caught the door so it wouldn't slam shut announcing her arrival. As she tiptoed to the back of the house, she stopped at a point where she was close enough to listen and recognized her mother's voice and Miss Ethel's. Peeking through the side window, Blanche saw them sitting on the patio chairs in the shade. Thinking Blanche was on her way to New Orleans, her mother had gone to her room and taken the photo album.

"Sherrie, these pictures are beautiful. I had never been to a wedding like that before. It was like something you'd see on television watching the stories. And the food! What they didn't have, they don't make. Everything anyone could want was there being prepared right before your eyes and being served hot. And that wedding cake! When Blanche and her husband cut through the layers and I saw all those fresh strawberries, blueberries, and blackberries in the middle, I couldn't wait for a slice. That icing was like a thick whipped cream. I never had a cake so delicious."

"Ethel, these pictures in the back is where Blanche will be living in New Orleans. I heard her husband tell his cousin the photographer was going to stop by while they were in New York and snap pictures for insurance purposes."

"Sherrie, this room looks like it's a wall of glass?"

"It is. You can look out that wall and see the Mississippi River."

"Oh, Sherrie, this room is fit for a queen."

"That's my room!"

"Your room?"

"Yes, Blanche and the boy keep begging me to move in with them. He had that room 'specially decorated with everything they thought I would like."

"Sherrie, I'll miss you, but I'll be picturing you enjoying this beautiful place."

"Though they keep begging me, I haven't made up my mind yet. I'll just wait and see. You know me, Ethel. I always was an independent person, but you know Blanche doesn't know anything about babies. That's probably why the poor boy is desperate for me to come there. He wants someone with experience around to help when they have children."

"Sherrie, this room is prettier than anything I've ever seen in magazines."

"You see they have four bedrooms. If I do move there, you need to come spend a weekend and see the place."

"I don't want to put Blanche through any trouble."

"It won't be. They have a maid service."

"Maid service? She's done far better than Tony could have ever done for her. With the child support he's paying, Blanche would have been helping him more than he would have been helping her."

Blanche took a deep breath in and held it in. So, he was after the little salary she was making at the small, Catholic school. Tony was still the user he always had been. She tiptoed back to the front door, opened the screen, and let it slam shut.

"Who's there?" her mother called out.

"It's just me, mother. I forgot the wedding album, and we need to get those proofs back to the photographer."

Her mother quickly entered the house carrying the album. "I was just glancing through it." She handed the album to Blanche.

"Thank you, mother. I'll see you Sunday night." As Blanche turned to exit through the front door, she thought, "Glancing through it, my foot! Bragging to Miss Ethel is more like it."

Chapter Forty-Four

As Blanche pulled in front of her grandparents' house, her heart saddened. She got out the car, leaned against the front passenger fender, and just stared at the white frame structure before her. She looked at the side yard and reminisced about the family gatherings that had been held there. How many years had she missed? After the baby was born, she would approach Aunt Nora about planning a family reunion. She wanted the chance to reunite with her relatives on her father's side. Hearing the creaking of the front door, she spotted Aunt Nora waving to her excitedly. Blanche hurried to meet her. They hugged each other before Aunt Nora led her inside. Entering the living room, everything was the same as Blanche remembered it. She recalled the aroma of her grandmother's almond pound cake baking in the oven and the smell of chicken frying in the huge iron pot on the stove. She tried to focus on what Aunt Nora was saying as she followed her through the house.

"I made up both the boys' room and the girls' room for ya' so just pick the one that you rather."

"I think I rather have the girls' room if that's okay with you, Auntie Nora."

"So be it. Let me help you with your things."

"No," Blanche put her hand on her aunt's arm to stop her from going back outside. "Adam will be here soon. He can take the bags in. Let's you and I have this time alone together."

Nora smiled and led the way to the old country kitchen where she had a pitcher of lemonade in the center of the table and a plate of cinnamon tea cakes. Blanche's face broke into a wide smile at the thought of enjoying these childhood treats again. She and Aunt Nora sat at the table talking about the years since they had last seen each other. When she heard the sound of Adam's car horn announcing his arrival, Blanche grabbed a tea cake and went out to greet him. As he approached the gate, she took her arms from around her back where she'd been hiding the tea cake and held it to his mouth ordering, "Taste!"

Adam obediently took a bite. His mouth savored the buttery flavor and the hint of cinnamon. Taking the rest of it from Blanche's hand, he asked, "What are these?"

"My grandmother's recipe for tea cakes…. Auntie Nora still had the recipe and made us a batch. She has lemonade for us too."

Blanche took his hand and pulled Adam down the short walk towards the house. She was almost skipping as they reached the steps. She had this childlike look of joy about her. She seemed at peace. Though he could have well afforded them staying in a hotel on weekends or leasing a temporary apartment there in Lafayette, he knew he had made the right decision approaching Nora. Blanche was the happiest he had seen her since they met.

The last day of school before the Christmas holiday, Melanie stopped by Blanche's office. As she entered, she reached into a bag she was carrying and pulled out a present for Blanche and placed it before her on her desk. Blanche looked up, gave her friend a smile, then reached into her bottom desk drawer and pulled out the gift she had brought for Melanie. They both laughed as Melanie took a seat and the two friends started opening the gifts they had promised not to buy.

"Oh, Blanche, thank you," Melanie fingered the silhouette of two young ladies sitting on a bench in a school yard seemingly sharing secrets. "It's the perfect gift and a beautiful symbol of our friendship. I can't wait to get my bracelet to a jeweler and have it added." She stood, walked over, and gave Blanche a hug.

After Blanche pushed aside the last of the tissue inside the gift box, she pulled out her gift. It was a Christmas ornament decorated with the saying, Our first Christmas together. Blanche's and Adam's names had been added to the ornament as well as the date.

"Melanie, this is perfect. It gives me a great idea as well. Adam and I were discussing last weekend how to decorate for Christmas. I'd love to start a family history and family event tree. Every time something significant happens, we could purchase an ornament to represent that event so each year we'd be adding to our collection. Can you imagine the amount of ornaments we may have by the time we pass it on to our children. I'm going to call Adam's cousin Kelvin and ask him to pick up an ornament in New York for me, one that would be symbolic of our honeymoon with the year on it. That would be so meaningful instead of just purchasing a box of ornaments from a store… Oh, Melanie, thank you so much! This is even more precious because it's the first piece for our collection."

Melanie moved her mouth into an odd stance, "I didn't know it was all that when I bought it…. If the store knew, I wouldn't have got it at half price."

The two friends laughed, hugged, and wished each other well in the New Year. Blanche put the last of her paperwork away, turned out the lights, and glanced around her office one more time. Her first office… And soon, she would be walking out for the last time…She regretted giving up her career a little but knew she could always go back to teaching or counseling once the baby was older. She closed the door and turned the lock. She had to learn to let go of the past, but she knew it would always be a part of her.

Arriving home, Blanche spotted her mother sitting on the front porch. She pulled under the carport and walked around the front of the house to greet her.

"Are you all packed, mother? We need to leave for New Orleans now."

"I'm not going. I'll be perfectly happy spending Christmas right here by myself."

Blanche sat in the chair next to her mother. "Then I'm not going either. Mother, we've never been apart for Christmas. Christmas is a time for family. I can't leave you alone."

"Stupid girl, Sister is waiting for you to drive her to New Orleans. If you don't go, Colin will have to make a six hour drive just to pick up his mother…. How selfish of you? Even worse, he might send that little red haired witch stepdaughter of his out here!"

"Then he'll have to. Neither Colin nor Autumn will mind coming to pick up Auntie. They'll understand I can't leave you alone at Christmas."

Sherrie got up abruptly slamming the rocker against the wall of the porch, "Since you're forcing my hand, I have to go. Get up, simpleton. Come help me pack!"

Smiling, Blanche followed her mother into the house and obeyed her orders as her mother sat on the bed yelling at Blanche what clothes to take from the closet, how to fold them, and where to put them in the suitcase. Of course, Blanche wasn't doing anything right. She pulled her red sweater out the closet, and her mother had specifically said the burgundy one. Blanche tried to control her grin as she refolded her mother's night gown for the third time. An hour later, they were finally heading to Aunt Barbara's to pick her up. When she pulled in front of Aunt Nora's, Sherrie turned to Blanche and her face reddened, "She's coming?"

"Yes, mother. Adam invited her to spend Christmas with us as well."

"I won't be in the same place with that woman."

"You don't have to. You will have your private room at Adam's. Auntie Nora will be staying at Colin's with Auntie Barbara."

Satisfied that Nora would not be in the guest room at Adam's, her mother settled down somewhat but still was abnormally silent as they drove to New Orleans.

Christmas morning, Blanche got up early and put an eplepai, a Norwegian apple pie recipe she had found at the library over the summer, into the oven. When it was ready, she cut a warm slice, topped it with whipped cream, poured a cup of café au lait, and brought the tray to her mother's bedroom. Sherrie was already sitting in the lounge chair by the sliding patio doors with the draperies drawn open watching the tourist walking in the French Quarter below. Her mother appeared to have adjusted to her new surroundings quite easily.

"Do you want anything else, mother? Colin and them should be here about noon. We'll have Christmas dinner then and open gifts after."

"You know I'm diabetic. Hand me my pills!"

Blanche did so gladly after hearing only the one complaint that morning. Shortly, Adam joined her in the kitchen, and she fed her husband bites of the eplepai as they worked together side by side preparing the Christmas dinner. As each dish was completed, Blanche would bring a sample to her mother in her bedroom for approval. "You need to add a little more cayenne in that, Blanche... You put too much thyme in the crabmeat dressing, but it's too late now; you can't take it out... That is too rich. Add a little more rice to it." Sherrie enjoyed being served in her elegant bedroom, and seemed to be quite at home giving Blanche orders still. Blanche didn't mind the type of orders she gave because her mother was an excellent Creole cook, and she had taught Blanche well. When it was getting close to noon, Adam added two extensions to the dining room table so Blanche could begin setting the table while he finished things up in the kitchen. The new condo was equipped with two ovens. Blanche had thought it an unnecessary extravagance until Adam took the roast from one and the turkey out the other. He tented both with aluminum foil until they were ready to transfer to a serving platter and be carved. By 11:45, the husband and wife team had everything ready for their first dinner party in their new home.

Though Sherrie stayed silent throughout their Christmas meal, Blanche was grateful she did leave her room voluntarily and join the rest of the family. Blanche purposely put the name plates so that her mother and her Aunt Nora were as far apart as possible. She kept Autumn on the opposite side of the table as well. Once everyone had their fill and the dishes were removed to the kitchen, Adam played Santa reading the names on the holiday gift labels and then placing it on the table in front of the appropriate family member. As each opened their gifts and seemed truly pleased, Blanche noticed her mother was making comparisons and sat back in her chair smugly feeling not only had she received the most gifts but that hers were also the most expensive. Throughout the meal and the gift exchange, Adam had set the sound system's radio to a channel that played only Christmas music the entire season. At times different family members would join in singing their favorite songs.

After all the gifts were open, Adam and Blanche warmed eggnog, and the family gathered into the living room to watch the one of classic holiday films. As different ones began nodding off during the movie, Colin announced it was time to make the trek back across the lake. Adam quickly offered his old condo and the guest room. Glancing at Maria, she nodded in agreement. Autumn and Aubrey would take the guest room there with Adam and Blanche. Colin, Maria, and the two aunts would use the old condo. As he turned over the access card for the old condo, Adam told Maria where he kept spare toiletry items such as tooth brushes. Colin insisted beignets and café au lait the next morning would be his treat. As everyone retired for the night and expressed how much they had enjoyed the day, Blanche noticed her mother was still not smiling, but at least she had stopped frowning as she went to her own bedroom. She even heard her humming one of the Christmas tunes.

As Blanche and Adam snuggled in bed that night, Blanche felt a flutter in her stomach. Startled, she stiffened.

"My love, what's wrong?"

"Feel here," Blanche whispered uncertain of what she had felt the first time.

As Adam placed his hand against her abdomen and the warmth caused the baby to kick again, he flinched as well before letting his hand rest gently against his wife's abdomen.

"Seems the baby is developing on schedule...."

"Yes," Blanche uttered in a husky voice elated over the first signs that the child she was carrying was well.

Adam leaned across and kissed her, "That was the best Christmas present of all."

Blanche snuggled back against Adam and fell asleep, her face glowing with happiness over how well the day had gone. Even the baby was jumping with joy.

Chapter Forty-Five

After the Christmas holidays, the relationship between Blanche and her mother seemed to improve. It was returning to a level equivalent of what they had prior to Blanche leaving to spend the summer with Autumn. One thing had changed, however. Her mother's domineering stance had lessened. She still placed demands on Blanche, and knowing she was diabetic, Blanche didn't mind as much when her favorite program got interrupted because her mother wanted a cup of tea. By the time the date came to attend the baby shower Melanie had planned, Blanche was feeling more confident her mother would not do anything embarrassing at her shower.

The baby shower was unlike any Blanche had experienced. Everyone was having a grand time as they actively participated in the games Melanie had planned and vied to win prizes. One of the most embarrassing to Blanche was when Melanie would melt a candy bar within a diaper in the microwave and then pass it around to the game participants to name the candy bar. The person who guessed the most fake baby poop correctly was the winner.

When the time came to open her gifts, Autumn and Aubrey got on each side of her, one to make a list Blanche could use to send her thank you cards and the other to facilitate the flow of presents to and from the gift table. Sherrie and her friends had a reserved table closest to Blanche's seat of honor. As Blanche opened the gifts, folks were asking various questions about the upcoming events. Who was her doctor? What hospital was she having the baby? When was she moving to New Orleans? It was when someone asked her if they selected baby names, Sherrie went into rare form again.

"If it's a boy, I like the name Drake and so does Adam so we'll probably stick with that."

Hearing Blanche's response, Sherrie spoke loud enough for Blanche to hear but not that everyone who had attended could.

"Drake?" she looked at each of her friends at the table and started laughing hysterically. "Y'all know Blanche's last name is Brown now. So if she names that child Drake, his name will be brown duck. Won't that be hilarious?"

Miss Ethel was the only friend at the table that joined in her mother's laughter, and when she did, Sherrie laughed harder as she continued, "And the way Blanche has been gaining weight and waddling around the house.. If he walks like his mother, he'll look like a duck too!"

Seeing Blanche getting upset over the chiding, Autumn leaned over and spat at Sherrie, "A more intelligent person would have thought of Sir Francis Drake, the explorer."

As Sherrie and Autumn locked eyes and Autumn's chin pushed out in defiance, Maria quickly walked over to Sherrie's table cutting her eyes at Autumn to cool down.

"May I get you ladies some more punch? How about a slice of the shower cake? Melanie is cutting it now."

Luckily, Sherrie and her friends began giving Maria their orders and didn't pay as much attention when the same guest inquired, "And if it's a girl? What names are you considering?"

Knowing her mother might hear and get insulted, instead of admitting they would be naming their daughter in memory of Adam's mother, Blanche responded, "We haven't decided on a girl's name yet."

"Then it has to be a boy," the guest laughed and luckily the questions and conversations went to more general subjects.

Though all had a wonderful time and Blanche was pleased with the each of the gifts she had received for the baby, her mother's comment plagued her mind. Having been a teacher, she knew how cruel children could be. Would naming her child Drake if it's a boy cause him to be an object of ridicule in the future? It was an issue she would have to discuss with Adam.

Initially when Adam had asked if Blanche would consider naming their daughter in memory of his mother Victoria, she had readily agreed. Blanche liked the name Victoria and was already thinking of her daughter as Vicki Brown. When he insisted they name their son after her father in exchange, Blanche shook her head adamantly indicating that was not a good idea. Though she loved her father dearly and James Aubert sounded fine, she was sensitive to the ridicule the child would experience going through life named after a famous singer. Adam had laughed heartily when he heard her father's first name and conceded they had to begin looking outside the family tree for a name that had less notoriety.

When she came across Drake in the book of baby names, Adam spoke it aloud a couple of times and commented it sounded strong. They had circled it in the baby book and hadn't found anything they liked better yet. It was Drake for now but brown duck? Blanche grimaced at the thought it could be a permanent label for her baby. Once again, her mother's actions had caused her plans to go astray.

The week following the Easter vacation, Blanche's replacement reported to the school officially, and Blanche began transitioning her work. After two weeks of reviewing files and conducting side by side coaching sessions, Blanche was confident the lady would be able to move forward with the plans she had in place and would prove an asset to the staff. The students were beginning to accept her in the new role as well. They were happy for Blanche that she was having a baby and doing something as exciting as moving to New Orleans. Once Blanche completed the last of her duties, she began spending her weekdays sitting home and reading books on the care of newborns and inspirational books on parenting.

After a couple of days, her mother interrupted Blanche's pattern with the suggestion that made Blanche feel she was finally accepting Adam and was happy over the birth of her first grandchild. As one of the shower gifts, Blanche had received a memory book in which she could record milestone events in the baby's life. She also had a picture album. Over breakfast one morning, Sherrie recommended they use some of the pages in the picture album to create a family history tree for the baby. They could include pictures of their relatives on the tree as well as their names, place of birth, and birth/death dates.

Blanche thought it was a wonderful idea and was excited about the new project the two of them could work on together. They would start with Blanche's family first using pictures Sherrie had gathered through the years and inherited from her parents. Blanche would ask Aunt Nora for photos of her father's side as well. After, they would tackle Adam's side of the family. Though it may raise sad memories for Adam, she was hoping Aunt Elaine could provide photos and information, and the research would close some of the gaps in knowledge Adam had about his mother's heritage. The only aggravation was Blanche having to reach up on the top shelves of the closets to constantly pull down the photo albums and boxes where old photos were stored. It seemed as soon as she put a box back on the shelf, her mother would remember something else and send her to retrieve it again. Her arms would grow tired some days from pulling things down and then having to put them back up. She didn't mind. She was so excited about her mother and her working on something positive together.

Chapter Forty-Six

Once she was off from work, Blanche had moved her appointments with Doctor Sarah to early Friday morning slots and would go to her Aunt Nora's immediately after, allowing them time together before Adam's arrival later that night.

As Doctor Sarah made notes on Blanche's chart, Blanche relaxed on the examining table pondering that the time would come soon that she would get to hold her baby in her arms.

"Mrs. Brown, everything is looking good based on my exam, but you are a week overdue now so I'm going to send you for a couple of tests just as a precaution. This will be your last office visit. If the baby doesn't come by Wednesday next week, I'll have the nurse make the arrangements for you to go to the hospital, and we'll induce labor. Do you have any questions?"

"So I'll definitely have the baby no later than next week."

"Yes, the baby is in position, and you are beginning to dilate so you probably will go into labor prior; but, if not, we'll set everything up for Wednesday. You can dress now, and the nurse will be in shortly to go over the orders with you."

After dressing, Blanche looked at the clock on the wall and noted that Adam would still be in one of his lectures. Instead of calling him on his cell, she would wait and give him the news when he arrived. After taking the orders from the nurse, she headed from the clinic area of the medical complex to the hospital lab. After drawing blood and providing a urine sample, she headed to her Aunt Nora's impatient to share the news with someone. As they prepared lunch together in the kitchen, Nora shared stories from the past.

"I swear, Blanche…" Nora made the sign of the cross against her breast to emphasize she wasn't lying. "Your father was so excited they day you were born. His chest was sticking out so far that I thought his heart was going to burst through. The whole time your mother was pregnant he kept talking about his son and how he would change the name of his business to add 'and son' to the legal name. All he talked about was teaching him the trade and how the business was going to be handed down through the generations now. We thought he was going to be disappointed your mother gave birth to a girl. But when the nurse handed you to him for the first time, he took those huge, strong hands of his and held you so gently. He pulled you against his chest and kissed your little cheek."

Nora paused a moment remembering the day.

"Then your Uncle Louie started teasing him about not having a son. You father looked at him and said,
'I'm not trading this baby girl right here for any of those boys in that nursery. This little gal is just fine with me."

Thinking she had heard her cell phone, Blanche walked from the kitchen to the living room where she had left her purse. Removing the cell, she punched the menu and saw she did have a missed call, but the cell indicated the number was unknown. Thinking it was a wrong number, Blanche shoved the cell back into her purse and returned to the kitchen to enjoy the chicken salad over a bed of crispy Romaine lettuce she had helped Aunt Nora prepare. As soon as they placed their plates on the small dinette table, Blanche thought she heard her cell again. Returning to the living room, she grabbed the phone in time to answer.

"Hello?" she asked inquiringly after seeing unknown pop up again on the screen.

"Is this Blanche Brown?"

"Speaking," she answered hesitantly thinking she recognized the voice but not able to yet place it.

"Blanche, I'm so glad I was able to reach you this time. This is Rose. Doctor Sarah's nurse…"

"Yes?"

"Doctor Sarah needs you to come back to the medical complex as soon as you can. Your tests results are in and she's planning to do a

Caesarean section this afternoon. I've arranged a surgery slot for you for 2:00 P.M."

Feeling Rose had contacted the wrong patient, Blanche challenged the instructions she was hearing.

"Doctor Sarah told me this morning I didn't have to report until Wednesday. She would induce if the baby doesn't come on its own by then." Not wanting to sound condescending, she tried to soften her tone as she continued, "I'm sorry, Rose, but I think you have the charts mixed up. You must have called the wrong patient."

Blanche was speaking confidently until her Aunt Nora came to her side. Hearing Blanche's response, a worried expression replaced the normal smile on her face.

"The charts are not mixed up, Mrs. Brown." She used Blanche's surname to emphasize she was speaking with the authority of the doctor. "The test results indicate the baby is in distress. The doctor feels it's best to take it as soon as possible."

"The baby's in distress... What does that mean?" Blanche's glanced at Aunt Nora for comfort as she heard Rose's reply.

"It means the heart rate is irregular; it's dropping.... Something is going wrong. We need to get the baby out as soon as possible. You're at the end of your term. If you're worried about the baby having the problems of a preemie, it shouldn't."

Blanche stared at her Aunt Nora as the news sank in. Her aunt grabbed the phone from her Blanche's hand.

"This is her aunt. Please tell me what we need to do."

As Blanche slumped into the armchair next to her purse, Nora listened intently to what Rose was saying. Blanche sat trying to pinpoint the last time she had felt the baby move. Was it already too late? She heard Nora's response, but it seemed her voice was from afar.

"We were just about to eat lunch so you called at the right time. She hadn't had anything to eat yet today so it's just as if she's fasted. We'll be at the hospital as soon as we can get there."

As Nora hung up with Rose, she asked, "Do you want me to call Adam for you?"

Blanche glanced at the clock on the wall, "He's giving an exam right now…. I shouldn't disturb him."

Nora could tell by the distant look on Blanche's face that she wasn't thinking clearly.

"Honey, you're about to have surgery. Your husband needs to know."

Nora punched up the address book in Blanche's phone, dialed Adam's number, and placed the phone to Blanche's ear. Seeing his wife's cell appear as the phone on his desk began vibrating, Adam stepped into the hallway to take the call watching his students through the glass pane in the door.

"Blanche? Is everything ok?"

As soon as she heard Adam's voice and question, Blanche began crying hysterically.

"My love! Please… You have to stop crying long enough to tell me what's wrong."

Thinking his wife had another altercation with her mother, Adam was tempted to hang up the phone and get back to his class. He would discuss the incident with her when he arrived in Lafayette later that day.

Raising his voice as loud as he could not to disturb the classes around him, Adam tried to induce a response, "Blanche, we can discuss this tonight, ok? I need to get back into class."

Hearing nothing but her cries, Adam was about to ring off when he recognized Nora's voice, "Adam?"

"Aunt Nora? I don't know what her mother did this time, but I'll be there as soon as I can."

"Adam, you need to get here now! The doctor ran tests, and the baby's in distress. They're cutting it out of her at two this afternoon."

Adam looked at his watch and cursed. It was already past noon. Traffic on Fridays was so heavy, the drive usually took him at least two and a half hours. There was no way he'd make it in time. He listened to Nora's words, but his mind was only on getting a proxy to take over his class and getting on the highway.

"I don't think she should drive. She's too upset. I don't have a license, but I'll figure out a way to get her to the hospital as soon as I can."

"Aunt Nora, please just call for a cab. Blanche should have enough money in her purse to cover the fare. I'm leave as soon as I get someone to cover my class!"

"Don't you worry none! I'll take care of her...."

"Thank you, Aunt Nora!"

As they rode towards the hospital in the taxi, Blanche's focus on her baby shifted when amidst the words of comfort her aunt was expressing, she asked her a strange question.

"Blanche, I know you resigned at your school. To pack up your things, you haven't been lifting boxes up and down on shelves, have you?

'Why?" Blanche's tears dried, and she answered her aunt in an angry voice thinking of the number of times her mother had sent her to pull the boxes of photos off the shelves in her bedroom.

"Nothing, honey... It's just an old wives' tale anyway..."

Nora patted Blanche's hand to comfort her as the cab pulled into the driveway by the hospital's admission entrance. She was surprised when Blanche's hand squeezed hers tightly, and her voice got stronger.

"Tell me, Auntie Nora. What is this old wives' tale? Some of them have a measure of truth."

Reluctantly, Nora shared, "The old people use to say you can't lift your arms over your head when you're pregnant... If you do, you'll wrap the cord around the baby's neck and cause it to smother to death."

She watched Blanche's reaction. Instead of the zombie like state she had been in, her hands crossed her baby bump, and her face changed to one of anger. Blanche jumped into action. As she confirmed with the driver the amount of the fare, she grabbed her purse, took out several bills, and handed them over the seat. Not waiting for change, she got out the car and started hurrying towards the admissions' door. Nora had to run to catch up with her. By the time Nora reached her, Blanche was already at the counter pulling her medical cards and driver's license out her purse. She spoke in an agitated tone informing the customer service agent the reason for her visit. The lady took the information, looked Blanche up in the computer, and instructed her on the admission process and where she needed to go next.

Blanche listened intently to the instructions and began walking with determination to the area where she had to check in. As they walked down the hall together, Nora whispered, "I'll call Barbara and have her tell your mother."

Blanche stopped short, and her face was stern as she spoke to her aunt, "NO! She's done enough... I don't want her here!"

Surprised by her reaction, Nora didn't press the issue until Blanche had completed the admission process, was changed into a hospital gown, the I.V. had been placed in her arm, and her demeanor seemed to be calmer. Glancing at the clock, Nora knew if Sherrie wasn't there in a half hour, she wouldn't be present when Blanche was rolled into the operating room.

"Blanche, if I don't call your mother now, she won't get here before they take you in to deliver the baby. Don't you want your mother with you when you have your first child?"

Blanche turned her face away from Nora and faced the wall.

"The only person I want to see right now is Adam. Mother doesn't care about me or my baby."

"Blanche, that's not true. Your mother loves you!"

"I don't feel loved right now..."

Not wanting to upset her, Nora didn't push the subject. When the nurse asked her to leave the room for a few minutes while she shaved Blanche for the surgery, Nora used Blanche's cell phone to call Barbara. Minutes before Blanche was rolled into the operating room, Barbara and Sherrie arrived.

In front of the nurse and Doctor Sarah, Sherrie was a completely different person. After leaning over to hug and kiss Blanche, she turned to Doctor Sarah, "This is my only child, Doctor. Please don't let anything happen to her even if you have to sacrifice the baby."

Not wanting to be ugly in front of the doctor, Blanche held back the words she wanted to tell her mother and pretended to be touched by her mother's actions. As they rolled her into the operating room, her blood pressure began rising.

Chapter Forty-Seven

Blanche blinked her eyes and looked about the room trying to ascertain where she was. The top half of the wall in front of her was painted white, and the lower part was covered with a pale green tile. The wall was devoid of any pictures. There was a curtain pulled on each side of her. Her back ached, and she wanted to adjust her position in the bed. Slowly things were coming back to her.

"Good! You're awake," a strange voice spoke as a nurse appeared and stood by the side of her bed, "You had a general anesthesia. After I check your vitals, we should be able to move you to your room shortly."

"Can I move my legs around?"

"Sure. You just can't try to get up yet. Rest...."

Blanche did as the nurse ordered and soon dozed back to sleep. When she woke again, she was being pulled sideways onto a stretcher and told she was being moved to a room. Still feeling groggy, she only nodded in response to the orders from the medical staff. As she was being rolled into what would be her private room, she heard the sound of familiar voices but didn't open her eyes. After being pulled into the hospital bed and the attending nurse for her ward checked her vital signs, Blanche dozed off once again.

Hearing the cry of a baby, Blanche's eyes blinked opened and she turned toward the sound. Adam was sitting on the sofa against the window holding a bundle wrapped in a blue blanket and feeding the baby a bottle. When he saw Blanche awoke, he stood and walked towards her.

"Thank you for the gift of my son," he stated as he leaned down and kissed his wife softly on the cheek before holding the baby up for Blanche to see him.

"Adam, he's alright?"

"He's perfect! You did a wonderful job, my love. Doctor Sarah said the cord was wrapped around his neck, and that's why they were getting indications the baby was in distress. If you had gone into labor and had a vaginal birth, we may have lost him. I'm sorry you had to go through a Caesarean Section, but the surgery probably saved him."

"Oh, Adam, may I hold him?"

Adam pressed a button on the side of the bed to move Blanche into a more upright position and placed their son in her arms. Blanche took the tiny hand into hers and kissed his fingers softly. Her son had his father's fine features, but his golden skin tone was lighter than Adam's. He had a full head of medium brown, silky hair with blondish highlights. The locks fell in a thick mass onto his shoulders. As he yawned, his eyes opened for a brief moment and Blanche caught a glimpse of green eyes. The baby reminded Blanche of pictures she had seen of tanned children with sun bleached hair playing on Caribbean beaches.

"Oh, Adam, he's beautiful!"

Sitting on the edge of the bed and placing his arm around his wife's shoulder, Adam pulled her gently against him and placed a kiss on her forehead. The moment between the three was short lived as Sherrie and Blanche's two aunts entered the room.

Nora and Barbara were immediately at Blanche's other side ranting on how beautiful the baby was. Sherrie stood at the foot of the bed observing but making no comment. Barbara pushed the subject.

"Don't you want to hold your grandson, Sherrie?"

As the nurse walked in, Sherrie said, "Give his mother some time with him first, Sister." She turned away, walked over to the sofa, and took a seat.

"Blanche and Sherrie will have him nearly every day for the rest of his life. I've been waiting too long for this moment. Give him to me," Nora demanded.

As Blanche handed her son over, Nora began cooing at the baby and rocking him slowly in her arms, "He's the prettiest baby I've ever seen. Blanche. My brother would have been so happy if he could have been here today to see him... We were all so worried about you, and thank God, everything turned out fine. Your husband must have been driving like a bat out of hell because he managed to get here in two hours. He was able to talk to Doctor Sarah right after your surgery."

Seeing her sister's face turn into a frown, Barbara spoke up, "Sherrie, Nora, we need to get out of here and give this new family time to be alone. We can come back tomorrow to visit."

"Ladies, would you like me to drive you home?" Adam offered.

"No, we'll get home just fine. Stay with your wife and child. This is bonding time!"

"Thank you, Auntie," Blanche smiled.

Nora turned the baby back over to Blanche as he started fussing, and Adam handed her a bottle of formula. Before leaving the room, Sherrie looked at Blanche and asked, "Are you still going to name that child Drake?"

Before Blanche could respond, Adam spoke, "Yes! That will be our son's name."

Sherrie made a huffing sound as she left the room. Drake began fussing, and wouldn't continue to drink his bottle. Adam took him from Blanche, and he settled down.

"Stress," Blanche thought. She knew she was worried about her mother accepting her son. His skin wasn't fair, and she had made it clear the name was ludicrous. As she looked at Drake content in his father's arms, she knew she had to leave her past fears behind for her baby's sake, but it was hard after so many years.

The day Blanche was to be discharged from the hospital, Nora called and offered her and the baby to move in by her house. Blanche started thinking of all the preparations she had gone through at home and all that would have to be moved: the bassinet, baby clothes, towels,

On Monday, Adam called the university and made arrangements for someone to proxy the exams that were scheduled the following week. After seeing Blanche was recuperating well from the operation, he had to return to the university to finalize the year. The couple fell back into their previous routine with Adam coming down every Friday and returning to New Orleans on Sunday night; but instead of sneaking over to Nora's, they continued to stay at Blanche's home, and Sherrie remained civil.

When he was two months old, Drake came down with a high fever. It took two days before the medicine his pediatrician prescribed kicked in. After being up with him nonstop for two nights, his fever broke but Blanche was exhausted. Her body felt sticky, and her hair was matted to her head. She longed desperately for a shower. With Drake appearing to be finally sleeping soundly, she took the chance of getting into the shower to wash her hair and bathe. After working up a thick lather with the shampoo, she cut the shower off while she massaged her scalp vigorously. When she was about to turn the shower back on to rinse and to apply the conditioner, she thought she heard Drake crying. Thinking to herself, "Mommy's coming, Drake," she quickly rinsed her hair and stepped from the shower donning her robe. By the time she walked out the bathroom, the house was silent. Worried she had left Drake alone for too long a time, she rushed to her bedroom and stepped back in fear when she saw the empty bassinet.

Every incident from her recent past rushed to her mind. She remembered overhearing her mother talk about old Miss Celine and the concoctions she made up. Blanche thought about the time she poured the tea her mother had prepared down the kitchen drain. She recoiled knowing she and Adam had almost lost their son and blamed it on the old wives' tale Aunt Nora had recounted about her lifting her arms. Remembering her mother had suggested they work on the family history tree project together, hearing the news her baby was in distress, and then Adam confirming the cord had been wrapped around Drake's neck, she became more frantic in her search for him.

She hurried down the hall praying nothing had been done to her baby. There was no sight of her mother or child in the living room. She went through the dining room and walked into the kitchen and found both empty. As she walked towards her mother's bedroom, her apprehension grew. Before she reached the door, she heard her mother speaking soothingly, a tone Blanche could never recall hearing.

"Yes, Granny is going to have to move to New Orleans to help take care of you. I'll just rent this old place out furnished... Yes, I'm going to have to move because all your stupid Maw thinks about since she got that relaxer last summer is her hair... Yes, that's all she cares about is her hair and having the hots for your Paw... Say, 'Yes, Granny. I need someone to take proper care of me.' ... I can't believe your stupid Maw left a sick baby all by himself so she can do her hair? Say, 'Yes, Granny. I have a stupid Maw.' ...And if she goes back to work, she'll have to stick you in a nursery and who's going to pay any attention to a lil' brown duck in a nursery? Say, 'Nobody, Granny. I'd be crying and wet all day, and I'll get diaper rash.' Yes, that's right. So, you're going to have to stay at home with me because no one is going to be looking out for a lil' brown duck. They'll be too busy playing with all the pretty babies.... Only your Granny is going to be bothered with a lil' brown duck."

Blanche peeked into the doorway and spotted her mother holding Drake in the rocking chair and rocking him softly as she talked to him. Not understanding a word his grandmother was saying but responding to the soft, comforting sound of her voice, Drake was cooing and smiling back at her. Blanche stepped into the room, and her mother looked up.

"I stopped doing my hair because I thought I heard Drake crying."

"The poor lil' duck was crying his head off. Go get me a bottle for him, Blanche. Then you can go back to dealing with your hair. Worrying about your hair when the baby's been sick? Some mother you're turning out to be.... Dumb, dumb, dumb. "

Drake cooed again and Sherrie took her grandson, kissed him, and put him up to her shoulder.

"Go on, stupid girl! Don't just stand there. Get a bottle for you son!"

"Yes, mother, right away." After Blanche turned her back, a smile crossed her face. The tightness in her chest eased as she walked to the kitchen to warm a bottle for Drake. She knew her mother would never break completely free of her old ways and outlook on life, but Blanche finally felt she was loved. And in her heart, she knew Drake was loved too. She exhaled slowly. Life would be good from now on. For the first time since her father died, she felt she had a family once again. She knew that, with each day, the bonds would grow stronger. As she returned to her mother's bedroom and handed the bottle to her, she got the exact feedback she expected. She would have been shocked if she heard anything different.

"Stupid girl... This feels too hot. Did you test it first?" Sherrie shook a drop of the milk onto her inner wrist to test the temperature before she gave the bottle to Drake.

"Here, my lil' brown duck. Granny made sure you won't burn your little mouth because you have a stupid Maw." As Drake began sucking the bottle, Sherrie looked up at Blanche, "What you're still standing there for? You think I can't feed a baby a bottle? Go finish with your hair!"

Sherrie emphasized the last two words saying them with a sneer.

"Yes, mother," Blanche smiled with her heart light as she walked back to the bathroom to condition and roll her hair and to finish her shower.

She thought about the day she had left home to spend the summer with Autumn. In only a year, so much had happened and so much had changed; but their lives had been changed for the better.... She remembered how she felt that day, and those same feelings returned. Her anxiousness since the day the baby was born had changed to a feeling of excitement about the new life they all would have together. She started feeling giddy about the possibilities that were ahead. She was light hearted as if a weight had been lifted off her chest. Even though she would patronize her mother, she knew that she was the one now in control. But most of all, as she took in a deep breath once again and exhaled it slowly, she suddenly felt free.... Free to be the woman, wife, mother, and daughter she wanted to be.

The End